The Tenth

The Tenth

JOANNE E. MOUDY

The Tenth

2nd edition

Copyright © 2013 by Joanne E. Moudy

Cover design by Matt Fischer,
copyright © 2013 by Joanne E. Moudy

Author photograph by Everett R. Moudy,
copyright © 2013 by Joanne E. Moudy

ISBN: 978-0-9913633-1-5

Published by Gated Creative

This book is dedicated to
Ashlyn and Siena,
the two brightest stars in the
midnight sky.

ACKNOWLEDGMENTS

First of all I need to acknowledge God, without whom I would not have had the wondrous gifts of life, liberty or freedoms graciously bestowed upon me. Through the good fortune of being born in America, I was empowered to reach for every star and fulfill my dreams. I'm living proof that when God closes a door, He simultaneously opens a window; except in my case, He opened several. God also blessed me with an amazing soul-mate, my husband, Ray, who's been my Captain and Chief Pilot for over three decades. Only through his support, advice and great cooking, did I manage to transcribe the vivid dream stuck in my brain. On days when I was too involved in writing to speak, he played golf, and on days when I needed a fresh look, he patiently read. Truly, Ray, you're the best man alive.

After the rough draft was complete, I nervously sent the book out to professionals, most of whom I'd never met, asking for their input and feedback. It is those people who inspired me to proceed and refine the work. Specifically, a huge thank you to CAPT Michael B. Stenger, U. S. Coast Guard, retired, for not allowing the float plane to go down in the Strait, Laurance Nils en, M.D., FACP, for his medical expertise and encouragement, and Richard W. Kemp for his honest support and fresh look at an old topic.

Being a new author, I didn't have an editor or publisher, so I turned to the only reliable resource I know of for finding what I need when I need it badly; prayer. Almost immediately, two key people were put in my path. Without them you wouldn't be reading these words. Thank you Matt Fischer, for being the best graphic artist on the planet! You captured the theme and boiled it down for the perfect cover design. You also built a killer Web site for Gated Creative. And a huge thank you to William Greenleaf, Greenleaf Literary Services, for being incredible in every aspect of the editing and proofing process. From our first phone call, I knew my manuscript was in great hands. I trust you implicitly. You're the best!

I also need to mention my intellectual property rights attorney, Rich Alaniz, who followed this all the way through. Time and time again, his instant and accurate responses protected my hard work and imagination. Thanks!

Each and every one of you made a difference in this book and I couldn't have done it without your help and support. It's an honor to know you all!

FOREWORD

When Joanne Moudy presented me with her novel manuscript *The Tenth*, I had no idea what to expect. What I found within its pages was a fast-paced story that, while fictional, explores important, real-world issues I feel deeply about.

America was founded a shining beacon on the hill, standing as a great bastion of hope to people of all nationalities and faiths. For over two centuries, multitudes have flocked to her shores for help, protection, and sanctuary. Unfortunately, the noble republic our Forefathers envisioned is becoming a victim of complacency and apathy of its people. Those intangible and invaluable freedoms and inalienable rights are being cast aside in favor of immediate but fleeting material self-indulgence. In one generation, the vacuum of social media, meaningless celebrity minutia, and government handouts are beginning to outpace our faith in God and our US Constitution.

As one privileged to be a member of the US House of Representatives, I want my phones to ring and to know my constituents understand and care about America's first principles. I want them to remember what made America great and how blessed we are as a country to have the US Constitution and Bill of Rights. I want them to remember every single day how blessed we all are as Americans to have been born in a free country where all men are created equal. The minute we don't remember or care is the minute we forfeit our ability to self-govern.

It is so very important for each of us as citizens of this country to remember how our governing documents came to exist in the first place. Although the process wasn't simple, the basic premise was. The men who penned them took power and control out of the hands of mortal men and placed it squarely at the foot of God, the ultimate Authority in all matters. Basic freedoms were unfurled and an entire nation flourished. By recognizing and honoring God as the Creator and giver of all human rights, we—in turn—recognized and respected that the image of God is stamped on each human heart. And in one of the most consequential moments in the entire history of mankind, every life was counted as precious. All life was sacred.

Now we find ourselves at a terrible crossroads. Secular socialism relentlessly bears down upon our Judeo-Christian principles and threatens to extinguish the very humanity which made America the greatest nation in the history of human kind. Political correctness intimidates our free people into the slavery of silence, which once again allows the survival of the fittest to begin to prevail over humanity. Instead of recognizing innocent human life as the most priceless gift on earth, we now ask the inconceivable: How much is innocent life worth?

America has fought in some heartbreaking wars, but the Affordable Care Act is bringing the battlefield home. Instead of uniformed soldiers fighting on foreign shores, today we force doctors, nurses, and hospital administrators to stand front and center in the moral dilemmas being rammed down our throats by bureaucrats. From a premature infant needing lifesaving resuscitation to an eighty-year-old retiree needing open heart surgery to a teenager awaiting an organ transplant, decisions which heretofore were based on the Hippocratic oath and the simple concepts of human worth and dignity suddenly become huge mathematical equations based upon dollars and cents. Make no mistake, our country is heading down a slippery slope which may ultimately define our civilization. This is just one of the travesties of socialized medicine and heartless secularism.

While most authors wouldn't even attempt to reconcile legitimate politics with humanity's responsibility to God, Joanne Moudy does not back away. Instead, she faces critical life-and-death dilemmas head on and strips complex social ideology down to its bare bones. She imaginatively creates an interface with the heavenly realm and our earthly realities, using every-day human struggles to show plausible alternatives to the future of mankind.

Moudy hits the nail on the head in this fast-paced thriller and isn't afraid to ask the reader to reexamine concepts of Heaven and Hell, and life after death. These are questions that our modern culture needs to ask because one thing is certain: If society moves away from the Creator to embrace the secular belief system wherein man is the only dominant animal on earth, it will shred the fabric of moral impulse toward one another and destroy what made America that last bastion of human hope on earth. If we do not wake up in time, our Judeo-Christian civilization and all the peace and hope it brings to humanity will be lost.

The Tenth puts forth the premise that only through under-standing the true nature of God can we understand ourselves and what ultimately awaits us on the other side. Only when we experience that moment of spiritual clarity will we understand the divine nature of the universe and the sanctity and unspeak-able miracle of all human life.

~ Trent Franks, Member of Congress

ANOTHER TIME, ANOTHER PLACE

"Come away from the water, Joseph. You know it is forbidden."

"I can sense it again, Lady Mary. And I do not like the feeling."

Joseph stares into crystal blue water sheeting endlessly over an unseen, impenetrable barrier. Cascading vertically, the liquid monolith of water known as Mayim follows a timeless passage. Flowing from the highest point in the sky into the deepest depths of the earth, Mayim stands as the only gateway.

Lady Mary of the Nine approaches Joseph from behind and lays her hand gently on his shoulder. "I understand. But what you sense or how you feel does not change Father's law."

"What I sense now is different. It is a darkness," he says beneath his breath. "A darkness approaching from their realm."

"Clear your mind, Joseph."

"It is difficult. I am drawn to identify what the darkness is."

"You know Mayim only opens one way. It is not our purpose to investigate the other side. Even if we could pass through, Father's law forbids it."

"I know. But nevertheless, I feel Mayim pulling at me. And I sense a darkness," he repeats quietly.

"Joseph, you must clear your mind. You have a passage approaching."

He turns away from the water to face Lady Mary, his mentor, a tall, slender woman draped in a white robe. Her long, flaxen hair gleams in the soft light.

Joseph looks into her mind. "Yes. You are right. It is time." He steps away from Mayim.

Lady Mary's deep blue eyes search the air, peering into the invisible. "The others are coming."

Without warning, the remaining eight simultaneously appear, with four on either side of Joseph, forming a half circle in front of the falling water. Dressed in their usual hooded white robes, they funnel their individual power to him. Once again, the Nine are complete. Their unity flows through Joseph, strengthening his purpose.

Lady Mary walks to an arched, crystalline alcove adjacent to the falling water and lifts an egg-shaped vase from a tripod on the sixth shelf. Twelve inches tall and eight inches wide, the perfect ovoid is one of the original Nine Vases created eons ago from the purest gold in the universe, in a time no one can remember.

Deep within the vase is inlaid the whitest, most chaste diamond ever mined. Cut from the Original Stone at the same time of the creating, the diamond and vase were forged together, ensuring neither could be torn asunder.

Balancing it between her hands, Lady Mary extends her arms to Mayim and fills the vase with the cascading liquid until it bulges over the top. With the vase cradled carefully in her hands, she walks to Joseph and stands behind him.

The eight others direct their thoughts to Joseph while he focuses on the liquid monolith. Staring straight ahead, Joseph gasps for his last breath just before his body seizes. Now rigid, he is frozen in position. From behind, Lady Mary releases the vase into the air, places her hands on his shoulders, and narrows her mind. Meanwhile, the vase floats upward and holds its position above Joseph, waiting.

Joseph cries out in pain. "No! Not . . . yet!" His head rises and jerks back, forcing his face upward. His neck muscles bulge, and his veins vigorously pulsate from the strain. Above him, the vase hovers, still waiting.

A brilliant beam of white light erupts through the vertical Mayim and angles like a bolt of lightning to pierce Joseph's chest. As it condenses and collects within him, it changes from a beam to a miniature galaxy that swirls through his body, illuminating his total being. His blond hair stands erect, as if charged by an electromagnetic field, while his body levitates six inches off the ground. Through it all, Lady Mary maintains her position and contact, with both hands on his shoulders.

As the swirling lights emerge from his body, they reconstitute and form a vertical beam in front of him. When his feet once more touch the ground, the beam pauses momentarily, balancing on a spot no larger than the head of a pin, then shoots upward and ricochets off the lofty ceiling to return straight back down to the vase above Joseph's head. The beam penetrates the surface of the bulging water, collapses to a small ball, and finally ensconces itself within the diamond at the bottom of the vase.

The vise-like seizure holding Joseph's body rigid dissipates. His head falls forward. His body, soaked with perspiration, goes limp with exhaustion. Lady Mary continues to hold his shoulders, supporting him from above, giving him time to recover.

Silence.

The passage through Mayim is once again complete. The other eight vanish, having finished their task.

"Rest, Joseph," Lady Mary says. "You must clear your

mind. There are many more passages approaching all of the Nine. I will return shortly."

The vase and its precious cargo are already floating in the direction of the sally port. Lady Mary follows behind it toward the great hall.

Rest is impossible, Joseph thinks as he steps closer to Mayim. He holds out his hand and extends his fingertips, now so close to the liquid that he feels the air moving in response to the falling water. All he has to do is touch it.

But for Father's law, I would know what is on the other side. There must be a way to find out about the darkness. There must be a way.

CURRENT TIME, SEATTLE, WASHINGTON

I lean my head against the white wall next to the open double doors of Trauma 2.

"You doing okay, Elizabeth?"

"Honestly, I'm beat and my legs ache from standing for eight hours, but I'll survive. How about you?"

"Same ol', same ol'. Some shifts I hate being in charge, but tonight hasn't been too bad so far."

I look at the clock across the hall and wonder if it's broken. "Don't tell anyone, Monica, but I'm thinking about climbing up on a chair and moving the hands on that clock over there. I swear, it's been stuck at two a.m. for hours."

"Well, if you do, my lips are sealed." She makes a zip motion with her fingers across her lips, and we both laugh a little. Shaking her short, bobbed red hair, she shows me a big smile. "Seriously, you need fifteen minutes?"

"What I need . . . is to win the lottery, go home, and drink heavily."

"I'll give you a buck for the ticket. But if you win, you have to share."

"The money or the booze?"

Monica's laugh is infectious, and we both bust open in exhausted hysterics. She pinches the bridge between her tearing eyes in an effort to regain her composure. "Oh, man. It feels good to laugh. What a night!"

I see some patients' family members staring at us. *Hey, nurses laugh, too!* I look back at Monica's freckled face and almost bust up again. Thankfully, she ignores my impending laughter.

"Tell you what," she says, "take five and go get a cup of coffee. The latte stand is still open. I'll cover your room."

"Thanks, that would be great. Besides, I need to pee."

"So whaddaya got?"

"Okay, bed one is a seventeen-year-old who OD'd on lots of 'colored pills' at a rave. His words, not mine. I lavaged his stomach, gave him charcoal, and he's on his third liter of fluids. Sleepy but stable. Parents are in the waiting room. I'm waiting for the house supervisor to find him a psych bed. He can be moved out if we need the space.

"Bed two is a multiple gunshot, right arm, left leg. Both through and through, mostly fatty tissue. Nothing particularly vital was hit. Probably some kind of gang initiation. He's stable. Med students are having a field day working on him." I roll my eyes. "Waiting to see if Doc wants to keep him.

"Bed three is the woman from Spokane who got here about two hours ago. Necrotizing fasciitis all over her belly. She weighs close to four hundred pounds, so we're waiting for one of the flotation-type oversized beds. Patient's a mess, though. Her belly looks like acid was poured all over it. Antibiotics are hanging, and she's had ten of morphine times four, none of which did much. Here's the rest of the newest syringe." I hand Monica the remaining five milligrams of morphine. "She can have as much as she wants, but it makes her nauseated. And bed four's empty. That's it. I'll be back in five or ten. You want anything?"

"Nope, I got it."

With my patients in Monica's capable hands, I waste no time speeding down the hall. I zoom past the two enormous circular desk systems that stand guard in the Emergency Department's huge entry, make a quick detour through Zone Three, swipe my security badge at the back entrance, and exit the inner sanctum. Five minutes is all I need to visit the locker room and get coffee. After my initial pit stop, I pause at the mirror, run a quick brush through my long brown hair, and swirl it up again into a bundle at the back of my head. I snap the spring-loaded plastic clip into place and go in search of caffeine.

The forty-bed ED is the hub of the hospital and the crown jewel which distinguishes it from all the other medical facilities in the region. With its Level One Trauma Center, Bayside Hospital in Seattle, Washington, is the only such facility in its four-state region. From Alaska to Idaho, critically ill or injured folks are evacuated to this place twenty-four hours a day, seven days a week, three-hundred sixty-five days a year.

I work the night shift, 6:00 p.m. to 6:30 a.m., three nights a week and sleep whenever I can during the day between shifts. But this is my third night in a row, and my tank's running on empty. Thankfully, I'll soon be heading to my little cabin on the peninsula for a welcome four days off.

"Hey, Elizabeth! The usual?" asks the petite blond coed we've affectionately nicknamed "Latte Lady."

"Yup. Gargantuan grande-quadruple-mocha-schmocha with extra whipped cream."

"You got it. How's your night?" she asks with a smile as she steams the milk.

"Not bad, but I'll be glad when it's over."

"This oughta help."

A minute later, I have my cup of heaven. "Thanks." *Ahh.*

Absolutely decadent. "Cheers! See ya next week." Sipping the hot, sweet liquid, I make my way back into the fray.

As I round the corner to Zone One, I hear the loudspeaker blare an all-too-familiar mantra: "Medics on the ramp. Medics on the ramp."

I know the drill. Either an ambulance is pulling into the parking zone outside the Trauma doors, or a helicopter is landing on the roof ramp beside the ambulance lanes. Either way, a Trauma patient has arrived, and I will undoubtedly get the case. I quicken my pace.

Monica updates me on our current patients. "They finished sewing up the gunshot guy, but he needs more IV antibiotics, so he's a keeper. Police are talking to him now. I already got a bed for him, and transporters are on the way. I'll call report for you if you want."

"Thanks, that would be great." I set down my coffee and take back the syringe of morphine. "What's coming in?"

"Stabbing. Female, I think. Pretty bad."

"Bummer." I look down the corridor. "Here come the boys now." Two medics are rounding the corner from the side entrance, pushing a gurney toward us. A third medic runs behind the head of the gurney, holding down the oxygen mask and rhythmically compressing the non-rebreather "ambu" bag. The patient's long dark hair is matted with blood and tangled in the mask's elastic strap.

Shaped like a giant U, the ED is divided into three separate Triage zones, with Trauma and patient rooms on the outside of the loop and equipment-based rooms on the inside. Zone One consists of two heavy Trauma rooms and X-ray, CT (cat scan), and MRI rooms. Farther down the hall is a single well-equipped surgical suite, and somewhere in the mix is the ED's lab and pharmacy.

Trauma 1 and 2 are both large, open rooms divided into four individual bays, each outfitted with state-of-the-art cardiac monitors, ventilators, and built-in vital equipment. In spite of a gurney and all the machines in each bay, eight or ten people can still huddle around a patient and work without feeling crowded.

The ED is always staffed with four board-certified emergency medicine physicians, a shift "trauma doctor" (usually a senior surgical resident), and an on-site neurosurgeon, as well as a lengthy list of registered nurses, nursing assistants, technicians, and support personnel employed by the hospital. Additionally, the university medical school and residency programs provide a perpetual stream of med students and residents.

On paper it sounds like plenty of staff, but there are nerve-racking moments when I feel totally alone, especially if I have a bad case. It's not unusual for a single patient to be so critical they require the attention of three RNs at once. So, in the Trauma rooms, I never take a moment of peace for granted.

"Bed four, boys." I help push the gurney, directing its head alongside the trauma bed. "What do we have?"

"Female, mid-twenties, no ID," the medic answers. "Multiple stab wounds to her chest and abdomen. Possible rape. Fresh bruises to her face. Defensive wounds on her hands and forearms." As he speaks, he locks the gurney rollers with his foot, pulls a bundle of lab tubes with multicolored tops out of his pocket, and hands them to Mark, my nursing assistant. "I think she's lost a lot of blood. Correction, I think she's still losing a lot of blood."

As he narrates, five people lift the thick plastic skid from the medic gurney to the trauma bed, and I cut what is left of the thin woman's bloody clothing off her. Peeling back the slashed fabric brings the stark horror of this woman's attack into full view.

Good Lord! It feels almost personal. *She's not much younger than I am. What a mess.*

The butcher showed no mercy, using a narrow blade to

stab the young woman's torso over and over. She may very well
die, and the clock is mercilessly ticking away. Adrenaline rushes
through my veins and catapults my mind into its well-rehearsed
mental gymnastics routine.

Just above the mask, the woman's eyes are unevenly
closed. As I pull each open to check for response, I note the hazel
irises and equal pupil sizes. It's a good sign. Her badly bruised
right temple and cheek show the only real color in her face: blue.
Her mascara is smeared, but her otherwise flawless skin is pale,
close to dusky. Not a good sign.

"One, two, three," I count, "roll!" In a well-coordinated
effort, I support her neck and head while we quickly roll her to
one side. Two med students remove the skid, and we roll her
back onto the sheet and settle her in place.

"Someone found her between a couple of cars on the
second level of the parking garage at the Northern Shopping
Mall and called nine-one-one," relays the medic. "One witness
said he heard her mumble a few incoherent words before she
passed out. She never opened her eyes for me. Considering
the time, she might've been down for a while. Probably a little
hypothermic.

"Her airway seems okay, and she's been mostly shallow
breathing on her own. Her initial sats were ninety percent, BP
eighty-six over forty-four, heart rate thready but palpable. I
started oxygen, got an eighteen in her right AC, normal saline
wide open, just started the second liter, oh-two on at four liters.
Once she was in the rig, her sats started dropping, so I bagged
her."

While he speaks, I place five leads on the woman's chest
and shoulders, dodging the multiple gaping wounds scattered
all over. Even though it's impossible to avoid the horror in front
of me, I try not to really see it. I recycle the cardiac monitor.

Monica and another RN join the effort. While one inserts a
large-bore IV catheter into the patient's left arm, Monica inserts

a urinary catheter so that urine will flow out and not engorge the bladder.

Meanwhile, someone from Respiratory Therapy (RT) appears and assumes responsibility for the patient's breathing, and a lab guy stands by, ready to grab the tubes and newly drawn blood samples.

Taking the lead, I fire down my list of memorized protocol orders. "Type and cross, CBC, full chem panel, and run everything else as well." I listen to the patient's chest for breath sounds and look over to RT. "I don't hear much on the right. May have a collapsed lobe, probably needs a chest tube. I know you're busy, but if we can get a blood gas, that would be helpful as well."

Monica hangs the urine catheter bag down on the side of the gurney, and we all notice it's filling up fast with dark, bloody urine. "Dang, look at that color." She unlatches the spigot on the bag and fills a small urine cup. After tightening the lid, she sticks it down into a plastic bag the lab tech is holding.

Ann, one of the ED's secretaries, reaches from behind the privacy curtain and hands over several sheets of nameless patient labels. Apparently feeling brave, she peeks her youthful face around the curtain. "Oh, gross," she mutters and ducks back behind the fabric.

"She got a name, Ann?"

"Not yet. But we're working on it." She's already bolting out the door. "Cops are here. I'll let you know when I have something."

"Keep them out with you for now. We don't need this circus to get any bigger."

Like a choreographed dance routine, all of this coordinated activity takes less than five minutes. Right on cue, Dr. Bennett, our chief doc tonight, walks in and stands at the bedside, shaking his balding head at the horrific sight. "Oh my goodness. What's a nice lady like you doing in a place like this?" Looking over to Monica, he says, "Get me an anesthesiologist. I think Brinkman's right upstairs. He'd be good." Bennett is board certified in surgery as well as emergency medicine.

"You got it. You want OR set up?"

"Yeah, and I need those labs back as fast as possible." He looks up at the monitors and then to the RT. "You feel like intubating her?"

"Sure, it'll save some time. Elizabeth couldn't hear any breath sounds on the right." The RT opens the drawers of his rolling "tool chest" and pulls out several different endotracheal (ET) tubes, weighs the options, and selects the correct size.

"Probably has a pneumothorax." Dr. Bennett migrates to the head of the bed and gently moves the woman's head back and forth, all the while palpating her neck and upper spine. Carefully laying her head back down, he says, "Feels stable. She needs a nasogastric (NG) tube put down as well. I have no idea what he did to her stomach or intestines." He adds, "Can we get X-ray in here now?"

"I'm right here," comes a voice from behind the curtain. "Just waiting for the opportunity."

I reach behind me into a drawer and pull out a long, flexible tube. "Here's the NG." The tube is inserted via the nose and passes through the back of the throat before reaching the esophagus and stomach. The airway originates in the mouth and goes into the trachea and bronchi. Even though the tubes have different functions, it's sometimes easier to insert them both when the head is flexed back and a bright light is shining down the patient's throat. "You want to put it down when you tube her?"

"Yup, let me get this in first." He cranks the woman's neck back into position and depresses her tongue with an angled steel blade.

To the X-ray technician, Dr. Bennett says, "You got it. I want chest, AP and lateral as best you can, then belly, arms, and thighs. And someone get portable ultrasound in here, too, and I want CT right after that. I need all the info I can get." With gloved hands, he palpates the woman's chest and belly, then puts his long fingers down into each stab wound to ascertain the depth and destruction. At one point I see two fingers completely disappear into a gorge. It's a little sickening to remember that this woman isn't anesthetized at all, just unconscious from the assault. "Someone tell Monica I want a pulmonologist, too."

"I heard that," she yells from the corridor.

"This is a mess," Dr. Bennett continues, shaking his head. "I count twelve stab wounds in her torso, a deep one in the right thigh—but it looks like he missed the femoral artery—plus a bunch of shallow ones. Check out her hands and forearms. Looks like she put up one hell of a fight."

I move over to see. Cuts and bruises decorate the underside of her young arms, and most of her fingernails are ripped and jagged. Still, the remaining few appear well manicured. *She takes care of herself.* I can hear Monica down the hallway barking orders into her radio, assembling the surgical team for the OR, and letting the CT room know we have priority.

"She's tubed," the RT says, "and the NG should be in place."

Using his stethoscope, the six-foot-three-inch Dr. Bennett bends over slightly and listens to the patient's lungs. "I got breath sounds on the left, but not much on the right. I need to get a chest tube in before we move her."

Using a 60 cc syringe filled with air, I attach it to the outside end of the NG tube. While Dr. Bennett listens to the woman's belly, I push a large volume of air into it, hoping it fills the woman's stomach and not some other organ.

"I hear the rumble," he says. "Okay, X-ray, go!"

I grab a sterile chest tube pack from a nearby supply shelf and bring it to the bedside, then slip into my lead-lined apron and neck collar while the X-ray technician maneuvers the rigid, cold film boards into place. Like a bunch of bees feverishly working the hive for the queen, we never halt our efforts. The clock on the nameless woman's life is still ticking down.

The radiology tech slides the exposed films into the mid-section of his rolling cart and says, "I'll do these right now. Dr. Gross is the radiologist tonight, and she's on top of it."

"Good." Dr. Bennett is already inserting the chest tube. "I need the wet readings as fast as possible."

Through all the jostling, poking, prodding, and insertion of the various needles, tubes, and airway, the patient hasn't responded. But just now, she makes a barely audible groan—a small but significant sign of life. This young lady is a fighter.

Dr. Bennett clips the second suture on the inserted chest tube and orders, "Let's get this woman to surgery, folks, now!"

In perfect timing, two surgical nurses enter and start to systematically take over the care of the patient, ensuring that everything we've done to this point will support their needs during the procedure. Since they will be circulating within the operating room, this is when they verify the equipment and sterile packs they've gathered for the surgeons are correct and sufficient to meet the demands of the Trauma repair. Some of their questions are repetitious, but better to be safe than sorry. I continue monitoring the patient while we roll the gurney from the bay, down the hallway toward CT and the operative suite. Shoving a mask on my face at the entrance, I push the end of the bed through the double doors.

Disrobed from his white lab coat, Dr. Bennett is already scrubbing at the enormous sink right outside the doors.

I stop at the sinks when I exit the CT room. "Hey, Doc, I told the circulators, but don't forget. We'll need a full rape kit once you have her stable, so try to preserve whatever you can."

"Got it." He looks over at me. "You okay?"

"Yeah, sure. Thanks for asking. How 'bout you?"

"Honestly, I hate this crap." His response catches me off

guard. "Even after twenty plus years of seeing crazy trauma, I never get used to the senseless violence."

"I don't think years matter. If they did, we'd stop being human, right?"

"Right." He drops the scrub brush in the sink and releases his large foot from the water pedal so that the flow shuts off. "I just hate to see an innocent victim pay the price for someone else's insanity. That's what I hate."

ANOTHER PLACE

Lady Mary walks behind the floating vase as it moves down the long marble hallway and through the last archway to its destination: the Room of Holding. As she passes over the threshold into the warm, softly lit chamber, Lady Mary once again hears the distant, barely audible ocean tides. Of all the countless rooms within Father's Cathedral, this is her favorite, where she feels most complete.

The vase floats to the center of the room and hovers above a large pool of water, the same water which flows through Mayim. The pool's vast, three-foot-high, pale marble perimeter holds the water in place above ground. The depth of the pool is uncertain, as the sides extend many leagues down into the belly of the earth. Although made entirely of marble, its dimensions are not rigidly established, but rather can change at will, expanding or contracting as needed, always accommodating whatever it holds.

Lady Mary gently rests her hand on the pool's edge and

keeps her eyes focused on the vase and its precious cargo.
Slowly, the water within the vase morphs from clear liquid
into an opaque, viscous substance, all the while softly glowing
from its inner illumination. When the contents are fully opaque,
the golden vase lowers itself into the pool and submerges
completely under the water. Lady Mary watches as the top
of the solid gold vase opens outward like the petals of a tulip
seeking the morning sun. The opaque substance frees itself of
the vase and floats out into the pool's water. Having released
the globular mass, the vase's task is complete. Imperceptibly, it
closes into its original seamless shape, returns to the surface, and
rises into the air above the pool before vanishing.

Lady Mary lingers at the edge of the pool for a few
moments, watching the opaque glob drift away and settle
somewhere in the dark depths of the warm pool, far beyond
anyone's vision. There it will wait, suspended in time, like so
many millions of others. So many millions.

No doubt the system is divine. The undulating ebb and
flow of the tides: absolute perfection. But the obvious can no
longer be avoided, and Joseph is right. Though all events in this
dimension exist simultaneously in the present, things are not as
they used to be.

The Realm of the Forbidden is changing. Something is
definitely wrong.

PORT ANGELES, WASHINGTON

Late September on the Olympic Peninsula is a beautiful time of year. Bathed in clear blue skies, the entire Pacific Northwest is in the midst of an Indian summer, the days warm and sunny. Located two thousand feet above sea level, my property abuts the base of Olympic National Park. From the wraparound deck of my cabin, on cloudless days I can see all the way across the Strait of Juan de Fuca to Victoria on Vancouver Island and beyond. Sometimes on cold, clear winter nights, even the twinkling lights of the manicured Cypress Mountain ski slopes north of Vancouver are visible.

Today is glorious and perfect for viewing the strait. While soaking up the sun from my favorite bent willow chair, I get the unexpected pleasure of watching four huge Canada geese fly in and skid across the water of my little pond. Such a racket they always make! Alder, my faithful golden retriever, doesn't seem to notice. Lounging beside me, he chews happily on an old ham bone.

"Are you really a retriever?" I ask, patting his head. "Sometimes I'm not convinced."

Hearing my comment, he drops his bone, stands up, and nuzzles my knee.

"Oh, is it time for a stroll? Okay, I could use one, too."

I grab a small basket and open the gate in the deck railing, allowing him to run ahead while we make our way down the back road around to the cherry trees. Along the way I sample wild blackberries and blueberries and even snag a few small, pink salmonberries. Alder gets his fair share as well, although he keeps busy running zigzags through the forest, chasing leaves. When we get down to the cherry trees at the bottom of the clearing, I feel it's necessary to test several varieties before picking enough for dessert later.

"Oh, Mac, I wish you could see this. It's just as you imagined." I take a deep breath and let old memories wash over me. "Maybe you can."

Alder runs alongside, jarring me from my thoughts. "Okay, boy. Here's a cherry for you."

He munches a couple before running off to check the geese. I pick more cherries. *Dang, I wish I didn't have to go back to work tomorrow. I hate to leave the mountain.*

During the climb back up the hillside to the cabin, my thoughts shift to the stabbing victim. *Such a tragedy.* I stroll past the seasonal blooming dahlias, magnificent in their colorful glory, and pick a few varieties for my table. A beautiful pale pink one standing particularly straight catches my eye. *Maybe I'll go in early tomorrow and check on her. See if she's doing okay.*

"Come on, Alder. Time for dinner." He barrels past me on the trail.

I'm just walking onto the deck when the phone rings inside. I hurry in and pick up. "This is Elizabeth."

"Hi there. It's Jackson."

"Oh. Uh, hi."

"Hey, I didn't see you at the gym yesterday and just wanted to be sure you're okay."

"Yeah, I'm fine." *And I don't need a minister checking up on me.*

"Oh, good. That's good."

"Anything else?" I want to hang up.

"Yeah, I was wondering if you've seen the new movie at Deer Park. If not, maybe you'd like to go."

"No, I haven't seen it." I don't even know what it is. "I don't usually go to movies."

"Oh, well . . . maybe we could do something else."

"I go back to work tomorrow. Maybe when my next days-off rotation comes."

"You want to set something up?"

No, not really. "I better not. Might have to work an extra shift or something. How 'bout if I call you when I have time? Otherwise, I'll see you at the gym."

"Oh, okay." His voice drops a notch, then resumes. "By the way, the church is buying bulk ski passes for the youth group again. They're a third off the regular price. You want one?"

Geez, is it ski season already? "Maybe. How soon do you need to know?"

"Sometime before the end of the month."

"Okay. I probably will." I like to ski but hate the drive, especially the return trip home when I'm tired. "Let me think about it."

"You sure you're all right?"

"Yes, Jackson, I'm fine. Look, gotta go. Alder's waiting for me."

"Okay, then. Take care, Elizabeth."

I hang up, wondering why he always calls. Granted, he's a nice guy and great looking. Sexy, even. *Get a grip*, I chide myself. And he does make me laugh, but what's the point? I take a deep breath and remember the pact I made with myself a long time ago. Mac was enough, and our relationship was forever. *Damn.*

A dark cloud seems to have moved over my afternoon. I shake it off. *No way I'm ever getting involved with another man.* The risk is too high.

Three o'clock the next afternoon finds me navigating my truck down Highway 101 toward Discovery Bay and on to Kingston, where I'll catch the ferry. On the seat beside me is my overnight bag, packed with three sets of nursing scrubs and essential gear. I'll be gone for my usual three-night rotation and am already homesick for my snuggly cabin and Alder. With any luck, the Indian summer will still be lingering, and I'll have another four-day break with great weather.

I reach the hospital at 5:45 p.m., with just enough time to look in the computer and find out where they've put my patient. I already know her name is Sandra and she's still in the hospital, although she's been downgraded from ICU to Telemetry.

According to a friend of mine on the Seattle PD, Sandra is a single, twenty-two-year-old grad student. She was doing some late-night shopping at the mall when misfortune took her into the path of the monster who stabbed and raped her. There were no witnesses to the incident, nor could she remember much. Without a description, all the police have been able to ascertain is that the guy was huge, strong, and maybe white. But the event has drawn significant attention, because DNA evidence links the perpetrator to several other vicious assaults and murders in Seattle within the last few years. According to the news, no arrests have been made, which I'm sure won't give Sandra or the other victims any peace.

I walk up three floors, find her room, and give a gentle knock.

"Come in."

I push open the door and peek around the privacy curtain. "Hey, Sandra, how ya doing?"

Seated upright in the bed, she pulls the bedsheet up to her neck and asks, "Do I know you?" Although her long brown hair is a little messy from rustling against the pillow, it's been washed, and all the blood mats are gone. Her cheeks have more color, and her pretty hazel eyes are wide open, examining me vigilantly.

Her trust level must be zero. "Sorry. My name is Elizabeth. I'm the nurse who took care of you when you came into Emergency."

Sandra is still attached to a portable cardiac monitor, but down to one IV site in her hand. "Oh crap, I don't remember any of that. Sorry." A small bouquet of wilting flowers rests on the air vent next to the window, pathetically providing the only color in the drab room.

I should have brought her some dahlias. "Nothing to be sorry for. I don't usually check on my patients, but I wanted to see how you're faring. I was worried about you."

"Thanks. I'm okay." She's still staring at me.

"Well, if it's any consolation, you look a lot better now than you did four days ago." Her facial bruises are fading, and the soft-tissue swelling has diminished. The dressings on her hands and forearms are gone, revealing rows of fine sutures.

"Yeah, well, I think my body will heal, but I don't know about my head." She pauses, pulling the blanket farther up around her chest. "I'm afraid to close my eyes. I still see that huge guy, yet I can't really see him. Sounds crazy, but I know he's there."

"Do you have family in the area? Friends?"

"Yeah." Tears well up in her eyes. "My mom flew in and will be here for a few days, but she's more of a wreck than I am. A couple good friends from the U have been here checking on me, but . . ." She shrugs her shoulders. "It's hard to relate."

"I can only imagine."

Sandra uses the edge of the sheet to blot the tears escaping from the corners of her eyes. "You probably know the bastard raped me."

"I heard," I say softly. I move closer to the bed and hand

her a few tissues. "Has anyone from Social Work been in to talk with you?"

"Yeah, some older lady came by, but it was hard to listen. Not to sound mean, but she made it all sound really clinical. But it's not, not to me."

That's gotta be Georgia. "Sorry."

She nods. "It's like the most personal thing in the world, you know? Anyway, it seemed like she didn't really care, and I sorta shut down."

You're right, she doesn't care. "Well, her job is to get you in touch with support groups. Did she at least do that?"

"She offered. Said she could hook me up with a counselor or a rape crisis thing, but I wasn't paying much attention. She left her card."

The last resort. "What about a minister or something?" *Not that they'd be much help.*

"Well, I haven't been to church since high school, and that was in Idaho. So . . . I don't really know anyone."

Me neither. And I don't want to know any.

She offers a forced chuckle. "I guess God's getting even."

Her statement surprises me. "Why would you say that?"

"Because I'm not . . . whatever I'm supposed to be."

"Oh, Sandra." I gently take hold of her hand. *I hate to break this to you, girl, but we're all on our own here. God doesn't care.* "I'm so sorry. I can't even imagine how I'd feel in your position, but you didn't cause this."

She averts her eyes to the wall behind me. "Then why do I feel so dirty?"

I have no answer. She tries to pull her hand away, but I hold on, and we sit there for a moment in silence.

I let go of her hand and look down at my watch. *Time to focus on the here and now.* "Look, what happened to you sucks. The whole thing sucks big time. But I saw you fight for your life in the ED. You're tough."

"I guess."

"And you're gonna survive this nightmare. You have your whole life in front of you—you know, grad school, friends, family." *You have to remember your life from before the monster.*

She nods, but keeps silent.

"There's no easy way to ask this, and it's none of my business, so you don't have to answer. But has someone offered you the morning-after pill?"

"Oh, that." Her voice drops a notch. "Someone offered it to me, but I can't bring myself to do it."

"Well, you still have a few days to decide." *Better to be safe than sorry.*

She looks down at her finely sutured hands. "I guess I'm going to have to figure something out."

I look at my watch. "My shift starts in five minutes, so I have to go. But if it's okay with you, I'll come back in the morning when I get off. I'll even bring you some real coffee." Showing her my warmest smile, I squeeze her hand. "You'll be okay."

Sandra manages to smile back. "That'd be nice. I'd appreciate it." She looks savaged, but not beaten.

"Okay then, see you in about thirteen hours."

I hurry to the ED, lost in thought. *God. God? If You're up there, answer me this: Why do You let bad things happen to good people?*

I don't get an answer. But then again, I didn't expect one.

———◆———

I meet up with Monica in the locker room. "Hey, girl, did you have a good four days off?"

She slams her locker door. "Actually, they called me last night; needed an extra hand. So, like a fool, I came in and worked. Really dumb. I should've said no. It was a nasty shift."

"Bummer. That's one good thing about living so far away. I can't make it in for the little 'extras.'"

"I'm so jealous! Hey, I'm in charge again. You want Trauma Two?"

"Perfect."

As I make my way from into T-2, my nervous system is assaulted by bright fluorescent lights, overhead loudspeakers, and hundreds of endlessly beeping machines. Almost hostile to the mentally sane, the environment within the ED immediately pushes me into sensory overload.

"I've got two patients," says Paula, the day-shift nurse. She points to an empty spot in the room. "That one's in X-ray. Motorcycle accident. Right leg fractured in at least five places. Ortho's already setting up. Chart's with the patient." She jabs her thumb over her shoulder toward the other patient. "That one's a fifteen-year-old who got mad at her parents. Go figure. Apparently she got a bad report card, was subsequently grounded, and decided to down a bottle of Tylenol to spite her folks. She took over a hundred pills."

"You're kidding. Don't these kids know there are some things worse than death—like a lifetime of dialysis three days a week, forever?"

"You're preaching to the choir, girl." Paula checks her notes. "I managed to wash out a lot of pill fragments and gave her charcoal, but I already explained to her folks she may have organ damage. Her labs are still way outta whack. Anyway, I did all the normal stuff, just got a psych bed assigned, and called report. Here you go." She hands me the chart. "Transporters are on their way."

"Thanks. Have a good night."

By 2:00 a.m. the department is slammed with patients displaying everything from a sore throat to gunshot wounds to cardiac arrest. I have one empty bed when the overhead speakers blare, "Medics on the ramp. Medics on the ramp."

My shoulder mic clicks, and Monica says, "Elizabeth, this will be yours."

"Okay. What is it?" I click back.

"MVA. T-bone, I think. Female. Nonresponsive."

"Here they come now."

At the end of the hallway, two paramedics are pushing a rolling gurney toward me, one holding an IV bag up in the air. A third medic runs behind the head, pumping an ambu bag to ventilate the patient, who does indeed appear nonresponsive. The female subject has a protective C-collar around her neck and is strapped down to a thick, rigid backboard.

"Bed one, boys." I push alongside, turning the gurney. "What do we have?" We maneuver it into place, and six people grab the handholds on the edges of the plastic board, lifting it and its passenger onto the trauma bed.

Positioned near the head of the bed, RT takes the breathing bag from the medic and switches the tube in the patient's mouth to the ventilator. Another nurse inserts a second IV line with a large-bore catheter into the patient's right arm. Chuck, my nursing assistant, cuts off the patient's clothing, puts leads on her chest, and hooks up the monitor. Someone I don't recognize puts a blood pressure cuff on the patient's left arm and hangs another liter of fluid. The entire transfer and initializing hookups take less than sixty seconds.

Dr. Bennett pushes aside the curtain. "What do we have?"

"Twenty-eight-year-old female," the first medic says. "Driver, alone. Broadsided by drunk driver. Car's totaled. Air bags deployed, seatbelt on. Fire department had to pry the door off. Patient initially responsive at scene, said she was on her way home from work. Initial vital signs one hundred over sixty, heart rate irregular, about eighty. Respirations twelve, shallow, but she was talking coherently to us from the car. She'd hit her head on the steering wheel, but it looked sort of minor. Anyway, as soon as we pulled her out of the car, she collapsed, never regained consciousness. We got her loaded into the helicopter, and then she stopped breathing. I intubated and bagged her on the way in. My guess is internal bleeding, based on the damage to the car. She got adrenaline and epi."

Why is it always the young ones? I wonder. Listening to the woman's chest, I can't hear a heartbeat. "I got nothing. How long ago did this happen?" *Damn, she can't die! She's just a few years younger than me.*

"Crap, she had a pulse on the ramp!" The medic looks at his watch. "Twenty-two minutes."

Dr. Bennett listens and looks at the monitor. "Cardiac arrest. CPR! ACLS protocol."

Chuck and another assistant climb onto short stepstools and alternate doing chest compressions while the RT takes care of her breathing and airway.

One of the med students starts to put gel on the woman's abdomen for an ultrasound, but I stop him. "Pay attention! She doesn't have a pulse. Don't you get it?"

He backs away.

"Anything else, Doc?" asks the medic.

"No. Thanks, we're good."

Having dropped their cargo, the medics push their gurney out of the room and let dispatch know they're back on alert. As they depart, Dr. Simmons, the shift Trauma doc, walks in and stands on the other side of the bed.

Dr. Bennett tells her, "You put in the central line." To me he says, "We need drugs. We're on the clock."

I've already opened the crash cart.

Red, a primary color. Red roses, Red Delicious apples, red balloons, red wrapping paper at Christmas. But there's another primary red: blood. Blood, the precious serum of life, juxtaposed with crisp white linens and white tile floors. Red blood, whose real home is in the arterial and venous system of the human body, but which pours out in trauma: soaking sheets, flooding floors, staining uniforms.

The human body holds six pints of blood. This doesn't seem like much until you have to clean it up. Mops and buckets or sometimes down on your hands and knees with towels and linens; either way, it's often impossible to sop up all the red. Tonight is no exception. Changing scrubs, I see that even my black leather clogs are stained with the familiar dark color.

Why, God? Why another needless life? I want to scream. *She didn't have to die.*

"You okay?" Monica asks.

I take a long, deep breath. "Not really." Putting my head

down, I remember things I want badly to forget. "It brings back a lot of difficult memories." *Damn!* "I hate drunk drivers."

"Sorry. I'm really sorry. I know it must feel personal."

"Yup, it sucks."

She gives my shoulder a gentle pat. "I've got to check on some beds for your other two guys, but let's get coffee and talk after shift change."

It's 4:45 a.m.

I can feel my mind steeling itself, locking horrific memories into tiny little compartments and throwing away all the keys. *Hang on, girl. Only a hundred and five minutes to go.*

We'd worked on the young woman named Maggie for two and a half hours, trying to save her. A night auditor for a local hotel, she'd gotten sick during her shift and was driving home. But she never made it.

Some drunk guy whose license had been revoked twice for DUIs was illegally driving home from his favorite bar, ran a red light, and smacked into the side of Maggie's car. Witnesses at the scene told police he must have been doing about eighty. He delivered such force upon impact that she never knew what hit her. Air bags and seatbelts notwithstanding, it's hard to survive that kind of devastation.

In emergency responder lingo, that kind of accident is called a T-bone because the oncoming car literally creates a T when it impacts the other automobile. It's one of the worst types of crashes imaginable, because car doors don't provide much protection against the front end of a massive oncoming projectile. Over the years I've seen hundreds of broken bodies from hundreds of collisions, and some are simply harder to survive than others. And I know what it means to lose a loved one.

I feel familiar tears welling up behind my eyes. *Oh, bullshit! I don't need this right now.*

I hate losing patients, especially the younger ones. I hate losing an infant, a child, a teenager, or a young adult. Heck, for that matter, I hate losing anyone under the age of eighty, anyone in the prime of their lives. It is so hard to watch their bodies fail. Death is absolutely final. Period.

As I clean up the mess and debris from Maggie's trauma, I try to shut out my surroundings, if only for a moment. The heavy air reeks of antiseptics and death, yet I have no choice but to inhale it as I struggle to collect my thoughts. Closing my eyes, I concentrate on the young woman named Maggie, who is now but a memory.

I hear footsteps and open my eyes to see Dr. Bennett in the doorway. "Pretty tough, huh?" he says. "Are you okay?"

Fighting back rare tears, I look up at the ceiling. "Everyone keeps asking me that." *Duh.* I blow my nose. "Yeah, I'm okay. And yeah, it's pretty tough."

"We did try everything, you know. You did good."

"I know we did. Thanks for saying that, Doc. You, too."

"Do you mind going out to talk to the woman's husband? I've got another suicide attempt in T-one."

"Yes, I mind!" I say abruptly. I hate giving family members bad news. I hate this part of my job. "Sorry, Doc. Sure." It has to be done. "Yeah, I've got time. I'll go talk to him."

"Thanks. I'll get in there to see him as soon as I can."

"I'll tell him." I click my shoulder mic. "Hey, Monica, can I get a social worker or a standby clergy to back me up on this death notification?"

"Probably Social Work, but I don't know about the clergy. I'll try, though."

I do my best to focus my thoughts as I walk down the hall. *I'm about to ruin this man's life. How can I make this easier?* I put my hand on the doorknob to the private waiting room and look up. *Please God, if you exist, if you're really out there somewhere, I could use some assistance.* I doubt He's there, and I doubt He'd help anyway, even if He is. Taking one last breath, I walk into the "quiet room."

Pale blue carpeting with a weird, angular pattern woven into it covers the floor. Two overstuffed couches face each other in the middle of the room, one on each side of a plain, polished wooden coffee table. Extra chairs line one wall, and in the far corner a coffee machine percolates on a rolling cart. This room has no windows, only overhead neon lights which, blessedly, are rarely on. Instead, nondescript lamps on the four end tables provide softer illumination, creating a more pleasant visual environment than what is immediately on the other side of the door.

A good-looking man of medium height, around thirty years old, stands from one of the couches and steps toward me. A terrible worry pains his otherwise placid face. His fists open and close nervously, as if he's working out cramps in his hands. From the look of his ruffled, short dark hair, I guess he's been uncontrollably running his fingers through it. No one else is in the room.

I close the door and progress the few steps to him, extending my hand.

"Hi, I'm Elizabeth, one of the nurses. Are you Mr. Donaldson?" I assume he's Kevin Donaldson, the loving husband of Maggie, but I'm winging this and need some breathing room.

"Yeah, I'm Kevin Donaldson."

"How are you doing?" He has a firm grip, and I return the same in kind, giving it all I have.

"Okay. Just wondering what's going on with my wife."

"You want some coffee?"

"No, thanks. I've had about ten cups already." He looks at me expectantly. "What's going on?"

"I've got some bad news. When Maggie came in tonight, she'd suffered a lot of trauma." I look into his brown eyes, struggling to find the words. "She . . . didn't make it." I wait for my words to sink in, knowing the rest of what I have to tell him will be a blur.

Mr. Donaldson sits back down on the couch and buries his head in his hands. I sit on the couch opposite from him and lean forward, resting my elbows on my knees.

When he's ready, he asks, "What happened?"

I take a deep breath. "Her car was hit broadside with a huge impact. The other car slammed into her door, and even though the air bags deployed, she was hit pretty badly. The medics did everything they could to stabilize her at the scene, but she had massive internal injuries and began to lose a lot of blood immediately. It took only about twenty minutes for the helicopter to get her to us, but she was unconscious when she arrived and pretty unstable."

I want to tell him that for two and a half hours, more than twenty people worked on his wife. I want to explain how we fought to revive her using Advanced Cardiac Life Support (ACLS) protocols with at least ten different drugs in varying orders to try and get her heart started again. That we inserted every line known to modern medicine, filmed and scanned her body, and opened her torso to try and stop the massive internal bleeding. That we dumped at least eight pints of blood and sixteen liters of fluid into her to maintain her blood pressure while CPR and RT never halted their perfusion or ventilation efforts. But we couldn't get a response. I want to scream at him, *"I'm so damn sorry! We tried everything!"*

But I don't do any of that. Instead I say calmly, "When she got here, she didn't have a pulse. We tried to revive her, but we couldn't get it back. We tried everything."

"Is there anything else you can do?" he asks, denying the obvious, forever hopeful.

"No, there isn't. I'm sorry."

Silence ensues, and we just look at each other.

"Tell me about her, Mr. Donaldson."

"Oh, God." He lowers his head for a moment, then looks back up at me. "She was beautiful. The love of my life. We've been together for eight years, married for four. We met in college." He stops talking and begins to cry.

"Do you have family nearby who we can call?"

"No . . . I mean, yeah, her mom and dad live in Olympia. I already called 'em, and they're on their way up."

"What about kids?" I hand him the tissue box.

"We don't have any. We've been trying for two years, but never got pregnant. She wanted a baby so badly." He pauses to wipe away the tears with the back of his hand. "All we wanted was a family."

I catch my breath. *Damn, I hate this.* "This is really tough. I hate to be the one to tell you."

"What?" He looks at me intently, tears streaming down his face. "What else?"

"As close as we can estimate, your wife was about eight weeks pregnant."

"Oh please, dear God." Mr. Donaldson hangs his head. "What about the baby?"

"I can't tell you much."

ANOTHER PLACE

"I hear the chasm awakening, Lady Mary."

"Yes, Lord Marcus. It is time for a crossing. I wonder if it will be complete."

"Ah. A very good question." He shrugs his broad shoulders slightly. "Like you, I could once anticipate such things. But alas, no more. Now it seems the outcomes are uncertain."

"Yes. The era of predictability seems to be fading away, slipping through our fingertips—much like a favorite shadow in the evening twilight, eventually disappearing in the dark." As they near the end of the marble hallway, she asks, "Lord Marcus, do you sense anything different?"

"In what context?"

"There seem to be more. More passages. More crossings. Even Joseph, my Sixth, is experiencing a progressively greater number."

"Yes, Lady Mary." He turns and focuses his deep-set dark

eyes upon her. His long, straight nose and high cheekbones are accentuated by his dark brown, shoulder-length hair. "There has been an increase in the numbers of my Seventh, as well."

"It is unpleasant to admit, but I am not surprised. I believe each of the Nine are being affected. What troubles me, more than the increasing numbers, is that most of Joseph's passages now involve some level of agony. The discomfort is beginning to affect him."

"I concur. But even more peculiar for my Seventh is that not only her passages, but also her crossings, involve suffering. And sometimes it is significant."

"Both directions? Oh, Lord Marcus, that definitely confirms a shift." Lady Mary looks up at him. "I believe something is wrong in their realm. Terribly wrong."

"Unfortunately, it seems likely. But if you separate out their timeline, you will recall that this has happened to them before. Their humanity has had many eras of great darkness."

"Let me reflect." Lady Mary turns away and, with her eyes closed, scans through the archives of earth-realm history, both forward and back. "Yes, I now see those segments. The most recent one seems very black indeed."

"Yes, that would have been about seventy years ago in their linear time."

"What I do not comprehend is why they would not try to stop its progress. Having been through such darkness multiple times, why would they allow their own humanity to suffer the horrors again?"

"In their seventy years, many have moved on. The newer ones in their realm may not yet detect the darkness. As you know, evil always hides its true purpose, tricking the unwitting and foolish with great ease. We have witnessed this phenomenon in other dimensions."

"If it worsens, what do you think Father will do?"

Lord Marcus shakes his head. "I cannot foresee Father's

plan. But it seems unlikely he would allow their evil to taint the Nine. They are too close to Him."

"But the only way to stop it from invading our world would be to close the gateway. Close Mayim." Lady Mary puts her hands to her face. "Oh, Lord Marcus, that would mean the end of our symbiotic relationship. The end of . . ."

"Yes, I know. But if evil disintegrates their realm and Mayim is left open, one can only assume that same evil could—and would—infiltrate our realm."

"What if the evil contaminates the waters before Mayim is closed?"

"That would be unthinkable. Why do you ask?"

"Because in addition to the increasing agony, Joseph also senses a darkness every time Mayim opens."

"My Seventh feels it as well."

"I assume each of the Nine do. Thus I am wondering if it is possible for evil to travel through with the light."

"Only the most remote possibility, and never before in our eons of history. As Councilors, we must remember that everything in the many realms of this vast universe is Father's, even darkness and evil. If there is to be such a dark storm, then it is of Father's making."

Lady Mary closes her eyes and lowers her voice. "Yes, of course it is. Perhaps my question is simply, what is the point?"

"Father does not consult me. But I trust that nothing happens by chance." Stopping just before the archway, he takes hold of Lady Mary's hands and scans her thoughts. "I see your mind is still unsettled. If it will give you comfort, I would be honored to stand with you today, if the Nine will allow it."

"That is very kind of you." She searches the air again, peering into the invisible. "The Nine approach."

Appearing first, Joseph stands in the center of the enormous marble archway, and the other eight immediately follow. Clad in their usual white robes, the Nine assemble in single file, waiting for the invisible barrier to open. Although no door or gate can be seen, this particular archway is the Cathedral's only portal allowing passage to and from the natural world outside. The portal opens only before and after each crossing.

"The gateway is open, Lady Mary. We cannot delay."

"With your permission, Joseph, Lord Marcus would like to accompany us."

Joseph raises his head enough to make eye contact with Lord Marcus. In unison, the remaining eight nod their consent. An extra Councilor is not typical, but the Nine do not object to his presence.

As he takes the first step outside, Joseph's foot touches down on a newly formed stone, then another, and another. The calling of the chasm directs the stones to weave a unique path, materializing just prior to each step forward and vanishing behind the last member of the caravan. This is a singular route which will never, in all the eons of time, be repeated.

Although each of the Nine has the power to manipulate certain aspects of time and matter, the stones are beyond their control. Outside the Cathedral walls, the path determines their destination. And today, under blue skies and a warm yellow sun, the course takes them southward, through the mossy grass of a lush green meadow.

Solemnly silent, Joseph leads the caravan through wheat-covered fields and rolling hills, matching his gait to the rhythm of the stone formation. Sensing they are very close, Joseph focuses even harder on the pathway. Just as he lifts his foot in preparation to step upon the next stone, the materialization halts. He carefully settles his foot back down on the final stone and relaxes his mind, clearing it of extraneous thoughts. There will be no more forward movement. Everyone understands; they have arrived.

It is now time for the eight behind him to focus their

thoughts. As they do, the stones begin to form outward, signaling them to spread out in a sideways fashion, creating a slight arc with Joseph at the center. Lady Mary and Lord Marcus are afforded just enough stones to stand on, apart from the Nine. As always, the Councilor is three steps behind the center.

A light breeze flutters the hems of the robes as they silently watch their surroundings for the first sign. Ever so slowly, the earth separates, and the edge of the great chasm appears, opening its expanse before them. Where moments before, the Nine stood upon stones in the midst of rolling hills, now their toes perch precariously at the utmost edge of the largest crevasse in the universe. So wide is the chasm that the sky overhead cannot reach past the middle. So great is its depth that the lowlands recede well beyond the frozen, fiery pits of the world's centermost point.

The familiar sound of the endlessly flowing river rises from miles below. The churning sound reaches Joseph's mind as the water turns and twists powerfully through its course.

Joseph's hands rise, with his palms up and his fingers spread, as though ready to receive an offering. *"Yes, Mayim, I am ready,"* he responds telepathically. He takes two steps backward, away from the rim and toward Lady Mary.

The four to his left turn toward him and put their right hands on the shoulders of the ones in front of them, while the four on his right use their left hands to do the same. The Nine, now physically connected, meld together, once again empowering the central figure. At this moment, that figure is Joseph.

An opaque, gelatinous ovoid appears and hovers above his waiting hands. He reaches for it and carefully balances the entity in his palms, watching the dim light from within begin to grow and dart about, like a firefly ricocheting off the sides of a foggy glass balloon.

Gaining strength from the other eight, Joseph directs

every nuance of his thoughts toward the light within, willing it to grow stronger and brighter until it outshines the midday sun. Uncontainable, the light bursts forth, shoots skyward, and explodes overhead. Spiraling above, the miniature galaxy swirls, dancing and playful. It lingers for only a moment before coalescing tighter and tighter and finally coming to rest on the stone steps in front of Joseph. The opaque ovoid is gone, and Joseph's hands drop to his side.

Standing before him on the stone is a beautiful olive-skinned girl about twelve years old. Her heels touch the edge of the chasm's rim. Slowly she becomes aware of her surroundings and evaluates her guide with deep brown eyes. Her thick, curly hair is set off by a delicately flowered sundress. Joseph knows that if given the chance, they would be friends. But there will be no chance; there never is.

Tilting her head, she says, "I am Keisha. I've been waiting."

Joseph does not answer, except to nod his head toward the chasm. With silent understanding, Keisha turns and sees the chasm for the first time. Without so much as a flinch, she recognizes the gulf for what it truly is, understanding it as clearly as the others.

As the caravan of the Nine, the two Councilors, and Keisha watch and wait, both sides of the chasm begin pulling inward, toward each other, warping together with great speed and purpose. The rolling hills on the far bank come into distant view, and within moments, so near are the two sides that one can clearly discern every detail of the opposite bank. The far rim looks much the same as the near edge, the day every bit as beautiful. Narrowing until the opposite rim is just a stone's throw away, the once-great abyss is now reduced to a minor divergence.

Two stones appear in front of Keisha and move out past the edge of the rim. Suspended in midair, the new path beckons her away from the safety of solid ground. Remaining on the rim is impossible, for the single stone upon which she currently stands is beginning to fade.

Joseph redirects his combined energies toward Keisha's path and wills her time sequence to pause. The stone beneath her feet remains, allowing her to linger.

On the far bank, walking along a path near the edge of the chasm, an olive-skinned man and woman come into view. The path redirects the couple to the rim and positions them to face across the narrow void, prompting them to see it now for the first time. They scan the party of twelve, their gazes ultimately focusing upon Keisha.

"Huh! I think I see her," the woman says softly. "I think it's her."

"How do you know?" the man replies. "Maybe it's some kind of trick."

"No. No, I think we were brought here for a reason." The woman bends forward, shading her eyes from the sun. "To find her."

Keisha, Joseph, and the others listen to the discussion between the man and woman.

"Yeah, but we never saw her, so how can you tell?" the man says. "Besides, it's been so long, almost thirteen years." He looks around him. "And I don't like this place. It makes me uncomfortable."

The woman looks at him. "Well, I can't help that." She looks back at Keisha. "I'd know her . . . because she was mine. Ours. Please, God, it's got to be."

"Well, just so you know, I don't quite get this. But I'm willing to play along if it'll make you happy. I just don't want to see you hurt again."

"I know. But it hurt both of us, remember?"

From around Keisha, a light breeze swirls momentarily, then wafts across the void toward the couple and ruffles the woman's hair. She barely inhales at first, then more deeply with each breath.

"I can smell her!" she screams. "I can feel her!"

Without paying the slightest heed to her footing, the woman steps eagerly out into the air over the chasm as stones appear beneath her feet. Running to the near side with all the speed she can muster, she quickly reaches the center of the void. But abruptly, the stone formation stops, and the sides of the chasm withdraw from each other, preventing the woman from progressing farther. As the path behind her has already dissolved away, she cannot retreat, and thus is suspended on a single platform of stone above the cavernous depths below.

She turns and looks behind her to the man still standing on the rim. "For Heaven's sake, come and help me! I can't do this alone. It must be together or not at all."

He hesitates. "I'm not sure."

"Please, please!" she begs. "I know this is right, I know it's her. It's Keisha!" Her words echo through the canyon. "Keisha!"

Reluctantly, the man takes his first step. With each of his forward steps, the pathway of stones reappears behind the woman, becoming wide enough for two to walk side by side. He walks out to the point where the woman stands. The edges of the chasm narrow once again.

Very near to them now, Joseph can clearly distinguish the couple's features and recognizes the drips of liquid running down the woman's aging face for the tears they are. He also understands what her tears mean to the universe. His hold on Keisha's time must be released, but he waits for one last indication.

At the nth moment, the man asks, "Keisha, is that you? Baby, is that you?"

"It is. I am Keisha."

Keisha steps tentatively out onto the stone path and takes a few strides toward the couple before bursting into a run. The stones behind her disappear from view. When she reaches the middle, the woman stretches out her arms and grabs Keisha with all her strength, pulling her onto their side of the path. Lost in a deep embrace, the three hold each other, crying and hugging. Joseph and the others watch in silence.

Before turning around, the three, still suspended over the chasm, look up to the near side and nod their heads to Joseph in acknowledgment. As the midair stones at their feet are dissipating, they have no choice but to retreat to the far rim. With one foot each on the opposite edge, the great chasm begins warping back outward, reforming the original abyss. The separation is once again a staggering, impassable void.

The Nine drop their arms, breaking the connection with Joseph. Without a word, he turns and leads them back along another path to the Cathedral.

SEATTLE, WASHINGTON

September's warm Indian summer endures another two weeks before the clear blue skies turn an incessant rainy gray. Fall colors fade to a snowy winter in the mountains. Aside from a half-dozen ski days with Jackson's church group, Christmas, New Year's, and winter come and go without much notice by me or Alder. Now spring is around the corner. The mid-March days are getting longer, and the snow is starting to melt off the lower Olympics.

Standing outside on the helicopter ramp at Bayside Hospital, I look across Puget Sound and watch the sun begin to set behind the dusky-blue snow-capped mountains in the distance. Somewhere on the other side of the range, my snuggly cabin and faithful retriever are waiting for me. One more shift tonight, and tomorrow morning I'll be heading home.

Reluctantly I walk back through the Trauma doors and head in to get my shift assignment. Monica stands behind one of the circular desks as charge nurse again. Putting her hands on her slim hips, she looks up from the assignment board and smiles when she sees me. "Hey, Elizabeth. I know it's your third night in a row. You want something easy, like Zone Three or something fast?"

"I'll take Zone One, unless someone else wants it."

"All yours. Go take report."

Passing through the double doors of Trauma 2, I find the day-shift RN. "I have a surprise for you," he says. "Three empty beds!"

"No way." The busiest time in the ED is always from midafternoon until about five in the morning. Rarely, if ever, are there three empty trauma beds at change of shift. I peek inside the double doors, and sure enough, all is quiet. "Cool. On the other hand, this could mean a really bad couple of hours if I get slammed with three at once."

We exchange information on the one patient, then he hands me his shoulder radio and some keys and takes off. Systematically I circle the room, checking all of my equipment and the crash cart, and restock supplies. Undoubtedly there will be a surge at some point.

Sure enough, around 6:45 p.m. I hear the familiar, "Medics on approach. Medics on approach."

On my way to the entrance to intercept them, I overhear the medic radio squawking, "Twenty-three-year-old female, picked up from a clinic, apparently undergoing a minor surgical procedure and started to code. Hemorrhaging vaginally, possible internal bleeding. I got seventy systolic, no heart rate, CPR in progress, two lines in, normal saline wide open, ETA two minutes."

Dr. Bennett, who's standing right beside me, picks up the radio phone and gives orders for medications. By the time he hangs up, we hear the sirens.

I walk to the triple doors and punch them open to watch while the ambulance pulls into the drive. Even before the driver hits the brakes, the back-end doors are opening. Two paramedics jump out, unlock the gurney from the rig, and roll it out to the pavement. A thick, rubbery mask hooked to a small oxygen tank with a narrow tube covers the woman's face. The slender blond woman is obviously pregnant, unconscious, and covered in blood.

One medic continues to do CPR chest compressions while Dr. Bennett, two med students, and I work right alongside to get the patient through the entrance, down the hall, and into the Trauma room. Even though we're paralleling a fast-moving gurney carrying a pregnant woman, we manage to run alongside and keep the heart rhythm going.

"Twenty-three-year-old female," a medic says. "Picked up from North Sound Planned Prevention Clinic today. Apparently there to have a second trimester abortion. Abortion doc said he gave her drugs to expel the contents of the uterus, but the uterus apparently ruptured and the patient started hemorrhaging badly. He guessed her uterus must have been previously damaged by another event, although he had no clue as to what."

"Obviously the guy did a real thorough pre-op exam," interjects the medic managing the woman's breathing.

"Whatever," the first medic continues, shaking his head. "Anyway, things went from bad to worse, and before the doc could figure out what was wrong, patient went into cardiac arrest. They had no choice but to call nine-one-one. Talk about a screwed-up mess."

As we reach T-2, Dr. Bennett does a quick detour to grab an OB kit from a nearby supply cupboard. Everyone else stays in place to assist. Within two minutes we have the patient transferred to the trauma bed, hooked up to a ventilator, and additional IV lines inserted. Through all of our actions, CPR never stops.

While hooking up the monitor leads on her bare chest, I can't help but notice numerous random scars all over the woman's torso. *What the hell?* True, she has short blond hair, but from this angle, I can see the dark roots. I look a little closer at her face through the airway.

"Oh, crap!" I blurt out as Dr. Bennett catches up. "It's the stabbing victim!" I can't immediately remember her name, but there is no way in a million years I could ever forget her or the injuries. "The one from five or six months ago. You know, the college student attacked at the mall?"

"What the . . . ?" Dr. Bennett says, looking at her torso. "Oh, those damn fool butchers!"

Sandra. Her name pops into my head. "Sandra! Her name's Sandra. I had coffee with her a few times when she was still in the hospital, and then we lost track."

Like bad déjà vu, we keep working on her. Since she doesn't have a pulse, the team works through all of the ACLS protocols. We're about halfway through and running out of options when we get a heartbeat. It isn't perfect, but it's enough to support life.

Monica comes back into the area. "Doc, I've got the OR team prepped, and anesthesia's setting up. I assume you want the OB/GYN guys down here, too?"

"Yeah. I want them to take the lead on this."

"Got it. Also, ultrasound's ready, and CT's standing by."

"Okay. I'll go scrub," Dr. Bennett says. "Damn it all, anyway. There's only a slim chance the baby's alive, but I need to know. Someone get a fetal heart monitor on her—right now!"

"You got it. You guys know who this is, don't you?" Monica asks.

"We figured it out," I answer.

"After everything we went through to save her the last time, this makes me sick," Dr. Bennett says.

"If the baby's alive, you think you can save it?"

"I'm hoping I can just save her. She's not out of the woods yet. The drug they used on her can cause all kinds of internal bleeding, and she had so many intestinal wounds from the stabbing . . ." He shakes his head as he walks toward the scrub sink. "But yeah, I'll do my best. Maybe something good can come out of this."

———•◦•———

My grueling shift is at an end, and I want to catch the 7:10 a.m. Edmonds ferry so I can get ahead of the traffic going out to the peninsula. But before I head home, I need to get something off my chest.

Almost six months have passed since my first encounter with the stabbing victim, Sandra. Yet every detail of her initial visit to the ED, all the energy and hard work we poured into her survival, is fresh in my mind, like it just happened yesterday. I can't for the life of me figure out why, but I'm angry.

A few hours ago, Sandra was rolled from my Trauma room into surgery, again barely holding onto life. This time the gynecologist had opened her up. Although he and Dr. Bennett managed to stop the massive internal hemorrhaging, her ruptured uterus and part of her intestines had to be removed due to irreparable damage. And in the course of saving her from the precipice between life and death, the baby she was carrying died.

So, it seems, this young woman in the prime of her life has yet two more tragedies to deal with. She'll never again be able to have children, and she'll never know the child she was carrying. The monster who attacked her six months prior initiated a chain reaction of unspeakable events, leaving a catastrophic trail of destruction behind.

Quite simply, the whole situation makes me furious. But why? Who am I mad at? The attacker? Sandra? The abortion clinic? God? I try to collect my thoughts as I walk to her room.

Tap. Tap.

I rap on the door. "Knock, knock. Hey, it's me . . .

Elizabeth." I poke my head around the curtain. "How ya doing?"

"Oh, hey." She's very sleepy, heavily sedated and still under the residual effects of anesthesia. An NG tube protrudes from her nose, intermittently suctioning out the contents of her stomach into a plastic canister, and she has multiple IV lines running into her neck and arm. A catheter bag siphoning urine hangs down from the bottom of the bedrail. The drapes are closed, and no flowers or cards decorate the depressing, porridge-colored room. I realize again how much I hate hospitals.

"How are you feeling?"

"I hurt," she croaks through the tube.

"Yeah, I bet you do."

She drifts off for a minute. I sit on the edge of the air vent and wait until she rouses again.

"Oh, hey. You still here?"

"Yeah. Is your mom coming up?"

Sandra shakes her head a little. "She's not speaking to me right now."

Why the heck not? "Sorry to hear that. That doesn't help."

"Nope. It doesn't."

"So, Sandra, what's the deal?" I ask quietly. "What happened?"

"I don't know." She rolls over at an angle to face away and through her foggy haze starts to cry a little. "I just couldn't do it. I thought I could. But, I couldn't. I just . . . gave up."

"You had my number. I wish you'd reached out to me." I feel unbelievably sad.

"It wouldn't have mattered."

"Yeah, Sandra, it does. *You* matter. You almost died last night."

"I wish I had died," she says in a barely audible voice. "Anyway, it's over now." She drifts off.

Once again, I write my name and phone number on a card

and leave it in her purse with a note to call me if she gets out of the hospital before I return in four days. Then I wipe the tears from my own eyes and leave. She never calls.

8

It's Monday, the last day of March. My life seems to be an endless, revolving cluster of Trauma shifts, one three-night series after another. The only bright spot in my existence is my time off, spent in solitude with a bottle of wine and Alder. As I park my truck in the employee parking garage, I sorely miss them both already.

Get over it and buck up, I chide myself. *Got to make a living.*

Arriving at the ED, I check in with tonight's charge nurse. "Hey, Tom, how ya doing? What's happening?"

"Same ol', same ol'." He raises his green eyes slightly to look at me. I figure he's about an inch shorter than my five feet seven inches. Height isn't all it's chalked up to be, though, and in his case, he uses it to his advantage. After winning a long list of gymnastic competitions as a teenager, he landed himself a full-ride scholarship to the university. Now in his late thirties, he still maintains the amazing muscle tone of a gymnast. "Last night was about normal. Tonight's a full moon, though, so it could suck."

I look at his blue scrub top tucked into his trousers. *He must do a couple hundred sit-ups a day.* "Are you on your second or third shift?"

"This is my third and final for this week. And I'm ready to get the heck out of Dodge." He smiles. "I want to go home to my family and pretend I'm a dad again."

"Don't blame you." *Kids. Sounds nice.* "Where do you want me tonight?"

"Truthfully, I'd like you in Trauma, but I've got a few nursing students here on their first rotation, and they need to see the other areas before we destroy their vision of the world."

"Oh?" *Here it comes.*

"Yeah, so if you'd take Zone Three, that would be great. Do you mind being shadowed?"

Yes. "You know I hate mentoring."

"Sorry. But someone's got to do it. I'll put Marilyn with you, plus three aides."

"Right. How many, and when are they coming?"

"I'll give you two, if that's okay. They'll be here at six thirty."

"Okay. No problem." *Liar.* I grab my stuff and head back to the locker room.

Zone Three is the clinic side of the Emergency Department, usually full of patients with colds, flu, headaches, lacerations, simple fractures, light burns, dental problems, or other equally annoying complaints which can't wait for the doctor's office to open. This area is also where the police and sheriff's deputies bring county jail prisoners needing medical attention.

Of course, as with all ED's in the country, we get our share of patients fondly referred to as "frequent flyers," consisting mostly of serious alcoholics too drunk to function, drug addicts seeking some type of pharmaceutical relief, or prostitutes wanting aid after evenings with questionable johns. The indigent street people also frequent our threshold, usually looking for nothing more than a warm bed or a not-so-warm meal.

Also built within Zone Three are two padded rooms equipped with hidden cameras, steel padded doors, thick glass viewing windows, and absolutely no equipment whatsoever, except a single gurney with side-welded eyebolts for restraints. These are "safe" rooms where violent, strung-out, delusional folks deemed a danger to themselves or someone else are temporarily lodged.

"Hey, Marilyn." I throw my stuff into my locker. "How've you been?"

"Hey back at you, Elizabeth. I've been absolutely great!"

"I haven't seen you in a couple of weeks. What's been going on?"

"Not much. My daughter's second birthday is next week, and hubby's off tonight, at home taking care of her." She flashes me a warm smile, revealing a set of flawless teeth. "All I can say is, he'd better finish the laundry."

A tall, slender African American woman, Marilyn has been on her own since she was sixteen. Through brains and tenacity, she miraculously managed to finish high school, then worked her way through the university nursing program. She fought for everything she's earned. Her husband of five years is a Seattle firefighter who usually works shifts on opposite nights so they can keep a close eye on their beautiful little girl. This means they don't have a lot of time at home together, but it's the price they're willing to pay to be good parents.

"Wow, almost two, huh?" I marvel at the unrelenting passage of time. "That's amazing. I remember when she was born. Got any recent pictures?"

"Oh girl, you know I do!" She reaches into her purse and whips out a small photo album filled with pictures of her adorable family.

"Too cute! Wow." *Mac and I talked about kids. A family . . .*

"I know. She's the love of my life."

Mustn't think about those things right now. I shake it off.

With our personal stuff safely stowed, we move out to Zone Three's desk area to get reports from the two day-shift nurses. It's rainy outside and will be dark soon.

"Hey, guys, I hate to tell you this," says one of the nurses, "but every room is already full. All sixteen beds."

"We figured," I say. "Any idea how many are waiting to be seen?"

"At least a dozen, maybe more. We were just about to start pulling gurneys out of storage to stick along the hallway."

"Yeah, I'm sure we'll need 'em."

"I'll help you," offers one of the day-shift nurses.

"That's nice, but you need to go home and rest. We can manage. Right, Marilyn?"

"Yup! Take off, you two. We'll see you in the morning."

They waste no time departing to the locker room.

"Ugh, look at this stack of charts!" I moan. "They were busy today. You ready for this?"

"You know me, I'm always ready. Let's get this show on the road."

Just then, the two nursing students assigned to our supervision round the corner, looking spiffy in their clinical white uniforms, with notebooks in hand. Seeing them, my first thought is, *Wow, they're letting twelve-year-olds into this program now?* They look so young. The reality is, both are juniors at the university, and thus at least twenty years old. But from my thirty-four-year-old perspective, they look awfully innocent.

I extend my hand and introduce myself. "Hi, I'm Elizabeth, and this is my partner in crime tonight, Marilyn. Welcome."

The male student reciprocates the handshake and identifies himself as Tony. The young woman, named Michelle, does likewise.

"We don't have much time for chitchat," Marilyn explains. "Do you guys have things you need to check off during this shift?"

"Yeah, we each need to start as many IVs as possible, assist with suturing, and give medications—if possible," Michelle answers.

"And we need to put in a catheter if we can, too," Tony says, "using sterile technique."

Marilyn and I nod.

"Shouldn't be a problem," I say. "Now let me tell you a little about this area." I familiarize them with the desk, video monitors, and carts, then guide them down the two long hallways, explaining the variations in clinic rooms on each side.

Less than five minutes elapse before my shoulder radio goes off: "Zone Three, Triage."

"Okay, kids, who wants to work with me?" I ask.

"I'll stick with you, if that's okay," Tony says.

"I've got the Triage, Marilyn. Come on, Tony, let's go see what's up there."

Reversing direction, I head for the two Triage desks at the front entrance to the ED, with Tony at my heels.

———

It's approaching midnight, and with the exception of one of the padded rooms, every other room, bed, and extra gurney within our zone is full. The entire ED is slammed, and the previous six hours have flown by. I desperately need to use a toilet, something I've been delaying for at least two hours but can no longer ignore. I also want a gigantic cup of coffee and some food, so I let Marilyn know that Tony and I will take ten minutes, and then she and Michelle can do the same.

After relieving myself, I manage to gobble my midnight snack of tuna salad with sliced water chestnuts, three pieces of sharp cheddar cheese, and a dill pickle, all in record time. Then I slam down some much-needed hot caffeine. Somewhat refreshed, I return to the desk area and send my cohorts off for their respective respites.

"Is that all you guys get for breaks in here?" Tony asks.

I look at his innocent face and realize he's just beginning to get the full picture of his future. *Seems like a nice kid. I hate to spoil it for him.* "Oh, once in a while we get twenty, but that's not the norm. If you want ED work, you need to accept it. Otherwise, pick a different genre like surgery or chemo, something more controlled."

"No, it's okay." He runs his fingers through his thick, wavy black hair and pushes his wire-rimmed glasses back up into position on his nose. "I'm just wondering."

"Let's go make our rounds." I turn and almost bump into two heavily armed sheriff's deputies rounding the corner. Between them stands a huge man in an orange jumpsuit sporting matching wrist and ankle shackles strung together. Inwardly, I sigh. King County plus orange jumpsuit equals violent criminal.

"Triage nurse said we could come straight back," one of the deputies says.

"No problem. I've got Room One open."

Retrieving the pink key coil from my pocket, I unlock the padded steel door to the first of the two secure rooms. Once inside, both deputies assist the man onto the gurney, then detach and untangle the massive chains and reattach them to the four side-welded steel points on the outside edges of the bed. The prisoner is now prone, legs spread, left arm up over his shoulder and right arm down at his side. Considering that he is at least six feet seven and 250 pounds, I don't have a problem with the four-point restraint system. If we're lucky, he won't be here long.

I give him the once-over, noting clubbed fingernails and the putrid smell of old cigarette smoke. *Ugh, heavy smoker.* His shoulder-length dark hair looks unwashed and greasy, but seems to fit with his pocked face and previously broken nose. *Doesn't like to bathe and obviously never got that nose set.* When he opens his mouth, I see at least two broken front teeth. *No dental work.*

Not feeling terribly compassionate, I throw a basic question out to the room, hoping someone will answer. "What's going on?"

"I feel like shit," responds the prisoner.

"Herman, keep it clean," a deputy says.

I raise my hand to signal that I'm not offended. "Can you give me a little more detail?"

"I don't feel too good."

"Where?"

"All over. Urp!" He lets out a huge, disgusting belch.

"I need more specifics. Stomach? Chest? Head? Back?"

He raises his voice a little. "I feel sick."

"Any pain, nausea, vomiting, or diarrhea?"

From the corner of my eye, I notice Tony retreating to a position closer to the padded door.

"I told you, I don't feel too good," the prisoner growls. "Like I'm gonna puke."

"Okay, when did this start?"

"Awhile ago."

It's like pulling teeth. "Did you actually throw up?"

"Nah."

"Any sharp pains?"

"Nah."

"Gas?"

"Yeah, I fart a lot," he snorts, laughing.

Cute. The big guy thinks he's funny. "Okay, I'll be back in a minute." I move away from the gurney, unlock the door, and lead Tony out of the cell. The two deputies stay behind while I relock the door.

I point to the small video monitor mounted above the desk shelving area and explain, "Once we're done, we can observe him from out here. If you notice anything weird, just holler. Everyone in the department has a key. "

"He's really creepy."

"Yeah, you're right. But honestly, some of the nicest patients we get are low-level prisoners. Not this guy, though. I have a feeling he'd just as soon slit your throat as smoke a cigarette. I also think he's faking."

Marilyn and Michelle are back, so I tell them about our new guest and describe the color-coded jumpsuit system to the students. I grab the thermometer, blood pressure cuff, and a few other diagnostic tools and lead Tony back to the room.

"If we do this together, we can be out sooner. You take his temp, and be careful he doesn't spit at you. And double glove."

"Right."

Donning two sets of gloves, protective eyewear, and a mask, we're ready. I unlock the door.

"Herman, I'm going to get your vital signs and see if we can figure out what might be going on."

"You can do anything you want to me, bitch." He sticks out his nicotine-stained tongue and wiggles it at me.

What an ass.

"Hey! Watch your mouth, Herman," a deputy says. He moves closer to the bed and holds the man's wrist still while I put the blood pressure cuff around his upper arm, which bulges with muscles. Even though he's in shackled restraints, I'm glad to have the extra security.

Meanwhile, Tony tries to take Herman's temperature via the ear canal, but Herman doggedly turns his head to one side, avoiding the probe. To his credit, Tony tries the other ear, but Herman fights that attempt also.

"Never mind," I tell him. "I'll come back with a rectal probe."

Tony nods and is stepping away from the gurney when Herman regurgitates a huge wad of mucus and hurls it at him. Tony's eye shield takes the full force of the loogie, and he quickly retreats toward the door. Apparently the prisoner is quite skilled at hurling secretions.

The other deputy steps forward, but I hold up my hand to stop him. "Okay, here's the thing," I tell Herman. "Two can play this game. I don't care if you get treatment tonight. I also don't care if you spend the rest of your life chained to this bed. Eventually, you're gonna need to pee and poop, and I don't care if you do it all right here." I point to the mattress. "I'm also guessing you smoke and will eventually want a cigarette, but you won't be able to take a draw chained to the bed. Now we can make this easy, or we can make this hard. Your call."

"Screw you."

"Okay, then. We'll be back in a while." I gather my equipment, unlock the door, and leave.

"Fuck you, bitch!" he yells as I close the door.

One of the deputies follows Tony and me. "He's a real piece of crap. Been in the prison system for years, starting with drugs, theft, several violent assaults, and escalating recently to blowing the head off a young man working in a convenience store. He's awaiting adjudication at County now. Multiple re-offender and hopefully going down for life this time, maybe even the death penalty." The deputy pauses. "Prison guards didn't think anything was wrong with him, but the clinic is closed and it's the guard's butt if something's really wrong."

"I figured. Same ol', same ol'. Sounds like a nice guy. I think we'll just let him stew in there for a while and see what happens. An hour in that position may soften him up a little."

"Works for me," agrees the deputy. I unlock the door for him.

"Tony, throw that eye shield and mask in the trash, get rid of those gloves, and go wash up. We'll talk about this later."

I do exactly the same thing, knowing I need to focus on other patients.

<hr />

Two a.m. Four more hours to go. I hang up a new bag of IV fluids for a patient with the flu.

As general fatigue threatens to settle in, I get a weird image of myself skiing down a steep, snow-covered mountain toward slick, icy moguls. The last run of the day is often the hardest, but I always take it, figuring if I can hold it together long enough, eventually I'll be out of the woods, sitting comfortably next to a fire in a bar at the bottom of the hill and sipping a hot toddy. On the other hand, if I catch an edge or hit a tree, I'll crash and burn, ending up at the bottom of the hill in a pile of muck. ED shifts are a lot like that.

"Zone Three, Triage," blares my shoulder radio.

Walking past the desk, I notice the video feed from Room 1 and see that the felon is apparently sleeping. Tony and I head for the front.

Determining a patient's level of acuity during the initial evaluation is the role of the Triage nurse and, if done astutely, can often mean the difference between life and death or life and limb. Whether due to training or incredible gut intuition, we're lucky to have several great Triage nurses on our staff. Typically, they don't miss much.

As I come around the corner, I notice a familiar face sitting on the other side of the Triage desk. The permanent black eyeliner and artificial black lashes are partially hidden by her black-framed glasses. I'm positive she dyes her shoulder-length hair, because coal black isn't a common natural color. Her black fingernail polish matches the lipstick she's just finished reapplying.

"Hey, Tammy, what's going on?" I speak over the back of the seated nurse.

"Hey, Elizabeth." The gothic beauty smiles at me. "I think I've been raped."

Tony emits a quiet gasp.

"Oh, bummer. Again?" I note a new gold ring through her left nostril.

"Yeah."

"Did you know the guy?"

"Kinda."

"Any injuries?"

"Nope, just think I've been raped."

Eyeing the Triage paperwork, I note it's complete. I also spy a small mountain of Tammy's previous ED files already stacked underneath the current one.

"Is she ready to go?" I ask the RN.

"Yup, and here's all her records from this year's other visits."

"Okay." She hands me a file about two inches thick. "Come on, Tammy."

When I glance at Tony, he appears baffled, but I have neither the time nor opportunity to explain. Fortunately, he remains silent.

"I don't have much of a room for you tonight, Tammy. What are you looking for?"

"I just want to be sure I don't have the clap or something. And I want the pill."

"Okay, but in order to do the STD kit, you'll have to wait for a room. We can't do that in the hall."

As we round the corner, the sea of occupied gurneys filling every inch of space comes into view. "Oh crap, you guys are really busy."

"Yeah, we are." I show her to the one and only empty gurney about halfway down the hall. "I won't make you change into a gown until we have a room available, but it might be five or six hours. Can you give me some urine?"

"That long? Oh, man!" She leans against the gurney. "Yeah, I gotta pee."

"Okay, you know where the bathroom is. Here's a cup and bag." I hand her the labeled items. "Do this first, and then I'll get a doc to come talk to you. Maybe we can get the medication ordered quickly. You need a warm blanket?"

"Thanks."

"Hey, I know we've talked about this before, but have you given any more thought to using protection?"

"It's such a pain."

"Yeah, but look at the hours upon hours you waste coming in here each time. That's a pain for you, too. It might save you a lot in the long run."

"Yeah, it probably would. But it's such a pain," she whines, repeating herself. "And guys I hang with don't like condoms."

"I'm not talking about condoms. They'd never know if you get the shot or take birth control pills. At least that way you can protect yourself against potential pregnancy."

"Yeah, but you know I don't have any insurance."

"I thought I hooked you up with a social worker last time and she got you an application for state Medicaid. You know Medicaid will cover the prescription. She did give you the paperwork, right?"

"Yeah, but I forgot to fill it out."

How can people be so irresponsible? "Do you still have it?"

"Not sure. Probably somewhere."

"Okay. I'm going to get Social Work back down here and have her help you fill it all out before you leave today. I want you protected and taken care of. Really, Tammy, you've got to do this for yourself."

She looks down at her hands and shrugs her small shoulders. "Thanks. That would help a lot," she whispers.

"Okay, pee for me and then sit tight, and we'll get your vitals and all the regular stuff. I'll go find a doc. By the way, are you really claiming rape? Because if you are, then I need to start the chain-of-evidence process."

"Nah, I just always say that so I can get in quicker."

"Got it, okay."

Turning around, I head back to the desk area. Tony hasn't said a word, and I figure he's confounded by what he's witnessed. We stop in the corridor, long enough for me to quietly explain. "Tammy's a part-time college student, part-time waitress, and she loves to party. But she's not a hooker. She just frequently goes out with guys who are jerks, has sex, and then regrets it afterwards. So she comes in here to get checked and get the morning-after pill."

"What a stupid reason to come to the Emergency Room."

"Yeah, and expensive, too. Half our patients don't need to be here. But they come regularly because they think it's their own personal 'free' clinic. Her little visit tonight will cost the hospital several thousand bucks, and they'll never collect a penny."

"So who pays the bill?"

"You and me. But don't get me started."

"This makes no sense. I mean, no one even needs a prescription to get the morning-after pill. Anyone can buy it for like twenty bucks at a pharmacy."

"Yup, I know. But the operative word there is *buy*. Listen, Tony, I'd be thrilled if she'd just fill out the stupid paperwork for Medicaid. Oh well. At least she's smart enough to stop the pregnancies."

We reach the desk at the same time Marilyn approaches from the other hallway.

"Is it just me, or does it seem like this shift will never end?" She rolls her eyes. "I so want to go home."

"In your dreams." I look at the two students and see the fatigue setting in. "Hang in there. It'll be over soon."

"It's not quite like on TV," Tony says.

"No, sadly, this is real life."

Noticing the video feed from Room 1, Marilyn and I both catch movement. Awake now, the guy in the orange jumpsuit is maneuvering his shackled right hand into the side pocket of his suit. One deputy is leaning against the outside of the padded door, and the other is on break somewhere.

"What the heck do you suppose he's up to, Marilyn?

Please tell me they thoroughly searched him before bringing him to the hospital." I turn to query the deputy.

"Holy cow! Look!" Marilyn points to the monitor. "The creep's got a lighter!"

"Oh, for crying out loud!" Within a split second, the restrained prisoner withdraws a small Bic lighter from his pocket, flicks it, and holds the tiny flame to the sheet. Before we can react, the sheet has caught fire. It will only be another few moments before the mattress, his jumpsuit, and his right thigh are engulfed in flames. "Hey, Deputy! We got a problem!"

The deputy turns and looks through the small window of the locked door. "Damn him! Open the door!"

"Not without reinforcements. Where's the other deputy?" If this is Herman's grand scheme for executing an escape, his plan has a major flaw. More likely, he's too stupid to live. Either way, his attempt to wiggle away from the flames is an exercise in futility, as the bolted shackles restraining him are definitely locked.

"He's on break," the deputy responds. "You've got to open the door!"

"No way. We've got thirty patients in close proximity, and I don't want anyone else getting hurt." I grab the police band walkie-talkie.

"You've got to. He'll catch fire!" the deputy exclaims, pounding his fist on the door.

As the flames begin to lick Herman's jumpsuit, his muffled cries for help reach the outside of the padded room. It didn't take long for reality to sink in.

"Hang on!" It's against hospital policy to open the door without at least two security guards present. I key my mic and the radio at the same time. "Security, Zone Three. Security, Zone Three." Glancing back to Marilyn, I release my fingers from the buttons. "What do you think? Does this qualify as 'walking pace' or STAT?"

She shrugs. "He threatened you, not me."

She's right, of course. As I recall the hurling mucus and obscene language, I conclude that this truly isn't life or death. I rekey the items. "Security, Zone Three. Security, Zone Three . . . walking pace . . . STAT." *A combination ought to work.* I look squarely at the nursing students and explain, "He did this to himself, and payback's a bitch. I guarantee you, he'll never light himself on fire or think about spitting at a nurse—ever again."

Since the guards have to come from all over the hospital, it takes about forty seconds for the detail to arrive at the door to Room 1. I'm ready with my key to dutifully unlock it. Two deputies and five huge hospital security guards armed with Tasers and a fire extinguisher enter the room, and I close and relock the door behind them. It's their job to wrestle with the prisoner and the fire. My job is to call the Burn Center.

Near 5:00 a.m., things begin to slow down a little. Somehow we've managed to clear out about half of the patients and put away most of the temporary gurneys. The corridors are beginning to look more like hallways again, and the noise is down to a low roar. My pile of patient charts totals forty-two in all, and I happily drop them all at the front counter for the charge nurse to review.

"Here you go, Tom. A little late-night reading."

"Oh, you are too kind, darling."

"Truth be told, I really don't like Zone Three."

"Me neither."

"But give me a good Trauma any day, and I'm happy as a clam."

"Well, thanks for taking it this shift. I'll note that you and your student need to be in a different section when you come back tonight."

"Oh, whatever. I'll survive either way." I'm about to say

something else when the medic phone rings.

"Bayside Emergency." *Click.* "This is Medic Six." *Click.* "Inbound with thirty-one-year-old female, pregnant, approximately four months' gestation, apparently had a spontaneous miscarriage at home while attempting to have what she thought was a bowel movement. Husband dialed nine-one-one." *Click.*

The ED doctor closest to the radio room picks up the phone and keys the talk button. "Go ahead, we read you."

Click. "At the scene was a massive amount of blood and tissues, and she's still bleeding. I got an eighteen IV in her left AC and normal saline running wide open. Vital signs are ninety over fifty, pulse of fifty-six. Oh-two sat is ninety-five percent on four liters, nasal cannula. Our ETA is four minutes." *Click.*

Tom says to me, "You've got the larger OB room open. Can you take her?"

"Sure. Hey, Doc, sounds like she's hemorrhaging. Can you be with me at the beginning?"

"Yeah. I'll wait right here and meet 'em at the door. Call for labs, order type and cross, and get a monitor in that room. Tom, get me the OB doc who's on tonight, and you might wanna alert the surgical team upstairs."

"You got it," we all say in unison.

Remembering my student shadow, I turn to Tony. "Why don't you stay with Doc and watch the process from the beginning? I'll go set up the OB room."

It is against department policy to stock many supplies in the Zone Three rooms, due to regular pilferage and theft by our illustrious clientele. So when equipment is needed, every piece has to be procured from storage and moved into the rooms. This chore gives me about three minutes to run and snag what I'll need, haul it to the room, and get it all set up. I find a portable monitor and suction, then grab IV equipment, solutions, blankets, and an OB cart. I also find a neonatal incubator, just in case.

I finish readying the room just as the medics, the doctor, and Tony come through the door with a female patient on the gurney. The top sheet is soaked with blood from her waist to her knees, and she is sobbing uncontrollably.

I remove the saturated top sheet and a blood-drenched second blanket and throw them on the floor. Between the patient's legs is a wad of bloodied, blue-flowered towels, probably from her home. One medic grabs those up in a bundle and sets them on the floor in the corner behind us. Together we all lift and transfer the patient to a clean bed covered with disposable protective pads known as Chux.

Shock is beginning to set in, and the patient is shivering uncontrollably. Tony steps forward and covers her with several warm blankets while I put a mask on her face for increased oxygen flow and attach the monitor and blood pressure cuff.

Very quietly I say, "Hey, darlin', you're gonna be okay. This really sucks, but you're gonna be okay."

She looks up and cries out through the mask, "I lost my baby!" Gasping for air, she cries out again, "I lost my baby!"

"I know. And we're not sure the bleeding has stopped, which probably means that either part of the placenta is still inside, or your uterus won't clamp down. So we have some work to do to make sure you stay safe and can get pregnant again." I wipe the tears from her eyes. "Do you understand?"

"I just want to die. I lost my baby." She turns away and resumes sobbing.

Someone from each department is now crowding into the sardine-can-size space, doing their assigned tasks. The registration clerk arrives with the patient's husband, who looks devastated. He rushes to her side, bends down, and holds his wife. "Don't worry, baby, we can try again. It's okay."

I feel like crying myself. What a tragic scene. We are all intruders into this couple's worst, most private nightmare.

Searching my eyes for answers, the husband starts

blabbering, "I'm Ralph, and this is Molly, but everyone calls her Molls. Last night she didn't feel so great and went to bed early, but woke up about midnight feeling like she had to go to the bathroom, but couldn't. The urge kept coming, and about thirty minutes ago she pushed really hard. By the time she realized what was happening, it was too late." He stops talking and looks around. "Is she gonna be okay?"

"I think so," I whisper.

The doctor has Molly's feet in stirrups and is examining her as best he can through all the blood. I notice the stainless steel bucket beneath the end of the bed is already half full of tissue, gauze, and blood. He stands up and gently puts her feet back down on the table. "She needs to get into surgery. Make it happen."

Tom, standing at the door, replies with his usual efficiency, "You got it. They're on alert. I'll take care of the details."

Doc explains to the couple, "Molly's having what we call a 'spontaneous abortion,' also known as a 'miscarriage,' which is what naturally occurs when something isn't quite right with the baby, the uterus, or placenta. You guys didn't do anything wrong, so get that idea out of your heads."

"Why, Doc? Molly hasn't had any morning sickness or problems. Even the ultrasound last week was good. What happened?"

"I don't know, and we may never know, but the important thing right now is to take care of Molly. She's bleeding, and it's not going to stop on its own. And we don't have much time."

"Okay." Ralph nods helplessly through his tears.

The reception clerk holds out papers and releases for Ralph, Molly, the doctor, and me to sign, and by the time we're done, the OR nurses are present and asking the same questions I've already asked the couple. Within another few minutes, the nurses are wheeling Molly out to the elevator and upstairs to the surgical department. I know from this point on, she won't remember much.

Ralph follows the gurney.

"Hey, Tony, I'll clean this mess up," I offer. "But if you'd go out and ask Marilyn to call Housekeeping, I'd appreciate it." As I put on a clean set of gloves, I notice Tony is still standing at the door. "What's up?"

"Didn't that bother you?"

What a stupid question. "Which part? What bothered you?"

"The blood everywhere. The sadness of that couple losing their child. It's sort of heartbreaking. At least, I think it is." He hangs his head despondently.

"Yeah, it sucks. Life really sucks." I feel an emotion coming over me that I don't want to feel right now. Looking at Tony's young face, I crank it back down a notch. "Okay, here's the thing. This is truly a setting where life and death often hang in the balance. It's kind of like being on the front lines of a battle-field. You know you're gonna get incoming, but you don't know when, where, or how bad they're gonna be. And sometimes you get broadsided or hit with a head shot."

"Well, I just asked a girl to marry me, and we talk about having kids and making a life together. Then I see things like this and wonder what's wrong with God."

"What's wrong with God?" I stoop to pick up some saturated linens from the floor and begin shoving them into a huge, clear plastic trash bag.

"Yeah. Why does He let stuff like this happen? Why does He allow bad things to happen to good people?" Tony lifts his glasses and pinches the bridge of his nose, halting would-be tears. "It doesn't make any sense."

I've asked myself that very same question a thousand times in the last four years, and I still have no clue. "I don't know, but here's my theory. I don't think God causes anything bad to happen. I think crap just happens. Really bad crap, be it terrible personal choices, bad karma, evil, or whatever, bad crap happens. Our lot in life is to figure out how to deal with it."

"But He could have saved the baby. Why did she have to lose it?"

"Look, Tony, I'm the last person you should ask, because I don't understand God either. Maybe the baby had a genetic defect, or maybe God had a different plan, or maybe a million other possibilities. I'm not philosophically astute enough to understand any of this." I can hear the pitch of my voice rising. *Calm down!* "But hopefully they'll survive." I bend over to pick up more bloodied trash.

"Yeah, I hope so. Sorry about all the questions. It just seems like none of this stuff bothers you."

Halting my trash collection, I stand up straight and look at him. Now I'm irritated. "Well, you couldn't be more wrong. Everything affects me." *Control your voice.* "I have nightmares about this godforsaken place. But it's my job, and I have to keep going, so I try very hard to stay as divorced as possible from it all so I can function." I take a deep breath and add quietly, "Otherwise, I'd be no good to anyone."

He nods and opens the door. "Thanks."

"Give yourself time, kiddo. You're gonna be okay."

He heads off down the corridor.

Turning my attention back to the room, I start sopping up splattered blood. I remember all the hundreds of cases just like this I've seen over the course of my career. *This is where my nightmares come from.*

There's a knock at the door. "Housekeeping," a voice says.

"Come on in."

I gather up the remaining soiled hospital linens and dump everything into a huge, plastic-lined linens can. Anything with human tissues will go to pathology, while used linens go to the laundry. Everything else goes in the garbage.

A Filipino woman enters with her rolling bucket and mops. She looks around at the mess. "Pretty bad, huh?"

"Yeah, but I'm almost done getting up the big stuff. I just have the towels over here to deal with now, and these belong to the patient."

Even though I doubt either Ralph or Molly will want these gruesome reminders, it is against hospital policy to discard any personal belongings. Everything from a torn rubber beach sandal to a royal crown has to be preserved and returned to the patient or family. Grabbing another clear plastic trash bag, I hold it open with one hand while I pick up the blood-soaked floral towels from the floor with the other.

They're heavy. Must be completely saturated. Casually, I start shoving the messy glob into the plastic bag, but something makes me stop—a faint sensation, or some barely perceptible sound.

What is that?

I hold the towels in midair, suspended at the opening of the garbage bag, while I search my senses. *Probably nothing.* I shrug off the sensation and continue to push the contents into the bag.

"Stop!"

The voice seems to come from a remote canyon somewhere behind my eyes. Though it's not truly audible, I definitely perceive the word. I look around to be sure no one is behind me.

Some instinct urges me to check the contents of the towels before I bundle them up. Withdrawing my hand and the wad of bloody towels from the plastic bag, I let the bag drop to the floor. With my free hand I guide the mostly clean bedside table to the wall near the door, shake open another Chux, and lay the unfolded waterproof barrier on top of the table. A glance back at the cleaning lady assures me she is focused on her work, mopping in rhythm to some rock music playing through her earphones.

Good. No need to gross her out.

Positioning myself between the table and the housekeeper, I carefully separate one of three towels from the bloody group and place it on the table. Opening it up, I see bits of black fecal matter, dried blood, and not much else. I turn it over to be sure nothing is stuck to the other side.

Nothing. It can go into the belongings bag. I place it into the plastic bag on the floor, then repeat the process with the second towel, gently opening it up to check its contents.

Nothing. *This is a total waste of time.* Like the first towel, I place it into the plastic bag on the floor, somewhat irritated by the paranoid compulsion making me inspect these items.

With both hands now free, I open the final bloody towel, expecting more nothing. But what I see stops me dead in my tracks. Frozen, I can't breathe.

"Oh, God!" I whisper. "She's beautiful!"

Lying atop the towel's field of bloody blue flowers is the most perfect human being imaginable. Granted, her dainty body is no more than six inches long and lies silent and still, but there is no mistaking her feminine qualities. I study her twenty delicate fingers and toes, each one a miracle. I shift my eyes to her serenely beautiful face. Gazing at her tightly closed eyes, I am filled with an incomprehensible sense of peace and tranquility.

Unexpectedly feeling protective of the baby's dignity, I take the edge of the bloody towel and cover her.

What am I gonna do with this? The thought of taking this beautiful child to pathology for tissue studies is abruptly revolting and unimaginable. *They might dissect her like a frog. Think, Elizabeth! Think!*

In twelve years of nursing, I've seen hundreds of severed body parts and dead people, including a few fetuses. But this one is different. This one is up close and very personal.

I need another look. I lift the towel again and peek at the

unmoving human form. She's not much bigger than my hand. "Please God, bless her. Bless her soul and take care of her," I whisper. I feel warm tears welling up in my eyes, but this time I don't try to hold them back. *Maybe she needs tears.*

In a reflex effort, I look up toward the ceiling, searching for a God I don't understand, a God I don't want to know. Tears are now streaming down my face.

"God, if You're there," I whisper, "if You're up there, please help her." I look back down at the towel again, then back at the ceiling. Floods of random, unrelated emotions jam my nervous system all at once. *I can't take this!*

Crack!

What sounds like a loud clap of thunder erupts right above me.

"What the heck?" I exclaim aloud. Ducking my head in a cowering reaction, I bend over the baby in a protective stance. I wait. *Maybe it's some weird electrical surge.*

I glance behind me at the housekeeper, but she's still mopping to her earphone rhythm. *That's weird.* It was definitely loud enough to penetrate her music.

Refocusing my attention on the baby, I straighten my back. *What am I gonna do with her precious little body?* I could lose my job if I don't follow hospital rules. I struggle to weigh the options of an enormous moral dilemma, maybe the biggest one of my career.

Crack! Boom!

"Holy crap!" I cower again.

I run my gaze from the blank wall ahead of me up toward the ceiling, searching for the origin of the sound. But my vision blurs, and suddenly everything manmade disappears from my view. Without thinking, I put a bloody gloved hand to my forehead, then pull it away in reflex.

"Ugh! Contamination!" I mutter.

But when I glance at my hand, I see that it's bare and clean.

My line of sight moves to the floor, where a lush carpet of green grass has replaced the stark white tile. Beneath my bare feet I feel soft blades of grass squiggling between my toes, bringing back pleasant, distant memories from my childhood.

I raise my head. I am standing on the crest of a small knoll, edged with abundant, free-spirited wildflowers turning their faces to the east. Off in the distance, snow-covered mountains are also waiting for daylight to illuminate their majesty. Somehow I understand that I'm about to witness a magnificent early-morning sunrise, the likes of which will never be repeated.

Raising my eyes to look through the pale light surrounding me, I detect a few twinkling stars remaining in the night sky. From somewhere far in the distance, I swear I can hear the sound of softly rippling water. Wanting to hear it better, I turn my head ever so slightly, straining my ears.

Oh my! I'll just lie down right here and listen forever. The water's hypnotic, rhythmic quality has already captivated me.

Flash!

I'm jarred from my trance as a bolt of pure white light shoots down from the eastern sky above, blinding me. I have no time to dodge.

Oh, Lord! I'm gonna die! I close my eyes tightly, steeling myself against the expectation of great pain. But none comes. Still, I hold my breath, waiting for the bolt's impact.

Nothing.

Unable to take the suspense, I squint one eye open and see that the lightning bolt has transformed into a swirling, multi-faceted pattern circling around me. I open both eyes and watch the light dance, awestruck. Feeling no fear, I uncurl my fingers and hold my hands out in an effort to touch the light force, to become part of it.

"Huh!" The light goes right through the palms of my hands, seeming to meld with my physical being. The longer I watch and touch it, the more playful it becomes, dancing around and within, ruffling my hair, moving in and out with my breath.

"What are you?" I ask.

The light pauses briefly, then gently swirls again.

It has a life of its own! I sense that it is searching for something.

"What are you looking for?" I ask again.

Then . . . a moment of truth. Pure truth. *It's searching for . . . my soul.*

"Yes." The response appears in my thoughts.

The magical light withdraws from within and around me, retreating to a few feet away. Unafraid, I watch in rapture as it once again straightens into a rigid bolt, takes aim, and heads directly for my chest. As easily as twilight turns to dawn, it penetrates my body, filling me with reverent veneration. Remembering the tiny child behind me, I turn just in time to see the bolt of white light leave my corporeal body and enter the baby's, now suspended in midair by some unseen force. The lightning bolt shrinks to almost nothing, then coalesces within the child, giving her a beautiful, eerie luminescence.

Catatonically I stand, waiting. I have no words, no thoughts, just a feeling of indescribable peace. A peace passing all my prior understanding. The peace of—*God.* The only word which comes to mind is *God.* It's the only word I need to know right now.

I cast my gaze eastward and see daylight brightening the eastern sky. As I shield my eyes against the sun, I peek through my fingers. But to my utter dismay, what I see is the bright exam lights suspended from the ugly acoustic ceiling panels. The sweet-smelling grassy knoll has been replaced by the stench of antiseptic cleaner and a mundane white tile floor. No longer in the serene tranquility of my vision, I am back within the confines of the stark world, engulfed in the all-too-familiar assaulting sights and sounds of human suffering.

Through heavy tears, I turn to glance at the housekeeper.

Although I feel as if I've been elsewhere for several minutes, she is in exactly the same location she was in prior to the first clap of thunder.

She didn't notice anything. Maybe she wasn't supposed to.

My brief sense of relief quickly gives way to dismay and sadness. Filled with longing for the pristine beauty of the grassy knoll, the pale morning sky, and twinkling stars, I fight to go back, aching for the serenely hypnotic effects of the rippling water sounds and the playful light dancing inside me. Desperately I want to reconnect with all of it. I want to reconnect with . . . God!

That's it! The One I gave up on. The One I've angrily dismissed so often. Tears flood my eyes.

Standing in bloody scrubs, bombarded with an ocean of emotions cascading over me, I feel my self-consciousness juxtaposed with reality. My very sanity hangs in the balance. Determined to regain a modicum of composure, I pull hard at my brain to reassert my analytical side, to put it back in control of the here and now.

I look back down one last time and am almost relieved to see the perfect remains of the miniature baby girl still resting on the blue towel.

Deal with this. This is real. What are you going to do? Such pure innocence, such pure hope. My thought processes are changing gears at the speed of light. *I've got to find her parents. She needs the respect of a proper burial.*

The cleaning lady is still busy wiping stuff down, oblivious to my actions, so I carefully transfer the baby from the bloody linens to a clean white towel and meticulously fold it all up to protect the contents as best I can.

It's all I've got. It'll have to suffice.

Exiting the exam room, I walk as casually as possible down the long hallway to the elevator. To my relief, no one is in it. I hit the button to the third floor. When the elevator door slides open, my field of vision tunnels toward the surgery waiting room door, through which I hope to find Ralph. There is no going back now. If the hospital finds out what I am doing, I'll lose my job. But this fact no longer seems to matter. What does matter—all I can focus on—is dignifying this baby girl's brief existence. I need to give her parents an opportunity to acknowledge the magnificence of their daughter, a precious life—now gone.

I hesitate outside the waiting room door, pondering the brief epiphany I've been given. A curtain has been drawn aside, offering me a sneak peek at another world. I'm in uncharted territory now, with no idea of my heading. Even worse, the foundation of everyday beliefs I've assumed to be humanity's truths are beginning to crumble.

"You okay?" Marilyn asks.

"Yeah, but that was really tough." I wipe my tear-stained cheeks and red eyes. I don't feel like talking or listening to anyone, let alone trying to explain what has just happened— and I definitely don't want to be in this chaotic place anymore. In offering the baby girl's remains to the father, I broke a major hospital policy, and all I want is to find a warm, quiet, dark spot to curl up in, to sit and think.

"Hey, look, it's almost six-twenty. Why don't you finish your paperwork, and I'll give report to the day shift. We're down to five patients anyway, and the students can help me."

"Really? Thanks, that would be great."

"When's the last time you used any vacation or sick days?"

"What? Um, I don't know, seven or eight months ago." My mind starts turning.

"Well, its none of my business, but maybe you should use some of it and take the next two nights off. You know, go home, hug your dog, take a walk around your beautiful property, pick some berries. Relax."

"Wrong season for berry picking." I fake a little laugh. "I hate to use sick time if I don't need it." Still, I have to admit, the idea is appealing.

"Well, maybe you need it."

I stand still, looking at her serene face. "Maybe you're right. Maybe I do."

"Good. Now go grab your stuff, get in your truck, and drive home. This place will still be here when you get back in a week." She hugs me tight. "You're a good friend, and I'm giving you my opinion as a nurse and your friend. Get the heck out of here for a while."

"I will. Thanks for understanding."

"I'll call you in a few days to check on you."

"I'd appreciate that."

After I finish my paperwork, I turn everything in and collect my bags. As I walk into the crisp morning air, still damp and sweet-smelling from last night's rain, I gaze across the parking ramp toward the Olympics. As magnificently beautiful as the Pacific Northwest is, it can't hold a candle to the scenery I experienced a few minutes earlier. I want to go back.

I throw my gear into my truck. If I catch the next ferry, I'll be able to pick up my dog from the sitter and be home by 9:00 a.m.

There must be a way to reconnect.

ANOTHER PLACE

Seated peacefully in the carved, high-backed chair, Lady Mary drapes her willowy arms over the curved rosewood armrests, allowing her fingertips to rhythmically trace the ends. Over and over, she feels the circular lines of the spiral pattern, now worn smooth as glass.

"For me, Lady Mary, it is like knowing a terrible storm is brewing in the distance, when only the first slight breeze can be sensed." Joseph points casually to one of the arched crystalline windows, causing a slight stir in the air. The shimmering silken draperies billow out like the lazy sails of a ship. "Nevertheless, the storm moves relentlessly forward, bringing with it a great darkness." He waves his hand over the streams of sunlight that dance off the multifaceted window prisms, momentarily casting darkened shadows over the delicately painted walls and halting the light's fantasy of colored rainbows.

Patiently, she waits for him to restore the sunlight. "What are you trying to say, Joseph?"

"This is unlike anything I have experienced before. Although I do not yet fully understand its nature, every time Mayim opens, it is there. The darkness rides along with the light."

"Yes, I have seen the images in your mind."

"Conversely, the storm itself is drawing me toward the water. If it is the darkness, it is already powerful, and its strength is increasing exponentially. It will not allow itself to be ignored."

"Joseph, to ignore the darkness is to—in effect—give it attention. What you must do is focus on the light. Only the light. The light is what has sustained you through the ages."

"But would it not be better to understand the problem before it reaches us, than to wait until it is too late?"

Knowledge. Such a struggle. "And if you could understand it, what would you do then?"

"I am not sure, but it seems imperative to discover the source of the disturbance."

"Imperative or not, searching out a darkness in their realm is simply not allowed, nor is it our responsibility. Such matters are not part of our destiny."

"Perhaps my destiny is changing, Lady Mary."

"Your destiny—our destiny—cannot change. We are what we are."

"Yet there must be a reason why I am so intensely aware of these dark sensations—why I am so drawn to them."

"Perhaps it is because you are stronger. The strongest. Since the very beginning, your senses have been more acute than the others."

"Lady Mary, you know me. You know my heart is pure. I just want to understand."

Knowledge . . . a gateway to enlightenment, or a path to eternal darkness? "If you had all the knowledge in the universe at your disposal, what would it change?"

"I do not know." He shrugs his shoulders. "Possibly nothing."

Closing her eyes, Lady Mary looks into Joseph's thoughts. *"Please tell me what you are truly searching for."*

"A way to warn the other side. A way to stop it."

"Warn the other side?" Standing abruptly, Lady Mary points her finger at Joseph. "How dare you even suggest interfering in their realm?" She searches his mind again, this time probing more deeply. *"Ah. Joseph! You already have!"*

Joseph turns his mind aside, blocking her invasion.

"Mayim is sacred!" she asserts. "Our pristine and holy world is protected by the barrier for a reason. By reaching through the water into their realm, you have broken Father's most sacred law."

"Do not forget who you are speaking to, Lady Mary. I am Sixth of the Nine."

"I know exactly who you are, Joseph. And you would also be wise to remember who I am. For you to use the enormous power and energy coming through Mayim for Father's greater purpose is one thing. It is entirely another for you to journey through and touch their impurities for your own benefit. Your actions foreshadow disaster."

He narrows his eyes. "Disaster is foreshadowed anyway."

"Perhaps it was foreshadowed in their realm, but your impetuous actions may have tainted ours."

"Lady Mary, I can feel the other side with every fiber of my being. I sense their darkness, and I want to know what it is."

She returns to her chair. After a long pause, she says, "So, what did you find? Did you get any answers?"

"Not yet." He closes his eyes. "But I think I made a friend."

"What kind of a friend?"

"A woman. I believe—if the circumstances are right—she may be of assistance."

"What circumstances?"

"Hers. But from what I can sense, she will need an ally—a man."

"Do not forget, Joseph, you and I are connected. Where one travels, the other must follow. You are taking me to a place I do not wish to go."

"Then stay behind."

"Impossible! You know the bonds of guide and mentor are inseparable. We cannot function without each other."

11

OLYMPIC PENINSULA, WASHINGTON

"Hey, Mike, it's me, Elizabeth. Hope I'm not calling too early."

"No, I've been up for a couple hours. What's up?"

"I'm wondering if I could meet you later today for lunch or something. I need to talk."

"I could do that. I'd like to catch up. Where are you now?"

"I just finished a shift in Seattle and am heading home, currently passing Discovery Bay. But I need to pick up Alder and take him home."

"So you've been up all night?"

"Yeah, but I'm pretty wired."

"Well, I know you're Superwoman, but eventually you're gonna crash, so why don't we meet for breakfast? Sally's got a knitting thing to go to, so she won't mind. Say nine thirty at Café Garden?"

"That would be great. See you there."

An hour later, Alder runs around the hillside while I light a fire in my red enameled woodstove to take the chill

off the interior of my cabin. The little stove is my sole source
of heat and a lot more dependable than electricity out here in
the boonies in the winter. I recently hired some local teenagers
to cut, split, and stack three cords of downed timber, so my
woodshed is full and I'm set for at least another year.

Hearing a familiar paw scratch at the door, I let Alder in.
"Hey, boy, how ya doing?" His beautiful auburn fur is wet with
the morning dew, but I hug him anyway. "You are such a great
companion!"

Starting with his head, he shakes his body from his ears
all the way to his tail, flinging water everywhere, which doesn't
bother me in the least. As a satisfied conclusion, he shows me his
wide smile. "That's my boy, always happy to see me!"

I close the door and cross to the woodstove to be sure the
fire will catch. Following closely, Alder plops onto the rug next
to the stove. I lie down beside him and put my arm over his
back, pressing my face into his damp fur. My eyes start to sting
again, and I feel tears welling up, like a dam ready to break.

"Oh, Alder, I thought I was over all this."

I roll onto my back and look up at the sixteen-foot-high
whitewashed pine ceiling, with the pale, glossy finish I labored
over so many years ago. Mac and I built the compact, 1,400-
square-foot A-frame cabin by hand, and every memory of the
one-year project is as fresh today as it was during construction.
Mac's brilliantly simple design resulted in a great room with two
small lofts at each end of the A, which serve as small bedrooms.
For the kitchen, he intersected a second A to the main design
and strategically positioned several enormous skylights in the
lofty ceiling, which, combined with carefully placed windows,
filled the interior with an abundance of natural light even on the
gloomiest of rainy days. I look toward the opposite wall, remembering the wing we planned to add for the kids. *Kids. Babies.
Children. A family.* But Mac left, and it never happened. *Let it go.*

I roll back toward Alder and hug him. "Gotta go, boy, so

keep the fire burning. I'll be back in about two hours." With my bag in hand, I lock the door and drive my truck into town.

I spot Mike's vehicle in the parking lot and pull up next to it. I've known Mike for years through the NRA and skeet shooting, and although he's almost twenty years older, he's one of my few close friends. He also unequivocally believes in God, although it's a subject I've never wanted to discuss . . . until today. Right now, Mike's the only person in the world I trust to talk to about what I experienced at the hospital.

Swinging my truck door open, I pause to take in the beautiful view from Front Street down across town and farther out to the Strait of Juan de Fuca. It's an amazingly clear day. Not only is the Ediz Hook Coast Guard Air Station clearly visible, but so is the southern coastline of Canada's Vancouver Island. I can even discern a few of Victoria's sparkling buildings reflecting the early sunlight back across the water. And halfway across the cold ocean water, the Black Ball ferry, *M. V. Coho,* is making its morning crossing. Truly a serene setting.

As I push open the door to the cafe, I hear the waitress's familiar voice. "Hi, Elizabeth! Mike's over there. You want a glass of Chardonnay?"

"Oh man, Kelly. You know me too well." *Skip the glass and just bring me the bottle.* "Not today. But I'd love an Earl Grey with honey."

"Coming right up."

"Hey, Mike, sorry I'm a little late." Removing my sunglasses, I expose my swollen, red eyes.

"Hi, kiddo, I missed you." Dressed in his usual knit turtleneck and jeans, he stands and gives me a long hug. His well-worn leather bomber jacket is draped on the booth's bench. "No offense, but you look like Hell."

"Yeah, I know. None taken."

"Have a seat." He beckons me to sit across from him.

"Beautiful day out there," I say, dropping my bag on the seat.

"Yup. Spectacular!" He adjusts his glasses and runs his fingers across his graying left temple. A retired military pilot, he's kept himself in amazing shape, right down to the military-style haircut. Maybe the reason I trust him so much is because he reminds me of my dad.

I lean my elbows on the table, rest my chin on my hands, and stare out the window into the garden. *Okay, now that I'm here, what the heck am I gonna say?*

Kelly sets a teapot and china cup on the table and promises to check back in a few minutes.

"So, Elizabeth, what's up?" Mike asks.

Any bravado I felt when asking him to meet me has vanished, and right now all I want is to curl up in a ball, roll into a dark cave, and never come out again. *Damn. Either you talk to him now, or you retreat and die alone, all over again.* I suck it up. "I feel like I'm on the verge of a nervous breakdown or something. Like my world is about to implode and destroy me."

Mike nonchalantly sips his coffee.

"I mean, I thought I had everything figured out. Everything. I was back on a kind of even keel. Then something happened at work a few hours ago that made me start doubting everything again. Either I'm going nuts, or I'm really going nuts."

Silence.

"You know, losing my mom and dad was tough enough. But after I lost Mac, it took me forever to function again. There were days, weeks, months—maybe even years—when I was so angry at God and the world, I couldn't see straight. Heck, some days, it was all I could do to get through a shower and brush my teeth. I was angry that Mac died, angry at the drunk idiot who smashed into him, angry I hadn't been killed with him, and angry at God for allowing it. And then I was angry at myself for being angry." I taste the bittersweet tea. "I mean, how stupid is that?"

"Probably normal."

I shake my head. "Dang, Mike. It was like a vicious cycle I couldn't get out of. Like some nightmare merry-go-round I couldn't get off of."

"Yeah, I imagine."

"And then, ever so slowly, I realized that life isn't fair. I could feel myself changing. My brain started compartmentalizing each segment of my life into neat little boxes. I stuffed memories of Mac and our beautiful love into one box, shoved my anger into another one, nursing into another, home survival into another, and so on. And I squeezed the entire concept of God into one final little box I never intended to open again.

"Ultimately, miraculously, I found a way to function again and 'do life,' which I equated with newfound peace. By taking long hikes and smelling the proverbial roses, I refocused on the 'one with nature' philosophy and convinced myself I was growing spiritually. It was absolute bull and I knew it, but it allowed me a way to reconcile Mac's death with God."

"How?"

"Instead of blaming God for causing his death, I concluded it happened because He simply wasn't paying attention—like Mac just slipped through His fingers. An oversight." I sip my tea. "That way, I didn't have to be angry at God. I just decided He sucked at His job. Meanwhile, I work in the really sick world of trauma, and usually thrive on it. And maybe the reason I do is because it makes me feel less traumatized than I really am."

"Sometimes there's safety in numbers."

"Exactly. But the problem is, I'm not sure I can go on much longer, because stuff is beginning to bother me. After my rotation, it's all I can do to crawl back to the peninsula, light a fire in my stove, and drink an entire bottle of wine. Drunk on my butt, I simply pass out. By the time I wake up again, it's all just a bad dream, which fits neatly into another little box in my brain. Then I go on with my life as a hermit and repeat the cycle."

Kelly approaches our table and refills Mike's coffee. "I hate to interrupt, but I don't want you to think I'm ignoring you. You guys want anything to eat?"

"Yeah, thanks. I'm starving. I'll have your eggs Benedict, well done, with hash browns on the side."

"Just a berry muffin for me," Mike says.

Kelly picks up the menus we memorized years ago and leaves us alone again.

"So what changed?" he asks.

"Oh man, you're gonna think I'm nuts."

"Try me."

I pour steaming tea from the pot into my cup, take a sip, and as analytically as possible, describe what happened. I don't exaggerate or embellish my narrative, because there isn't any need. What I experienced was crazy enough just as it was. When I get to the part about being transported to the grassy knoll and sensing the sunrise, the tears start forming. By the time I get to the lightning bolt, dancing lights, and floating baby, the dam bursts.

Quietly sobbing, I conclude, "As stupid as it sounds, it seemed God, or something like God, reached out and touched me. But I don't know why."

"Wow, kiddo, what a night." He hands me a bunch of extra napkins. "But you should know, there isn't anything 'like' God. And why wouldn't He reach out and touch you?"

"Uh . . . um. Because I'm nobody. I don't matter to Him. I never have."

"Why do you say that?"

I shrug. "He left me alone—always, utterly alone. My mom when I was six, my dad when I was twenty-two, and Mac when I was thirty. He always takes away what I love." I hang my head. "So I must not matter."

"Oh, Elizabeth, God doesn't orchestrate life to hurt us or cause us pain. And personally, I believe you matter more to Him than most."

"Well, He sure has a cruel way of showing it."

"You missed my point. God doesn't desert us in our struggles, He stands with us. And He never gives us more than we can handle. That's a rule. Maybe in your case, He needed you to be strong for a singular purpose."

"Like what? What could God possibly want with me?"

"I have no idea. But I'm guessing He's been with you all along, from the first moment of your life, patiently waiting to awaken you. I'm also guessing, whatever it is He wants, you're about to find out."

"Isn't there a way to have God without all this emotional stuff? I mean, I hate this crying crap."

He considers this. "So you sort of want to know Him, but also want to maintain your distance, not get too involved?"

"I guess." I shrug again and sip my tea. When Mac died, Mike kindly arranged the funeral for me. Over the years, he and Sally have invited me to go with them to their church on several other occasions, but I always decline. I never want to step foot into any church ever again. "Probably sounds stupid."

"It doesn't work like that. It's usually all or nothing."

I lower my head. "Then I don't think I want it."

"Well, you may not have a choice."

I bite my lip. "You know, I'm pretty sure my parents had me baptized when I was a baby. But I don't think it took."

"God never forgets."

"What if I'm just going nuts?" I suddenly have a vision of myself bundled up in a straitjacket, huddled in the corner of a white room and covered in my own secretions. I shudder. "You know, bonkers?"

"Do you feel like you are?"

Good question. "No." If I do, I'm not going to admit it. "Actually, I feel like maybe I've been nuts and am just waking up. Or like I've been in some kind of coma and now can open my eyes. It's a strange sensation."

He cocks his head to one side. "It's been a long time coming."

I shake my head ruefully. "I wish I shared your enthusiasm."

Our breakfast arrives, and even though my appetite has waned, I manage to eat every delicious morsel on the plate. It feels good to stop talking and focus on the best homemade breakfast on the peninsula.

"You know, Elizabeth, there are a lot of crazy ideas out there about God's purpose. Everything from a repairman 'fix-it' guy we call on when we're in trouble, to a police-type guy whose job it is to protect us from ourselves, to some kind of benevolent grandfather whose purpose it is to grant us three wishes." Mike drinks down the last of his coffee and sets his mug on the table. "But none of those are even close. God is simply . . . God. All powerful, all knowing. Immutable, everlasting, ever dependable. He quite simply, just is."

"Is what?"

Mike looks at me intently. "In charge."

"Well, if He's in charge, then why does He let bad things happen?" Tears flood my cheeks again.

"Oh, sweetie, He doesn't. God created a fixed natural world and then created man, endowing him with free will, which is the key to everything. God specifically gifted humankind the freedom to make choices and thus influence our own destinies. We are allowed to create or destroy, seek or hide, love or hate. We make billions of choices every second of every day, ad infinitum. And every single choice alters the outcome of life. Your life, my life, all humanity."

"Then He's not really in charge."

"Yes, He is. Take the drunk who hit Mac. God allowed him to choose his life. The drunk chose to get plastered in the bar the night of the accident, then drive his car and smash into Mac. Those were all choices the drunk made, not God. God didn't want it to happen, because He loves Mac and you. But to intervene would have been to cancel out all of His creation and humanity."

"Maybe He could have made just one exception," I say softly.

"Look, Elizabeth. Our life, as God knows it, has already happened. It's already occurred. We're the ones experiencing this." Mike waves his hands around, indicating the world. "We're the ones passing through life waiting for it to happen, not Him. He sees our entire existence from start to finish in front of Him. He is the Alpha and the Omega."

My circling brain is having trouble concentrating. "You say God's in control. Well, how do you know? I mean, how can you tell?"

"I have faith."

"In what?"

"That God exists. That He is omnipotent and omniscient, and that He loves me."

"But how can you be sure?"

"Here's the thing, Elizabeth. If you believe in God, then it's all or nothing. There's no partial acceptance. It's not like there's an on-off switch."

I have no response.

"Think about the conundrum you're in. You believe in God enough to stuff Him in a box and ignore Him, yet you doubt His existence because you think He ignored you or didn't live up to your expectations. But that makes no sense. If you believe in a God, then you must acknowledge what He is: all knowing, all seeing, all powerful." Smiling, Mike adds, "Therefore, He can't 'not know' something." He laughs. "Sorry about the double negative. But you get my point?"

"Yeah."

"Okay. Well, if He's perfect and in control, then it's reasonable to assume that every minute detail of life, of *your* life, is part of His plan."

"I guess. That makes sense intellectually."

"Probably, but it's different knowing something in your head and feeling it in your heart."

"Yeah, I have great experience at disengaging the two."

"Don't beat yourself up. We all do."

"So how do I reengage?"

"I don't have all the answers, but I'd guess that you're gonna have to open up your heart a little. You're gonna have to accept Him on faith."

"Yeah, faith. That's the hard part."

"Not really. All you have to do is start paying attention."

"Attention to what?"

"God's little miracles. Like the one you were part of this morning."

"So you think it was real?"

"Absolutely." He smiles again. "God wanted your attention, and I think He got it."

"Well, dang! If it was a miracle, why do I feel so devastated? Why can't I stop crying?"

"Maybe your compartmentalized dam broke."

But it's so well-crafted to keep everything away.

"Elizabeth, by your own account, anger was a big part of your life for a while. It's a pretty powerful emotion. Maybe you needed it for energy or for survival. Maybe the divisions in your mind were really just a lot of walls protecting you from your own anger."

"Maybe." He's dead right on target. My deep-seated anger never went away. True, the beast is chained to the darkest corner of my belly, and I pretend it's slain, but it still lurks there. Lately, it's been harder to keep at bay. "Maybe."

"And like a house of cards, maybe a breeze just knocked a few over."

"I'm not sure I'm ready for this. Reality seems really confusing right now. Almost scary."

"I bet." He reaches across the table and takes hold of my

hands. "But actually, it isn't. Just remember, sometimes bad things happen to good people, but that doesn't mean God causes it."

Oh, Mike, could you be right? I just said those same words to Tony and didn't believe any of it. Now I'm not so sure. "Maybe you're right."

He pulls my hands farther across the table. "God is pure love, pure life, pure truth. What He is, is beyond our comprehension and wildest imagination. Without Him, life here on earth would be nothing short of a living Hell."

"So what do I do now? What do I do about the hospital? I broke a bunch of rules, giving the baby's remains to the parents. I could get fired."

"If I were in your shoes, I'd never mention it again. I doubt if the parents will say anything, and there's no reason for you to. Sometimes silence is the better part of valor."

"Yeah, you're right."

"Now, you go home and don't open a bottle of wine. Hug Alder and get some good sleep. Then tomorrow you come over to our house for dinner, and we'll talk about this some more." He waves to Kelly for the check. "I got this. Best breakfast conversation I've had in ten years!"

ANOTHER PLACE

"Lord Marcus, we have a problem," Lady Mary announces. "The Council must be assembled."

She allows Lord Marcus to reach into her recent thoughts and hear the conversation with Joseph.

"Ah, yes. This is most disturbing. Too long we have delayed." He projects his thoughts to the other Councilors. "They will meet."

Positioned in a perfect circle, nine crystalline thrones fill the small, round chapel. Thin, golden thread-lines are woven through the high backs and armrests of the sculpted ice-blue chairs and exit out through the legs to the silver floor below. The threads then converge like the spokes of a wheel on the centermost point of the room, where they weave themselves into golden vines around a shiny silver pedestal. Atop the pedestal rests a small, geodesic sphere of pure carbon. Long ago harvested from the midnight sky, it is the most divine diamond in all the realms of the universe.

Overhead, nine flying buttresses arch inward, supporting a domed sterling silver ceiling. Beneath each arch is a crystalline window, perfectly faceted to reflect a multitude of prismatic beams that stream through from every direction. The individual beams precisely triangulate off the colorless ceiling and reflect back toward the pedestal at the heart of the chapel. As the confluence of colors converge into the diamond orb, they create a singularly brilliant light of perfect white.

Slowly turning on its silver axis, the sphere rotates nine times. With each rotation, a Councilor appears in his or her assigned chair. As always, their heads and faces are covered by the deep hoods of their white robes—a sign of respect in the presence of the white light. When all Nine are assembled, the diamond ceases its movement. Except for the distant sound of falling water, the room is silent.

Lord Solomon raises his head, but his hood covers every feature except his long white beard. He places his aging hands upon the rounded ends of his chair's armrests. The golden threads within the chair sparkle to life. "Who has gathered us?"

"It is I," Lady Mary says from across the circle, lighting her own golden threads. "I have need of your collective wisdom. But before I begin, Lord Marcus would like to speak."

The other members of the Council nod their hooded heads. The communication continues.

"Thank you." Lord Marcus's words bring his golden threads to life. "Most respected members of the Council of the Nine, I cannot hide from you that I sense a change in the Realm of the Forbidden. Things are somehow different. This shift or change, whatever it may be, is affecting our world and the essential role of the Nine."

"Yes," Lady Ruth says, "I feel it also."

"I believe their destiny is shifting, and it may eventually affect the entire universe."

"Nonsense, Lord Marcus," Lord Solomon says. "Destiny

cannot shift. It is what it is. Father plans for all outcomes, all eventualities. While we may not like the way our universe moves, it is all according to Him."

"Yes, Lord Solomon. But—"

"There is no 'yes, but.' To postulate that destiny is somehow shifting to something unplanned is to exclude the omnipotence of Father. Our role in Father's plan is to assist the Nine and protect the purity of those entrusted to our care. Nothing more, nothing less."

"Then we have a problem," interjects Lady Mary. "Joseph has found a way to breach the barrier between the two realms. He has already reached through."

Lord Solomon stands abruptly and retreats from the circle. With his hands clasped behind his back, he begins to pace. While he strides around the perimeter of the circle, the golden threads do not shimmer. No one speaks.

Finally he returns to his chair, but remains standing behind it. As he rest his hands upon the crystalline posts atop the chair's high back, the golden threads once again brighten.

"Lady Mary, why would Joseph do such a thing?" he asks.

"Because he is strong. Because he has always been able to feel the humanity in the Realm of the Forbidden whenever he nears Mayim. And now he senses a grave change, a terrible shift. He believes that shift will bring absolute destruction upon everyone."

"What arrogance!" Lord Solomon exclaims. "How can he possibly know what is in their future?"

"He cannot," Lady Mary says, "but there is no doubt that a darkness has penetrated the barrier, along with the light. He feels it intensely. I have felt it through him, as well."

The other eight nod their heads in agreement. The words, "Yes, yes," echo through the chapel.

"I must admit, my Ninth has felt it as well," Lord Solomon says. "And she is quite uncomfortable with it."

"Hmm, even your Ninth. That is odd," Lady Mary murmurs.

"Yes, usually we are not affected by such disturbances. Regardless, why would Joseph do such a thing? He is as bound by Father's laws as any of us."

"Like all creatures, he has free will and thus can choose to act either within our laws or outside of them." Lady Mary looks down slightly. "Unfortunately, he has elected to act on his own."

"You say he breached the barrier," says Lady Ruth. "What exactly did he do?"

"He made contact with a woman and allowed her to witness the beginning of a passage."

"So not only did he reach through to the other realm, he allowed one of them—an impure—to penetrate ours?" Lord Solomon asks.

"I am afraid so. Although Joseph does not yet know the nature of the darkness, he believes the woman may be of some assistance. The question now is, how do we mitigate the damage he may have done?"

"Actually, Lady Mary, the real question is," Lord Marcus says, "will Joseph stop?"

"I do not think so. He has tasted the other realm and believes he can alter their destiny. He believes he can prevent their demise and restore the symbiotic balance between our worlds."

"If he will not stop, how do we mitigate the potential problems?"

"By assisting him." Lord Solomon looks up at the ceiling and then back at the diamond sphere. "That is the only solution. You must assist him, Lady Mary."

"How?"

"By protecting the woman."

"Why would she need protecting from Joseph?"

"Not from Joseph. From his powers. As with each of the

Nine, an integral part of Joseph's being is his power, a simple necessity required for his role as the Sixth. Since it is customary for him to manipulate time and space in our world, he may even consider his abilities rather banal. Yet he is the strongest of the Nine. The real danger is, he has no idea of the cataclysmic damage those simple powers can do if unleashed in their realm."

"How do you know?" Lady Mary asks.

"Because eons ago, I sensed a darkness as well." Exhaling deeply, Lord Solomon looks down at his hands. "I also crossed once."

Silence.

"What about Father?" Lady Ruth says.

"It is only we who are ignorant. Father is aware of everything." Lord Solomon gazes into the perfect white light emanating from the sphere in the center of the room. "It would be wise to remember that the earth-realm has teetered on the brink of extinction several times in the past. Yet each time, Father chose to save it." He looks across to Lady Mary. "Yes, you must assist Joseph and protect the woman."

Without announcement, the diamond orb slowly turns in the opposite direction. With each reverse rotation, a Councilor vanishes.

PORT ANGELES, WASHINGTON

By the time I get back home, it's almost eleven. The slow-burning fire in the woodstove is radiating a nice glow, and my cabin is toasty warm.

I call my boss at the hospital. "Hey, Angela, how ya doing?"

"Not bad, Elizabeth. What's up?"

"I'm not feeling well and need to sign out for my next two shifts. Sorry."

"No problem. Do you have a ride home to the peninsula?"

"Actually, I felt really crappy this morning and caught an early ferry. I figured if I was gonna be miserable, I wanted to be home and near my regular doc."

"Cool. Just so you're safe. I'll mark you off for tonight and tomorrow, and we'll see you back here on your next rotation."

"Thanks."

Heeding Mike's advice, I skip the wine and draw a hot bath in my Jacuzzi tub. A long soak in the sudsy water is exactly what I need. Only after my skin prunes up does it seem prudent to get out. I dry off with a warm, fluffy towel, lather my skin with lotion, and get into my soft flannel pajamas. After I'm certain the fire is cranked down to a low smolder, I climb into bed with Alder at my side and immediately drift off to sleep.

I must have slept all day and half the night, because when I stir, it's pitch black and raining outside, and I'm stiff from being in bed so long. So dark is the room, I'm not sure if my eyes are open or not. As I pull myself out of my fog, I flounder to find the bedside lamp. Eventually I locate it and click the knob. Nothing happens.

"Oh, dang, electricity must be out."

I fish around in the magazine basket next to my bed until I find my flashlight and flick it on. *Finally!* Stepping into my slippers, I move down the steep, narrow stairs to the main room. The only faint light in the cabin comes from the fire in the woodstove, which is barely smoldering. I unlatch the door, and it immediately roars to life. The flames light up the room enough for me to find my battery-powered lantern, matches, and emergency candles. When they are all lit and placed around the two rooms, I have enough dim light to see the general area.

"I wonder how long the power's been out?"

Alder's response is a bark and a lunge at the door.

"Okay, boy, you can go outside." As I open the front door, it slams back against my hand. "Wow, this storm must have come out of nowhere! Don't go too far, now. It's really yucky out there."

The wind is gusting so hard, the downpour seems to be shooting sideways, parallel to the ground. Alder, already charging out into the driveway, finds his own personal tree. I duck back inside and shove the door shut against the gale, then use the bathroom and find my watch.

"Holy cow, three thirty? Wow, I slept over thirteen hours! That's some kind of record for me."

Alder scratches at the door, and I let him back in.

"You're soaked!" I grab a big towel. "No way you're getting back up on my bed like that, boy." Laughing, I hug him while I dry him off.

Fortunately, when we built the cabin, Mac had insisted on a huge propane tank for our cooking stove and hot water heater. Since I'm on a well and have a generator for backup, all of my essential needs can be met during power outages. I light the cooking stove and heat a kettle of water. Before long, I'm snuggled up in my favorite overstuffed chair next to the fire, cup of tea in hand. It's too dark to read, so I just sit, listening to the howling wind and the torrential rain on our metal roof.

"It's a bad storm, Alder. Trees are gonna come down tonight. That's probably what happened to the power."

Sometimes the electricity is out for a couple of days, but usually the public utility guys have the power back up fairly quickly. It happens frequently enough that I'm used to it and don't worry. I curl my feet up in the chair under the afghan and wait in the muted candlelight.

Crack! Boom! Crack!

The startling sound causes my head to jerk up abruptly. "Crap, that thunder was close." I accidentally tip over my mug and reflexively jerk away, expecting it to be scalding hot. But it's not. Instead, the liquid saturating my pajama leg is cold. *Weird.*

Reaching over to feel the top of the stove, I'm surprised to find it stone cold as well. *Weird.* My mind wrestles with this discrepancy. *There should at least be some residual heat.* It's still pitch black outside and my candles are down to the nubs, burned out. I turn on my flashlight to check the time.

"Five a.m.? I must have fallen asleep again." I look around for Alder. For the first time, I notice he isn't with me. "Alder? Alder? Come on, boy, where are you?" I move around the room with my light, searching for him.

Nothing.

I check the front door.

Locked.

I go into the little walk-through closet which leads to my bathroom and find him huddled underneath my hanging clothes, shaking uncontrollably. "What's going on, boy? Storms never bother you." I reach out my hand to pet him, but he looks up past my shoulder and growls, showing his teeth. "It's okay, boy, it's me."

Reaching down again, I grab onto his collar and give a firm tug. He resists, but eventually allows his eighty-five-pound body to be dragged back into the main room near the stove. As soon as I release my grip on his collar, he makes a move to go hide again.

"What's gotten into you, boy? What's going on?" While speaking in the most soothing tone I can muster, I attach the permanent tie-down lead to his collar. "You just chill out here for a few minutes while I restart the fire."

The pelting rain and howling wind are still raging, but I need more wood and kindling. I hate the thought of going outside, but there's no way to avoid it. With a groan, I slip into my boots and throw my rain parka on over my pajamas, then open the back door and run to the woodshed. When I've piled as much wood in my arms as I can carry, I dash back into shelter. It takes less than thirty seconds, yet my jacket and pant legs are soaked.

"Dang, it's crappy out there!" I yell.

I reach the woodstove with my arms full of split fir and drop it all into the tinder box before slipping out of my wet boots and jacket. I should change my drenched pajama bottoms, but I need to get the fire restarted first. Alder is standing up, leaning and pulling as hard as he can against the tie-down lead, shaking again.

"It's okay, boy." Working as fast as I can, I scoop out the previous fire's stone-cold ashes, rip up some cardboard and paper, add kindling, and ignite an extra-long match. The flames spark up, offering not only light and heat, but also a small modicum of relief.

"I better get some more candles. These are done. I'll never believe that advertising again. 'Twenty-four-hour candles,' my ass." In the kitchen I snag another box of the tall wax cylinders and pause at the counter to get matches. When I casually glance through the huge bay window looking north down the mountain toward town, I catch sight of the next farm.

What the . . . ? Lights are on inside the farmhouse and in the little community way down the hill near the highway. "What the heck?"

Since I'm on the same utility power grid as the other houses and farms, this odd deviation makes no sense at all. I pick up the phone to speed-dial PUD, but my line is dead. Reaching into my bag, I find my cell phone and try that.

Nothing. Nada. No service.

"Okay, Alder, now *I'm* worried." My senses kick into high alert. I dig into the special side pocket of my bag and retrieve my Walther PK .380 pistol, which I always carry. I need no light source to check if it's loaded, so often have I practiced the maneuver with this weapon. Using a two-finger release, I eject the eight-round magazine, pull back on the slide, dump a round, reseat the clip, pull the slide back again, and release the hammer. The safety is in the "off" position. I fish for the extra magazine and stuff it down into the elastic waistband of my flannel pajamas. Holding the Walther at my side, I methodically recheck all the doors and windows, then finish lighting the remaining candles. Finally, I move my chair behind the woodstove as far into the corner as possible and sit with my back to the wall. Vigilantly I wait in the shadows, my gun resting on my knee. I am ready.

Still hooked to the tie-down, Alder continues violently resisting against an unseen foe. Standing and panting hard, he moves to huddle next to my chair. I reach down with my free hand and pat his head, wondering what he senses.

It's okay, boy. I don't know what's going on, but it's okay. Please, let it all be okay. Let it be light soon and the storm be over.

Within moments, the silence is broken by a steady dripping sound.

What now?

Smack dab in the middle of the room, water is dripping from the apex of the ceiling. This new problem momentarily distracts me from Alder and my protective posture.

"Oh, crap. A leak? No way!" Since Mac insisted on a fifty-year metal roof, a leak is something I've never worried about. But there is no mistake: I can see water streaming down. *Damn. I do not need this!*

I lay my Walther on the ground and fetch the mop bucket from the laundry room. But I stop dead in my tracks a few feet from the dripping water, now certain I'm going crazy.

Although I can see water coming down, it doesn't appear to be dripping from the ceiling, and nothing is hitting the floor. I listen again and realize the dripping sound is gone. *Was it in my head?* I have no idea. The only thing I'm relatively certain of is that no water or moisture is actually touching the floor. More like the small waterfall is suspended in midair, without a source, without an end. I barely hear the sound of the mop bucket rattling against the hardwood floor as it hits.

Searching my analytical mind, I dig for answers. *This makes no sense. It's like a* Twilight Zone *episode.*

"Who's doing this?" I yell.

Alder is freaking out even worse now, pulling as hard as he can against the lead, trying to run away from the scene. I kneel down and hug him, trying to comfort myself as much as him. "I get it, boy. Something scary is going on, and we're caught in it. Don't worry, I won't let you down."

Then, as if hit with a tranquilizing dart, Alder stops his violent shaking and lies down peacefully. Crouching next to him, I rest my cheek against his head near the floor and get shocked by the creepiest of sensations. I can feel another hand on his head next to my cheek.

"Holy crap!" I jerk my head up, narrowly missing the top of the cast-iron stove. It's too dark to see any details, but I definitely felt someone else's hand on Alder's head.

Almost peeing in terror, I reach around behind me and latch onto my gun. Muscle memory kicks in. With my hand firmly on the grip, I bring it to my side, ready to fire into the darkness.

Oh God, I'm really gonna die this time.

From an unknown region of my mind comes an immediate response, deep and calm: *"No, you will not. You are safe."* I can't hear the voice, exactly, but I sense it to be a woman's, and her words feel true.

Fingertips touch my forehead. I freeze, trying to disappear into my surroundings. Unable to breathe, I wait, certain my wildly beating heart can be heard for miles. Even in the darkness I should be able to detect the silhouette of a person so close, yet no one is visible. I take a gasp of much-needed air. The hand tilts, and ever so softly the fingers trace the features of my face, the way a blind person might discern someone's identity.

I am afraid—terrified, actually—but somehow, my body begins to relax. The hand opens, and the palm gently caresses my cheek. It feels like a woman's hand.

As the palm holds my face, conflicting sensations fight within me. Like two ends of a magnet unable to exist without each other, thoughts from the opposite ends of the universe battle in my mind. Extremes of fear and safety, terror and peace, hatred and love argue for what seem like an eternity. Slowly the steely grip of panic dissipates, leaving behind a weird assurance of safety.

Finally, exhaustion overcomes what is left of my sanity. Unable to control my emotions any longer, I surrender to the warm cocoon of serenity that is weaving itself around me. Invisible, yet definitely present, the cocoon surrounds and envelops my total being, reenergizing me and refocusing my vision and hearing.

"I've felt this before." *I love this feeling.* "I've been here before."

"*Yes,*" the woman responds from deep inside me. "*This was your sanctuary.*"

Everything about the envelopment is vaguely familiar, yet not really. *Yes, I know this place. I can almost remember. Just . . . not quite.* So long ago. So deeply buried is the memory. I search. *A faraway distant land? A world separated?* The answer gently comes. *Neither. This is . . . it feels like . . .* But a new sound distracts me.

"I am Joseph." The voice comes from somewhere near the dripping water.

The words surprise me, pulling me from my cocoon-like state. I'm definitely hearing this voice. It is a real sound. But from where?

"I am Joseph," he repeats, and my mind fills with the image of a mountain abbey choir singing an enchantingly rich cantabile. I try to analyze the source. *Far away? Close?* It sounds hesitant, like it's searching.

Gathering what little courage remains, I respond, "I'm Elizabeth."

"I know. Do not be afraid." The voice is like a solo in the choir. "I have been listening to you. Seeking you."

There it is again—the beautiful sound of rippling water. I begin to cry. It's too much. I feel like I'm going to collapse.

From my kneeling position next to Alder, I sit on the floor and set the gun down beside me. "You know me?"

"Yes."

"Where are you?"

"I am here," the voice says quietly, "on the other side."

"Other side of what?"

"The water."

Oh, yes. Of course you are. I don't understand, but accept it as reasonable. "Who are you?"

"I am Joseph."

Of course you are.

"I am the Sixth."

Submissively, I agree again, yet have no clue why. "What is 'the Sixth'?"

"A guide."

Of course. Wait! Hang on. The woman's hand caressing my cheek is beginning to fade away, and with it, the illusion of blind acceptance begins to fail. I reanalyze the scenario. *I'm totally lost and have no idea what he's talking about.* Thoughts of aliens, space invaders, ghosts, and ax murderers blaze through my brain uncontrollably in rapid-fire succession.

"No, I am not any of those concepts. But that is interesting."

"What is?"

"How quickly and randomly your thoughts change."

He can read my mind.

"Yes, I can. And it would be easier for me to communicate if your mind were still."

"I don't know how to keep it still."

"For a moment, try to focus only on me. On my voice."

"Okay." I feel something pulling at my thoughts. "Who are you, really?"

"I really am Joseph."

"And you're a guide?"

"Yes."

"A guide for what? Who? Uh, for whom?"

"For those who come."

"Come from where?"

"Through the water."

He's playing with me.

"No, I am not. I cannot."

I really hate that you can read my thoughts. "Look, I don't understand. Can you explain?"

"I cannot play with you, because it is impossible for me to lie."

"Why?"

"It is against my nature."

"Look, Joseph, go back to the 'guide' thing. Can you explain that?"

"Those who pass through the water must have a guide. Otherwise, they cannot come."

"You mean the water dripping down?"

"You see only a few drops of the whole."

"But where do the ones who pass through come from?"

"Your side."

"Our side of what?"

"The universe. Your side is but one dimension of it."

"How many dimensions are there?"

"More than two."

Changing tactics, I ask, "What is it you want?"

"I want to understand."

I sigh with irritation. "Understand what?"

"Interesting . . ." His voice trails off.

"Now what's interesting?" I ask.

"How easily you become frustrated."

I'm not frustrated. Becoming even more frustrated, I say, "I'm just confused."

"It is simple, Elizabeth. Your world is significantly changing. I need to understand why."

"Changing? Is it . . . bad?"

"Yes. And I do not understand how you can allow it."

"Me? I'm just a person. I don't even know what you're talking about."

"I tried to show you."

The epiphany I had in the hospital replays in my mind.

"The hillside and the sunrise?"

"Yes."

"Were you the bolt of white light?"

"No. I just allowed you to see a little."

"It was beautiful."

"Yes. It is perfection."

"So, what's wrong? What's bad?"

"Certain things which happen in your world affect ours. As long as life remains stable, our two sides coexist symbiotically, with mutual benefits."

"But?"

"Your side is becoming unstable," Joseph says. "If the irrational instability escalates, it will be catastrophic."

I have no idea what you're talking about.

"Elizabeth, I believe you are the one."

"The one what?"

"The one who can stop it."

"Stop what?"

"The . . . the . . ." The voice seems to falter.

"The what?" I hear my voice tensing up. "Joseph! What do you think I'm supposed to stop?"

"I do not know yet. I can only discern the very edge of the coming storm."

The way he speaks the words "coming storm" makes me shudder. I feel afraid, although of what, I don't know. *I need to break this off.* My urgent thought brings an unexpected reply.

"I must go." His voice fades, as does the sound of the rippling water. Seconds later, all trace of the invisible, caressing hand on my cheek has evaporated.

Will you come back? I wonder.

Silence ensues, and an eternity passes. Joseph seems to be gone, leaving behind a cold, vacant loneliness. I rise to my knees and collapse into my chair. Exhaustion overcomes me as I curl up under the afghan, yet rest is impossible. I can't settle my thoughts into a coherent thread. With this second encounter, the certainty of another realm of life leaves me wildly unprepared, unprotected, and vulnerable. I hate the feeling. The whole universe and my reality have simultaneously been destroyed and recreated in the blink of an eye.

God—the question. God—the mystery. *God—where are You?*

From a tightly sealed window, a faint breeze manages to sneak through and drifts in my direction. The delicate air gently swirls around my head. It feels familiar. I let it settle on my heart, knowing it has found my soul.

"HERE," comes the silent answer. *"REST NOW."*

I sigh, expecting the room's warm, stale air to fill me with familiar sorrow. But instead, what passes through my nostrils is fresh, sweet air tasting of joy and hope. I want more. As I breathe deeply, my lungs fill with the miracle of breath, and the wonder of life reinvigorates every cell in my being. The more I inhale the soothing sweetness, the more peace I absorb.

As I rock myself rhythmically in my favorite chair next to the fire, I notice the sun is just cresting the treetops visible through the skylights. It will soon be daylight.

"The storm's over, Alder. It'll be a beautiful day." I reach down to pat my faithful friend, who is now sleeping soundly without a care in the world.

———•◆•———

I must have dozed off again, because when I wake, it's sunny and bright outside and the fire is out. *Weird. Douglas fir usually burns longer than that. Whatever.* I rebuild it, then walk to the shed to get more wood. The ground around the woodshed is completely dry. *Okay, this is very weird!*

After brewing a pot of coffee, I shower, clean up around the cabin, and start a load of laundry. Although I'm now wide awake, my head feels like it's been in a dense fog for the past twenty-four hours. Since "preparation" is my middle name, I restock batteries and candles, just in case another storm hits. But as I reach the first candle, I stop. While the wick is black, it hasn't burned down; no wax has melted. I check the rest, and all are the same. *Another mystery.*

The phone rings. I pick it up eagerly.

"Finally! I've been trying to reach you all night!"

"Hey, Mike. What's up?"

"Are you okay?"

"I think so. I fell asleep after our breakfast yesterday and slept through until the middle of the night when the storm hit. I must've slept sixteen or seventeen hours. Power went out, and so did the phone. Everything's back on now. I was just gonna take the ATV out for a ride and see what kind of damage we had. No telling how many trees came down."

"Um, Elizabeth?"

"Yeah? What? Did something happen to your house in the storm?"

"Kiddo, there hasn't been any storm. The weather's been perfect for the last two days. You know, since I saw you two days ago."

Two days ago? What's he talking about? "Mike, quit with the jokes. You know I don't like them. This was the worst storm in ten years! And I was just with you at breakfast . . ." I calculate the hours. "Twenty-two hours ago. Then I came home and went to sleep."

"Elizabeth, look at your cell phone and tell me what the date says."

Before I even check it, I have a bad feeling creeping up my back. I click it on. "What the heck?" Sure enough, the date is one ahead of where it should have been. I don't know what to say.

"Hang on for a minute, Mike." I set the phone down and run outside to the garden area. It's damp from the normal morning dew, but shows no signs of having been assailed by gale-force winds or saturated by rain.

I sprint back inside and pick up the phone. Through my quivering voice and new tears, I cry, "Mike, something's happening to me. I think I'm losing it."

"Yeah, we were really worried when you didn't show up for dinner. I tried calling all night, but your phone just rang and rang. I couldn't even get the answering machine to pick up. Then another really weird thing. About eight, I decided to drive out there to check on you, but the car wouldn't start."

"Sally's new sedan?"

"Yeah! No reason it shouldn't have started. So I tried my truck, and it wouldn't start either. I went back in and called a mechanic friend from church, but he couldn't get here till this morning. And when he did come by at six this morning, both vehicles started up immediately. Now he thinks I'm a crazy old fart with dementia." He laughs, but I can tell he's baffled by it.

"Did Sally see that the cars wouldn't start?"

"Uh, no. Actually, now that you mention it, she didn't. When you didn't show up, we ate, cleaned up, and then she curled up with her knitting and a movie. She never came out to the garage to look."

Every detail of the last thirty-six hours I can remember turns over in my brain. And now this: an entire day of my life is missing.

I'm afraid.

I try controlling my voice, but it quivers anyway. "Can you come over? And please bring Sally if she wants to drive out."

He muffles the phone. "Hey, sweet lady, you feel like taking a drive out to the country?" I can't hear her response. "We'd love to come. See you in an hour."

"Thanks, Mike, I really appreciate it."

I'm about to hang up when he asks, "You need anything from town?"

"Nah." I reconsider for a second. "Yeah, actually, I need a gallon of milk and some half-and-half."

"Anything else?"

"No. Thanks, Mike."

"See you in a bit."

I spot my gun on the floor where I dropped it at some point during the encounter with Joseph. Retrieving it, I loop my belt through the holster and settle it all on my waist. *Better to be safe than sorry.*

I find a pen and my rarely used personal journal and write down all the details of the past few days I can remember. Real or imagined, I don't want any memory to fade, and this seems the best way to keep them fresh. If I am going crazy, maybe someone can figure it out and help me regain my sanity.

14

About an hour later, two vehicles pull up the drive: Mike and
Sally's beautiful new silver sedan and a dark green SUV I immediately recognize as Pastor Jackson Morgan's.

My privacy is going up in smoke. *Of all the people!* Jackson,
the guy from the Chapel in the Pines Church who's always
checking on me. *You have got to be kidding.*

The first time I met him was after Mac died, when he
spoke at the funeral. Since then, it's been four years of bumping
into him at the gym and his repeated invitations to go places.
Except for skiing, I've successfully managed to maintain a
distance. *A minister? I'm gonna get you for this, Mike.* I stuff my
fists into my jeans pockets and wait on the porch.

"Hi, guys. Hey, Jackson." *Dang, he looks good.* The thought
slips unbidden into my head. I look down at my feet. *Sorry, Mac.*
I look back up. Well-built and at least six feet three, Jackson has
a rugged, salt-of-the-earth appearance, probably the result of
lots of hard work. Wearing his usual attire of long-sleeved plaid

shirt, jeans, and hiking boots, he looks more like a logger than a minister. *Too bad ministers can't be married. Oh crap, where'd that thought come from? Sorry again, Mac.*

"Hi, Elizabeth," Jackson greets me. "Long time, no see—like, since February when you came skiing with the group."

"Wow, has it been that long?" I know perfectly well how long it's been.

"Yeah. Haven't even seen you at the gym lately. I hope you know, I left a couple of messages. Got kind of worried." I see him eyeing my sidearm. He smiles. "I hear you've been shooting a lot."

"Yeah. My priorities shifted for the new season. I've got competitions coming up. When I'm not at the range, I spend most of my time up here, chilling out." *And as good as you look, I don't want to be involved—with anyone.* "I'm kind of bad about returning calls. Sorry."

"Well, no matter." He gives me a genuine smile and then reaches out and hugs me warmly. "It's good to see you again. I've missed you."

Reluctantly I hug him back and inhale a deep breath. *Oh, I miss being held.* "Yeah, uh, I've missed you, too," I say into his shirt, and let go. *Ah, dang. He even smells good.* I try to shake it off. *Get a grip!*

"Nice gun," he says, releasing me. "I've told you before, you can call me Jax."

"Oh yeah, I forgot." *A pastor named Jax? Doesn't seem right. Whatever.* "Hey, Sally, I'm so sorry about last night. I know how hard you work cooking dinner for guests. I think I really screwed up."

She hugs me tightly, too. "Not to worry, dear." Sally is always impeccably dressed, and today is no exception. Wearing a pinstriped oxford shirt, a coordinating mid-length wool skirt, and leather boots, she looks like a middle-aged fashion model. Every short hair on her head is perfectly curled, giving the impression that she just stepped out of a beauty shop. *How does she do it?* "I've brought the food along today, and we can have a nice little picnic later. Mike's got it all in the car."

I hold the door open and wait while everyone files inside. After putting away the groceries they've fetched for me, I stoke the fire, offer coffee, and generally try to stall my way out of talking about the obvious.

"So, how was the drive up, Mike?" *And why did you bring Jackson?*

"It was normal. Elizabeth, we're here to help. So quit with the lame delays and come sit with us. Let's figure out what's going on."

I heave an audible sigh. "I wish I knew." I unhook my holster and set my gun on the counter. Before sitting down, I put a huge box of Kleenex on the table, just in case the flood starts again. "I spent the last hour journaling what I think has been occurring, but honestly, I'm a little worried about my sanity."

"Mike filled me in about what you told him two days ago," Jackson says, "but why don't you start over and explain it to me yourself, in your own words."

Not again. And especially not to you. A downhearted depression settles over me. "Man, I don't feel like going over it all again. I mean, I can, it's just a lot to try to describe."

"Humor me. Please."

"Okay." Starting at the beginning, I recap events at the hospital, including the epiphany I experienced, how I broke hospital rules, and my breakfast with Mike. Plunging into what I've remembered since then, I recall my strangely long periods of sleep, waking up to the monsoon-type storm, the localized power outage, and Alder's inexplicable reactions. I get right up to the point of the waterfall in my house and stop. *It's now or never. Either I'm nuts, or worse.* "Then I noticed water dripping from somewhere close to the ceiling, and had contact with someone or something named Joseph."

Everyone leans into the table, as though ready to catch me. *Great. They think I'm nuts.* I look at Jackson's face for a clue. *Please don't make fun of me. This is so hard.* But when I see the serious expression on his face and the concentration in his deep blue eyes, I realize that's the last thing he would do. *No, it's okay. He's taking me seriously.*

"Go ahead," he encourages me.

I take a deep breath and reluctantly describe the waterfall suspended in midair, the sudden calm which Alder and I both experienced, the woman's hand caressing my face, and the juxtaposed emotions arguing within my mind. "It was weird, like two forces fighting for control, but I didn't understand the reason."

"What happened next?"

"The conflict stopped, and I felt all warm and fuzzy inside—safe, like I was wrapped up in a cocoon or something. Shielded." I think back to the sensations. "What's weird is that I know I've experienced this feeling of sanctuary before, but for the life of me, I can't remember when or where. Anyway, just when I felt the very best, I heard Joseph." Referencing my notes, I read aloud what I wrote about the conversation and add, "After he was gone, I felt lonely. Really empty."

"Anything else?"

"Yeah." I avert my eyes. "Uh, sorry to be so blunt, but I don't ever pray. Mostly, I try not to even think about God."

"No need to apologize."

"Yeah, well, I guess He's sort of been in my face the last two days, and I think maybe I did."

"Did what?"

"I silently asked a question, like, as in a prayer, or something. I asked God where He was."

"And?"

"I know this sounds nuts, but I think I got an answer. It started with a little breeze out of nowhere inside the room.

Every window was closed and locked, so no way it came through from outside. Anyway, when the wispy air got close, I inhaled a little. It smelled amazingly sweet." I pause, taking a small breath to remember the aroma. "Somehow familiar." I think hard. *What did the fragrance remind me of?* "Anyway, I took a deep breath, which was wonderful. Each time I inhaled, I wanted more. The air seemed somehow essential, and it made me feel different."

"Different how?"

"That's the really crazy part. It seemed to fill me up with . . ." *What is the right word?* "With hope." *Yeah, that's the right word.* "Hope."

Silence.

How can I make this next part sound coherent? I take another deep breath. "Then I felt a response to my question. I knew where He was because I *felt* Him say, 'Here.'" I put my hand over my heart. "I mean, how can you feel a word?" I hang my head as the tears run down my cheek. "Then He told me to rest."

When I finish speaking, the three sit quietly, staring at me. *Yup, I'm bonkers.* No one speaks. I get up and make more coffee.

"Refill, anyone?" I turn toward the table, but am barely able to hold the carafe in my shaking hand.

"Uh, sure." Jackson stands and walks to the counter, kindly taking the pot.

Sitting back down, I hold my head in my hands. "It's just so weird. And honestly, if someone else was telling me this story, I'd think they were either making it up or hallucinating."

"Elizabeth," Jackson says calmly, "Even though I don't know you as well as I'd like to, I do know you, and I don't think either of those is the case." He looks into his cup. "No, I'm more inclined to believe you've had real spiritual experiences."

"You mean spiritual, like, with God?"

"Yeah, that kind of spiritual." He winks.

"So you think all this is—was—real?"

"I think so." He seems to be debating.

"But?"

"I'm not sure about Joseph. He's a little hard to explain."

"How so?"

"Something you said. I'm just not sure. But all the rest, I think you've had contact with God."

"But why? Why would He contact me?"

"Why wouldn't He?"

"Because I don't know anything!" *God would never want me.* "You'd be better, Jackson. You're a minister, or pastor, or reverend, or whatever you are. For Heaven's sake, Mike's even a deacon, and Sally runs a women's group. You'd all be better!"

"Ha!" Mike interjects. "The Bible's full of stories about God choosing unlikely candidates for His purposes."

I wince. "Oh, ouch."

"No offense on the 'unlikely' part."

Jackson starts laughing, and then we all do. I laugh so hard that tears flow again. The levity is much needed in the midst of such a heavy discussion. But when the laughter stops, the current situation pushes the humor away.

"I just want to hide."

"I don't think that's possible," Jackson says softly, "not any longer."

"What could He want from me?"

"Everything. Nothing. Whatever He wants. Whatever He needs."

"No, seriously, this idea is stupid. Look, I don't know anything about God, or—or the Bible, or anything! I have nothing to offer Him."

"Therein lies your error. You have everything to offer Him."

"Like what?" *What can You possibly want from me, God?* I feel my frustration rising at this unexpected challenge.

"I have no idea, and that's the cool part. This is God's plan, not mine, not yours."

"Why is that cool? I think it sucks." *Sorry, God.* I look up to the ceiling briefly. *Why is it that God is always up?*

"Here's the thing, Elizabeth. We can't predict, out-think, or quantify how God moves the universe. To say that God works in mysterious ways is the biggest understatement of human thought. He works in His way, always to a defined purpose."

"So?"

"So, if He's calling your name and wants you for Himself, He's gonna do whatever it takes to get your attention."

"What if I just ignore it?"

"I think He'd call harder." He laughs again, a good belly laugh. "Besides, can you simply ignore what's been happening to you?"

"No, it's pretty much in my face."

"Right. So what we need to do is learn as much as we can from what you've experienced. Maybe then we can figure out what's next."

"Oh, next." I sigh. "I don't think I can take much more."

Jackson reaches across the table and puts a warm, strong hand on mine. "Don't worry, we'll figure this out together."

Gazing into his intense eyes, I find myself searching for answers to questions I've never even thought of before. Surprising thoughts flood my brain, and I momentarily forget where I am.

I think back over the four years I've known Jackson. He's always seemed like a true gentleman, and we could probably be good friends—really good friends—if I gave him half a chance. But ever since Mac died, I've never given any man a chance, especially Jackson.

Was that a mistake? I wonder . . . No, it's not a mistake. Things must remain as casual as possible. And yet . . . This is the first time I've ever taken a good, hard look at him as a man. What I see is very appealing, and that realization scares me.

What am I afraid of? Him? Me? Disappointing Mac? Another

broken heart? I try to straighten out my thoughts. *No, I know what it is.* Whenever I see him, it reminds me of Mac and the funeral. *Oh, God. Will I ever let it go?*

Seeming to pick up on a cue that I'm struggling, Sally stands and smoothes out the few new wrinkles in her skirt. "I believe it's time for lunch." In her slight Southern drawl, she organizes the team. "Mike, you go get the basket. Jackson, you take Alder outside for a run. Elizabeth, let's eat outside. We need plates, silverware, and napkins."

"Okay, no problem." I withdraw my hand and shake off the mystery of Jackson. "And I seriously need a glass of Chardonnay." *Actually, I'd like to get drunk.* "Wine or beer, anyone? Oh, sorry, Jackson. You probably don't drink."

"Of course I do. I'd love a glass of Chardonnay."

Huh? Really? What else did I miss? "Any other takers?"

"Sounds good to me," is the general response. In short order, the picnic table is covered with a blue-and-white checkered tablecloth and set with the necessary utensils. We munch on a wonderful meal of cold roasted chicken, potato salad, grilled asparagus, and fabulous olive bread from the Sunny Farms Bakery. Exactly what I needed.

About halfway through the meal, the wine—having a slightly deleterious effect on my exhausted brain—encourages me to blurt out, "What if Joseph is from some other planet or parallel universe or something? Like, what if he's torn the fabric of time or whatever separates worlds? What if he's not supposed to be here?" Several wild tangents are forming, and my brain feels like it's misfiring.

"Interesting thoughts," Jackson says.

"I mean, think about it for a second. What if he's not"—I search for words—"not from God or Heaven? What if he's like a predator or alien or something?"

"Look, anything's possible. But being a man of God, I don't look for answers in fantasy where God doesn't exist.

Having said that, most of what we believe about the details of our afterlife is pure speculation. No one knows for certain. But what's really hooked me, what I keep coming back to, is how you felt after both experiences. Especially your account of the baby girl and how you reacted."

"Yeah, that was amazing." He's right. The memory allows my mind to settle again. With the warm sun on my back and the wine in my head, I begin to feel unusually relaxed. "So, what do I do now? Any advice?"

"I'm still giving thought to that question." Jackson swirls the wine in his glass and smiles at me. "And you'll be the first to know when I have an answer."

I believe him. Something in his voice lets me believe. *This is all new.* I can feel the layers of my walls eroding, and for the first time, I find myself looking for an opening.

———◦◦———

By two o'clock, picture-perfect weather and glorious sunshine bathe the Olympic Peninsula. Situated six miles up the mountainside, my twelve acres of wooded property are often shrouded in clouds—but not today. Far beyond the sculpted tree line below and north past Highway 101, the beautiful Strait of Juan de Fuca glistens in the afternoon sun, beckoning on to the Pacific Ocean. Reminiscent of the Emerald City of Oz, Vancouver Island's faraway coastline and Victoria's city buildings reflect back the sparkling sunlight. Like a masterpiece of art, the brilliantly contrasting colors alone are enough to jar the senses. I stop to breathe in deeply the peace and serenity of this spectacular scene.

Bellies full and our meal finished, we opt for a lazy stroll around the upper trails, perhaps to feel less guilty about stuffing ourselves. Alder traverses the hillside, running his usual pattern of zigzags and playing tag with his tail. As I walk among the towering Douglas fir and cedar spires, it's easy to remember why Mac and I chose this land for our home. True, it took years of hard work to carve out the little pasture setting and build the cabin, but we knew it would be the right spot to raise our children. *Our children. Yeah, Mac, we were supposed to have a family.*

As we circle around to the front of the cabin, Jackson's voice pulls me from my thoughts. "Sorry, guys, but I've got to leave. Duty calls."

"Oh, no problem." I find myself wishing he could stay longer. It's been nice to talk to him again. "Sorry for the inconvenience, but I'm grateful you came out to help me sort this through. It means a lot."

"I'd love to stay longer, but I've got to get back to the office for a meeting. I'll check on you tomorrow."

"Tomorrow?" As much as I hate to admit it, that might be nice. "You will?"

"Yeah, I will." He rubs his chin. "Unless you object."

I look down at my feet. *What am I feeling?* I look back up at him. "No, I don't mind."

"Good. When do you go back to work?"

"Technically, I start my four nights off tonight, so not until Monday afternoon. But I have almost four months of paid leave, so if I need to, I can take additional time off."

He raises his eyebrows. "Wow, you must not miss much work."

"No, never." I lower my head. "Honestly, I don't have much else."

"Well, maybe we can change that. I'll see you tomorrow." He gives me another bear hug. "You'll be okay. Don't worry."

I reluctantly reciprocate the hug and find it doesn't feel half bad. Again I wonder what I'm feeling.

Sally and Mike have been talking off to the side. Turning to me, Sally says, "I think I'll hitch a ride into town with Jackson. Mike's gonna stick around for a while."

"Oh, Sally, that's sweet. But you don't need to do that,

Mike. I'll be okay, really. Go home."

"Nope, I came prepared and intend to stay until coffee tomorrow morning. I'm staying to be certain you get a good night's sleep. And that's final."

Protesting is futile, as it seems this has been their plan all along. As Jackson pulls out of the driveway, I wander back inside to clean up the kitchen.

"Jackson's a good man, you know," Mike says, stoking the fire. "He was really sorry about Mac."

"I know. Doing the service must have been hard for him."

"It was hard for him to see you in so much pain. That was hard for all of us." He hangs up the poker and adds, "You know, he asks about you all the time."

"He asks you about me?"

"Yeah, does that surprise you?"

"Kinda. I mean, he calls here a lot, always checking on me. Half the time I don't answer. Probably sounds rude, but I can take care of myself."

"He knows that. I think he just cares."

Cares how? Never mind. Duh, he's a pastor. "Oh, sure, I get it. Too bad he can't be married. He'd make a good husband."

"What are you talking about? Ha! That's funny. Pastors can be married. He's just never found the right person. And trust me, he's looked and been approached."

What? "Oh man, all this time I thought it wasn't allowed." *What an idiot I am.* I think back to a decade earlier when I used to date and remember the list of requirements I'd created. I purposely set the bar high for prospective men, knowing few would ever meet it. *Intelligence, education, hard work, sex appeal, charm, manners, and single. Hmm, maybe Jackson's got a shot.* "Hey, Mike, I don't know much about your church." I laugh. "Wanna trade some trauma info for church info?"

"Not really, but I'd be happy to tell you whatever you want to know about what we believe and how we worship."

"I'd actually like that."

We relax in front of the woodstove while Mike gives me a crash course on Christianity and how Jackson's church differs from others. I listen with interest about the development of the church, rituals, scripture, doctrine, and differences between the various denominations. Surprisingly, I find it all quite fascinating.

"So Mike, you're the only guy I trust to ask this."

"Go ahead."

"Don't laugh now. I'm sure this will seem like a stupid question. But how, exactly, do you pray?"

He strokes his chin. "I'm not sure I understand your question. Are you asking about kneeling versus bowing or something?"

"No. Well, maybe. I don't know. Mostly I wonder . . . like, what do you say? I mean, if a person is praying to God to ask for something personal, isn't that being petty? Isn't that wasting His time?"

He bends forward in his chair and rests his elbows on his knees, looking at me in all seriousness. "First rule of prayer is that God already knows what you need and want. He knows your heart and soul, probably better than you do. So it's not like you're keeping any secrets. Second rule of prayer is that He wants—emphasis on *wants*—you to ask Him for what you need. He's ready, willing, and accepting."

"So then, if He already knows, what's the point in asking?"

"To open a dialogue with your Maker. To open your heart to His responses. To begin to hear what He wants to tell you."

"So give me a clue about what you say."

"Well, prayer is really personal."

"Oh, sorry."

"No, no. I don't mean it that way. Why don't I give it a shot right now?" He bows his head and closes his eyes. "Dear Lord, Elizabeth and I are having a conversation right now about

You and prayer, and we could use some help. We ask that You give me the right words to say and give her the wisdom to understand, so that we may both come to know You better. We also ask Your help and guidance in figuring out what's been going on the past few days. In Christ's name, amen."

"Wow, that was simple."

"What did you expect?"

"I don't know, something more involved, I guess. Talking to God has always seemed daunting. But that sounds like a regular conversation."

"Precisely. A normal conversation with the Creator of this magnificent universe. It's all He asks. To be acknowledged as your Creator and to be loved, as He loves us."

"So basically, a person could pray anywhere. You don't need to be in a church or on your knees." I think about that. "So I could just pray in thought, right?"

"Absolutely. There are no hard and fast rules, Elizabeth. Only that you try. It's very easy once you get started. Almost like He's an invisible best friend who's always with you. He's my confidant, my guide, my source of strength, and I know He loves me for who I am."

"Wow. I never looked at it that way."

"That reminds me." He reaches into his bag and pulls out a box wrapped in tissue paper. "Here. We got you a gift."

"What's this for?" I unwrap it. "A Bible. Oh, Mike, this is beautiful!" I flip through it. It's hand bound in brown leather, replete with pictures, maps, and detailed explanations. "You know, I've never owned a Bible. Truthfully, I never even wanted one." Flattening my hands out on the cover, I try to feel the words inside. "But now I feel like I need one, badly."

"We figured. And here's a couple of extra items for you from each of us." He hands three bookmarks to me, each one inscribed with an inspirational message.

"I recognize this one, the 'Footprints in the Sand' poem.

I love it. Oh, Mike, this means so much to me. I can't thank you enough. I'm really touched by your kindness." I feel tears welling up again.

"It's from all of us, and our pleasure." Standing, he claps his hands together. "I believe it's five o'clock, and I'm opening a bottle of your finest red. You want some?" He heads for my small wine supply in the laundry room.

"Sure. I've got a frozen pizza I can cook for dinner. Would that be okay?"

"Absolutely. I love frozen pizza."

Needing no further prompting, I fire up the oven, shred extra cheese to add to the toppings, and slide it in to cook. After chopping some romaine for a Caesar salad, I set the table and feed Alder while Mike searches the Internet. Just before the buzzer goes off, I reload my wood supply in the tinder box.

Even though it's the third of April and the day is sunny and in the mid-sixties, I know as soon as the sun goes down that the temperature will drop to the low forties. Since nights don't warm up much until late July, my little woodstove runs constantly almost ten months of the year. That's totally okay with me, because even though it requires extra time to clean out and reload, the radiating wood heat is soothing and friendly.

"What're you looking for on the Internet?"

"I'm searching 'six,' 'guides,' and ghost stuff. Just trying to cover all the bases."

"Any luck?"

"Not exactly. There's a wealth of info about ghosts, most of it speculation. I think we'd get more info from an Edgar Allen Poe novel."

The timer sounds, and I check the pizza. "Chow time!"

We easily devour the gourmet meal of pepperoni pizza, salad, and some anonymous brand of red wine which actually isn't half bad. Considering my normal routine is solo, it's a nice respite to have company.

"Do you ever get lonely up here on the mountain?"

"Yeah, sometimes." *You can't hide from yourself up here.* "But Alder keeps me sane, and I have the high school kids who come up once a week to work around the property, so that's a fun diversion. I also have a few close friends like you and Sally."

"You don't have to defend yourself. It just seems kinda solitary."

"It is. But honestly, when I get done with three back-to-back Trauma shifts, I'm so fried, I need silence." *Face the truth: you can't hide anymore, and you're lonely.* I shake off the thought. "Anyway, I guess there are times when being a hermit is okay." *No, it's not okay.*

"It must be like a war zone in the Emergency Room."

"Yeah, sometimes that's exactly how it feels." Leaning back, I cross my arms over my head. "The worst is when you fight hard to save someone's life. The whole team works on them for hours, but for whatever reason, they don't make it. And then you have to immediately turn around and greet a new patient who's there for some stupid reason. There's no debriefing, no consolation, no nothing.

"I remember once at a different hospital, working on a child who'd fallen into a swimming pool. We tried for two or three hours to revive the little girl. Her parents were right there and absolutely devastated. The lead doc wouldn't give up. Heck, no one wanted to call it. But eventually, we had to. Such a tragedy.

"Meanwhile, since the staff was pretty much focused on saving the child's life, a bunch of other noncritical patients got neglected and had to wait. We got really backed up. Literally, one minute I was zipping the little girl's dead body into a black bag, and the next I was in a room with an elderly man who'd forgotten to refill a prescription. The old fart was an impatient ass, fuming that he'd had to wait. To make matters worse, since the facility was so small, the other patients watched the lifesaving efforts from their rooms. So, even though the guy knew a child had died, he laid into me for inconveniencing him.

"Truthfully, I almost lost it. I almost decked him. But instead I smiled, took copious notes, and put his chart at the very bottom of the pile for the doc, and mysteriously, it stayed at the bottom. I think the old fart waited another three or four hours for his stupid little pill." I chuckle at the magic of a little retribution.

"Wow. Can't say I blame you." Mike sips his wine. "Don't hospitals have chaplains or clergy to help during a crisis like that?"

"Not too much anymore. Maybe the Catholic or Seventh Day Adventist hospitals do, and a few others I'm not familiar with, but the regular public hospitals don't. Most don't even have chapels anymore. So in dealing with trauma and death, the general staff and patients' families are left to their own devices. It's tough some times."

"I don't know how you do it. Nine months in Vietnam was enough gore and stress for me. I couldn't do it week after week for twelve years."

"Sadly, I don't know how to do anything else. Besides, sometimes the good guys win and we save the patient, so the trade-off is worth it." I think for a moment. "And I love it. Ninety-nine percent of it."

"I know you do. It shows."

Having finished everything, including the bottle of non-descript red wine, we clear the table and wash the dishes. After stoking the fire, I take Alder out for one last run. An early moon is rising, and it looks to be a clear, crisp night. To the west, the treetops are silhouetted against the glow from the city lights of Port Angeles. Except for the familiar constellations of Orion's Belt and the Big Dipper, I have an eerie feeling I could be in any number of distant planetary locations in the universe. *Where are you, Joseph? Do you see the same sky I see?*

Back inside, I hang up my jacket and pull out sheets and

a blanket for Mike. He is already up in the other loft, pulling down the Murphy bed. After it's made up, we alternate turns in the bathroom, and I slip into my snuggly flannel pajamas. Although it's only 8:30 p.m., I'm exhausted, and Mike says he feels the same.

"Don't be alarmed," I say, "but I'm sleeping with my Walther PK on my bedside table. So try not to scare the crap out of me if you wake me up."

"Good. Then you won't be alarmed that I brought along my HK forty for good measure. I always carry it these days."

"Awesome. Nice gun. I feel better already." *Great minds think alike!*

"By the way, when's your next competition?"

"In about two months. I just got my Kimber back from the gunsmith, and Irene and I have been practicing at the tactical range in Seattle. She's so fabulous! We'll be ready."

"Maybe Sally and I will come watch. I'd love to see you kick butt."

"Me, too." I grin and switch off the lights. "Thanks for keeping me company, Mike. See you at coffee."

I leave one nightlight on downstairs, in case he needs to find anything. Then I head up the narrow steps to my loft as Mike goes up to his.

As I slide between the sheets and snuggle underneath the down comforter, the radiant heat wafting up from the woodstove below instantly relaxes my muscles. With Alder's furry body at my side, the dry warmth is intoxicating. Exhaustion overcomes me, and my thoughts once again return to the beautiful baby, Joseph's words, and Jackson.

Jackson. *Dang it all, Jackson! You found the chink in my armor.* I can't get him out of my head. I roll onto my back and look up at the ceiling. *Face it, you're attracted to him. But why?*

Is it because he listened to everything I said and wasn't judgmental, or is there more to it? I'm sure counseling people about their problems is part of his job, but his reaction to me seemed more involved, more personal. Maybe I'm just making more out of it than there really is. Still, thinking about him makes me feel . . . better. *Elizabeth*, I chide myself, *you can't get involved.*

I think back again over the four years I've known him. *Maybe I was attracted to him all along, and that's why I worked so hard to keep him at bay.* But what's so great about him? *Give it up. It'll never work out.*

Rolling on my side, I bury my face in my soft down pillow and feel tears welling up behind my eyes once again.

Oh please, God, help me!

15

Crack! Wham! Bang!

I sit bolt upright in bed, but it's pitch black. I can't see a dang thing. My mind scrambles to orient itself and shake off the cobwebs of sleep. *Oh damn, not again,* I think, as memories of recent events flood back. I feel for my gun on the table next to me and wrap my fingers around its grip. Then I search for Alder at the end of my bed, but he isn't there.

"Alder! Alder, come!" I command. I hear his patter of paws and feel a welcome cold nose at my thigh. "Good boy. Get up here." He jumps up on the bed and lies next to me.

"Elizabeth, you okay?"

"Huh? Oh geez, Mike, you scared the crap out of me! I forgot you were here for a moment. Can you see anything?"

"Nope, you must've lost power. I got a light. Come on down." He shines the light up the steps.

"Thanks. Hey, shine it up here a sec." I find my own flashlight in the basket and flip it on, then make my way down the steps. "What the heck was that loud crack?"

"It sounded like a big tree hit the ridgeline of your roof. I haven't gone out to check yet, but it's a good thing you guys built this house like a tank."

"This makes no sense. Wait! Stop." I grab his arm. "What time does your watch say?"

He shines the light on his wrist. "About midnight thirty."

"What's the date?" I hate to ask, but I have to know. It was the evening of April third when we retired to bed. I hold my breath while he strains his eyes to see the tiny numbers.

"The fifth." He bends his arm around so I can verify the number.

"Damn, I lost another day. Or rather, *we* lost another day."

"What the heck? We just went to sleep."

"I know. And it was clear and beautiful outside. No way a storm or high winds were in the forecast. I wonder if the phone works." I walk to the woodstove, feel the top, and open the door. "It's stone cold. Not a single warm coal left." I move on to check the phone. "Line's dead again."

I find the matches and move around the room, lighting candles and lanterns, while Mike tends the fire. Within a few minutes we have sufficient light from the blaze and candlelight to navigate. I grab my jacket, slip into my boots, and start out the front door. I need to find out what's happened to my house.

Mike is right behind me, and once we get clear of the porch, we turn around and aim our lights at the roof. Sure enough, lying across the midsection of the A-frame ridgeline is an enormous cedar.

"Oh, Mike. It's fallen right across the roof. It must be a hundred feet tall!" I trudge around to the backyard. "Holy cow! It's over the propane tank."

Mike aims his light in the same direction. "That's not good."

The propane tank sits on a small concrete pad roughly

twenty feet from the back corner of the house. The tree originally stood uphill, approximately thirty feet above and beyond the tank. When it crashed down, it hit the top of the roof at a forty-five degree angle to the center ridgeline. This angle puts the propane tank right underneath the giant tree, halfway between the roots and its midsection. The rest of the tree and most of its branches are suspended out over the other side of the roof. The roof ridgeline is acting like the balancing point of a giant tree seesaw.

"I've got a good lumberjack I can call in the morning." I aim my light up at the tree and scan it, searching for any breaks in the trunk. "Hopefully it's stable and won't break in half."

"That must be what took out your power and phone."

"Nope. Everything's underground." I trudge back to the other side of the house and aim my light at the driveway where the power and phone lines are buried. "Looks like the transformer's okay." Pointing down the hill, I add, "Lights are on in town."

"Looks like the next property has lights, too."

"I'm getting tired of this." Feeling a sudden chill, I pull my jacket up around my neck and head back toward the door.

"I hope Sally's okay."

"Me, too." I stop to think about the time for a minute. "Hey, Mike, don't you think she'd have come back out here to check on us if a whole day went by?"

"Yeah, 'course she would've."

"So maybe the time thing isn't real." I want answers. "I'm gonna get my keys and see if the truck starts."

"Good idea."

We both go inside to fetch our keys. Mine are in my bag in the kitchen, and Mike's are up in the loft. As we meet back at the front door, I hear a dripping sound. *There it is again.* "It's starting," I whisper.

"Looks like you have a pipe leak," Mike whispers back.

"No pipes in the ceiling. It's Joseph." I aim my light up, and sure enough, a small stream of water is dripping from about a foot below the apex. Then I aim my light down at the floor, and just as before, it's dry. "See, it has no visible beginning or end. Isn't that weird?"

"Oh man, that is weird," he whispers. "Where's the sound coming from?"

"It's just like last night. I have no idea. Except maybe it's not a real sound."

"So, what do you wanna do?"

"Actually, I just want to sit down and wait. Are you game?"

He shrugs. "I guess so."

"Alder, come here, boy," I command as quietly as I can. To my surprise, Alder comes down the stairs and stands at my side, tail wagging. "Wow, he doesn't seem to even notice. Like he's not afraid. Maybe it's some primordial animal intuition or something."

"Maybe. Maybe not."

"Well, he's definitely not reacting like he did the last time it started."

Mike scans his light over the dripping water. "Elizabeth, this is so surreal."

I take another look. "Yup, it really is."

With our flashlights switched off, we sit in front of the fire and wait. The firelight casts an eerie glow on the falling water, making it seem luminescent. At least an hour of vigilant silence passes in the dim candlelight while we watch the phenomenon of water dripping from nowhere. Unable to take the suspense any longer, I get up to use the bathroom and make some tea.

"If we're gonna wait, we may as well be comfortable." I yank a couple of throw blankets from the linen cupboard, grab the two mugs of hot tea, and come back into the room. "Here you go," I whisper, handing the items to Mike.

"Thanks. Hey, I have an idea. Why don't you call out to him?"

"Actually," I say, "I want to feel this water."

I take three strides to the dripping liquid and hold out my hand. My fingertips are very close, no more than half an inch away. It appears to be just water, yet I am afraid to touch it. I hesitate, debating.

What if touching it makes it go away? What if touching it brings evil? What if I get sucked through a vortex? What if? What if? What if? My mind is fighting itself. *Enough!* I close my eyes and take the plunge.

I catch my breath. The sensation is pure ecstasy—pure, unadulterated joy. Pure love. No worries, no cares, no . . .

Poof! The connection is severed. Opening my eyes, I see my fingers still penetrating the dripping liquid, but the sensations have ceased—like I've been cut off. I withdraw my hand. "Oh please, don't go away! Please, God, or Joseph, or whatever you are, please come back!"

"I am here," a distant female voice responds. The sound seems to come from within me.

"Mike, can you hear that?"

"Yes, but it's inside my head," he whispers. "Sounds like a woman."

"Exactly!" I really want to communicate with this entity. Peering through the dim light toward Mike, I see that his eyes are closed. He is smiling delightfully.

"Mike?" I whisper. "Are you okay?"

"I feel something wonderful. Like a hand on my heart." He places his own hand over his heart and gently pats his chest.

"Elizabeth."

I turn my head back toward the water.

"It is me, Joseph."

"Yes!" *Thank you, God!* I look at Mike. "Did you hear that?"

"Yes, barely. But it's a different voice. There's two of them."

"Two?" *Of course.*

"Two. The one from within—touching my heart—is

calming. The other is hard to hear. The waterfall seems to block some of it."

"Waterfall?" I lower my voice to a whisper again. "I can't hear it."

"Yes. Definitely a waterfall."

"I can't hear it," I repeat. "You think the rippling water sounds like a waterfall?"

"Elizabeth, focus! Ask Joseph what he wants."

"Right." I turn my head back to the water. "Joseph, what can we do for you?"

Silence.

"What do you need?"

"To stop it." As he speaks, I once again hear the beautiful sound of rippling water.

There it is! I love that sound. Falling water? Maybe. I'm not sure. "What do you need to stop?"

"Things are changing. A darkness is coming." His voice is becoming stronger, more clear.

Definitely male, English. Oh wait, maybe I just understand it as English. Maybe he really speaks Martian. After all, what do I know?

"No, I communicate what you understand. We share a common consciousness."

I hate that you can read my thoughts. "Where are you?"

"On the other side of Mayim."

"What is . . . Mayim?" I ask.

"The sacred water. The water is called Mayim."

"Are you in Heaven?"

"No. I am in the place of Holding."

"Holding?" *Maybe it's Hell.*

"No, it is not." The image of a magnificent crystalline structure on a faraway hillside fills my mind. "Good, Elizabeth. Your mind is able to see. I am inside the Cathedral in the place of Holding."

"Where is it, this Cathedral and Holding?"

"In a world adjacent to yours. Here, on this side."

"Of the water."

"Yes. Our world is on the other side of Mayim."

This is stupid. I'm not getting anywhere. Think!

"Calm yourself, Elizabeth. I will answer your questions."

I feel the feminine hand on my face again and immediately begin to relax. In place of my irrational, random fears, logical questions begin to form in my head one at a time.

"Joseph, please tell me about yourself."

"I have *been* . . . for as long as I can remember. I am the Sixth. The Sixth of the Nine."

He told me that the last time. "So there are more? You're not alone?"

"I am frequently in solitude, but never truly alone. I am one of the Nine unique parts that create the whole. We cannot function if we are separated, and thus are always connected to the other eight."

"So you each have a different number?"

"Number?" Joseph asks.

"Name?" I fumble.

"Function. We each have a different function."

"What is your function?"

"As I told you before, I am a guide for the ones coming."

He thinks I'm an idiot.

"That is not true. I think you can help me."

Please, stop reading my thoughts!

"It is impossible for me not to read your thoughts. I am sorry if you find it unpleasant."

"I do." I feel the woman's hand gently caressing my cheek. "But I'll survive. How can I help you?"

"I know for certain that things are changing, which should not. They must not."

"What is it? What's changing?" *Maybe our side tore the fabric separating us, or . . .*

"There is no fabric to tear."

My frustration rises again. "Joseph—look, I have no idea what we could be doing that could affect you."

"Elizabeth, a small connection still exists between your dimension and mine. Through it, I have learned to sense you. Perhaps you can sense me."

"Only when you show up, like now."

"Ah." He hesitates before continuing. "Can you not see it? Can you not feel it?"

See what? Feel what?

"The difference."

"Joseph, every day is different! I have no idea what to even look for." I try a different tack. "What changed on your side?"

"There are more . . . passages." His voice drops a notch. "And many are agonizingly painful now."

I wonder what a passage is. "Why is it painful?"

"I am unsure. Pain used to be rare. But now it seems they can anticipate the end and know the pain is coming to them. Then they bring the pain with them."

"What's a passage, and who's 'they'?"

An extra-long pause ensues, and for a moment I think he is gone, but I can still hear the rippling water and see the surreal liquid dripping from below the ceiling.

"Joseph?"

"Patience, Elizabeth. I am searching for a way to explain it." He hesitates again. "Ah, yes. A passage is when one must travel from your side to mine. The gateway is Mayim."

"Huh. Travel?" *So we can go back and forth. This could be cool.*

"No. Travel through Mayim is only one way."

Oh. He means death. Crazy, disorganized ideas of Heaven and Hell jump all over my mind.

"There is no death."

Flashing anger rises from the soles of my feet to the tips of my fingers. "I *know* there is death." *Mom, Dad, even Mac.*

"They are not here. Mac is not here. He is safe."

Don't lie to me. "I've seen it too often not to know!" The anger that surges up from within me rages like a wildfire out of control. My deepest privacy has been invaded. *Get out of my mind!* I scream in silence.

"Elizabeth, you must trust me. There is no death."

I don't want to believe him. "I don't even know who you really are, or what you are." I begin to cry. "But I know there's death. I've felt the aftermath of it all my life."

"What you feel in your current existence is only temporary. Because your time is linear and your nature fixed, you cannot see what is beyond."

I feel the woman's gentle fingers caressing my cheek. *Please, don't take my anger away. It's all I've got left.* Unable to resist, I let out a huge, long sigh as the anger subsides. *Okay, I give up.* "Why should I believe you?"

"Elizabeth, there is more to your existence than your physical life in your dimension. You and all of humanity have a much greater purpose."

Somehow I know what he's saying is the truth. *He's got to be right. If this world is all there is, then what's the point? It would make no sense.*

"As I said, I am the Sixth of the Nine. We exist solely for the others. We are not here for you. And this is not about Mac."

"If you aren't here for me, then what can you possibly want?"

"We are here only for the Pure."

"I don't understand. What does that mean?"

"Only the Pure, until they are released."

"Released? Like from a prison?"

"No, not a prison. A protected Holding."

"How long are they held?" I ask.

"Since linear time does not exist on this side of Mayim, the question is irrelevant."

"How can time not exist?"

"Look at it this way. In your world, each moment is sequential. Each present moment builds upon the last, creating the past. In our world, everything happens at once, although events can be expanded, contracted, and rearranged."

Time warping?

"Not exactly. More like—immaterial. Those in Holding are released at their own appointed moment. It is a moment of their own choosing."

"So what am I supposed to do?"

"Help me stop . . . ah-ha!" Joseph seems surprised, which surprises me in turn.

"Ah-ha what?"

"I just sensed the root of the darkness. I know what it is." As he speaks these words, his voice drops another notch. "One is coming who must not." He sounds heartbreakingly sad. "We must stop the one coming who has no—"

But his voice and the dripping water are abruptly gone, and so is the feminine hand on my cheek. In their place is a suffocating silence. Barely breathing, I sit in the chair and feel salty tears stream down my face.

Oh God, how could You do this to me all over again? Why did you take Mac away?

The answer comes roaring at me as if from the deepest part of the universe, thundering through my brain, catapulting me into another realm of consciousness.

"I DID NOT TAKE HIM ANYWHERE. HE IS WHERE HE HAS ALWAYS BEEN. HE IS WITH ME."

Stunned, I am unable to breathe. After what seems an eternity, I gasp and ask meekly, "God? Is that really You?"

"FOREVER."

As His answer comes, so does the same sweet aroma from before, coupled with a sense of incredible peace. I am beginning to understand.

16

ANOTHER PLACE

"Why do you keep following me, Lady Mary?"

"Joseph, you know I must."

"You are interfering."

"No, I am fulfilling my role."

"You seem to be counteracting me, as though you are trying to shield her."

"I am shielding her."

"But why? I am simply trying to open Elizabeth's mind so that she can understand her realm and see life for what it is."

"She is unprepared for your intrusions."

"But I would not harm her. Such things are not within my nature."

"I am not protecting her from you, Joseph. I am shielding her from her own emotions."

"I do not understand."

"That is because you are not aware of sensations these humans feel."

"What sensations?"

"Anger, hatred, and fear. Fear is the worst because it leads to all the others."

"What is this fear?"

"An uncomfortable sensation. Although they have been given ways to find and comprehend the true meaning of their existence, it alludes them. Since they cannot see their final outcomes, they fear virtually everything."

"How unfortunate."

"Yes, it is. Therefore, Elizabeth must learn to trust you; otherwise she will turn away and work against you. That will not serve the greater purpose."

"I see."

"All she needed was comfort and love, which I provided. Remember, not only am I your mentor, I am also a caretaker."

"Lady Mary, why is the earth-realm forbidden?"

"Ah. A very good question." She closes her eyes and touches her finger to the center of her forehead, retrieving a vision from the archives. "Apparently, it has not always been so. Once they were as pure as we are, and travel between our worlds was welcome. Full of rich clarity and truth, all who dwelt there lived in harmony with life, nature, and Father, as we do here."

"What changed?"

With her finger still on her forehead, her eyes narrow. "Someone within their world felt a darkness approaching from a lower realm. He crossed their barrier, hoping to investigate and understand the darkness. He believed that through understanding its nature, he could control it."

"What happened?"

"His arrogance allowed the darkness to latch onto him like an evil parasite. It quickly took total control of his being. When he returned from the lower realm, he carried with him an evil so insidious and potent, it almost destroyed their world."

"Why did they not stop it themselves?"

"The dark evil permeated the fabric of their humanity until they could see nothing else. Soon their knowledge of the Light was all but extinguished. Except for the gateway through Mayim, Father barricaded their world from the rest of the pure realms. That is why they must endure their separation." She releases her finger, returning the disquieting visions to their proper place within the archives. Her voice softens. "Father, the Spirit Wind, and the Most Holy are the only ones who can move freely within and around their humanity."

"When I reached through Mayim, why did you not stop me?"

"I sought the wisdom of the Council and acted upon their advice."

"You called the Council? This matter has been discussed within the chapel?"

"Yes."

"Was that necessary?"

"Absolutely. I am as concerned as you, Joseph. The Council acknowledges that there has been a shift in the earth-realm. Every member of the Nine feels it. Something is transforming their world. What the Council is unsure of is whether or not the shift can be halted. Either way, it seemed unlikely you would desist."

"What was their advice?"

"I am to assist you. Perhaps this time the darkness can be stopped."

"I believe it can."

"Obviously. But none of us yet understand what is approaching."

"Actually, when I reached through just now, I saw the outline. I am beginning to understand what the darkness is, what it represents."

"May I see the image?"

"Not yet. It keeps changing." Joseph looks down at his hands, then back at his mentor. "Lady Mary, do you think I am wrong?"

"I think Father is in charge of the universe. I *know* He is. It is, after all, His. I believe that if a darkness is coming again, He is aware of it." Lady Mary pauses. "I also know we are His, to use as He sees fit."

"What should I do?"

"Control your powers. Until you understand the magnitude of your strength in their realm, you must proceed with utmost caution. Even if alterations in her time and space are necessary, you must not bring harm to Elizabeth. I will do my best to allay her fears. We all agree, she may be able to help."

17

"Mike!" I whisper. "Did you hear all that?"

"I think so. The waterfall was loud, but I think I got most of it. What a great smell—just like my youngest daughter smelled when she was born. Goodness me, I couldn't get enough of her scent!"

Of course! The hope-filled scent reminds me of a newborn baby, the sweetest fragrance in the world.

Jumping over to Mike, I pull him out of the chair. "Come on, we've got to get all this down before we forget anything."

Unexpectedly, the electricity returns, the lights come on, and the microwave oven beeps. I walk over to it to set the time. "Hey, what time does your watch say now?"

"Four fifteen sharp."

As I'm setting all the clocks, Mike joins me in the kitchen. "Note the date." He holds out his arm.

I look closely at the tiny numbers on his watch face. "It's a four. We're back to the fourth." I struggle for an explanation.

"Looks like it." Mike verifies the date on his cell phone, which miraculously has a full signal again. Indeed, the date does appear to be correct.

"So we didn't lose a day, after all. Maybe time is flexible, or . . . irrelevant on the other side." Illogical as time flexing seems, at this point it's the only plausible answer.

"Maybe. I agree, Elizabeth, let's write all this down—now!"

After writing for more than an hour, I set down my pen, and Mike stops typing on his laptop. Even though daylight hasn't broken, we're wide awake, and there is no way either of us is going back to sleep. As I make the first pot of coffee, the sun crests the treetops. It looks like it will be another clear, cold spring day. While Mike showers, I feed Alder and take him outside for a little romp so I can check the status of the fallen cedar. My breath crystallizes in front of my face as I trek around the house.

In the daylight, the tree looks even more massive than when shrouded in darkness and shadows. The lower trunk is at least five feet in diameter and probably closer to one hundred fifty feet in length. Shuddering at the thought of this mammoth tree crashing down on the roof, I realize once again just how brilliantly Mac designed the house. As a structural engineer, he certainly did his homework. An average stud-framed house would have been decimated by the crushing load of this cedar. But mine seems to stand in defiance of the massive weight and laws of gravity. I smile at my memories of Mac, missing him yet again.

Yanking myself out of the past, I go back inside and phone the lumberjack. Unfortunately, he's swamped with another job and can't get to me until the following week. Mike walks out of the bathroom just in time to catch the end of my conversation. Without saying anything, he grabs his cell phone and goes outside. Disheartened, I pull out the community phonebook and start looking for another logger.

Deep into my search, the phone rings. It's Roger, calling to say he'll be out to the house in a few minutes.

"That's great! Thanks, Roger." I'm hanging up when Mike comes back inside.

"What's great?" he asks.

I explain the phone call. "I'm grateful, to say the least, but it's a little odd."

"Well, maybe he had a change of heart. Now, why don't I fix breakfast while you go shower?"

Standing under the hot water, I feel my body relax as the steamy essence cascades over my head, shoulders, and tired muscles. Although I've taken thousands of showers, this one feels incredible. As I listen to the sound of the water falling from the shower head, I decide Mike is right. The sound I heard during Joseph's visits was definitely that of a waterfall, not a rippling brook as I originally surmised.

I could stay in the shower all day, it feels so glorious. But since nothing lasts forever, I capitulate to reality and reluctantly turn off the water. The phone rings as I'm slipping into my normal daily garb of corduroy jeans, a lightweight turtleneck, and a nautical-style sweater. Bringing my morning preparations to a close, I dry my hair and brush my teeth.

I hate to wear makeup and don't own much. I simply never see the need. Likewise, I wear only one piece of jewelry. One year after Mac died, I took the wedding ring off my finger and slid it onto my only gold necklace. It hasn't been off my neck in over three years. Stretching the collar of my shirt out a little, I reach in and pull the chain to the outside. Even though the sweater covers the ring, I know it's there, and that's all that matters.

"Who was on the phone?"

"Jackson. He was checking on us."

"Oh, that was sweet. Did you tell him we had another encounter?"

"Nope. But I told him about the tree, the propane tank, and the power failure."

I pour myself some more coffee. "Yeah? What did he say?"

"That he'll be out here in less than an hour. And he's bringing Sally, too."

"Oh, for Heaven's sake, he doesn't need to come back out here!" *Although it would be nice to see him again.* "I'm okay, and I've got Roger coming up in a little while to take care of the tree. I'm sure he has better things to do."

Mike hands me a plate. "Eat, madam!"

The plate is full of a steaming omelet with lots of melted cheddar cheese, fried potatoes, and an English muffin. "Oh, Sir Mike, you are too kind." I curtsy. "Wow, this looks great, and I'm famished. This Joseph stuff gives me an appetite." I scoop fresh salsa on top of the omelet and dig in. "Excellent. Just the way I like it."

"Thanks." Mike points his fork at me. "Actually, he doesn't have anything better to do."

"Who?" I look up from my plate and lick jam off my finger. "Jackson? What are you talking about? It's Friday morning. He has church on Sunday and a large congregation to care for. I'd think he'd be busy as all get out."

"Oh, for sure he's busy. Crazy-busy like the CEO of a corporation working for God. And lots of folks need or want him for something or other. But that doesn't mean those things are better for him to do."

I stop chewing and sit with a quizzical look on my face.

"Not too bright, are you?" He smiles.

"What?" I smile back, although I'm not sure why. "Okay, what did I miss?"

"That Jackson cares about you."

"Oh, yeah. I got that when you said it last night."

"No, actually, you didn't get it. He really cares, *cares* about you . . . *you.*"

I suck in a little air with my coffee and start coughing.

When my throat clears, I ask, "You mean, like, he's interested in me?"

"Now she's catching on, boys."

"Mike, stop it! How the heck would I have known?" *I kept him at a distance for a reason.* "Remember, I didn't even know he could get married until you told me." *Plus, I don't date, although I might want to reconsider that.*

"Well, now you know."

"Yeah, but Mike, you know how I feel about church. If I got involved with him, it would mean opening up emotions I'm uncomfortable with. It's almost better to leave things as they are."

"Which is what, exactly?"

"Casual friends." *Lonely.* The word hits hard, but I can't go there yet. "You know, meeting at the gym, a few ski days, occasional lunch or something. Maybe that's better."

"Maybe. Maybe not. Anyway, let's just say he's been trying, he's been waiting, and he cares. Neither of you need me running interference. You'll figure it out."

I hear a large four-wheel-drive diesel vehicle coming up my road. "Must be Roger."

Throwing my boots on again, I go out to greet the big, rugged man as he jumps out of his faded green 1974 diesel truck. Wearing brown coveralls and heavy boots, he pulls his wide-brimmed metal hard hat off its hook and slaps it down onto his close-cropped brown hair. I notice he's shaved off his beard since the last time I saw him.

"Hi, Roger."

"Hey, Elizabeth." He reaches back into the truck for a few small tools and stuffs them into his pockets. Roger has some kind of advanced degree in mechanics, teaches at the community college, and has a wide reputation for being able to fix or rebuild anything with an engine. But he's also an independent logger, owns a D-6 Cat, and is known for his meticulous approach to removing timber. Mac hired him to create the clearing on our property for the cabin, lawn, pond, and tiny orchard. Roger did it perfectly, evaluating every tree in order to maintain our privacy with a buffer forest, while maximizing our view to the north.

"So, how've you been?" I hold out my hand, anticipating his strong handshake.

"Great, great." His huge hand wraps completely around mine, and I wince at the strength of his grip. He looks up at the cedar branches suspended in the air over my roof. "Yup, you got a downed tree." A man of very few words, he wastes no time striding around to the back.

Roger rarely speaks more than necessary, and during the two months he spent clearing our building site, we never exchanged much in the way of chitchat. I did know he was married and had a couple of kids, but beyond that, not much. Whether he is really shy or simply quiet, however, doesn't matter. He is definitely the man for this job. I follow him around the house.

"Well, you're really lucky."

"She is?" Mike inquires, coming out the back door. "Hey, Roger, nice to see you."

"Hey, Mike." Roger doesn't seem at all surprised to see him, which I find a bit curious. "How's Sally?"

"She's fine. Jackson's bringing her up."

"Yeah, I talked to him this morning."

I briefly wonder why he would have spoken to Jackson, but don't want to seem nosey. I change the subject. "You said I was lucky?"

"Yeah." He turns back to the cedar and points to where the tree previously stood. "This big boy fell from behind all those others, which makes no sense and is a little unusual. It's not like its roots were exposed or weak, and it isn't diseased. Actually, looks like a really straight, tall timber. And there wasn't any wind last night, so what made it come down, I have no idea."

Neither Mike nor I comment.

"Anyway, you're lucky, 'cause all those huge Douglas firs in front of it seem to have sort of blocked or slowed its crash." He points to the area fifty feet up the hill. "See those other limbs on the ground? The cedar took all those with it." He turns back to face me. "I can do this. You want to sell the wood or use it?"

"How much do I have here, and what's the price of cedar today?"

"This single tree will fill my self-loader, and if I drive it to a guy down south of Tacoma, I can get at least fifteen hundred per thousand board feet." He's already striding back to his truck.

I run after him. "Refresh my memory, Roger. What does that equate to?"

He jumps up onto the bed of the truck, opens up a huge, rectangular metal locker, and hefts out his Stihl chainsaw with a five-foot blade attached. "Well, you're looking at about six or seven grand for the tree. Like before, your part is sixty percent of the load."

"Wow. Price is good now, might as well sell it. And cedar burns so hot in my stove, I prefer hemlock or fir anyway."

He jumps back down to the ground, checks the gas in the saw, and does a practice pull. It fires right up. Turning it blade-tip down, he leans on the top. "I'm gonna check the other trees while I'm at it and make sure nothing else will come down. Still can't reckon why that one did."

"It's a mystery." I'm in no mood to offer any explanation. "I really appreciate you doing this, Roger. It's a little scary."

"Don't mind. I'll need a ladder. You still got that extension one?"

"Wow, I can't believe you remember. Yup, I never give away good tools. It's in the toolshed."

We turn at the sound of a vehicle coming up the drive and see Jackson pulling his SUV up behind Roger's truck. Roger waves before striding off. Sally opens her own door and heads straight for Mike, looking impeccably groomed as usual, but this time my eyes immediately divert to Jackson. His broad shoulders and narrow waist are accentuated by a starched, pale blue oxford shirt tucked into jeans. The cuffs of his long sleeves are rolled up twice, exposing sinewy forearms. *Dang nab, he looks great.*

Standing with his hands on his hips, Jackson looks from the tree to me and back again several times. Based on his furrowed brow, the sight of the massive tree hanging out over the roof and porch must be alarming.

Suddenly he reaches out and hugs me tightly, while my arms hang uselessly at my side. "I was so worried," he says, burying his face in my hair. "I'm so relieved you're safe."

I figure this will be a regular, friendly hug, but he doesn't let go. *Mmm. He smells so good.* I inhale just a little extra and feel his warm breath on my neck. I relax slightly and inexplicably find my hands moving up his back, reciprocating the hug. There is something surprisingly tender about his embrace and the warmth of his soothing breath. It reminds me of . . . Mac. *Oh, Mac.* Feeling awkward, I pull away and shove my hands back in my pockets.

"Thanks," I say. "Thanks for coming out again. I'm really sorry for the trouble." *Geez, this is more embarrassing than that miserable high school prom date sixteen years ago.* I look down at my feet.

"Elizabeth. It's no trouble." He cocks his head to one side. "You know, I'm a very honest man. And I'm not sure how to break this to you, but you mean a lot to me." He takes hold of my hands and wraps his own hands around them gently. "A lot."

If Mike hadn't just warned me, I wouldn't have seen this coming. "Wow. I don't think I ever knew that."

"That's okay. I figured you needed time, and I'm very patient when I need to be."

"Hmm. Honest and patient." My walls are definitely crumbling. *Why do you have to be so perfect?* "Quite a rare combination these days."

He releases my hands and puts his up in the air, mimicking a holdup. "You got me, ma'am. Guilty as charged." He holds out his elbow to escort me to the cabin. "Shall we go inside?" When I hesitantly put my hand through his arm, it doesn't feel half bad.

Sally and Mike are talking intently in the kitchen when we enter. Roger is climbing around on the roof above, and there is no mistaking the idling chainsaw's low-level hum.

"Sorry, guys, it's going to be annoyingly noisy for a while," I say. "When that saw cuts loose above the metal roof, you won't be able to hear yourself think."

"We could go to our house," Sally suggests. "Get out of here for a couple of hours."

"I hate to leave in case something happens to Roger or my house. Chainsaws, roofs, propane tanks, and partially downed trees are a recipe for disaster. So I'll stick around at least till he's off the roof, but feel free to get out of here if you guys want to."

"I agree with Elizabeth. I'm for staying put," Jackson says. "With all the weird stuff going on, we shouldn't abandon him."

"Uh, Jackson, you don't know the half of it," Mike says. "I was just filling Sally in. You'd better sit down."

He looks at Mike and then me. "You mean you had another encounter?"

"Yeah. But I need more coffee first," I answer. "Anyone else?" I pull two mugs from the cupboard and fill them before cleaning the pot and starting a fresh brew. I have a few priorities in life, like 800-thread-count Pima cotton sheets, huge plush bath towels, flannel pajamas, and the best dark Sumatran coffee that money can buy. Anyone who comes to my house for coffee either loves it or hates it; there is no in-between.

Resuming our seats at the kitchen table, Mike turns his laptop toward Sally, and I hand Jackson my journal. They both read while Mike and I sip our coffee in silence. When they finish reading one source, they switch material and read the other account, while Roger stomps around and cuts overhead.

"Unbelievable," Sally says. "I mean really, if I didn't know you guys, I'd think you were making all this up as an elaborate hoax."

"Yeah, it's pretty amazing," I say with a smile. "But you know the really cool thing? Mike was here and witnessed it all. I keep thinking of all the stupid Hollywood shows about creepy close encounters, where no one ever shares the experience of the hero or heroine. I'm so glad Mike could validate the event. As ridiculous as it sounds, I feel vindicated."

"I can understand that," Mike agrees. "But I'm glad I was here for a lot of other reasons, one of them strictly selfish. It was an amazing experience. And it absolutely, unequivocally confirmed my faith in my Creator. Never before have I felt such a presence or peace."

Jackson seems deep in reflection.

"Jackson, what do you think?" I ask.

"Honestly?" He rubs his chin. "I can't doubt either one of you. It's not my place. We each know God in our own way, and if you believe you've had an encounter with Him, then that's enough."

"But?"

"But, nothing. Mike believes he heard a woman's voice from inside his mind and felt God's hand on his heart. I have no reason to doubt him." He points to me. "You've now had three separate spiritual encounters. The first one didn't involve any voices, but it does seem like it had a huge impact on your beliefs. The latest two involved Joseph and a female. Those same two events ended with what you describe as God."

"Yeah, that's right. They both did."

"Well, I have no reason to doubt your interpretation."

"I'm not convinced." *What's wrong? What are you holding back?*

"I believe you," he assures me.

"Yeah, okay. But there's something you're not saying."

"I guess I'm worried about Joseph. He's my concern. What he says is my concern."

"Why?"

"For a lot of reasons, not the least of which is his power over time and space and his ability to read your thoughts."

"Yeah, that bugs the heck out of me. But maybe it's how he communicates."

"Maybe. But I wouldn't want him in my head."

"What else?" Mike asks.

Jackson rubs his chin. "Well, let's assume for a moment that Joseph is very real and exists in another dimension. Granted, his words are cryptic at best. Nevertheless, we can glean a few clues—like, even though he denied being in either Heaven or Hell, he seemed to know what they were."

"I hadn't put that together, but you're right, he did."

"But honestly, the biggest strike against him is that he never mentions God. Instead, God came to you after the last two encounters."

I think about that. "Yeah, you're right again."

"Why do you suppose that is?" Jackson asks.

"I don't know."

"I don't either, except that I can draw a few conclusions. First, assuming God created and controls the nature of the entire universe, then we have to include Joseph's dimension within God's scope of power. Vis-à-vis, there is nothing God wouldn't know or be able to stop in either world."

"Right," Mike says.

"Second, God created mankind in his own image and blessed each of us with the gift of choice; our free will. God also created the angels and gave them free will as well. Considering how much power Joseph seems to have, I'm lumping him into the angel category. But remember that Lucifer fell because of his free will. He challenged God."

"Oh." I grip my cup uncomfortably. "You think Joseph is the devil?"

"No, that's not what I'm saying. But think about this for a sec. Every time he makes contact with you, it's cataclysmically disruptive to your environment. So I'm inclined to believe there's a boundary between the two worlds for a reason, and maybe it's a bridge he's not supposed to cross."

I nod. "Yet he's doing it."

"Right. Because he says he needs your help to stop something that he's worried about. So maybe he thinks he's right and God's wrong. Or maybe he thinks he can alter God's greater purpose."

"Why would he do that?"

"I'm not sure. Maybe he just thinks he knows better than God."

Like a lot of humans do. "But when God shows up afterward, doesn't that indicate He's aware of Joseph and his actions?"

"Yup. And it also tells me He's protecting you."

"Wow, what a thought." *I don't think God's ever looked out for me before. Why would He start now?* "But if Joseph is doing something wrong, why wouldn't God just stop him?"

"For the same reason God doesn't stop us from making bad choices."

Choices. Choices made every minute. Each one leading to an infinitesimal number of possible outcomes. An incredible vision of the entire neural network of the universe pops into my head. I see trillions of lighted pathways leading to trillions of junctions and bifurcations, and each new direction continuing to newly forming possibilities.

"*Yes, Elizabeth.*" I hear Joseph's voice in my head. "*This is what it is about. Choices ad infinitum. And when you are ready, I will show you the way."* The mystical image and the message is mind-boggling—almost too much to comprehend. Both the vision and the voice disappear.

Shaking it off, I counter, "Okay, wait a second. If Joseph's breaking some kind of rule or something, I don't think he's doing it out of maliciousness. He seems genuinely concerned about a problem he believes we're causing. He sounded almost brokenhearted."

"Apparently." Jackson looks into his cup.

"What do you think he meant by 'passage for the pure, only the pure'?"

"Good question, and I'm not sure."

"You're a pastor. Can you make an educated guess?"

"Yeah, but I might not be right."

"Please, tell us anyway."

"I think he means pure souls. In other words, souls which are innocent of sin. The ones yet to be born." He shrugs his shoulders. "My personal beliefs aren't necessarily shared by conventional theologians. But it's how I feel."

"So, like souls that haven't been formed yet?"

"No, that's not what I mean. I believe every new life is given a soul from the moment of conception. I'm talking about human life—yet to be birthed. Life in the womb. That life is innocent, at least in my way of thinking."

That seems to make sense. How could a soul in the womb be anything but perfect? "Like the baby girl I saw," I whisper.

Jackson reaches for my hand and answers, "Exactly."

"So now what? What am I supposed to do?" I feel like crying again.

Jackson inhales deeply before speaking. "We wait. I'm fairly certain he'll be back."

Just like the Terminator.

18

Sometime before noon, Mike and Sally depart for home, and Jackson leaves for his office while Alder and I curl up for a much-needed nap. I use earplugs to block out some of the constant, undulating din and roar of Roger's chainsaw, so deep slumber comes promptly. I get a peaceful four-hour respite, without foreign voices or cataclysmic interruptions.

After shaking the sleepy cobwebs from my brain, I wash my face, slip back into my boots, and trek up the hillside behind my cabin to the spot where Roger is cutting. Climbing over huge cut logs, I pick my way through piles upon piles of crisscrossed tree limbs. *What a mess.* The site of the terrible twisted mass of cedar and fir boughs is disheartening.

Roger looks up and nods when he sees me coming.

"Hey, Roger, how's it going?"

I don't think he's heard me through the idling saw. I wait until he shuts it off, then repeat myself.

"Well, I still can't reckon why this big boy came down," he

says. "It was really healthy. But I'm about done for today." He points down the drive. "Looks like Jackson's back."

"He is?" Surprised, I turn to look. *Well . . . cool!* "Oh, ah, yeah. He probably came back to check on your progress." I don't know why he's returned, but I'm glad. "It's almost four thirty. Long day for you. Here, I brought you some water."

"Oh, thanks." He glances sideways at his five-gallon water jug, stuck between some downed limbs. "Can always use a cold one." He takes the bottle from my hand.

"How do the rest of the trees look?"

"Great. No problems up here in this area. But this one didn't have any problems, either." He points to some trees west of my house. "You might have a problem with a few of those. They're pretty close."

"You think?"

"Yup." He picks up a couple of tools and stuffs them in a bag that he throws over his shoulder. "I'll leave the jug and be back tomorrow with the Cat and loader. At least your propane tank is safe. Shouldn't be a problem when I drag these logs out, but it might mess up your backyard a little."

"Geez, Roger, don't worry about it. I'm just grateful you came out today, and I'm sorry you gotta come back tomorrow, on Saturday."

"Makes no difference to me. Only day I don't work is Sunday."

"Oh." I look around at all the downed boughs. "It looks like some of the limbs are big enough to use for kindling or firewood. I'll get some extra kids up here this week to cut it and clean all this up. Whatever I can't use, I'll have 'em make a pile down in the clearing, and we'll have one heck of a bonfire!"

"Yeah. Well, see ya tomorrow." Balancing easily on the various logs, he strides off toward his truck, reminding me of Paul Bunyan. He's cut all day, first on the roof and then later on the lower trunk. I watch him stow his huge saw in the locker, wave to Jackson, and climb into his truck. He has to be exhausted.

"Thanks, Roger," Jackson yells from the porch, waving. "See you later."

"He's such a hardworking guy," I say as I move to stand next to him.

"Yeah, he really is. Salt of the earth."

"I understand he's a heck of a mechanic, too."

"Yeah, I know." He gives me a funny look. "He's helped me restore a few things, including a Model A sedan we're working on right now."

"Really? Wow, that's cool. I didn't know you liked to work on cars."

"Young lady, there's probably a few things about me you don't know." He has a twinkle in his eye. "For instance, I'm particularly fond of French sauces and great food. And I took the liberty of making dinner reservations for us at six o'clock tonight at C'est Si Bon."

"Seriously? That's my favorite fancy restaurant! Actually, it's where Mac and I ate after we got married." Everything feels weird and uncomfortable again. I haven't been out on a single date since Mac died, and this feels like some kind of betrayal. "Oh, ah, I don't know . . . maybe I should stay here in case Joseph comes back."

"Listen, Elizabeth. I really like you, a lot. I also know how much you loved Mac. This isn't about him at all, or my need to replace him. It's about life, your life and where you want to go from here."

I give him a wry grin. "I guess you saw through my lame defense." The grin falls away. "This is just strange for me, because I don't date. It feels somehow wrong."

"Who said it was a date?" He looks at me, pulling back his head.

Oh crap, I really screwed this one up. "Oh, man. I just assumed it was. Now I feel really stupid. Sorry."

He bursts out laughing and grabs hold of my shoulders. It's an honest laugh that warms my heart. "Of course it's a date!"

This makes me laugh, too. "You brat." I punch his shoulder.

"I say we try one date and see what happens. No pressure, no commitment, no nothing except an excellent dinner, some great wine, and a chance to get away from here for a couple of hours."

It seems like a nice diversion. "Should we call Mike and Sally?"

"I told them I was taking you out to dinner, but we can include them if you want. Your call."

Oh heck, what do I have to lose? It's just one dinner. "They're probably tired and need some alone time. Maybe we should just go by ourselves."

"You read my mind."

"Something you should know about me, though—I hate to get dressed up. So is casual okay?"

He spreads his arms down and out to the side, showing me his jeans and boots. "Considering that all I brought with me today is what you see, I'm thinking casual is perfect."

"Cool."

"So go wash up, or whatever you need to do. I'll feed Alder and stoke the fire, and we can leave whenever you're ready."

Since most of my wardrobe consists of nursing scrubs, turtleneck shirts, and a few sweaters and jeans, my choices for something nicer to wear are slim. *This is pathetic. I have got to find time to get off this mountain and go shopping one of these days. And I should take Sally. She always looks great.* I manage to find one clean shirt hanging in my closet which doesn't appear too wrinkled. *This should be okay with some clean jeans.*

After taking a quick sponge bath, reapplying deodorant,

and putting on my blouse, I'm faced with a plethora of stupid questions. *Shirt tucked in or left out? Belt or no belt? Dang, I wish someone would dress me.* I tuck it in and put on a leather belt.

My next quandary is hair. *Ponytail or straight? Up or down? Ugh! I hate these kinds of decisions.* I twist my long brown hair into a knot and use a lovely old wooden hair comb to secure it in place.

Two down, one to go. I open my little red makeup bag and pull out the only three items it contains: mascara, blush, and lip gloss. I try to decide. *Mascara or not? Maybe just a little.* I apply a few strokes to my brown lashes. *I guess they seem longer.* I brush pink blush onto my high cheekbones and groan. *Looks like I'm flushed.* I wipe most of the blush off. Finally, I apply the pale lip gloss and rub my lips together, relieved that the gloss, at least, is the right color. As I survey myself in the full-length mirror, it seems that my current state is about as good as it's going to get. *I need a fairy godmother.*

This is why I don't give a dang about dating. It's too much work. Heaving a big sigh, I sit down on the edge of the tub and hold my head in my hands.

Barely audibly, I speak to the air. "Dating? Oh, Mac. Mac, are you there? I could really use a little help right now." Tears sting my eyes. "I love you so much and miss you terribly." Another deep sigh. "Babe, you know what's in my heart. What am I supposed to do now? I've had to be so strong for so long. The honest truth is, I'm tired of being so alone. Really tired."

I reach into my blouse and pull out the chain with my wedding ring on it, holding it tightly in the palm of my hand. A simple, solid gold band signifying an unending commitment to my true love. "I loved you, Mac, but you left this earth ahead of me and moved on." I rub the ring again.

Death, the final resolution. *Or is it? What if Joseph is right? What if there is no death?* The alternative is almost too much to fathom. *But what if there isn't? What would that mean for those of us still living? What if . . . ?*

Taking a deep breath, I stand up and wipe my eyes. *So much for the mascara. Guess it's the thought that counts.*

Reaching for the doorknob, I glance in the mirror. Something I see catches me off guard, making me stop. A new image comes into focus, a perspective I've avoided since childhood. I retreat from the glass and examine every minute detail of the image before me. There is no avoiding it. *It's me. The real me, stripped to my essence.* Vulnerable, fragile, heartbroken, and totally alone. The real me.

The sobering awareness of what my life has become is overwhelming. "Oh God, please help me. Please take away this pain." I lean on the counter and fight back the tears.

A faraway voice whispers from deep inside my mind. *"My child, you hold the key. The path is right in front of you."*

The words knock me to my core, because I know them to be true. Long ago, I locked the shackles surrounding my heart into place. It was my choice alone that chained me to a dark, disillusioned life. Having sentenced myself, I was my own warden.

As the image in the mirror fades, a new one takes its place. I see a stone pathway in front of me, bifurcating into two different directions. The options appear in vivid color. I can tighten the screws around my heart, continue the torture, and insidiously bleed out a little more each day. Or I can unbolt the locks, step out of the chains, and taste freedom.

The choice is ridiculously simple: death or life. It seems like a good time for a prison break.

I turn off the light, open the door, and look up. "Thank you, God."

19

"Everything to your liking, *mon ami*?"

"Absolutely perfect, Armand, as usual."

"You know, Pastor, I don't want any trouble with zee Big Guy upstairs, so if you don't like, you tell me!" Armand lets out a huge belly laugh.

I burst out laughing, almost spitting my wine across the table. Jackson holds my hand under the white linen table cloth. Looking at Armand out of the corner of his eye, he leans close to me, feigning secrecy. "You see, I have a lot of pull in this world."

Armand reaches over and pours a bit more of the Cabernet into each glass. "You two enjoy, and I'll check back on you in a few moments." He moves efficiently around the room, checking on each table individually.

"Such a nice guy," Jackson says. "Immigrated with his wife, Jolie, from France when he was about twenty-five. Then they settled up north here on the Olympic Peninsula and started a small cafe downtown. Eventually had enough money to buy this property and open up C'est Si Bon. Aside from a few local college kids working here part time, they do everything themselves. Amazing."

"That's why I love this country so much. Land of the free, home of the brave, and an opportunity for anyone willing to try."

"Yup. How's your rack of lamb?"

"Truly a little slice of heaven." I let the decadent taste linger on my tongue. "Mmmm. The sauce is so subtle, it literally melts in my mouth."

"Good."

"How's your steak?"

"Nothing better than 'man's meat.' Add to that a green peppercorn sauce, and you pretty much have a perfect meal." He picks up his wine glass and holds it out to toast. Reciprocating the gesture, I pick up mine. "Here's to the wonders of life!"

"Hear, hear." I clink my glass and take a sip. "Delicious. It must not have a screw-top lid."

"Actually, you'd be surprised. Some of the best wines today have screw-top lids."

"How do you know so much about wine? I thought clergy had rules about drinking."

"We do. We only drink the good stuff." He winks at me. "Okay, start asking."

"Asking what?"

"All the questions you have about me being a minister. I don't mind. I get questions all the time. And I'd much rather you ask me outright than wonder."

"Well, funny you should mention that, because until last evening, I didn't even know you could be married. I thought you had to be celibate or something, and I felt bad that you couldn't be with someone. But Mike was kind enough to set me straight and explained a bunch of stuff about churches, and your church in particular. I must say, I felt pretty ignorant."

"Good for Mike! But don't feel bad, lots of people have misconceptions. There are simple but huge differences between Christian denominations, and every generation seems to elicit new interpretations of God's Word."

"Like what?"

"Right now, two big issues facing many churches are homosexuality and abortion. My parishioners opted against both of those and thus voted to split from our guiding council. Other denominations have other issues, and that's just the Christian faiths. Throw in Judaism, Buddhism, Hinduism, Islam, and the rest, and you have a confusing bunch of doctrines and rules. I studied theology for six years as a post-grad, and I still get confused."

"Wow. Okay, now I don't feel so bad. Maybe I can learn a few things. By the way, I forgot to thank you for the beautiful gift."

He looks up for a moment. "Oh yes, the Bible. That's my favorite thing to give. Glad you liked it."

"I haven't started reading it yet, but I will. Honestly, though, it seems a little intimidating. Like learning a foreign language."

"It is at first. But the Good News is the crux—actually, the entire theme is Good News." He puts his fork down. "It's all about God's promises of hope, forgiveness, and life everlasting."

"I remember a few old stories and fables I learned in Sunday School. I was about five or six, and I think it was fun, but then, after my mom got sick, Dad didn't take me to church much anymore. Since then, it seems like most of my time in church has been spent at funerals."

Armand is back at our table, pouring a bit more wine into each glass. "*Mon ami*, still doing okay?"

"Yes, sir," Jackson answers. "It's fabulous. Our compliments to your lovely wife. The sauces are perfection."

"Ah, great. I'll let her know." He pauses and looks at me.

"Madam, I think we've met, but it has been awhile, has it not?"

I blot my mouth with the white linen napkin before speaking. "Yes, it has. I'd forgotten how delicious your food is and how perfect the setting. I love your garden! It's every bit as romantic as I remember."

With a twinkle in his eye, he swirls his hand in the air. "Ah, yes! Here we always have love in zee air." He sighs deeply and then strides off to check the rest of his customers.

Jackson takes hold of my hand again and squeezes it. "You doing okay?"

His hand is warm and feels strong around mine. I look at his broad shoulders and lean, rugged face. "Actually, I think I'm doing just fine."

"Good. I'm glad." He takes a sip of wine. "So I'm guessing that given your unhappy reasons for going to church later in life, you probably connected the church itself to your sadness."

"Yeah, probably."

"And consequently, you missed all the good parts."

"Truthfully, I stayed away on purpose."

"Well, my dear, this is your lucky day. Go ahead, ask away."

"Sure you don't mind?"

"Not in the least."

Huddled with Jackson at our secluded table, I ask questions and listen intently while he answers. He discusses his theological education, training, assignment to his current position, congregation, and personal philosophies. The more he explains, the more intrigued I become, and the more questions I think of. We talk through dinner, dessert, and brandy, and probably would keep right on going except we look up to find we are the only ones left in the restaurant. Jackson signals for the check and pays the bill. After saying goodbye to Armand and his adorable wife, Jolie, we stagger out to Jackson's SUV. Fortunately, we don't have very far to drive.

"I'm gonna take you home and pour you into bed, young lady."

"I think I'm a little tipsy."

"You and me both."

"Great dinner, Jackson. Thanks so much."

"My pleasure."

Ten minutes later, we're on my front porch. "Give me your keys so I can open the door for you."

Leaning against the front post for support, I dig into the depths of my bag for the necessary item. "Why is whatever I need always at the bottom of this stupid purse?" I empty my bag's contents out on the porch bench. "Finally!" Producing the necessary set of keys, I hand it to Jackson.

"Okay, in you go, girl." Obligingly I enter as he flips on the light and whistles to Alder. "Come on, boy, let's go out for a quick one." Without hesitation, Alder bounds forward past Jackson, out the door. "You go get ready for bed," he tells me.

Teetering toward the bathroom, I grab a clean set of flannel pajamas on the way. "Wow, I must have had a lot more wine than I thought," I say to the mirror. "Dang that Armand, he's a sneaky one." I wash my face, brush my teeth, and slip my white terry-cloth robe on over my pajamas. Still conversing with my reflection, I note the long-sleeved button-up pajama top over the matching pink-flowered pants. After brushing out my long hair, I pull the robe's collar up around my neck and retie the belt. "Definitely not sexy."

Hearing the two of them back in the house, I wander out to the main room. Jackson is holding a little black pouch which looks suspiciously like a small ditty bag.

"What's up?"

"I'm staying here tonight."

My head clears a little. I walk over to him and put my hands up in protest. "Look, Jackson, I had a really great time tonight, and I like you, but I'm not ready for anything more yet."

"Look yourself, Elizabeth. I'm not suggesting anything else. I'm staying because one, I'm a little tipsy also and don't want to drive thirty miles into town. And two, if you have another encounter with Joseph, I want to be here."

"Oh, okay. Sorry." I point to the opposite loft. "There's a Murphy bed in that loft."

"I know right where it is." Moving toward me, he grabs me by the shoulders, turns me around, and directs me to my narrow stairs. "Up you go." As I follow his command, Jackson's right on my heels. "Now get to bed and pull the covers up."

He watches me get into bed and switches the light off for me. "Your Walther's in the drawer next to you, but I suggest you leave it there until the wine wears off. Flashlight is right here. If you need anything else, just holler."

"Thanks. I had a really good time."

"I did, too." He bends over and kisses me gently on the forehead. "Sweet dreams, Elizabeth."

I'm asleep before he makes it down the stairs.

ANOTHER PLACE

"Lady Mary, may I speak with you?"

"Of course, Lady Ruth. What is it?"

"I am greatly disturbed by a recent crossing my First of the Nine had. I feel you should be advised."

"What occurred? Is Tabitha safe?"

"Yes, she is quite safe, but it was distressing. Thirty-eight in all."

"What? Thirty-eight? Oh, Lady Ruth, how is that even possible?"

"I do not know. But as you said to the Council, something terrible is happening in their realm. If you will allow me, I will show you the event."

"Yes, of course. Please proceed."

Lady Ruth and Lady Mary dissolve and reappear in the crystalline chapel with the diamond orb. Seated in their assigned chairs, they each rest their hands upon the ends of their crystal armrests, and Lady Ruth opens her mind to Tabitha's most recent event. As Lady Ruth begins her recollection, her golden threads light up. But unlike a meeting of the full Council, this time the diamond orb can be avoided. With her threads lit, she pushes the images through the center of the room, focusing solely upon Lady Mary. All the while, Lady Mary sits poised, ready to receive the sequence.

Through a light memory mist, the chasm comes into view. Aligning herself behind Lady Ruth's eyes, Lady Mary becomes one with her. Immediately in front of her is Tabitha, cloaked and hooded, standing at the edge of the chasm. As the current center point of the Nine, she has the assistance of four others on each side of her.

Tabitha raises her arms, opening her small palms in the familiar position, awaiting the offering. An opaque mass appears and hovers above her hands. As Tabitha reaches for it, a second ovoid appears, then a third and fourth, and a fifth and sixth, then more and more until there are thirty-eight in all.

Thirty-eight! Oh, Father! My First cannot control this many. She will be unable to guide them across. What has happened to the world of the Forbidden?

Lit from within, the thirty-eight masses begin to glow brightly until the intensity of each one is as strong as the overhead sun. With the focused assistance of the remaining Nine, Tabitha does her best to balance her powers toward all the ovoids at once, but the separation between them causes unexpected distractions. Each one is worthy of individual attention, yet she is unable to bring any forth.

"TABITHA! NONE NEED TO AWAKEN."

"But Father, what about their paths?"

"THERE WILL BE NO NEED FOR STONES. I WILL CARRY THEM ACROSS."

"Then yes, Father, I am ready." Tabitha balances the thirty-eight objects hovering in front of her.

"LADY RUTH!"

"Yes, Father?"

"REFOCUS YOUR THOUGHTS UPON THE CHASM. I WILL ASSIST TABITHA."

Understanding the unusual change in format, Lady Ruth redirects her attention to the chasm. The far edge of the enormous gulf once again begins to warp inward, ever lessening the expanse between the rims, until the span is no more than a modest ravine, close enough for her to easily discern minute details on the other side.

Coming into view from the far left, a fiftyish, dark-skinned woman swaggers toward the rim. At the same time a tall, dark-skinned man comes into view from the right. They stand looking at each other for some moments, but neither one seems to recognize the other. After a few moments, they turn to face the near side. The woman looks toward Tabitha, then back at the man.

"Who are you?" she asks him.

"I'm not sure. Who are you?"

"I think I'm lost."

"Yeah, looks that way. Who are they?" he asks, pointing his finger toward Tabitha and the others. "And what are those lights?"

"I have no idea," the woman replies. "No idea at all."

"So what are we doing here?" the man asks loudly.

"I don't know, and I don't care. Standing here is annoying!" she says as spittle sprays from her mouth. "I've got things to do and a life to live."

"Well, I'm kinda confused. I don't think I'm in a hurry to go anywhere, but I'd sure like to know what's going on."

"I'll tell you what's going on." The woman raises her voice. "This is some kinda shitty dream, and I wanna wake up."

"If this is a dream, it's the weirdest one I've ever been in," the man says with a laugh. "Are you sure we haven't met before?"

"Who knows? I've met lots of men in my life. No way I could remember 'em all." Increasingly irritated, the woman shouts across the ravine, "I need to wake up!"

"Look, lady, I don't think this is a dream, and I don't think it's about us."

"Yeah, well, whatever this is, or wherever we are, I want out!"

From behind the man, a second man now appears, walking toward them. He has lighter skin and reddish-blond hair.

The newcomer turns first to the woman and looks at her for a moment, then toward the first man. He looks back at the woman and says, "I wondered if I'd ever see you again."

"Oh, damn you!" she replies. "Is this your doing? Did you bring me here? You stupid idiot! What the hell do you want with me now?"

"Nothing. Nothing at all," he says quietly. "I just thought . . . I hoped you might want to see me."

"Yeah, right! Go screw yourself, you moron. When I said 'Adios,' I meant it."

"I was a fool to believe." The man hangs his head. "I hoped things would change."

"Not a frigging chance! This is such bullshit. Now let me go."

"But I didn't bring you here."

"Yeah? Then what the hell are we all doing here?" The woman tosses her head back and throws her hands up in the air. At the top of her lungs, she screams across the ravine, "Hello! Anybody home? What the hell are we looking at out here?"

For the first time, the second man's gaze shifts from the woman to the group across the gap. "Oh no," he says faintly. "It can't be!"

The woman barks sarcastically, "It can't be . . . what? What's wrong with you now?"

"I never knew," he whispers. A breeze carries his voice across the gulf to the near side. As the breeze reaches Tabitha, it brushes by the edge of the first two ovoids and pulls them out above the chasm until they hover near the center. The fair-haired man steps out over the ravine, moving forward until he is close enough to touch them. All he has to do is raise his arms. Reaching for the ovoids, he grabs them both tightly, then turns and races back to the far rim, protecting his precious cargo and ignoring the woman.

The lights within each ovoid begin to grow until their brilliance can no longer be contained. Exploding up and out of the top, the lights shoot skyward with enormous energy. As they reach their zenith, they coalesce and angle back toward the ground, then touch down beside the man. Part of the light beams reach out for the man's heart, and immediately the man and his two beams vanish from sight.

"I understand now," the first man says to the woman. "I did know you. You never considered us."

"What the hell was there to consider?"

"A lot."

"What a crock! You're just guys."

Ignoring her, he steps out over the ravine. "I don't know which one or two or three are mine, but please release them. I take responsibility."

"What the hell are you doing?" the woman says.

Nearing the center of the gulf, he watches three ovoids float toward him. When they are close, he reaches for them as the other man did, and holds them tightly as he runs back to the far side. Soon the man and his lights disappear as well.

Twenty or so other men arrive and stand next to the woman.

"Oh crap, I can't take this," she says.

Barely acknowledging the woman's existence, each of the men glance across the ravine, then quickly look away. Whether out of embarrassment or lack of interest, none advance toward the open space in front of them.

"I don't know any of you, and I don't know what I'm supposed to do," one of the men says to Tabitha. "But I think . . . I think I have others to meet and atone for as well." He turns away and vanishes from sight.

"Just like that?" the woman screams. "Just like that, you're gonna leave me here alone? Fucking men."

The remaining men solemnly nod their heads toward Tabitha and vanish as well.

Without warning, a strong wind gusts up from behind the woman, pushing her out over the ravine onto a few newly formed stones. The woman screams, "I'm not gonna do this, damn it!" She turns around to go back, but the far edge has already withdrawn from her, and she is now miles into the center of the chasm, standing on a single stone suspended over a bottomless void.

"Oh, bullshit! Look, whoever you are, I had to fend for myself. There's not a damn thing in my life but me. The last thing I needed was baggage. I don't know what crap you're trying to pull here, but I'm not playing. Get me the hell out of here."

No one moves.

"I don't deserve this! I never did nothin' to anyone."

A light breeze comes from behind Lady Ruth, brushing past Tabitha, and encircles the remaining thirty-three ovoids. The breeze lingers for a moment, swirling gently around the opaque masses. Then, forming a single gust, it picks up speed and sails out to the woman, hitting her with a wind so strong it almost blows her over and off the fading stone she is perched upon.

Struggling to keep her balance, she refocuses on Tabitha and with a puzzled look yells, "Hey! It was no big deal! I didn't want them! It was nothing! Everyone does it. I did it as often as necessary, and I'd do it again if I wanted. Who gives a shit?"

Halting her rants for a few seconds, she hears the sound of rushing water, churning and raging as it courses down the river in the depths of the canyon miles below. Another gust of wind rises up, this time from the river bottom. With great speed, it encircles the woman, enveloping her being. As the wind whips and spirals around her, it strips away every defining feature, every nuance of her individuality, until nothing remains except a nondescript humanoid form. When she is finally silent, the wind fades away and dissipates back into the canyon. Sentence has been rendered.

As the sides of the chasm are now quite far apart, the group on the near side is not certain what has become of her. Only Father knows she denied Grace and thus is destined to relive the realities of thirty-eight innocent deaths over and over, until the end of time.

"*RELEASE THEM!*" Father commands to Tabitha.

Tabitha complies, and the remaining ovoids drift out over the great chasm, maintaining their luminosity. About halfway across, each one bursts forth, shooting upward to a great height, like a magnificent fireworks display. A prism of colors explodes toward the far side, spreading out in an arc of brilliant light. Coalescing back to the ground, the thirty-three points of multicolored light weave playfully in and out, swirling about each other in random patterns of pure energy.

The lights pause in their excited activity and redirect themselves to Tabitha, sending her a wave of energy. Then, resuming their intimate activities, the points of light rise and dance in the air far above the other rim. Just before the last light disappears from view, Tabitha thinks she hears children laughing, but she can't be certain. Turning, she leads the group back to the Cathedral.

Lady Ruth pulls her mind back from Lady Mary, ending the connection. Departing the crystal chapel, they once again stand in the Great Hall.

"I am at a loss, Lady Ruth. Surely this must be an egregious event."

"No, it is not. Sadly, numbers such as thirty-eight have become average for my First. Without Father's interference, Tabitha would not have survived."

"Joseph is correct. A terrible darkness is upon the realm of the Forbidden."

"Yes, Lady Mary, I agree. And it will spread to ours."

21

Rah . . . clack, clack, clack, clack, clack. Rah . . . clack, clack, clack, clack, clack.

"What the heck?" I roll over and see the sunlight streaming through my small skylight above. I smell coffee, feel warmth from the woodstove wafting up, and hear someone bustling around in the kitchen below. It takes me a minute to get oriented and remember that Jackson stayed the night. Simultaneously I realize that the annoying sound hacking through the air is undoubtedly Roger's caterpillar tractor making its way up my quarter-mile drive.

I lean over and peer through the rails of the loft, feeling like a kid on Christmas Eve. Jackson is in the kitchen below, busily preparing some delicious-smelling delicacy at the stove. *I could definitely get used to this.*

At that moment, he looks up through the bar opening and spots me peeking at him. "Good morning, sleepyhead. Coffee?"

"Definitely." I slide my feet into my slippers, put on my robe, and make my way down the stairs. Alder is waiting for me at the bottom, with a wagging tail and a huge smile on his face. "Hey, boy, did you have a good night?" I hug him tightly around his furry head.

"He did. And so did I. That's a great bed up there, really comfortable. I slept like a baby."

On my way to the kitchen, I can hear the washer and dryer running in the laundry room and notice the time is 8:30 a.m. "You're doing laundry?"

"Yeah, thought I'd wash your sheets and the towels Mike and I used. Hope you don't mind, but I took the liberty of using your shower." He hands me a steaming cup of coffee. "Cream's on the table."

"Thanks. No, of course I don't mind. But you didn't have to do my laundry."

He points the spatula at me and says, "What's to do? I stuck the stuff in, added soap, and turned it on. Besides, I can multitask. By the way, I think Roger's here."

I pause for a sip of coffee before pulling my robe up around my neck and changing into my boots for the walk out to greet Roger. Far below, he has veered off the drive onto a forest trail, presumably to preserve my driveway's hard-packed pea gravel and binder. On his slow approach through the buffer trees, he's already reached the grassy clearing and is now in a steep climb to the upper site. I wait and watch while he skillfully maneuvers his equipment toward me.

He stops at the upper edge of the yard where it borders the parking pad and climbs off. "I tried to figure another way, but can't. So it looks like I'll have to drive the Cat across your parking pad to get back there. Probably have to cross it a few times." He picks up a long piece of grass and sticks it in his mouth. "Might chew this gravel up a bit."

"I figured."

"Might need another load of quarter-inch with binder after I'm done."

"I was going to get some this spring anyway, 'cause I need it down there at the bend." I point to a spot on the drive about three hundred feet to the west. "The gravel guys are pretty good about spreading the mix with their dump trucks, and I'll have the boys finish the edges."

"By the way, Elizabeth, I checked on cedar, hemlock, and fir prices last night, and all of them are up, especially cedar. So as long as I'm here with the Cat, I figured I'd ask if you want any of those others taken out at the same time."

"Oh, wow, I haven't given that idea much thought. Can I think about it and let you know?"

"Sure. But I mulled it over some last night, and if I were you, I'd pull those few out that are closest to your house, especially on that side." He points over my roof to the trees on the east. "Seems like they block your morning sun, anyway."

"True, they do."

"And they're close enough to do damage if they fall over like that one." He indicates the fallen cedar he cut up yesterday.

"Yeah, I get your drift. I just hate to take down any of these trees. They're so majestic."

"Hey, it's your land. You don't have to. Just a suggestion."

"Okay. I need to get dressed, so I'll think about it while I'm in there." I walk back to the porch, then holler at him before he revs up the engine, "Would you like a cup of coffee before you get started?"

"Nah, I'm good for now. Maybe in an hour or two."

"Whenever, just let me know." I laugh at his predictable response. It's always been the same, and to this day I can't recall him ever coming into the house or accepting anything from Mac or me except payment for his services. But that's just Roger.

I leave my boots at the door and head back to the kitchen to sip my coffee. "He's asking me if I want any other trees taken out."

"Oh, really? What do you think?"

Mac built the kitchen using the same method of construction as the main portion of the cabin. It has a fourteen-foot center ridgeline, three huge skylights, a six-foot-wide bay window, and double glass French doors leading out to the deck on the north side. The east wall boasts a series of trapezoid windows, the upper angles of which perfectly match the roof line. The design brings in natural light even on the gloomiest of cold, gray days. Overhead, the tops of the tall timbers are always visible through the long, angled skylights. If a tree fell on the end, it would definitely cause damage.

"I hate to make decisions like this alone. If Mac were here, he'd know exactly what to say." *But he's not.* I realize I need a shower and excuse myself.

After completing my morning routine, I wander back out to the kitchen, but Jackson isn't around. Noting his SUV is still parked next to my truck, I slip into my boots and jacket and walk out through the back laundry room door. That's when I see the two of them deep in conversation, each one pointing to various trees and making notes on a scrap of paper.

"Hey, guys, what's up?"

Jackson answers, "I was just asking Roger if he could make an educated guess about which of these trees might pose a real threat to you in the event of a bad storm. He's got some good points."

I get an uncomfortable feeling in my gut, like my privacy is being invaded and my personal space violated. "You didn't need to get involved in this, Jackson. It's my problem, my decision." I hear a little streak of edginess in my voice.

He nods. "It's absolutely your decision. No question about that. But sometimes the more accurate information you have, the easier the decision can be." He smiles at me. "Hey, I'm just out here on a fact-finding mission."

The hair on the back of my neck calms down, but I still feel somewhat intruded upon. "Not to sound skeptical, but exactly what do you know about forests or lumber?"

Stuffing his hands in his pockets, he takes a deep breath and looks at Roger, then at the ground.

"She doesn't know, does she?" Roger asks.

I look from one to the other. "Know what?"

"Well, it was bound to come out sooner or later," Jackson says.

"What? What's going on?"

"Ever heard of the Blue Sky Lumber Company?"

"Yeah, of course. They're huge. Here, there, all over the world, multinational."

"Well, it was started by my granddad, Jackson the first."

"Yeah," Roger chimes in. "And he's my granddad, too."

I compare the two of them and for the first time notice the similarities in stature, rugged features, and coloring. "You mean you guys are cousins?"

"Yup," Jackson says. "My dad and Roger's mom are siblings. We were brought up in the worldwide timber and lumber business together. But neither of us liked the business stuff or the nonstop lifestyle. Fortunately, our parents were kind enough to allow us to choose our own paths."

"I keep my hand in by working quietly in the forest, which is what I really love. And Jax helps me on occasion when I've got a big job."

"So you guys are like . . . millionaires?"

"Nope. We're like two guys who chose a different path." Peeking at me from the corner of his eye, Jackson adds, "Sorry to disappoint."

"One reason I work so hard at teaching, doing mechanics, and logging is 'cause I wanted to prove to myself I could do it on my own," Roger explains. "Nobody handed me a dang thing except an opportunity for a great education. Once that was completed, I was outta there." He looks down at his rough hands, stained with grease and engine oil, then at his worn logging jeans, and looks back up, smiling, "Don't lie, now. Do I look like a millionaire?" He points a greasy finger to Jackson. "Does he look like a millionaire?"

I have no idea what to think, let alone say. *These guys are so full of surprises, I need a map to find my way.* "No."

"Don't feel too bad," Jackson says. "Roger and I don't have the same last names, and we don't advertise. Only a handful of people on the peninsula know about our background, which is just how we like it."

"Well, I need to get back to work." Roger holds up the drawing in one hand and points to the trees with the other. "So we think you should pull out these five trees. They could pose the most threat to your house in a bad storm. Otherwise, I'd leave the rest. Still leaves you with a hundred feet of buffer and plenty of privacy, so you shouldn't feel much of a difference."

I study the drawing and try to calculate the fall of each tree. He's correct. If a bad storm blows them over, they'll crash right into the east end of my kitchen where all the large windows are situated. "Okay, I give in."

"I'm gonna drag out what I cut yesterday and then start cutting the rest. Probably take me a few days. And again, your backyard's gonna be a mess afterwards."

"Don't worry about it. It can be repaired in May."

"You should make about twenty grand off this, if it's any consolation."

"Oh, cool! I forgot about the money. Twenty grand is always a nice bonus."

———◆———

"Elizabeth, I have something I want to show you," Jackson says as he puts the last dirty breakfast plate into the dishwasher.

"Really? Like what?" I'm still focused on the berry pancakes and wonder where the spicy sausages came from. My stomach's so full, I could take a morning nap.

"I'd like to take you for a little ride, if you don't mind. And we can take Alder."

"Oh, yeah?" I pull myself back to the conversation. "Okay, I guess I'm up for a drive. Where are we headed?"

"Let's just say we're going somewhere really nice, and let it be a surprise."

"Ooh, a mystery." I rub my hands together. "You know I'm big on mysteries."

"Yup, and you need to bring a warm jacket, gloves, and a hat."

"Oh. Up to the mountains?"

"Now don't spoil my fun." His sly smile reminds me of a little kid with a garden snake in his pocket. "We can leave anytime you're ready."

"Okay, let me check on Roger and lock up." It occurs to me that Jackson has church on Sunday. "Hey, don't you have to get ready for your sermon tomorrow?"

"Wow, aren't you the concerned one."

"No, seriously. It's your job, and I don't want you to mess it up on my account."

"Okay, seriously. We just finished the Lenten season and Easter. I'm starting a new five-week series, and my sermon's done. Actually, it's been done since last Monday, and the rest of the service is pretty organized. I do need to run by the office later today to check on some things, but my staff is in touch with me all the time."

"They are? Oh. I never heard your phone ring."

"We have this cool new thing called 'text messaging.' Really modern."

"Ha, ha, very funny. I'll get my jacket."

We drive the six miles down the mountain to Highway 101, make a left, and head toward town. After stopping for gas at a convenience store, Jackson continues into Port Angeles, going all the way through town and out the other side.

Assuming we're headed toward Forks, I'm surprised when he makes a right turn onto Airport Drive. Even though its name implies a major hub of activity, the Fairchild International Airport isn't known for a large operation or a huge amount of aviation. But since it gets daily traffic from Canada in addition to the local flights from Seattle, it was given the rather grandiose "international" label, which I always find a bit amusing.

"So, what? We're gonna watch the planes land?"

"Not exactly."

He pulls onto a side road bordering the chain link fence which encloses the entire airport and weaves around the end of the runway to the side where private airplane hangars are located. At the security gate, he swipes a card and steers the SUV through to a hangar about halfway down the road, where he parks and switches off the engine.

"We're here. This is it."

"You own a plane?"

"In fact, I do."

"So you really are a millionaire."

"No, I'm not. But I figured you'd get that idea."

"So, what's the story?"

"The story is this. I work hard, I'm single, I don't have many expenses, and I spend my money on things I like. One of them is this plane I want to show you."

I shrug. "Okay." What he says makes sense. *I work just as hard as anyone else and spend my money on things I like, too.* I can't find fault with his logic. *Who am I to judge?*

Ever the gentleman, he walks around to my side and holds my door open, then lets Alder out.

"Come on, Alder, let's go for a ride!"

"A ride?" *Oh man, I'm definitely not ready for this.*

"Yeah, I want to take you someplace." He unlocks the door to his hangar and flips on the lights, allowing Alder and me to enter first. "After you, m'lady."

Inside is a gorgeous silver floatplane with blue trim. "Wow! What is it?"

He lets out a little laugh. "A 1956 de Havilland Beaver, completely restored by Roger and me. I call her *Ladybug*." He walks around the front and pats her cowling.

"You guys rebuilt it all? This is remarkable! I bet you have a blast taking it out. Do you fly a lot?"

"I do."

"How long have you been a pilot?"

"Well, let's see. I started flying when I was about twelve or so. My dad owned a Cessna four-oh-two."

"I have no idea what that is."

"Oh, sorry. It's a small, twin-engine workhorse." Jackson points to a photograph of another airplane hanging on the wall behind a table and chairs. "Dad would take me out all the time to show me the wilderness areas and timberlands our family owned. He's always been protective of old-growth trees and forests, and anal about ensuring his loggers never screwed up."

Jackson continues walking around the plane checking on things. "Anyway, Dad taught me how to fly, but I was too chicken to go alone until I was about eighteen. When I found enough courage to do my first solo flight, my parents had a big surprise party for me in the hangar afterward." He laughs. "You'd have thought I'd won a Nobel Prize or something."

"That's so cool! Sounds like your parents are sweet—like they love you."

"Oh, they're the best. Dad is funny, though. He has two mottos for life: 'Waste not, want not,' and 'You want it, you earn it.' So my sister and I grew up with that kind of mindset."

"Maybe he was trying to make you appreciate what you had, not take it for granted."

"Oh, absolutely." He chuckles again.

"What's so funny?"

"Nothin', really." It seems like he's reviewing an old

memory of some bygone day. After a minute he continues, "I remember in high school when I was applying to various schools across the country. Dad agreed to pay for whatever university I got accepted into, and wouldn't you know it, I got Yale. It was really cool for me, really expensive for him. But he was proud of me and no doubt could afford it." He adjusts something on the plane. "Anyway, shortly before I was set to depart, I worked up the nerve to ask him about a car. 'Dad,' I said, 'I think I'm gonna need a car when I'm back there so I can get around and stuff.' Dad looked up from his morning paper and said, 'Maybe so, maybe so.' I thought, Cool! Dad's gonna buy me a car. But then he withdrew one of the note cards he always carried in his left shirt pocket and wrote down some figures. Dad angled the card toward me and showed me the numbers. 'For a used car,' he said, 'this is about what you'll need to earn in order to make the payment and pay for gas and insurance. And I don't know if Yale charges for parking or not, but you may need to figure that in as well.' Then he went back to reading the paper.

"Honestly, I just stood there for what seemed like an eternity, trying to figure out answers to multiple questions, each one circling around in my brain at the speed of light. Why wouldn't he buy me a car? Could I work, pay for one, and make grades at the same time? Would the trade-off be worth it? They had tons of money, so why wouldn't he do this for me? The circular thoughts went round and round."

"So what happened?"

"Well, my dad looked up at me and said, 'On the other hand, there's a perfectly good twelve-speed racing bike in the garage which is paid for, requires no gas or insurance, and will get you to and from all points on the campus. And it will fit in the back of the four-oh-two when I take you.' He was right, of course, although I hated to admit it. He'd offered the perfect solution, and the bottom line was, I didn't really need a car."

"Sounds like he was hard to argue with. I'd like to meet him and your mom someday."

"I'd like that, too, and I've got a sneaky feeling you will. Anyway, to finish answering your initial questions, I've got about five thousand hours and fly a couple times a week. And yes, she's really fun."

Drawing me closer to the passenger side, he opens the door to let me look inside. I'm surprised to see how roomy it is. "Wow, six seats?"

"Yeah, and a fully updated state-of-the-art navigation system. She's a workhorse and can go virtually anywhere."

I turn to face him. "I'm truly impressed, and you have every right to be proud of it. I never would have guessed. This is amazing. Truly amazing."

"I'd really like to take you and Alder for a ride. We can make it a short one, but I'd like to take you."

What else does this guy have up his sleeve? "Well, we've come this far, we may as well get a ride in your *Ladybug*."

"Great! If you push that red button over there, the hangar doors will open. I'll get the tow."

"Not to sound stupid, but how do you get the floatplane out of the water and into the hangar?"

He lets out a little laugh. "If you'll look closely, you'll see the small wheels on the underside of the pontoons. They're partially retractable. *Ladybug* can land on either the land or the water."

"Well, that's cool."

"Indeed it is." He attaches a small electric cart to the front of the plane and tows it outside the hangar, detaches it, and goes back inside to lock up. When he returns, he lifts Alder up and over the floats and then helps me get seated as well.

He hands me a set of headphones, gives me a quick safety briefing, and starts the engine. After using the radio to announce our takeoff, he taxies to the end of the runway, runs the engine up, and we start rolling down the runway. We're off the ground in less than five hundred feet and fly out over the west end of the city.

The day is almost as clear as the previous few have been, and the scene below is surreal. We fly across what looks like a miniature model of a quaint oceanside community, complete with a harbor, sawmill, old-fashioned homes, tree-lined roads, and forested mountains in the background. Out to the north is the Strait of Juan de Fuca and beyond that, Canada, where once again the emerald city of Victoria is visible.

Jackson gradually angles the plane north, flying toward Vancouver Island.

Ever skeptical, I ask via the intercom, "Is it safe to fly out over the ocean?"

"Ahhh . . . yes. It's a floatplane." He tilts his head toward me and winks.

"Oh, right. Sorry, I forgot."

He chuckles. "No need to apologize. Have you ever been in a private plane before?"

"No. I don't fly all that much."

"Are you comfortable?"

"Yeah, the seats are really nice. Hey, what happens if a passenger has to go to the bathroom?"

"Ha! Typical! We find a spot to land and take care of the problem. Why, do you need to go?"

"No, just curious."

Cruising along at an altitude of 2,500 feet, Jackson flies us steadily north. In no time at all, we quickly reach the halfway point between the U.S. and Canadian coastline, yet he makes no sign of reversing course.

"Are we going to Canada?"

"As a matter of fact, yes." He points a finger to a spot on the southwest tip of the island. "That is what I wanted to show you."

"What? I thought you wanted to show me this plane."

"Well, yes and no. Let's just say I wanted to introduce you to *Ladybug* and show you my home."

"Your home? Wait, I thought you lived at the church, at the house they provide for you."

"I do. But I have a little place up here that's all mine. It's my real home, away from the world and all of its demands. It's where I come when I want to rejuvenate and be alone."

"I totally get that." No doubt his position as senior pastor puts an enormous strain on him, just like my insane job. "I'm sure you cherish your solitude and respite as much as I do."

We've only been airborne about fifteen minutes when he begins to descend toward the coastline. He flies north, passing the spot he indicated, then makes a wide turn to the west, banking about thirty degrees so he can see the approach below. Continuing to descend while he completes a huge U-turn, he angles back toward the east, then meticulously lines the plane up for a landing on the water within a small, hidden cove. The cove only becomes visible after Jackson turns the plane from west to east. I doubt anyone sailing along the southern coastline could detect the cove's existence.

"Hey, Jackson, what about US Customs or Canadian Customs? Don't you have to stop somewhere to clear them?"

"Normally, yes. But since Canada has no office near my Canadian property, I agreed to undergo an extensive background investigation. Now I'm considered a 'trusted agent' by both governments. As long as I announce my travel plans, they only do occasional spot checks."

"Well, that's convenient."

As Jackson gently maneuvers the plane onto the smooth water, I get a good look at the immediate area. The surrounding low mountains, covered in tall, stately timbers, give way to a small clearing along the shoreline. In the center of the clearing sits a quaint, two-story New England-style cottage, situated about two hundred feet from the rocky beach. Complete with shuttered dormer windows upstairs, two huge bay windows downstairs, and a wraparound porch, it looks like a magazine advertisement for a getaway bed-and-breakfast establishment.

I wait until he's shut off the engine and removed the headphones. "Geez, Jackson, this is like the cover of an architectural magazine or something!" I unbuckle my seatbelt. "It's beautiful."

He sits back in his seat, heaves a deep sigh, and relaxes noticeably. He reaches over with his right hand and takes hold of mine. "I'm so glad you like it."

"Who wouldn't? It's spectacular!"

"Yeah, it is. It's been a five-year project, a total labor of love, and it's just about finished."

"It looks pretty finished to me." I automatically open my door.

"Ah, Elizabeth, I don't think you want to get out that way."

Looking down, I realize that if I step out, I'll fall into the bay. "Oh, right. I knew that."

After he climbs out, he attaches a mooring line from the dock to the float and reaches across to grab my hand, helping me out of the cockpit.

"Actually, it's all done, except for one or two more things." His voice trails off as he turns and opens the back door to let Alder out. Even though he's a big man and physically fit, I'm surprised at how easily he lifts my eighty-five-pound dog up, out, and over the float pod, and gently sets him on the dock.

"Come on, boy, let's check this place out," I urge. Wasting no time, Alder bounds down the wooden planks toward the shoreline.

"Come on, girl, let's check this place out," Jackson echoes.

"Funny." I comfortably slip my hand into the elbow he offers me. "Lead the way."

While Alder runs all over the beach, checking out one

pebble after another, Jackson escorts me up a lovely, rock-lined path to the cottage. Once on the porch, I turn to look back at the scenery. What lies before me is a spectacular view of a small, intimate cove, hidden by a tree-lined peninsula that stretches all the way from the eastern side around to the western edge, leaving only about a forty-foot opening out to the Pacific beyond. The calm, protected water is a brilliant blue and contrasts starkly with the deep green trees behind it. A few puffy clouds linger in the sky, and the sun is almost at its peak overhead.

"Boy, a person could get used to this. How do you ever find it in your heart to leave here and go back to life in Port Angeles?"

"Come on, let me show you around." Behind the leaded-glass front door is a spacious entryway with a wide, circular staircase set back about twenty feet. Both the entryway floor and stairs are made of solid cherry planking finished to a warm, hand-rubbed glow. The room is open all the way up to the second-floor ceiling, and two large, rectangular skylights brighten the entire area.

To the right is the dining room, and to the left is a cozy living room with a massive stone fireplace. Two large, colonial-style rocking chairs sit on each side of the fireplace, and a muted, multicolored woven rug completes the arrangement.

"Jackson, this is really lovely. All the cabinetry is gorgeous."

"Thanks. I did most of it myself."

"No way!"

"Come on, let's finish the tour." He reaches for my hand and guides me around. Before yesterday, I hadn't held hands with anyone in so long, it seemed strange. Yet I'm slowly getting comfortable with the practice and, surprisingly, it now feels pretty wonderful.

As we walk around, I begin to notice the warmth subtly

wafting up from the stone floor. "I love the heated floors. I'm guessing it's radiant?"

He nods an affirmative.

"What a great idea."

"The whole house is solar, except for my two propane tanks. I ran circulating hot water through the floors, so even in the middle of winter I can walk around in my bare feet and feel warm. I also put a large woodstove in the basement, which I can use as a backup heat source if necessary. So, with all that and the well, I'm pretty much off the grid and self-sufficient."

After showing me his library and den, he says, "Let's see the kitchen next, and then we can tour the upstairs." He leads me past the stairway to the back of the entryway, and we move through French doors to an enormous kitchen. As I scan the room and see the stainless steel appliances and multiple hanging pot racks full of copper pots and skillets, I decide that as much as I hate cooking, even I wouldn't mind it in this setting.

Aside from a bay window opening out to a grassy backyard, every wall is adorned with abundant cabinetry. In the midst of the kitchen is a huge center island covered in solid maple butcher block, surrounded by comfortable bar stools. The remaining countertops are white granite.

"Wow, this should be on the cover of a magazine, too. It's amazing!" I get a sweet vision of myself rolling out sugar cookie dough for Christmas cookies. Scanning the area a second time, my eyes rest upon a sparkling crystal vase full of fresh-cut flowers, sitting right in the middle of the center island. To my surprise, leaning against the front of it is a pale blue envelope with my name on it. The lettering is done in flowery calligraphy. *Now how the heck did he manage that?* "What's this?"

"Oh, I have no idea. Maybe you should look."

Gingerly, I pick it up and notice a small box wrapped in pale blue paper immediately behind it. "There's more?"

Jackson shrugs his shoulders and remains silent.

My heart begins beating a little faster, and I'm fairly certain I'm blushing. Although a bit self-conscious, I am thoroughly enjoying the adventure. "Hmmm. What do we have here?" Wanting to take it one step at a time and savor the moment, I slowly turn the envelope over. Unsealing the flap, I withdraw a beautiful note card, hand painted with a red, orange, and blue bird-of-paradise. On the inside, in perfect old-style calligraphy, is written a simple note.

Welcome to my small slice of Heaven.
May you be as comfortable in it as I am,
~ Jackson

"Oh my goodness," I whisper, "I don't know what to say."

Without giving me time to think, he reaches for the small box and hands it to me. "This is for you. I've waited a long time to give it to you."

"Jackson . . ."

"Before you protest or say anything, just open it."

"Okay." I untie the thin silk ribbon, undo the wrapper, and open the box. Inside is a tiny, blue velvet jewelry box, which I pull out. Holding it in the palm of my hand, I can neither move nor breathe. *I'm not ready for this.* Part of me wants to run away and hide, while the other part wants to explore possibilities. Slowly I open the lid.

"Oh, Jackson. I don't know what to say. It's so beautiful. I had no idea."

"I figured you didn't have one, and maybe it was time you did."

I lift the delicate platinum chain and examine the cross suspended from it. Also platinum, it's set with one single, perfect diamond in the center. Very simple, very elegant, and absolutely the perfect gift.

"Would you mind?" I ask, handing it to him. Turning

around, I face away and pull my long hair to one side.

"Not at all." He reaches over my head and places the chain around my neck, securing it at the back. "There's a mirror in the hallway if you'd like to see it."

Before I let my hair fall back into place, he kisses my neck gently, sending a warm shiver up my spine. When I lightly rub the cross between my fingers, I inadvertently feel my wedding ring underneath my shirt. I drop my head down a little. *It's time to let you go, Mac. I hope you don't mind.* For some reason, I don't think he does.

As I turn back to face Jackson, my mind shifts to the present moment and the man in front of me. *There is so much to this guy.* Without thinking, I hear myself blurt, "I think I'm falling for you, Jackson." The words are out before I can stop them.

Tilting his head back, he looks up at the ceiling with a smile. "Now I'm the one who's surprised." He puts his strong arms around me. "But just so there's no confusion, I fell for you a long time ago." He hugs me tightly and buries his head in my hair.

———

Holding hands, we ascend the cherry steps to the second-floor landing, the midpoint of a wide, U-shaped balcony that wraps all the way around the entryway below. Each side extends to the front of the house, terminating at tall windows. The overhead skylights give the area a gloriously open, roomy feel.

"Who designed all this?

"Mostly me and Roger. We worked on the plans for about a year and got 'em pretty close. Then I took the sketches to a draftsman and had him make it all work."

He opens the double doors to the huge bedroom above the dining room and smiles. "And this, my dear, is the master bedroom."

"Oh, wow. This is stunning! I love the dormer windows and window seats. And where did you find that four-poster bed? It looks hand carved!"

"Actually, I had it made."

"That must've cost a bundle. It's gorgeous!" The sheer white canopy and side drapes are tied to the head posts with beige satin ribbons. "I don't know who did the rest of your decorating, but they are really good."

"Thanks. I'll tell my mom you approve."

"No way! She picked all this out?"

"Yeah, she's pretty good at lots of stuff. Come on, you've gotta see the bathroom."

"I'd love to."

Pushing open the door, he reveals a brightly lit white granite bathroom with double sinks and a ball-and-claw-foot soaking tub. The all-glass shower is large enough to hold six or eight people at once and is fitted with multiple heads and knobs. "Geez, Jackson, you could have a cocktail party in there! It's gorgeous, just like everything else."

"Yeah, this is a fun room. I like all the natural light."

Back on the balcony, he leads me around to the other side and opens another double door to a guest bedroom facing the rear of the house. Following the theme of the master bedroom, it also has dormer windows and a hand-carved four-poster bed. He takes my hand and leads me back out onto the balcony to the last set of double doors. This room faces the front of the house, but there is nothing else in the rather large room. "Is this a bedroom, too?"

"Yeah, and it connects to the one behind it through this double bathroom." He pushes the door open to reveal a large, interconnecting bath.

"So why no furniture?"

"Oh, I don't know. I guess I'm kind of waiting for an idea."

"Well, I'm sure it will be lovely, whatever you do. It's large enough for two twins, a queen, or even a king. Heck, you could fit both my lofts in here."

"Yeah, maybe. I suppose I could put just about anything I want in here. Don't you worry, I'll figure it out eventually." He takes a deep breath and smiles at me. "I'm hungry. Let's go downstairs, and I'll whip something up."

"Sounds good."

He takes my hand and leads me back down the graceful stairway into the kitchen.

"How large is this place, anyway?"

"About four thousand square feet, give or take a little."

"Wow, that's pretty big. Almost three times bigger than mine."

"Yeah, but I built it for my future. You know, maybe a family, retirement, old age, all that."

Family? Yeah, I get that. I think about Mac again, but for some reason it doesn't hurt as much. Suddenly a pang of unexpected jealousy rears its ugly head. *Wait! He said family. He means his family. Am I a day late and a dollar short?* I push the feeling away. "Oh, don't get me wrong. It's not a bit ostentatious. Quite the contrary, it's perfectly done. And honestly, why not? I think if I could afford it, I'd do something similar."

He uncorks a bottle of cold, crisp Chardonnay, pours a few ounces into a crystal wine glass, and hands it to me. "Enjoy!"

"Aren't you having any?"

"No, I still have to get us back across the water. I'll wait until dinner tonight."

Two hours later, Jackson lands the plane safely in Port Angeles, taxies to the hangar, and secures everything while Alder and I supervise.

"I hope you don't mind," he says, "but I need to stop by my office at the church on the way."

Since the word "church" is synonymous with the word "death" for me, my brain begins to disengage. *Come on, Elizabeth, don't shut down. This day's been so perfect. Please don't spoil it for yourself.* "No, of course. It's okay."

"Cool. It will only take a few minutes." Jackson drives on for several minutes. "Going into a church is hard for you, isn't it?"

"Yeah, I guess. It's never been a happy time for me. It usually signifies that someone's died. First my mom, then my dad, and then Mac. That's church for me."

"What about weddings? Baptisms? Confirmations? Christmas Eve service? Or my favorite—the reason for it all—Easter?"

"I don't go. I mean, I've been to a few weddings, but as for the rest, I steer clear."

"Maybe I can show you the other side of church."

"Honestly, Jackson, for me it became a simple case of fear. I think deep down I believed that if I avoided church, nothing else bad would happen to me. Kind of a weird phobia, which probably sounds lame, but that's it in a nutshell."

"Considering your tremendous losses, it sounds very reasonable. But given my line of work and your recent connection to Joseph, maybe it's time to introduce you to a different perspective." He pulls his vehicle into the church parking lot.

Just as I remember it, the church is styled in the old-fashioned way, with a steeple and bell tower over a high-pitched roof. Tall glass windows flank both sides, and a full-length covered porch extends out over the quad-door entryway. Flanked by tall cedar and fir trees, the setting is picturesque enough to be on a jigsaw puzzle. I've forgotten how pretty this place is.

Jackson walks around to open my door and give me his hand. "Come on, Elizabeth. No time like the present to get over your fear of heights. And I promise not to let you fall."

Obligingly, I accompany him into the office while Alder

stays in the SUV.

"Well, hey there, Elizabeth! Long time, no see!" Jane, his effervescent secretary, greets us as she walks out from behind the counter and hugs me warmly. "I've really missed you."

I barely recognize you. How the heck do you even remember my name? I awkwardly fumble for an appropriate response. "Ah, yeah, Jane. I missed you, too."

"No matter. It's good to see you, and you look great." She turns her attention to Jackson. "Pastor, here's the mail, and here's your notes for tomorrow. Also, the Simpsons did the flowers for tomorrow's services and wanted to be sure you knew."

While Jane continues rattling off news and updates, I find the ladies' restroom. When I come out, I hear the choir practicing through the open double doors leading to the narthex of the sanctuary. Filtering through the space, the peaceful sound beckons me to enter. *Not yet. Maybe another time.*

Wanting to run away, I turn back toward the office but see that Jackson and Jane are still going over stuff. I realize that I'm not ready to let all my walls down. If I capitulate, it might mean I've been wrong—again. But the lovely choir voices continue, drawing my sight back to the double doors. *Oh, screw it! It can't be that bad.*

Taking a deep breath, I wander through the doorway and into the quiet, serene setting. Afternoon sunlight filters delicately through stained glass windows, and wooden pews stretch outward from the middle aisle, where a stone baptismal font stands at the center of the room. Suspended from a high beam at the front of the church is a simple wooden cross, beneath which is a modest, two-step stage. In the center of the raised platform, a stone altar is adorned with two single candlesticks and a large Bible. To the left is a stone lectern, presumably where Jackson speaks. *I'd like to hear him speak.*

Standing behind the last pew, absorbing the serenity, I feel a strong hand gently touch my shoulder, awakening me from my thoughts.

"We can go now, Elizabeth. If you're ready."

"Oh, yeah. Sure."

"How 'bout I pick up a few things, take you home, check on Roger, and then cook you dinner? I've got some steaks and a decent bottle of wine. What do you say?"

"I'd love that. But what about your services tomorrow? I don't want to distract you." *Please argue with me. I'd love to spend another evening with you!* From a distant recess in my heart comes an inexplicable understanding. I want to be with him. I feel better when I am.

"I'll tell you what. You let me do the worrying, and you can make a salad."

The small alleyway next to the church parking lot leads to the modest home provided by the church. Waiting with Alder while Jackson runs inside gives me time to contemplate Joseph and the events of the past six days. *What a whirlwind!*

As Jackson points the SUV toward my home, the quiet drive up the mountain lulls me into a peaceful state of relaxation, and soon I'm drifting off to sleep. Although I fight to stay awake, I can't help but nod off a few times. The third time I close my eyes, I see him.

Joseph.

22

"Joseph."

"Elizabeth. You made it."

Clad in long white robes and innocently beautiful, Joseph stands near a gently cascading waterfall with his hand outstretched, fingers barely touching the misting spray. He appears to be about sixteen or seventeen, but I innately know he is older than generations. An illumination radiates from within his being, creating a celestial effect all around and through him. As his light envelops me, I am filled with an understanding of how utterly insignificant everything is compared to the infinity of the universe.

"Where am I?" I ask.

He pushes back his hood and allows me to see his serene face, unmarred by the struggles of life, as only the innocent can be. "This is my side of Mayim, my side of the water."

"Are you an angel? You look like one."

"No. I am the Sixth. We are similar, but not the same," he clarifies.

I can see no details except for Joseph and the falling water, as if I'm peering through the lens of a tightly focused camera. Everything else is blurred, hidden from my vision.

"Why am I here?"

"It is easier, and it might help if you understand."

"What? What am I supposed to understand?"

"I exist for one reason: to ensure the passage of the Pure, who come here to wait until their journey can continue. Without me and the other eight, multitudes would suffer and be eternally lost." He pauses, giving me time to process his words. "We are the Nine for a reason. Nine in all—no more, no less."

"Yes. You told me about the Nine."

"You must understand that there are Nine on your side as well. We exist only for them. One of us for each of them."

I don't understand. "But Joseph, we have no one in our world like you."

"I did not say they are like us. I said they are Pure. Innocent. We are here for them."

"They must be invisible, because I've never heard of them."

"They are not invisible, merely unrecognized or forgotten. But though humankind may not recognize them, they most definitely exist. They are everywhere."

"Everywhere?"

"*JOSEPH!*" speaks a passionate voice.

"Father! I did not expect you."

I can see nothing, and the voices are fading.

"*YOU SHOULD NOT HAVE BROUGHT ELIZABETH.*"

"But Father . . . "

"*MY SON, THIS IS NOT THE WAY.*"

———————

"Elizabeth . . . Elizabeth."

The passenger door is open, and Jackson is leaning on the door jamb. I feel a gentle hand on my shoulder, "Hey, lady, we're here."

"Joseph . . ." Opening my eyes, I realize we are on the gravel parking pad in front of my cabin. "Oh, wow. I just saw Joseph."

"Yeah, I guessed you were dreaming a little. You were sort of mumbling in your sleep." He squats down on his haunches. "What did you see?"

"An angel." I think of his appearance. "At least, he looked like I imagine an angel would look, with blond hair and piercing blue eyes. Very peaceful, and dressed in long robes, like a monk. Physically he looked about sixteen, but I know he was older, ageless maybe. He was standing in front of a waterfall, in a room of some kind, but all the background was blurred, so I don't really know."

"Did he say anything?"

I nod. "He told me again about being part of the Nine, and then said there are Nine on our side as well."

"What?"

"Yeah. But the Nine here aren't exactly like them. Joseph said his Nine exist only for ours. He said they're everywhere."

"Hmm. I didn't expect that."

"Me neither. It sounds like a symbiotic relationship or something."

"That's a switch."

"Yeah." I think about the voice at the end of the dream. "And then . . . I think God came. He seemed displeased."

"At you?"

"No . . . I think He was disappointed that Joseph showed me their side."

"Interesting," Jackson says as he helps me out of the vehicle. "Let's check on Roger, and then we can talk about it some more."

In our absence, Roger has made enormous progress. Standing on the back of his truck, he's packing up his chainsaw and equipment for the day but stops long enough to wave to us. Having already dragged out the multiple thirty-foot sections of the first cedar, he has a nice stack piled off to the side of my yard. After stacking the logs, he apparently switched his efforts to felling the other five trees and worked his usual magic, bringing each one down precisely where planned. His strategy caused minimal damage.

"I'm gonna leave my Cat up here and will be back on Monday to finish this," he says. "I'll bring the loader up on Tuesday and should be all done by the end of the day."

"Okay, Roger. No problem. I won't be around after Monday afternoon 'cause I have to go back to Seattle to work, but just do whatever you need to."

He looks at Jackson and then me. "You guys have a good time?"

"Yeah, actually, we did. I showed her *Ladybug* and my house."

"Whaddaya think?" he asks me.

I shrug. "I hate it, all of it." We all laugh. "What do you think? It's fabulous, of course! I understand you helped restore the plane and had a hand in the designs and building of the house. All I can say is, you guys did a great job. It's really lovely, on so many levels."

"Well, good, that's good." He turns to leave. "See you in church tomorrow, Jax."

"Right."

"Thanks for everything, Roger," I call after him. "I really appreciate it. Everything."

We follow him around to the front, where his truck is parked, and watch him load up and drive off.

"Is he just really shy?" I ask.

"Not so much when you get to know him. I'd say he's more private than anything else. He cherishes his anonymity and privacy. Why?"

"Oh, nothing. It's just that he did a lot of work for Mac and me, clearing this part of the land. He was here six days a week for almost two months, and in all that time I couldn't get more than a few words out of him. We only had the travel trailer, but I'd always offer him coffee or a meal or whatever, but he'd never accept. So I wondered."

"His mom and the man she married were like my parents. They worked hard every day and traveled a lot for business, so we each had nannies and housekeepers to help fill the voids. I think we both grew up just wanting quality time with those we love the most and solitude in our private lives.

"Roger's a great husband to Nan and a fabulous father to their three kids. He coaches Little League and youth skiing, and takes 'em hiking or fishing almost every weekend in good weather. And he adores their new baby girl. He's devoted to them."

"Do you have regrets about the way you were raised?"

"Not so much regret as wanting to do things a little differently when it's my turn. Our parents were—are—very kind and supportive. There was never any doubt they loved us. But they had tremendous obligations that superseded our daily lives. When my sister finished her master's and opted to stay with the family business, she decided not to have a family because she didn't want the emotional conflict. Roger and I chose our own paths away from the business. And the best part is, our parents understood."

I pause for a moment on the deck and lean against the railing, watching Alder run around the pond. "Where are they now?"

"The company's headquartered in Houston, and they all live in a beautiful suburb about ten miles from each other. But since they own land and mills all over the world, they're constantly traveling to keep close watch on their enterprises. The sad thing is, they may be moving everything overseas in the near future."

"Why would they leave Texas?"

"It's not Texas, it's the United States." He sighs heavily. "It's complicated, but suffice it to say that their business—actually all business—is being strangled by the federal government, specifically the EPA."

"Why? What did your parents do wrong?"

"Absolutely nothing. Granted, some loggers are idiots, but not my folks. As a matter of fact, they've always managed to stay ahead of environmental rules by proactively protecting the environment through their own corporate advocacy programs. But under the recent administrations, the EPA has grown into an enormous federal cancer now churning out thousands of regulations cleverly designed to end our free market system. Their regulations make it harder and harder for anyone to stay in business in the US. If the agencies don't back off, I predict it's only a matter of time before Blue Sky packs up and moves away. Along with a lot of other great companies."

"Wow, that's a drag."

"Yeah, and then there's the other little item they've recently become embroiled in."

"What's that?"

"The new federal healthcare laws. Decades ago, my parents established a self-insurance trust fund program, which provides medical benefits to every employee working a minimum of twenty hours a week. Low cost, great insurance. A win-win situation for thousands of employees."

"Yeah?"

"The only two things the insurance specifically didn't cover was the morning-after pill and abortion, because neither my parents nor the board members believe in abortions of any kind. In thirty-five years, they never had one single complaint about the insurance."

"What about contraception, like birth control pills and shots?"

"Those were covered. They never saw a moral conflict in using birth control to prevent conception."

"So what's the problem?"

"Day by day, we see the nuances of the insidious new law becoming clear. The law's ultimate goal was not just the takeover of our healthcare system, but also to eliminate God from our lives, to evict His existence. By enforcing the horrific law, each government employee becomes complicit in rejecting God, forcing its citizens to overtly defy God and their personal religious beliefs."

"You lost me."

"My parents will be forced, *forced*, by the regulations and courts—to pay for, and thus participate in—aborting human life. They will be *forced* to kill innocent babies, babies still in the womb." He slams his hands down on the railing. "My parents will be *forced* to choose between God and murder if they want to stay in business."

I put my hand on his back to comfort him. "Can't they just ignore it?"

"Nope. They're already being sued by the feds for not complying. The lawsuit will cost millions. Thousands of Americans who work for our company, in one form or another, will lose their jobs. They'll lose everything." He leans against the deck railing and lowers his head. "And that equates to millions of lost jobs around the globe. Such a needless tragedy, caused by bad government policies." He pauses and looks down. "It just never ends."

"What?"

"Evil. No matter how close a people come to eradicating it—and our forefathers did a pretty good job of keeping evil at bay—it always returns." Closing his eyes, he puts his head down for a moment of silence and then looks up, smiling. "And that, my dear lady, is why my faith in God is so important."

"What does He have to do with government regulations

and your parents' company fighting bad policies?"

"It has everything to do with it. Whatever happens or doesn't happen, wherever we are at a given moment in time, it's always, *always* part of His amazing plan. And He has great plans for us."

"So you're saying God already decided everything before we were born, and we're just living out some type of puppet show?" I can feel the old anger rising. "And a sick, cruel puppet show at that."

"Not at all. That's not what I said, nor what I believe. Let me say it this way. My faith tells me I was created in His image with an innate ability to differentiate between good and evil, right and wrong. The ability to differentiate is, quite simply, our humanity. It's the *understanding* that links us directly to God.

"God also gave us the gift of choice. He didn't have to. He could have made us all a bunch of robots, blindly doing His bidding. But there'd have been no point. Instead, He planted the seed of knowledge deep in our hearts, then sat back and watched us choose. The conundrum is that although we innately *know*, we can choose to ignore that very undeniable truth. Bottom line, God made us with a full capacity to live and love, knowing He might be disappointed."

"Why?"

"Because He loves us. He wants us to find our happiness in Him and in our love for His Son, Jesus Christ. But we must choose which way to proceed. I freely chose to trust God and accept His Son as my Lord and Savior. Only through God can anything Holy or good come from life's tragedies, and only through His promises can one find peace about events we have no control over."

I mull this over. "Trusting something I can't see is hard for me, Jackson. Me, myself, and I have been all I've had for so long, it's hard to count on anything intangible."

"Yes, it is. That's the hardest part about faith. But if we

want to be freed from the earthly bondages of worry, despair, and fear, then we must choose to let go of the reins and trust Him."

"Well, I can attest to one thing. Prior to Monday, I believed God was an absentee landlord. But since then, I think maybe He's a lot closer. Now it feels really personal."

"It is! And you know what? This is my favorite topic, and we can explore it a lot more over time." He puts his arm around me. "But right now, I'm starved. How about I start the grill?"

"Sounds like a plan." I holler down the hill, "Alder, come on, boy. Dinner!"

It's half past eight by the time we finish eating and clean up the kitchen. A nice fire fills my little cottage with toasty heat, and Alder is settled in for the night. I know Jackson has an early wake-up call and assume he will be driving home soon.

"I hope you don't mind," he says, "but I'm gonna stay here again tonight."

"Really?" *What a great idea!* "What about church tomorrow?"

"I've got an alarm and a clean set of clothes in the car. Like a Boy Scout, I'm always prepared." He gives me a big hug and then lifts my chin with his finger. "I'd like to kiss you."

"I'd like that, too."

He puts his lips to mine tenderly. This is my first kiss in four years, and I can feel my body responding to his warm embrace. As I kiss him back, he pulls me closer, and our kiss turns deeper and more passionate. From the depths of my belly a fire is beginning to burn, a fire I haven't felt in a very long time. We stand together, exploring each other's lips and mouths, neither one of us wanting it to end. I finally pull away and bury my head in his chest.

"I'm glad you brought your alarm, Jackson, because I'd like you to stay." I pull him toward my loft.

"Wait, Elizabeth. As much as I'd like to go up with you, I'm gonna play by the rules."

"What rules?"

"God's rules."

"Oh."

"So I'll sleep up there." He points to the other loft. "And you sleep over there." He points up to my loft.

"But Jackson, we're adults." I hold his hand and pull him toward me.

"Yes, we most definitely are. And if ever the time is right, I'll make mad, passionate love to you, over and over. But that time has not yet arrived."

"Bummer."

"Not at all. I look forward to that moment with great anticipation." He embraces me again and kisses me deeply. It seems like we fit together perfectly as he envelops me in his strong arms. The longer he holds me, the more I want him.

Am I in love? How can I be, after only a few days of being with him? Do things like that actually happen in real life? Rapid-fire questions fill my head in a familiar circular pattern. I stop the inner debate. "So, why are you staying? Won't people talk?"

"I don't care what people say, only what God knows to be true. But since you asked, I'm staying because there's a very good chance that Joseph will return, and when he does, I want to be here."

"Oh yeah, Joseph. I almost forgot."

"Now, go get into your flannels and get ready for bed. We both need as much sleep as possible."

"Yes, sir."

23

Through the crisp, cold air I can see my breath, yet I feel no chill.
Under a cloudless, sunny sky, I meander along a narrow stone
path through a pristine alpine valley. Snowcapped mountains
rise majestically in the distance, and thick woodlands cover the
lower hillsides.

For a brief moment I wonder where I'm heading, but the
thought quickly vanishes. As I crest a small hill, a sparkling blue
mountain lake comes into view. I halt my steps to take in the
spectacular scene. That's when I notice the others immediately
in front of me.

I count ten in all, although the one in the rear seems
somehow separate, older. The silent group walks single file
through the valley, straight into a light mist which soon
envelops everyone, including me. The mist turns to a heavy, wet
blanket of murky vapor so dense it obscures all but the stones
beneath my feet. Even the group before me becomes difficult to
discern when their long, white hooded robes blend into the fog.

A voice from somewhere inside my head tells me, *"This is where the universe turns cold, soulless hearts into stone."* A shiver runs through me.

Abruptly, the procession stops. I watch as the first nine spread out in a sideways pattern, forming a curved line on each side of the central figure, whom I assume to be male.

Slowly the vapors begin to dissipate, bringing into view the very edge of the earth, or possibly a mammoth chasm; either way, it is the end. I feel woozy just seeing it from a slight distance. It seems unimaginable that the nine in front of me can remain at the brink of such an enormous fracture in the earth without backing away. Yet there the line remains, the front edges of their sandals hanging out over the rim.

The fog swirls around the group, forming a lens-like funnel into the distance. The visual opening is ahead of the central figure, the person standing behind him—and me. The four on each side of the middle person turn and raise their arms in unison, touching the shoulders of the ones before them, connecting to the central figure. As they connect to him, he takes two steps backward.

Raising his arms, he turns his palms upward to the sky. A swirling mist momentarily obscures my view until a bright light bursts forth from his hands and shoots upward with great force and speed. When it seems the light can rise no farther, it draws together and coalesces to a spot in front of the one in the middle, right on the edge of the chasm.

The mist gradually clears, and in place of the light stands a brown-haired man of medium height, about the age of forty. He wears the same robes as the others.

"I am Douglas," he says.

The one facing him lowers his arms and tilts his hooded head, indicating the chasm behind Douglas. As Douglas turns, the far side of the gulf begins to warp inward, toward our side. These aren't slow changes, but dizzyingly rapid morphing.

Wherever I am, this world is vibrantly alive! As I watch the far rim, I feel the ground beneath my feet move forward in a smooth, gliding motion, gaining speed and powerful momentum as it progresses. Within seconds, the once great void is reduced to a mere river canyon, and the far rim is no more than a stone's throw away. Every landscape detail appears to be identical to this side, and I wonder momentarily why such a great separation is needed.

Just then, an elderly, stooped woman with gray hair walks unsteadily into view on the far side. She is alone. Coming to the edge, she stands a little straighter and looks across the ravine. Her eyes rest on Douglas. She tilts her head to one side, then the other, as if lost in thought. The old woman mumbles something inaudible and looks down at her feet, then back up at Douglas, then down and back several more times.

While she contemplates, a huge man with mangy, matted hair and a severely scarred face and right hand appears to her left. Locked in heavy iron shackles about his feet, hands, and neck, he stands perfectly still. All the shackles are chained together and attached to an enormous black ball on the ground beside him. The ball rolls ahead of him, forcing his feet toward the woman and the edge of the rim.

Recognition dawns on the woman's face as she turns to face him. "Oh, you! I'd know you anywhere, you evil bastard!"

"I know what I am," the man snarls. "I told you I'd find you again, little girl. You could never hide from me. Even now I can taste you, all of you." His maliciously creepy tone turns my blood cold, and I shiver unexpectedly.

"You monster!" The woman feebly raises her frail arm to slap the man's scarred face, but something stops her hand in midair. Unable to complete the task, she tries with her other arm, forming a fist and swinging wide. But again her effort is prevented by an invisible force. Over and over she battles the barrier, screaming and raging, but to no avail; she simply can't make contact.

"Ha! Face it, you little bitch. You can't fight me. You couldn't then, and you can't now."

Eventually she halts her attempts, and her screaming turns to uncontrollable weeping, followed by quiet sobs and halting breaths. "You ruined everything." Her sputtering desperation subsides, and the cathartic event passes. She stands a little straighter and looks a little younger.

"Ha, ha, ha! No jail could ever hold me, and I always remembered you, especially you."

But the woman no longer seems to hear his taunts. "Look what you did to me." She looks down and then up again. This time her eyes focus on Douglas. "Look what you did to us."

A wisp of air rises from the depths of the chasm and circles around the woman. Inhaling, she turns away from the man. As she inhales again, I see subtle changes occurring. Defying the years which have passed, her bent frame stands erect, her shoulders move back, and her head rises. She inhales more deeply, and every feature begins to transform, erasing the cruel, sagging wrinkles of life. Thick auburn hair replaces thinning silver strands, and a full bosom graces her chest. Very much in the prime of her life now, the lovely young beauty stands poised, unmarred by tragedy.

Douglas returns her gaze, and their stares lock in place.

Tentatively the woman asks, "Is that you?"

"It is I."

"You're . . . you're a man. A grown man. I never knew." She lowers her voice. "I never wanted to know."

"I know."

"Would this have been your future?"

"If given the chance."

"I'm so sorry. I couldn't go through with it. Oh, I'm so very sorry."

Without responding, Douglas takes one step out over the

edge of the rim, waiting for the stones to form in front of him. He takes a few more steps and turns to look back. But the stones between himself and the rim are already gone. Now suspended in midair upon the one stone beneath his feet, he waits.

The woman on the far rim looks down at the few stones in front of her and then up at Douglas. Whether it's indecision or confusion, she hesitates briefly and then seems to reach a conclusion. Without looking aside, she speaks to the brutal man. "I think we have to do this together."

"Me, go out there? Fuck you!"

The corners of her mouth turn up into a tiny, knowing smile as she takes a single step out onto the stones in front of her. Pausing, she waits while the huge black ball attached to the shackles on the man's feet slides forward to the stones forming in front of him. He has no alternative but to follow the ball. Out over the chasm he is dragged.

While they stood on the rim's edge, a connecting path existed between the woman and the shackled man. But when he steps out from the rim, the connection evaporates and their paths immediately bisect, bringing the woman toward Douglas and veering the man to the left into a swirling fog, far away from the others.

Douglas methodically takes one step forward and then another, neither hurrying nor hesitating, his gait matching the formation and disappearance of the stones at his feet. Eventually he stands less than a foot from the woman, yet the separation might as well be a universe. Neither moves. Silence ensues.

From his periphery, Douglas can still detect the man in the fog, but seems to pay him no attention. Quite the contrary; his eyes appear focused only upon the young woman.

In a soft voice the woman says to Douglas, "I am sorry. Please try to find it in your heart to forgive me."

"It is not for me to forgive. It is only for me to live. To have had my life."

Hearing his words, she puts her hands to her face. "God forgive me, God forgive me!" Falling to her knees, she screams out, "He didn't deserve this! Take my life! Please take mine!"

From the depths of the chasm comes a faint breeze, swirling gently around and through Douglas. His chest rises and falls while he inhales the refreshing air. He closes his eyes and says, "Yes, Father, I understand."

Reaching out across the small separation, he takes hold of the woman's hand. A single row of stones forms between their feet, bridging the gap. He steps next to the woman, closer to the far rim, and pulls her to her feet. The stones form a path wide enough for the two to walk side by side, guiding them to the other side.

The shackled man begins to scream. "You bitch! You can't leave me here! I should have killed you when I had the chance!"

Douglas and the woman, now lost in quiet conversation, pay no attention to the shackled man still suspended over the center of the great chasm. Reaching the far rim, Douglas turns briefly to look at the group of nine and nods his head. The central figure in the linked group returns the gesture.

Whether the fog blocks the man's raging, or his existence is now simply insignificant, his vile threats can no longer be heard. Either way, he remains suspended over the void while Douglas and the woman fade out of sight.

As rapidly as the ground closed the immense gulf, it now reverses its efforts, warping outward with great speed to reform the gargantuan chasm. From nowhere, a rolling, thick fog surrounds the group of ten and me, obscuring everything. Dropping their hands, the hooded figures break their physical links and turn to form a single-file procession behind the center. As new stones appear at his feet, he leads the entire party away.

Off to one side, I watch the group of ten walk by, all seemingly unaware of my presence. As the second-to-last one passes, he gives me a slight glance from under his hood. Joseph.

When the last one moves past, I follow, picking my way through the fog. A terrifying scream echoes from somewhere behind me. It is an inhuman cry, born from the cold realization that sentence has been rendered. I somehow understand that his stone-cold soul, eternally bound to its fate, will never again touch the universe.

The fog lifts, and I can once again see distant snowcapped mountains, stately evergreen trees, and brilliant blue sky overhead. As I walk in the sun's warmth, surrounded by the beauty of the day, thoughts of the man's blood-curdling screams fade away.

"ELIZABETH." I sense a deep, gentle voice. It is somehow familiar. *"YOU CANNOT BE HERE."*

I stop and look expectantly around, but the source evades me. *"Who are you?"* I ask in my mind.

"YOU KNOW ME."

The voice must be in my head. *"Yes, I remember now."*

"YOU CANNOT BE HERE."

"Where am I?"

"ON HOLY GROUND."

"How did I get here?"

"THROUGH YOUR DREAMS."

"But I didn't ask to be here."

"I KNOW. AND NOW YOU MUST GO BACK."

"But why? Why must I leave?"

"MY CHILD, IT IS NOT YET YOUR TIME."

"Please tell me. How do I leave?"

I feel a firm hand on my shoulder.

"Wake up! Elizabeth, wake up!" Jackson shakes me until my eyes open.

I'm annoyed at being pulled from my dream. "What?"

"Wake up! We're having an earthquake!"

"Oh, Jackson," I say, sweeping the sleepy cobwebs out of my brain. "This is a bad one."

"We need to get downstairs, under the beams. Let's go!" He already has my slippers and robe as he helps me up. "You can put these on downstairs."

The nightlights are still on. "Thank goodness we haven't lost power—yet."

I grab my gun and flashlight and follow him down the narrow steps. Seeing pictures and photos bumping around on the walls and hearing the china and knickknacks rattling in the cupboards gives me the willies. When the windows begin vibrating, I know it's getting worse. "Oh crap, I hate these." I run for the big table at the end of the room, and we dive underneath. "Where's Alder?"

"Not sure. I figured he was up in the loft with you."

"Alder! Alder!" I pan my flashlight around the base of the woodstove, which is still producing a nice warm glow. "Come on, boy!"

Nothing.

"He's probably hiding in the closet. That's where he goes when he's afraid."

"I'll go check," Jackson says, moving to get out from under the table, but I hold his arm.

"No, just wait till it's over. He'll be okay." *Please be okay, Alder.*

But the tremors continue, shaking my little cottage to its core.

"Puget Sound has so many fault lines," I yell above the noise, "it's a wonder Seattle hasn't fallen into the ocean."

"I know, and this has been going on for several minutes."

"Wait a sec. What if it's not really an earthquake? What if it's Joseph?"

"What?"

"Joseph!" I shout. "Joseph, if you're there and you're causing this, please stop! You're gonna hurt us!" Worsening tremors cause the table above us to skitter across the floor. "Oh God, please don't let the house come down."

Abruptly, Jackson crawls out from under the protection of the table and stands up in the middle of the room. Silhouetted against the glow of the fire behind him, arms raised and fists clenched, he yells above the deafening vibrations, "Joseph! In the name of the Father, the Son, and the Holy Spirit, I command you to stop!"

"Are you crazy! Get back under here!"

Ignoring me, he continues his demand with even more fervor. "Joseph! In the name of Almighty God, I command you to stop!" Reminiscent of Moses parting the Red Sea, Jackson stands with unwavering determination, arms outstretched, eyes skyward. Even more fiercely, he repeats his command a third time, turning slowly as he speaks.

Miraculously, the tremors calm, and the house becomes

quiet once again. From my hiding place, I strain my ears to hear new sounds, wondering if the quake is really over. Thankfully, the silence is growing—and that's when I hear the waterfall and the familiar voice.

"Elizabeth."

"Jackson!" I whisper. "It's him, Joseph!"

He nods. "I hear him."

"Yes, Joseph, I'm here. What do you want?"

"To stop it. And to understand."

Coming out from my hiding place, I stand beside Jackson.

"Joseph, what do you need to understand?" I ask.

"Someone called out to me in the name of 'the Father.'"

"That was me. I'm Jackson. I commanded you to stop."

"Yes. I know you."

Jackson and I exchange glances.

"Upon whose authority did you use Father's name?" Joseph asks.

"I have as direct a connection to God, our Father, as anyone else," Jackson answers. "He is as much a part of me as I am of Him."

"But you are impure. I know He moves within your world, but He would not allow your impurities to touch Him."

"True, we suffer from sin. But you are wrong about touching God. In our Father's infinite wisdom, He gave us a gift—a way to reach Him. While some of us may not recognize them, our Father and His Gift are with us continuously."

"What kind of a gift?"

"His Holy Son."

"Ah. The One who moves with and beside Him," Joseph says quietly. "The One we do not see."

"Joseph, please listen," Jackson says. "I sense you come from far away and your travel here is difficult."

"It is not that we are far away, only that we are separated. It does require much control."

"Are we separated for a reason?"

"Your realm is forbidden."

"Is travel here allowed?"

Silence.

"If it's forbidden, then why do you come?" Jackson asks.

"To seek Elizabeth."

"Each time you 'seek' her, it causes a dangerous rift in her world—disturbances in her time and space."

"It was the only way to bring you two together."

Jackson and I look at each other again. *Nothing happens by accident.*

"Why did we need to be brought together?" I ask.

"It was imperative. Absolutely essential. It will make all the difference."

"Imperative or not, you could hurt her," Jackson says.

"That . . . was not my intent."

"I assumed not. Is there another way?" Jackson asks.

"Another way?"

"Can you contact Elizabeth without causing damage?"

"I have been trying. I am sometimes able to reach her—when her mind is quiet."

Dreams. "Yes! I've definitely dreamed about you."

"Dreams? Ah, yes. The problem is, reaching you is unpredictable. I cannot always control where you go or what you see. And it is better if we are alone."

I shoot Jackson a sideways glance. "Why do we need to be alone?"

Silence.

"But Joseph, someone else is always present when you're around, whether it's here or there," I say. "I can always feel someone else."

"That would be Lady Mary. She explained to me about your fear."

"Who is Lady Mary?"

"My mentor. She is the caretaker for those I guide."

I'm so lost.

"Think of it this way: she is a comforter for your humanity."

I'm still lost.

"Remember the hand on your face?"

"Yes." *How could I forget?*

"Did it not relieve your fears and anxiety? Did it not calm you?"

"Yes. But Joseph, sometimes there's another. Sometimes I also feel or hear God—at least, I think it's God."

Silence.

"You aren't really supposed to be here, are you?" Jackson asks.

Silence.

"Joseph! I don't care about the stupid rules. You're here now, so what do you need?"

"I will come to you in your dreams," he says quietly.

"You're making me crazy!" I hold my head. "What do you need from me?"

Silence. The sound of the water begins to fade away.

I heave a sigh. "He's gone."

"Shhh! Just wait."

Finally Joseph answers. "I believe Elizabeth can prevent the beginning of a great darkness."

"A great darkness?" Jackson echoes.

"Yes. It is looming. If it is not stopped, it will cover your world. It will be the end."

A great darkness? The end? "Joseph, the end of what?"

We hear a pathetically sad exhalation, and then his measured words. "All . . . you . . . know."

Jackson and I look at each other in stunned silence.

"I must go."

"No, wait!" Jackson cries out. "What starts it? What starts

the darkness?"

As though from a great distance, Joseph utters, "The Tenth. The dark forces are organizing. Soon they will create the Tenth."

———◆◆———

"What time is it?" I ask as I pan my flashlight around the room, searching for Alder. "And where is my dog?"

"Two o'clock. Yeah, where is he?"

Jackson looks in each loft, while I look in the bathroom and under the clothes hanging in my closet, but he isn't there. Systematically, I go through my cabin, flipping on lights and looking under things. When I get to the kitchen, I am surprised to find him peacefully asleep next to the back cabinets. "There's a good boy," I say, rubbing his head.

"I don't think he even noticed the quake, Elizabeth."

"That's so weird. He hates them and usually gets completely freaked out."

"Maybe it wasn't a real quake. Maybe it just seemed like one."

"You mean like the storm I thought I had, and the power outages."

"Yup."

"But why? What's the point?"

"To isolate you, or bring us together. Either way, it's to focus your attention."

"Well, he got it. And I really don't want to be *focused* again! I'm tired of all this."

"I imagine you are. Come on, I'll make us a cup of tea."

"I'd rather have a slug of scotch."

"No. Herbal tea is better for sleeping."

While he puts the kettle on, I curl up on a kitchen chair, hugging my knees. "How did you know what to say to him?"

"I'm not sure. Training, I guess. Except I figured I had nothing to lose. Even the devil listens to God."

"Well, it seemed to make him stop."

"Yeah, perhaps." He seems deep in thought.

"What do you think he meant about the beginning of the darkness and the end?"

"That's a great question."

"Can you make an educated guess?"

"Only based on what the Bible teaches us from the Book of Revelation. But I'm not sure that's what he was referring to."

"He sounded almost afraid. Especially when he said 'the Tenth.'"

"Yeah, I noticed that, too." Jackson hands me a hot cup of tea and the honey scoop. "Here, put a big glob of this in it."

"It kind of creeped me out." I drizzle honey in my tea and pass the scoop to him. "Who are the dark forces, and what do you suppose a 'Tenth' is?"

"Aside from the obvious"—he winks—"I believe both of those are very good questions—questions for which I don't have answers." He leans his cup toward me to signal a toast. "Here's to a good mystery. Drink up, my darling."

"Jackson, I need to tell you about my dream. It had a creepy bad guy in it, and I've seen him before, recently. He came into the ED and lit himself on fire." I tell him about the dream as best I can remember, although by now it seems jumbled and illogical.

When I finish, Jackson says, "I'm pretty sure we dream about people or events we're trying to work out, and maybe the guy bugged you more than you thought."

"Maybe. Anything else?"

"Yeah. The nine figures in a row. In the first dream, Joseph told you he was part of nine in his world. So that group was probably the nine. And maybe the one who seemed older was a counselor, or whatever."

"Yeah. Go on."

"Well, he said there are nine in our world, too, right?"

I sip my tea as a creepy feeling forms in my gut. "Yeah."

"So, what if our side has a new one? What if that's what he meant by the Tenth?"

"But if we have nine like him, wouldn't we know it?" I ask.

"I'm not sure that's what he meant. I think this goes far beyond nine people."

"Then what does he mean?"

"Not sure—yet."

We sit in silence, sipping our tea until the last sweetened drop is gone.

"Jackson, I don't want to sleep alone. I'm not trying to be cute, and we don't have to do anything. I'm just afraid and want to know you're near."

"I hate to admit it, but I feel the same."

"I've never been through anything like this before, and I'm starting to freak."

"I'll get my blanket and come up to your loft."

A few minutes later we're lying on my bed, me under the covers and Jackson above them, wrapped up in his blanket. With his arms around me and my head buried in his neck, I drift off to sleep.

Unfortunately, his 6:30 a.m. alarm sounds much too quickly, interrupting the most enchanting few hours of sleep I've had in years. My right side is numb from resting in one position against his warm body, but even so, I don't want to budge from the spot.

"Sorry, darling. I've got to get up." Jackson stretches his long arms and yawns.

"Can't we just skip the world today?" I murmur.

"No, we can't. At least, I can't."

"Bummer." I bury my head deeper into his chest.

He pulls away and sits up on the opposite side of the bed. "Why don't you get ready, too, and come with me? We can go to breakfast after the two services."

"Oh, ahhh . . ." I scramble for an excuse. "I don't really do church."

Turning back toward me, he leans down on one elbow. "Well, you better learn how to 'do church' if you're gonna be with me." He gently slaps my thigh. "Come on, girl, no time like the present to take a chance."

I flop my arm over my head, wondering why I'm so resistant. *Maybe it wouldn't be so bad. Maybe I'd be okay.*

Jackson walks around to my side of the bed and pulls my hands to get me up. "Come on, you can do it."

"Fine, okay. But only if you promise breakfast afterwards."

"Deal. Now hop in the shower while I take care of Alder and make us coffee."

Going to church with Jackson is not what I expected. Of course, there are no caskets or pallbearers. Neither are there tears or sorrow. Admittedly, I retain a few isolated recollections of attending Sunday school as a little girl, but those have always been overshadowed by the one memory of consequence I could never forget: a Tuesday morning in church at the age of six when I listened to a strange man talk about my mommy. His words meant nothing to me, and I never understood. I still don't. When my daddy and I left the building, my sadness was inconsolable, and I cried for days. In my young mind, church became enmeshed with my mother's departure, and I knew for certain I didn't want any part of that experience again.

After college, when my dad died of cancer, I was compelled to reenter a church for another funeral. That depressing service only reinforced the misery I associated with places of worship. Then Mac died. For the third time in my life, I listened to meaningless words that offered no comfort and no understanding of why I had been left standing alone once again.

Why I shuddered at the thought of going into a church, any church, has never been a mystery. But today, as I sit through two very different services, I am met with the unexpected:

uplifting music, a cheerful atmosphere, and happy parishioners who seem genuinely glad to be in attendance. I watch in awe as they warmly greet one another, shaking hands and inquiring about families and loved ones. I enjoy watching all the children play together, and the healthy-looking teenagers discussing life's many questions. While the ambiance is appropriately solemn, joy and gratitude abound. Yes, church today is a totally new experience.

Then there's Jackson, I find myself thinking as he stands at the pulpit to speak to the congregation. *Jackson, the man I'm rapidly falling in love with.*

He is amazing. Without notes or script, he speaks from his heart about what matters most to God—the reason for faith so clearly explained, anyone can understand, even me. Remembering the voice from my dream that said, *"You know me,"* I realize the obvious; I do know Him. I've just forgotten.

After the second service, Jackson invites Mike and Sally to join us for brunch at Café Garden. Although the restaurant is crowded with Sunday patrons, Kelly escorts us to a back booth apparently reserved for Jackson. While he tells them of our previous day and a half, I sit in silence, deep in thought. My gaze drifts to him; I see his lips moving, but I can't hear a single word. All I can do is gaze, as I did when he delivered this morning's sermons.

"Elizabeth, are you there?" Jackson asks, waving his hand in front of my eyes.

"Oh, sorry. I was just thinking." I grab his hand under the table and join the conversation.

After our delicious meal, we say goodbye to Mike and Sally and climb into Jackson's SUV.

Jackson turns his electric blue eyes on me. "I know you go back to work tomorrow afternoon, so what would you like to do for the rest of the day? What's your pleasure?"

"Honestly?"

He grins. "Of course. I'm always honest."

"Hey, don't you have to go back to church for something this afternoon?"

"Normally I would, but since I haven't taken much time off in the last six months, I'm letting my associates run things today. I'll be back at it tomorrow."

"Oh, well, in that case, I'd like to go home . . ."

"Oh, okay."

"Wait—you didn't let me finish. I'd like to go home, pack a bag, load up Alder, and go back to your house."

"Really?"

"Yup, that's my pleasure."

"Awesome!" He leans over to kiss me.

Everything about him feels right. Thank you, God.

On the ride to my cabin, we devise a plan. I'll pack a bag for one night at Jackson's, plus load my truck with what I'll need for three shifts at the hospital, then follow him to the airport. I'll be able to leave from there and head straight to the Kingston ferry, saving at least an hour. He'll keep Alder with him for my three-day absence, which is great because Alder will be much happier with him than in the doggie motel.

Under a cloud-covered midafternoon sky, we make our way across the strait toward Vancouver Island. As we climb and gain a little altitude, we fly into thick clouds, which don't seem to bother Jackson in the slightest. He focuses on his instruments and directs us systematically to his protected cove until we land safely. Cutting the engine, he lets the plane drift alongside the dock and jumps out to secure it to the mooring. I guess he's executed this routine so many times, it's almost rote.

Once inside his comfortable home, I get settled in the guest bedroom while Jackson builds a fire in the massive stone fireplace. With impeccable timing, he uncorks a bottle of Chardonnay and pours two glasses. It tastes of oak, nuts, and possibly apples.

Apples? Hmm. I'm not sure, only that it is delicious and has a label I don't recognize.

"This is really good," I gush while ogling the bottles in his temperature-controlled wine closet. "I've never even heard of most of these brands."

"Truthfully, I fly down to Napa Valley a couple of times a year and visit some small boutique wineries I'm familiar with. I sample wine for a few days, buy cases of the ones I like, and bring it all back."

"Wow, what a life."

"Don't make fun of me now."

"No, I'm not. I wouldn't. I'm just thinking what a nice life you lead. You've got a great job where people love you because you give them hope and something to believe in, a loving family, and friends all over the place. And that's not even counting the amazing diversions like your antique car, *Ladybug*, and this beautiful home."

"Yeah, it's all good." He looks at me and cocks his head to one side. "So where are you heading with this?"

"I'm not heading anywhere. Just stating the obvious. From all outward appearances, you have it pretty perfect, and you seem to take it all in stride."

"I try to take life one day at a time and enjoy whatever comes. But my life isn't perfect. It could be, but it's not."

"What's wrong with it?"

"Now you're asking a very personal question." Smiling, he walks toward me and takes hold of my hands. Looking down at me, he moves one hand up to my shirt collar and gently reaches underneath for the platinum chain around my neck. As he pulls the cross out from beneath my shirt, his touch feels electric. The sensation is growing stronger with each contact. "I'm happy to see you wearing this."

"I love it. It's beautiful."

"So are you." He runs his fingers through my hair and strokes my neck.

His touch! I close my eyes to relish the shivers running down my spine. My desire for him is growing exponentially, and I wonder how I could have been such a fool for so long. *Not anymore.* "Jackson, do you think it's possible to fall in love with someone overnight? Or go from friends to lovers in a heartbeat?"

"Yes, I believe it is. Most definitely."

"How would a person know if it's real?"

"Well, I don't know, because it's never happened to me, nor would it."

"Oh." I feel awkward again.

"It wouldn't happen to me, because I've been in love with you for almost four years. And once I fell for you, there was no going back, and no one else would do."

My jaw drops. "You . . . what? Really?" The magic of his words swirls around in my head. "Why didn't you ever say anything?"

"Oh, darling, I did. All the time. I purposely scheduled my time at the gym each week to coincide with your workouts, I frequently asked you to lunch, always invited you skiing, sent you cards for your birthdays and holidays, called to check on you, and generally racked my brain trying to figure out any excuse to see you. But you turned me down at almost every crossroad."

I think back over the past four years. "Honestly, it wasn't on purpose." But I know the real reason. *Time to fess up.* "Mostly, I was afraid. I kept my distance from everyone. I didn't want to know anyone cared."

"And that, my dear Elizabeth, made it all the more intriguing for me."

"I can't believe you stuck it out. I'm deeply flattered."

"I'm a very patient man. I prayed for God to bring you into my life or me into yours, and I trusted that eventually it would happen."

"I'd like to be in your life now, if you don't mind."

"No, I don't mind. The question is, how much in my life?"

I know what he's asking: *How deeply can I commit to a relationship with him? Am I over Mac? Can I accept Jackson as my soul mate and partner?* These are the same questions I've been asking myself. And I think I've reached a conclusion.

"I'm falling in love with you, Jackson. No, let me reword that. I'm already in love with you." The words are out, and it seems okay. I'm not afraid. "What's weird is that it seems easy to go from being friends to being in love. Does that make any sense?"

"Perfect sense."

"So now what?" I know his faith won't allow us to live together before marriage. "Where do we go from here?"

"So now I ask you to marry me."

He says it so simply.

I've never heard those words before. After two years of living with Mac, one day we just decided to get married. So we got a license, found a justice of the peace, and said an oath on a Bible. This is all new.

"Are you gonna? Ask me?"

"Would you mind?"

I feel my voice grow weak and small. "No, I don't think so."

"Stay right here." He lets go of my hands and walks back to his office, where I can hear him opening the wall safe. He returns a few moments later with a small box similar to the one he gave me the previous day. Opening it, he withdraws a velvet jewelry case and opens the lid, hiding the contents from me. While he gets down on one knee, he turns the box around, presenting an emerald-cut solitaire diamond ring.

"Oh!" Total surprise prevents me from saying anything coherent.

He doesn't miss a beat. "Elizabeth, my beloved, would you do me the honor of accepting my hand in marriage?"

I'm stunned. Stunned by the proposal, the ring, the fact that he's gotten down on one knee, everything. *Is he my knight in shining armor? Can I be happy with this man for an eternity?* All my instincts say *yes*—I trust him to take care of my heart and protect my darkest secrets.

"Yes, Jackson, I would be honored to accept your proposal of marriage."

He takes the ring from the box and slides it onto my finger. It fits perfectly.

"I love it! It's so beautiful, so simple, and I can't believe it fits." I wonder briefly how he knew my ring size, but figure he worked it out somehow.

I pull him up from his kneeling position and put my arms around him. Over his shoulder, I can see the ring on my finger; I like looking at it. "I think you need extra kisses for this," I say softly.

"Elizabeth, you will be Mrs. Jackson Howard Morgan, the third. How does that sound?" He kisses me deeply.

"I think Mrs. Elizabeth Kathleen Morgan has a nice ring to it as well." I kiss him back. I'm amazed at how much I love to hold him. Our bodies seem to fit together so perfectly. *Is it possible that two people can be made just for each other?* I don't know, but in our case, it sure seems likely.

We lie on the sofa in front of the fire and snuggle together until after sunset. Folded in his arms, I allow myself to slide into a peaceful security I've never felt before. While my relationship with Mac was full of love and mutual respect, I never permitted myself to feel dependent upon him for anything. Even after we were married, I intentionally maintained a level of autonomy and self-reliance, which I later realized was a roadblock to a deepening bond. Intuitively, I know Jackson can maneuver around any emotional barricade and lovingly dismantle my defensive walls, one brick at a time.

Somewhere between a state of utter relaxation and light sleep, he nudges me gently. "I hate to break this up, but I'm famished. Since you are now officially my fiancée, I'll whip something up for us."

"Hmmm, fiancée, huh? I like the sound of that." I allow him to lazily pull me up from the sofa, and we kiss one more time. As if a total separation can't be tolerated, we hold hands while we walk to the kitchen. "I feel like I'm a teenager again. A teenager in love."

He turns and holds me tightly. "That's what real love does," he whispers. "It makes people young at heart." He pulls away. "Now let's get serious. What sounds good?"

"If I were home, I'd probably have a gourmet meal of peanut butter and jelly. So anything other than that would be a step up."

He laughs. "As enticing as P. B. and J. sounds, I think I can do one better. How about linguini with sautéed scallops and a baguette?"

"Only if you insist. Twist my arm."

As he easily maneuvers around the kitchen, it's obvious he thoroughly enjoys cooking. Since I am a minimalist at meals, having a natural chef around will be a definite asset. My mind shifts to the storm, lost time, the fallen cedar, Roger, and the earthquake, then settles on Joseph—Joseph, the one who's brought all this about. He is the focal point of the mystery. But what is he, really?

"I hate to bring this up," I say, "but what do you think Joseph meant? Is it possible I'm part of an evil plot and don't even know it?"

"No, absolutely not. Get that out of your head."

"So what do you think he meant?"

"I don't know yet, but I intend to find out." Coming to my side, he places a finger under my chin and kisses me gently. "Be patient. We'll figure this out together."

"Okay. It's just a lot to digest."

I sit and sip my wine while he heats the water and chops garlic for sautéing. "So, Elizabeth, when would you like to get married?"

He speaks the words so casually, I almost spit my wine out. "Um, I don't know. What do you think?"

"Well, it's currently the seventh of April, and we'll need a few weeks to prepare, so I'm thinking around the middle of May." He looks up at me from the cutting board. "How about the second Saturday? How does that sound?"

I deliberate for a moment. "Sounds wonderful! For the life of me, I can't think of anything better to do on that particular day."

He gives me a lopsided grin. "Funny. Way to make me feel secure."

"You know I'm only kidding. Where do you want to have the ceremony?" I already know what his answer will be, but ask anyway.

"If it's okay with you, I know a great little church in Port Angeles, and I'm pretty sure they can work us into their schedule."

"So who would officiate? I mean, since you can't, who would you want?"

"Well, I think we have two choices. We can ask my associate pastor, who would be great, or we can ask Roger."

"Roger? Why would we ask him?"

"Because he went through seminary school, too, and is an ordained minister."

"What? You can't be serious!"

"Don't sound so surprised. Just because he's a man of few

words doesn't mean he has few talents. Quite the opposite is true."

"So why isn't he a pastor like you?"

"He gets too nervous in front of people and could never get over it. Plus, he got his bachelor's in mechanical engineering and liked it almost as much, so he decided to pursue that instead. Ultimately, he ended up doing stuff he really loves and is comfortable at."

"Wow. Once again, you could blow me over with a feather!"

"So who would be your choice?"

"I'd be honored to have Roger do it, if he's willing."

We spend the rest of the evening discussing plans for our wedding. Considering that one week ago, I was a lonely widow seemingly doomed to solitude, I'm having a hard time accepting this enormous shift in my life as anything but surreal. But the more we talk about it, the more genuine it becomes. We decide on a private ceremony with just a few close friends and relatives, followed by a larger reception at C'est Si Bon. I have a few minor hurdles to deal with, like a wedding dress, bridesmaids, flowers, and invitations, but I figure somehow, it's all doable.

"I think we need to make a few calls," Jackson says.

"To who?"

He's already started dialing. "Hi, Mom, how ya doing? . . . Yeah, I'm okay. . . . Sorry to call so late, but I need to give you some news. . . . No, nothing's wrong. Actually, everything's perfect."

He tilts the phone out from his ear so I can hear both sides of the conversation. "I asked Elizabeth to marry me."

"Well, good for you!" responds a woman's cheerful voice. "I sure hope she said yes. Wait, let me get your dad. He'll love this!"

I can hear her muffle the phone on her chest while she yells, "Honey, pick up the phone! It's your son. He wants to tell you something."

Repeating the news a second time, Jackson fills them in on our engagement and plans. I listen to the animated discussion with great interest. It's obvious they care deeply about one another and have a close bond.

"Is she there?" his mom, Rebecca, asks.

"I'm right here," I answer. "I've been listening to the whole thing."

"Welcome to our family, my dear," Jackson Sr. says. "I think my boy's waited a long time to ask you."

"I guess I'm the only one who didn't know how he felt."

"That's okay," Rebecca says. "All the best things in life are worth waiting for. I'm so happy for you both. This is just thrilling!"

"I must agree," I say. "It really is!"

"Okay now, kids," she continues, "can I help with any plans or arrangements? You know that's my favorite thing in life to do."

"Um, I don't know. I don't want to impose."

"Actually, Mom, that'd be great. Elizabeth has to work, and so do I, so we'd love to have your help. It would mean a lot to both of us."

I shoot him a curious glance, but he holds up his hand and continues, "Also, she needs a dress and a few items for the honeymoon, so maybe you'd like to accompany her on a shopping trip and pick out some stuff. That way you two can get acquainted."

"I'd love that!" She sounds so excited, I understand why he suggested it. "Now let's see, we could go to New York or Los Angeles, but—"

"Mom, reality check here. We're on a budget and she can't miss work, so we'll probably have to keep it local."

"Oh, right. Sorry about that—you know how I get going. Seattle has great shops. I'll start looking."

Jackson Sr. breaks in. "Now son, I haven't discussed this

idea with your mom yet, but I think we'd like to give you your honeymoon as our wedding present."

"Jackson, that's a great idea!" Rebecca says.

"Then it's settled. You figure out the destination and time, and we'll do the rest."

"Wow, you guys, that is really generous!" I say.

"By the way, Elizabeth," Rebecca asks, "what do you think of the diamond?"

"Oh, um . . . it's huge and gorgeous, and I've always loved emerald cuts."

"It was my grandmother's, and I can't think of a better place for it than on your finger."

"Oh my! I had no idea. I'm truly honored and will cherish it forever."

"If you don't mind my asking, who's gonna give away the bride?" Jackson Sr. asks.

I bite my lip. "I don't know. I hadn't thought about that." I rack my brain and look at Jackson. "Probably a friend of mine named Mike."

"Is that Mike who's married to Sally?" Rebecca asks.

"Ah, yes."

"Great! We know them, and he's perfect."

"Now about your reception . . ." Jackson Sr. says.

"Dad, you heard me. Our wedding, our budget."

"Well, since your sister never got married, I feel a little cheated out of my right to spoil someone with a reception. What do you say we pitch in a little?"

I shrug my shoulders and defer to Jackson.

"Okay, Dad. That'd be great. Thanks."

We all chat for another twenty minutes before saying goodbye. They insist on visiting immediately to coincide with my days off so Rebecca and I will have ample time to shop for a dress and work out the reception plans. They are so happy and positive about everything, I feel my own level of excitement and anticipation skyrocketing.

"We need to talk to Roger and tell Mike and Sally," Jackson says, "but we can do that in the morning."

"Agreed."

"As for sleeping, I suggest we fold out the couch in the living room, build a roaring fire, and sleep next to each other like we did last night. What do you say?"

"Absolutely perfect."

26

Through a gray afternoon drizzle, I make my way to the Kingston ferry terminal and wait in line while the boat docks and offloads the westbound vehicles and passengers. The unsettling events with Joseph and his hints of foreboding about the "beginning of the end" weigh heavily on my mind. Using my favorite mental technique, I try to compartmentalize, forcing Joseph into a tiny little box at the back of my brain.

You can't think about him at work, and you absolutely can't mention it to anyone. Put him away until Thursday morning, and then you can worry about it.

I close my eyes and refocus on Jackson: wonderful, dreamy Jackson. As I open my eyes, the first thing I see is my left hand on the steering wheel and the stunning diamond adorning my finger. I've never seen any stone as lovely, and find myself admiring it over and over. *I wonder if I'll ever get used to it.*

An attendant waves me forward in the line.

Finally. Let's get this show on the road!

Totally unenthused about leaving the peninsula to go back

to work, I want the next three days to fly by as fast as possible. I navigate the truck across the huge loading ramp and downward into the belly of the ferry to the final parking spot, where I turn off the engine. As I look up through the windshield, the scene in front of me vanishes, and in its place appears a terrible vision. It's the parking lot outside the ED, and a woman is lying dead next to my truck. I look more closely and see that the woman is . . . me.

Oh, God!

I try to look around the body to determine what happened, but the vivid image evaporates, giving way once again to the vehicles in front of me. I tell myself nothing's gonna happen. *I'm fine. Just make it through the next three days.* Still, the vision gives me the creeps. I shake it off.

As I refocus on the previous week, the nonstop events seem more like an illogical fantasy than reality. *What a crazy whirlwind!* On the one hand, my new relationship with Jackson resembles a wonderful fairytale I can't get enough of. On the other hand, the events with Joseph have been filled with intermittent anxiety, despair, and curiosity, all at once. And then there's God: a voice lost, a voice found.

Focus on Jackson and God. I stuff Joseph back into his designated compartment and try to swallow the key.

The crossing between Kingston and Edmonds takes less than forty minutes, but provides ample time for me to refill my coffee and use the ladies' room. Once on the Edmonds side, I switch to some kind of mental autopilot, hit I-5, and head straight south into the heart of Seattle toward Bayside Medical Center. It's located smack dab in the middle of Capitol Hill, a once-classy upscale locale. Decades before, the area was affectionately nicknamed "Pill Hill" because of all the hospitals, clinics, and medical offices in such close proximity to one another. Sadly, over time, it slowly became more inner-city, and currently isn't a neighborhood I'd choose to walk around in at night unaccompanied. Even so, it still sports quaint shops, local markets, and unique delis and is safe enough during daylight hours.

I turn off the freeway at James Street and head straight east, up the hill to Broadway and the hospital. Parking on the upper garage, I grab my bag, lock my truck, and head inside. Not knowing who is scheduled as charge nurse tonight, I've arrived a little early so I can request the Trauma side.

"Hey, Monica," I call out, relieved to see that she's coming on shift when I spot her in the locker room.

"Hey back, Elizabeth! Good to see you. You feeling better?"

"Yeah. Mostly just run-down and exhausted. The extra few days off made a big difference." I reach up to open my locker.

"Whoa, girl! What the heck's on your finger?" She moves toward me and grabs my hand. "Oh my goodness, Elizabeth. That's got to be three carats!" She gawks at the ring, then at me, then back at the ring. "Is it real?"

I try and fail to stifle a big grin. "Yeah, it's real." It feels odd confirming that something is different about me today, but obviously my pending wedding isn't going to be a secret for long. I hold my hand up in the air to display the ring in better light, adding, "It is pretty big, isn't it?"

"Uh, ye-ah!"

"Well, my fiancé is just as fabulous."

"Oh, man! I want all the nitty-gritty and more. Please let me take you to breakfast in the morning after we get off! I want every juicy detail." She hugs me tightly and then stands back. "I'm so happy for you. This is wonderful!"

"Thanks. I'm really happy, too!"

"It shows. You have a glow I haven't seen in you for a long time." She hugs me again. "Of all the people in the world, you deserve this." Opening the door to leave, she looks back at me. "I hope this isn't a secret, 'cause you know what a big mouth I have."

"You're the first one I've told, but I figure that by the end of the week it'll be on the evening news." We both laugh. "By the way, since you're charge tonight, can you put me in Trauma?"

"You got it. See you out there."

I put my stuff in my locker, load my pockets with my usual gear, drape my stethoscope over my shoulder, and head out into organized chaos.

Word of my engagement spreads like wildfire through the department, bringing more congratulatory hugs and ring inspections than I thought possible. The news even makes its way through the police, fire, and medic circles, which surprises me. Considering how much I otherwise value my privacy, tonight I enjoy every single moment of the encouraging attention.

The nicest reaction of all comes unexpectedly from Dr. Bennett. Although I've always known him to be a very kind, compassionate man, we've never spoken about anything personal. So I'm surprised when he makes a special appearance in my Trauma room.

"Oh, hi, Dr. Bennett." I note his crisp white lab coat, personalized with blue script lettering embroidered under the left lapel. "What can I do for you?"

"Nothing. I just stopped in to tell you how happy I am for you and your upcoming marriage." His deep voice and Midwestern drawl make the words sound incredibly sincere.

I put my chart down. "Thanks for saying that. It happened kinda fast, but it definitely feels right. And I've know the man a long time."

"What does he do, if you don't mind my asking?"

"I don't mind. He's the senior pastor at a Christian church in Port Angeles."

"Of course he is." He looks down and rubs his chin thoughtfully with one hand.

"What does that mean?"

"Oh, just that it makes perfect sense." He puts his hands on my shoulders in a fatherly manner and continues, "Elizabeth, I've known you since before Mac died, and I've watched you struggle with your broken heart and spiritual doubts. I've prayed for you at every turn, every step of the way. I knew God had a wonderful plan for you. It was just a matter of time."

Stunned again, I wonder how many people in my small world have seen things in me which I refused to acknowledge or let surface. "You prayed for me?"

He nods. "Every shift, every day, every time I thought about you. I pray for everyone, but especially, I've prayed for you."

"I had no idea. I guess I should say, 'Thank you.'"

"You're welcome, but the real thanks probably should go to the Big Guy Upstairs." He points toward the ceiling. "Prayer works. I've seen it time and time again."

"Are you some kind of minister, too?"

"Me? No, just another sinner. But I'm a Christian sinner, savvy enough to know my place in the world, as well as my limits. All the rest is up to God."

"Wow. I might want to talk to you about something sometime." I hear one of my patients groaning.

"Anytime. Now if you don't mind, I'll give you a quick hug, wish you all the best, and be on my way."

"Thanks again."

At the double doors he pauses and turns back. "Please send me an announcement. I've got the perfect gift."

Overwhelmed by his kindness, I want to stay in my thoughts for a few moments longer, but it isn't to be. The groaning becomes a loud moan, and I know the patient needs more pain medication. *Ah well, time to focus.*

Mondays typically aren't as busy as weekends, but due to the pouring rain, slick roads, or simply bad karma, by midnight the entire department is slammed with patients. We have a three-hour wait for non-emergency walk-in patients, and the four gurneys in my section have been steadily occupied by a stream of patients presenting a wide variety of illnesses and injuries. So far, nothing too bizarre has jumped out, which is fine with me.

Tony, the nursing student, is still on his rotation and once again assigned to shadow me. He looks much more at ease tonight, and it's impressive to see the improvement in his overall skills and confidence in such a short period of time.

Monica rounds the corner. "Hey, Mrs. Morgan, can you move any of these patients?"

"Ha! Funny girl. Yeah, actually." I point to a male patient who accidentally made a jagged cut in his hand and wrist with a router. "He can go home as soon as his IV antibiotic is done. Everything else is finished, and his ride is waiting for him."

"Can we move him out into the hall?"

"Why, what's up?"

"Motorcycle accident coming in. Really bad. Missing a limb or something."

"Oh, sounds lovely. Yeah, sure, let's move this guy. If I get overwhelmed, can you finish the discharge so he doesn't lie there for hours?"

"Absolutely."

Tony and I move the router patient out to the wide hallway while Chuck, my nursing assistant, cleans up the area and moves another trauma bed in. No sooner is all the equipment wiped down than I hear the familiar words over the loud-speaker, "Medics on the ramp, medics on the ramp."

"Watch these other ones," I say to Chuck. "I'll be right back." I speed down the corridor toward the ambulance entrance with Tony hot on my heels.

Three medics and a cop are just coming through the automatic sliding doors, pushing a gurney between them, as we round the corner.

Oh Lord, what a mess.

The patient has an ambu mask over his mostly skinless face and is being force-fed oxygen. The left side of his head is smashed in like the shell of a boiled egg that's been tapped against a hard surface. With all the blood, guts, and road rash, the most distinguishable characteristic is his overall stature. Based upon his size, the patient is male and somewhere between the ages of twenty and forty. What's quite clear is that he's badly beaten up.

"This way, boys. Let's go." I grab the foot of the rolling bed and steer it toward my room. "Tell me what we've got."

"Thirty-three-year-old male riding a motorcycle, drove straight into a brick wall. Possible suicide attempt. No helmet, no leathers. Must've had last-minute regrets, 'cause from the road marks, he slammed on the brakes, skidded, and slid sideways."

"I'm guessing he didn't stop in time."

"Nope. He slammed into the wall broadside and flew about fifty feet. Lots of head trauma and skull fractures. He's a mess."

When we reach the room, I push the gurney up next to the trauma bed. Since the patient already has a C-collar around his neck and is strapped to a backboard, it's easy to lift the entire package up and over. This accident victim queues up every head, neck, and spine precaution in existence, and treatment protocols are already synced.

The medic continues, "Not much movement at the scene. Vital signs minimal, thready pulse, respiration about five per minute, shallow and labored. His left arm is severely fractured. Surprised it's not severed. I'm sure he needs blood."

As the Trauma team arrives, I strip away the remnants of his shredded jeans and knit shirt, picking the larger pieces out of raw muscle sinew. Though I'm normally immune to such sights, I'm repulsed by the sight of his mangled forehead and face, bloody and caked with gravel and asphalt. *Looks like he's been scalped by savages.*

From gross observation, it appears he suffered crushing injuries to his right side when he hit the brick wall sideways. And like the force from an ejection seat, the speed must have catapulted him out in a reverse direction, hurling him down the concrete, where he sustained horrific impact and sheering injuries to his left side. Much of his left eye socket, cheek, and jawbone no longer exist, presumably ripped from his face during his slide across unforgiving pavement. What remains of his left arm is oddly bent, indicating multiple fractures. Below his torn jeans, he's missing the left shoe and part of the foot. This guy was the eight ball in a quintessential bank shot, and quite probably every vital organ in his body is damaged.

The medic drones on, "I got an eighteen in his right arm, IV wide open. Found this in his pocket." He produces a small plastic bag of white powder. He looks up toward the door. "Hey, Doc."

Dr. Bennett walks to the bed and dons gloves while the medic repeats his monologue. Meanwhile, I get ready with the crash-cart supplies while the team struggles to insert all the routine lines. Working as fast as possible, we address the most serious, life-threatening problems first.

Ann, our sweet department secretary, walks in shielding her eyes from the horror. "His name is Arnold Johnson, and his wife is in the waiting room. Here are his labels." Ann wastes no time in departing.

A police officer enters the arena at the same time and adds, "Probably doesn't matter, but this may not be a suicide. Apparently this yoyo likes to party. Cousin was at the scene, higher'n a kite. Said they were playin' chicken with a wall. We got the cousin in custody for possession and general stupidity, among other things. And it was the cousin's bike."

I stick a label on the clear plastic bag the medic is still holding and watch him hand it to the officer.

"You can add this to your evidence," the medic says. "I pulled it from his jeans pocket."

Dr. Bennett repositions to the head of the bed and gently feels the man's neck and head. He starts barking orders. "Okay, folks, enough chatting. This guy's bad." He looks at the officer. "Everyone out who's not essential." To the staff he says, "I can feel cranial fractures, his neck's unstable, and I'm sure he's got a pneumothorax as well as other internal injuries. I want a stat C-spine so I can decide where to put the airway. He needs a vent, labs, type, and cross with at least six units banked, and tell surgery to be ready."

Monica, who's standing by the door, issues her standard reply, "You got it," and escorts the officer out of the room.

"And I want neuro stat and a cardio-thoracic surgeon, and put the bypass team on alert. I got a feeling we're gonna need 'em all." Looking over at me, he winks and whispers so that only I can hear, "Now's a good time to pray."

The patient's respiration is minimal at best and won't support life for long. While X-ray shoots the neck and back films, known as "C-spine," a senior resident inserts a central line into Arnold's right groin and quickly sutures it in position. Another resident moves an ultrasound wand over the patient's belly to check for soft tissue damage. There's plenty. No matter how much we poke and prod him, the patient remains completely flaccid, nonresponsive.

It takes less than six minutes to get the call from Radiology that the patient has three fractured vertebrae in the lumbar region and another one in his neck. The radiologist, Dr. Gross, has also identified a lower skull fracture near the base of the brain and multiple fractured ribs.

I key my microphone. "Monica, where's neurology? We need 'em now!"

"I don't think he's gonna make it," Dr. Bennett says, watching the monitor. "His heart just stopped, and his belly's still expanding. Let's go, folks, CPR!" He looks at the respiratory therapist. "Trach him."

Chuck jumps up onto a stool and starts regular compressions, but immediately stops. We all hear the crunching sound emanating from the patient's chest. The ribs have split and probably splintered inward. Chuck's hands still rest on the patient's sternum. He looks at Dr. Bennett. "What do you want me to do, Doc?"

"Try two rounds and see if we get anything."

Doing compressions on a chest with splintered ribs potentiates nasty risks like punctured lungs, a punctured pericardial sac, or even a punctured heart. But the only alternative is to do nothing and allow certain death.

Chuck proceeds with two rounds while I push drugs into the IV line and the resident sticks the adhesive paddles on. As a last resort, we shock him at settings of 200, 300, and 360 joules. No response. It's over. Arnold is dead. The badly damaged, unrecognizable thirty-three-year-old has expired less than ten minutes after arriving at the hospital.

Dr. Bennett calls the time of death, and we all cease our hive-like activities. From the corner of my eye I notice Doc leaning over the body, speaking to himself for a moment. Then, almost imperceptibly, he makes the sign of the cross on his own chest and briefly touches his thumb to Arnold's forehead. I think back over all the years I've worked with Dr. Bennett and wonder if he's been invisibly doing this all along.

"He's in a better place now," he says.

"It's so sad. So needless."

"Yup. The result of a bad choice which will no doubt affect the lives of hundreds of people."

Bad choice. His words ring loud in my ears, reminding me of what Jackson said two days earlier. Immediately, the vision I had of the neural network of the entire universe pops back into my head.

"Yes, Elizabeth. This is what it is all about."

"Joseph?" I look around.

"Yes." I am briefly able to focus on one particularly bright pathway among the network's interwoven complexities. But it suddenly goes dark. *"Another life extinguished. Humanity's choices, ad infinitum."* The neural network image and the voice are gone as quickly as they came.

I hear Dr. Bennett's voice. "Clean up what you can," he tells me. "Then let's you and me both go talk to the wife. I'll meet you in five."

"Okay." I shake off the vivid vision and key the mic to tell Monica the plan. Then I say, "Tony, take a break and be back in thirty. Chuck, take all the lines out, wipe him off as best you can, and cover him with a clean white sheet. The family may want to see him before we bag him up. Monica's gonna watch my patients. When I get back, you can go on break." I start cleaning up the mess on the floor.

"Okay," they both answer.

Dr. Bennett meets me five minutes later. "You doing okay, Elizabeth?"

"Yeah, I just hate stuff like that."

"You mean trauma?"

"No, not trauma. Stupid people and bad outcomes. Irreparable damage and irreversible death."

"Me, too. It's the worst part about being a doctor."

Arriving at the all-too-familiar, blue-carpeted "quiet room" entrance, we pause to ask reverently for a little guidance. Doc opens the door for me.

Inside the room, four people are waiting: an older, well-dressed white couple who look to be in their late fifties, a young Hispanic woman in her late twenties, and an adorable little boy coloring in a book. They all look up expectantly as we walk through the door.

"Are you the family of Arnold Johnson?" Dr. Bennett asks.

The older gentleman solemnly stands. "I'm Ralph Johnson, Arnold's father. This is my wife LouAnn, our daughter-in-law, Christine, and our grandson, Peter."

"I'm Dr. Bennett, and this is my nurse, Elizabeth."

Dr. Bennett explains everything to the adults as delicately as possible, excluding the gory details. Since labs aren't back yet and an autopsy has not been done, we have no proof Arnold was high on crack, so that isn't mentioned. It seems prudent to allow the family as much dignity as possible.

They all seem like friendly, hardworking people who don't deserve to hear the terrible news we have to break. Looking at the innocent little boy, I can relate to how his world will never make sense to him again. No child deserves this.

Christine sits down and buries her head in her hands. "You don't have to lie to me," she says. "He was probably loaded or something. This is so stupid. What am I gonna do?"

Arnold's mother sits down next to her and puts her arms around her. "It's okay. We're here for you." Both women start to sob.

I place the tissue box between them.

"I just found out I'm pregnant," Christine says. She looks up, tears streaming down her cheeks. "I was gonna tell him tonight."

Oh, God. What a disaster.

A few minutes later, a social worker arrives and agrees to keep Peter occupied while the adults pay their respects to Arnold's body. Still plagued by my own horrific nightmares, I know beyond a shadow of a doubt that the visual images of his torn and ruptured body will leave an indelible impression upon each person. This is a night they will never forget.

Monica assigns another nurse to look after my other patients while I finish the details on Arnold. After the family departs, I move to the closet and pull out a folded black bag in a sealed clear plastic wrapper. I notice Tony hanging around.

"Is this your first traumatic death, Tony?"

"Yeah. No. Actually, it's my first death."

"It sucks, doesn't it?"

"Yeah. It's so cold. So final."

"It is that."

"What happens to him now?"

"We put a tag on his toe, put him in this bag, and take him to the morgue."

"Oh, crap."

"Here, you can assist. It might help the shock wear off."

I open the package, unfold the bag, and find the toe tag inside. I stick one of Arnold's labels on the tag and attach the wire to his right big toe, which is partially severed. Then I unzip the black bag and open it up wide. It's kind of like a large garment bag, but it doesn't hold anything you'd ever want to wear. "We'll have to sort of roll him around to get him into it. Grab some more gloves."

Returning from his break, Chuck joins the effort. Together we get Arnold into the bag and onto a transport gurney. I zip the bag closed and cover the entire thing with a clean white sheet. *Who are we fooling? Everyone knows this is a dead body.*

"Come on, Tony, let's go to the morgue." We steer the gurney toward the back elevator. "Punch the down arrow."

We descend two levels into the bowels of the medical center and exit the elevator at the lower basement, where the real boogieman lives. Past the main pharmacy through two deserted, dimly lit corridors, we halt in front of a locked door identified as MORGUE by its placard. I unlock and open it. Unlike the scenes portrayed by Hollywood, this is the real McCoy.

Inside are long steel cabinets resembling large, wide pizzeria ovens. About two feet in height and seven feet in length, the cabinets are stacked one on top of the other, floor to ceiling. The individual doors pull down and lie flat, allowing the bodies to be lifted and slid in sideways. Once the body is in, the door closed and the latches secured, no doubt remains about the finality of death.

Tony and I leave the morgue in silence. There just isn't much to say.

27

"Hey, don't forget about breakfast," Monica says as she comes through the double doors into Trauma 2. "We get off in fifteen minutes and can run to the omelet place around the corner. My treat, while you tell me all about your engagement."

"Yeah, I should get out of here on time. I only have this one fellow left, and he's easy." I adjust his IV site.

"Did someone say 'breakfast'?" a familiar voice asks.

I look up from my patient and am shocked to see Jackson standing in the doorway. "What are you doing here? How'd you get in?"

"Well, that's a fine welcome, if ever I heard one!" He flashes a wide smile that almost makes my knees weak.

Dang, he looks gorgeous. Bless my soul! What a sight for sore eyes!

"Oh, so this is your Prince Charming. I'd marry him, too!" Laughing, Monica holds out her hand. "Hi, I'm Monica, and you must be Jackson. Very nice to meet you."

"The pleasure is all mine. I hope you'll allow me to take

both you hardworking nurses to breakfast."

"Jackson, I'm really glad to see you, and we'd love to have breakfast with you." I pull him to one side and lower my voice. "But really, what are you doing here? And how the heck did you get past security?"

"First, I wanted to see you, so I flew over. It only takes about thirty minutes, you know. Second, I'm acquainted with a few people in this hospital, so getting past security was easy. Now, about breakfast—I'll be waiting out front for you two ladies." He winks and walks out.

"Oh man, Elizabeth, he's perfect! I'm swooning! Does he have a brother? What a doll!"

She's right. "Yeah, he really is perfect."

As promised, Jackson takes us to breakfast. Over a delicious meal of waffles, sausage, and chamomile tea, we have an animated discussion of our wedding plans and engagement. An hour later, bellies full, we say farewell to Monica. She and I both need sleep.

"Come on, Mrs. Morgan, let's get some sleep," Jackson says as we walk back toward the hospital.

"What do you mean? I sleep at the hospital between my shifts. You can't be there with me."

"I know. That's why I got a hotel room. And it's right around the corner."

"What?" I stop on the sidewalk and turn to look at him. "Are you nuts?"

"Yup. Crazy in love with you, and I can't help myself."

"Oh, Jackson, this is stupid. Really stupid. We're gonna spend more in one night than I just made. That makes no sense."

"What makes no sense is that you're standing here arguing with me about something I've already done." He smiles and hugs me. "I missed you and just couldn't take the separation."

"I missed you, too. Okay, I give in. By the way, where's Alder?"

"At Roger's, playing with the kids."

Back at the hospital, I grab the overnight bag from my truck and gear from my locker and get into the car Jackson is driving. "This is nice. Is this a rental?"

"No, this is my Seattle car."

"A Seattle car?" I look at the leather seats and well-appointed interior. "It's nice."

"Thanks. It's all-wheel drive, great in the snow and steep city hills, and carries a fair amount in the rear. My parents come here a lot and use it whenever they're in town. I keep it at Boeing Field." He bends toward me in the seat and puts his warm hand on my neck. "Sounds like you had a rough night. Want to talk about it?"

"Not really," I say, inhaling deeply. "Stupid decisions, stupid outcomes. It's tough to watch people destroy not only their own lives, but their loved ones', too. The saddest part is, the ones left behind will never understand."

"I'm here for you. If you want to talk, just let me know. Now you need some sleep."

28

I'm standing in the large, semicircular foyer of an elegant art-deco-style performance center, dwarfed beneath the vast ceiling. Intercepting arches adorned with romantic Renaissance-style frescos top the embellished promenade, replete with lavish, eighteenth-century-style velveteen furniture. Brocade tapestries drape gracefully around the outer multistory windows, and lush carpeting woven with giant fleur-de-lis designs extends throughout the foyer's inner circle. Tall, wide sally ports embossed with carved plaster ribbons and bows offer a grand entry to the main venue.

Three times the theater lights blink off and on. I look down at my hands and see I have no ticket.

A girl dressed in a frilly pink chiffon dress, a dark pink satin belt, lacy ankle socks, and white Mary Jane shoes approaches. Her long dark hair is woven into thick braids. She stops in front of me, furrows her brow, and says, "You need to decide." With her nose up in the air, she disappears through the nearest portal.

"Pay no attention to that twit," says a bent old woman wearing a black silk cape. Crooked fingers grip her goose-head cane as she struggles to ambulate towards me. Despite her difficulties, she manages a warm smile. I try to bridge the gap between us but am unable to lift my feet. By the time she traverses the distance, the uppity girl reappears.

"It's starting!" the girl says, tapping her foot. "Are you coming or not?"

With a glance in the young girl's direction, the old woman tilts her head and gently pats my arm. "It's not yet your time, dearie." Shaking her head toward the main hall, she hobbles past me through the foyer and exits the building.

The theater lights blink off and on three more times.

Able to lift my feet, I take a few steps toward the venue entrance. But without a proper pass, I can proceed no farther than the nearest archway. At least from my vantage point I am able to see most of the theater's seemingly infinite rows of tiered seating, although the stage is disappointingly far away, a distant miniature.

The structural design is perfect in its elegant simplicity. Flying buttresses cap the cavernous interior, arching over high ceilings, and, like the foyer, are elaborately decorated with colorful frescos. Inserted into the angular walls at each descending tier level are fifty arched sally ports, which connect the main theater to outer arenas consisting of vastly unique frontiers. Each one, while individual in its construction, nevertheless contributes significantly to the whole of the theater.

Supporting the arch points, foundational white marble columns reverently point skyward like giant old-growth redwoods. Art-deco sconces, cleverly embedded within the walls and stairs, provide subtle, indirect guidance in times of darkness. Built strong to withstand the adversities of time and conflicting interpretations, this entire masterpiece is obviously an iconic architectural achievement, perhaps the only one of its kind.

Through the multitude of portals, I watch as thousands of attendees pour in through the fifty portals and search for their assigned seats. Slathered face makeup disguises their features, as if they are trying to hide their true identities. The women, flaunting decadent wealth and lacking all subtlety, wear lavishly beaded gowns and drag furs behind their spiked heels. Gaudy, jewel-laden tiaras perch upon swirling beehive hairdos, screaming import and stature. Watching the women, I see them openly envy each other, yet I suspect they secretly despise themselves.

Equally showy in their finely crafted tuxedos, the men prance like peacocks in their starched, gem-studded, brilliantly-colored ruffled shirts and matching gloves. Complete with black top hats and long, silk scarves, they strut about, tapping the ground with carved ivory walking sticks.

The audience sips champagne from crystal flutes and chatters animatedly as the orchestra warms up in its darkened pit below. A single blink of the lights, and darkness settles over everything.

Silence ensues. The anticipation is palpable.

From the deep recesses of the stage, a single bright spot illuminates the way for the maestro as he strides deliberately to the director's platform. Without acknowledging the audience, he bows his head, indicating that applause is expected. The response is a resounding, thunderous standing ovation.

From my distant vantage, he appears to be but a wisp of a man, with slicked-back graying hair, narrow mustache, and a goatee. A man of immense power, he wears the finest-quality long-tailed black tuxedo, a crisp white shirt adorned with large jeweled studs, gloves, and a monocle on a gold chain.

By lifting a single finger, he silences the entire room. After a slight nod, he turns toward the musicians and raises his thin baton. On his downward stroke, the music starts. My own anticipation quickly turns to horror as the first note emanates pure cruelty. Instead of Mozart or Beethoven, angry screeches of discordant, chaotic sound fill the room.

Oh my God, make it stop! I scream silently, covering my ears. *How can these people stand this?* But adoringly, the enthralled audience wails back and forth, weeping tears of joy and applauding quietly. *How is it possible that I can miss the unheard melodies they seem to love?* Desperately wanting to escape the agony, I try to leave, but my feet are glued to the floor again.

My attention shifts to the stage, where a random series of lights brings performing groups into focus. Three massive sumo wrestlers lumber out from a main wing, standing side by side, arms locked in solidarity. Nine ballet dancers clad in black silk capes over black tights and leotards pirouette out from an opposite wing. They each sport crisp white neck bands below their expressionless faces.

Initially, these small groups move in unison to a common purpose, supporting each other against would-be foes. But with minimal instruction from the maestro, they change their routine, leaping and lumbering in opposition to each other. As they vie for superiority, their precious synchronism is erased.

Next, more than four hundred colorful acrobats emerge from the multitude of sally ports and fill the stage, half from the right side and half from the left. At first they tumble and jump concordantly, but a simple wink from the maestro, and they begin flipping their partners high into the air, disregarding the landings. One hundred opera singers come into view from another wing. Although the music is confusing, they seem to partially harmonize until the maestro directs them to blare unrelated, discordant arias. Fire-eating men and women with individual spotlights perform until they spontaneously combust, and knife throwers hurl long, shiny blades, impaling whoever is in their path. Destructive chaos reigns, and the stage is transformed into a bloodbath.

The maestro now turns toward the audience and points his thin baton to a rear corner of the theater. With a downward stroke, the corner of the building begins to crumble inward, barely perceptibly at first, then with growing speed. He points his wand to the opposite rear corner and makes a second downward stroke, causing it to insidiously crumble inward as well.

The maestro redirects his energies to the orchestra again, signaling them to play louder. The multitudes in attendance appear unaware of the slow destruction of the theater's back corners, as the crumbling continues and white dust billows into the room from the falling debris. Not even the fine concrete powder coating their bodies, nor the large chunks of falling wall plaster crashing down on them, can capture their attention. All remain riveted on the maestro, oblivious to the ruin.

As the majestic rear cornerstones fall, the beautiful arched ceiling loses its support, causing it to tumble downward. Thousands of the enthralled patrons are annihilated beneath the crushing collapse. Now silent, they are eternally entombed.

Then the spotlight falls upon a new, smaller stage right in the middle of the audience. At the center of the spotlight, a young, blond-haired boy is wrestling a horned bull.

Joseph!

Ignoring the booing audience, his eyes find me through the vast darkness at the back of the theater. We look at each other, and our gazes lock.

"Can you see?" he asks.

"I see how magnificent this once was," I reply.

"Yet as the magnificence wanes, this last bastion of hope becomes a monument only to the lies, corruption, and power of evil."

"Are you saying evil is always victorious?"

"Yes, when it grows unchecked. Evil can only be stopped by those it is focused on destroying."

"But they seem to embrace their fate. Look at them—they are relishing the orchestrated cruelty and death."

"Good, Elizabeth. You are beginning to understand."

"It is hard to face."

"But it is imperative that you do."

"Why? What can I do? I don't even have a ticket."

"You do not need a ticket to awaken to the truth."

"The truth?"

"Yes. The orchestra playing for the maestro believes he is akin to a god. Their music portrays that image to the performers and the masses until they believe the lie as well. Eventually, few remain who can see the small, dark man for what he really is."

"What is he—really?"

"A statue of red, hot coals wrapped in a skin of temptation. His smoldering smiles promise everything. All they have to do is embrace darkness and relinquish their souls."

"But why would people willingly give away their essence?"

"Because they cannot see past their own existence. They have lost sight of the Light."

"Is there nothing we can do to stop it?"

"Not unless humanity awakens." He closes his eyes. "Feel fortunate. You alone get a glimpse of the likely future. Now, witness the finality."

As the maestro lowers his baton, Joseph allows the bull's thick horn to impale his belly.

"Joseph!" I scream as his image fades.

This moment of gore only heightens the audience's thrill as they clap and cheer. They seem to love every movement. Feeling only agony, I avert my eyes from the hideous sight before me and look up, past the partially destroyed building to the brilliant sun and blue sky overhead. Clouds zoom by, darkness follows, and daylight returns, repeating the cycles in rapid-fire succession, time-lapse-style.

I understand. *Evil takes only prisoners. Time takes none.*

As my gaze readjusts to the grand interior now enmeshed in cruelty and destruction, I understand that Joseph was right. No one seems concerned about the maestro's unchecked power. Quite the contrary—the masses are permitting him to destroy this bastion of beauty and are celebrating the demise of the dead and buried. Whether ignoring their impending doom or welcoming it, they perversely champion him.

As the orchestra plays more vigorously, the maestro points his wand to the performers and increases their furious tempo. With each stroke, the surviving dancers, singers, and acrobats frenetically swirl faster and faster while the orchestra clashes and bangs, keeping pace with the wand's direction.

The noise continues as the maestro turns his back to the stage to face the audience, his expression one of deep satisfaction. Raising his baton toward the right side of the theater, he issues a single downward stroke, and the beautiful walls begin to crumble. Since the rear cornerstones have already collapsed, it isn't long before the walls perish as well. Unable to bear up under the weight of the destruction, the strong marble pillars crash inward. Mercilessly, the maestro flicks his wrist in the opposite direction. The unstoppable debris floods outward through each of the fifty sally ports, contaminating the interior of their venues as well.

As the destruction at the rear of the theater moves its way forward, the first-class patrons—yet unaffected—continue their applause. But alas, progression is unavoidable, and escape becomes impossible. Bizarre to the end is the death of the final few, who catatonically sip champagne while dust billows into their crystal flutes and mouths. Eventually, the debris crushes every last one.

For his grand finale, the maestro turns back to face the remaining performers and lowers his baton one last time, bringing down with it the front of the theater and crushing the beautiful stage and everyone on it or near it. Not a stone remains standing, except for his raised platform. Having accomplished his magnum opus, he raises his hands and bows.

Unscathed, the small, dark man is the only survivor.

From the rear archway, I observe it all. It is too late for protestation, too late for remonstration, and much too late for reconstruction. All is lost.

Hearing footfalls behind me, I turn. I am surprised to see the foyer intact and the grand promenade still standing. A kindly old gentleman with a familiar face approaches from the far side. It's good to see him, and I momentarily forget about the tragedy within the theater.

"Daddy! What are you doing here?"

"No, Elizabeth, the question is, what are you doing here?"

"I don't know. I had no ticket. Is this Heaven?"

"No, this isn't Heaven, but you'll know it when you feel it."

"Oh. Is Mommy okay?"

"Yes, she's through there." He points to a faraway door.

"Can I see her?"

"Not yet. Elizabeth, you should leave now."

"Those people in there." I turn to look back at the mountainous pile of rubble and debris. "They all died."

He shrugs his shoulders.

"But why?"

"Choice. They chose to allow evil to orchestrate their destruction. Evil destroyed all they knew. And Elizabeth, the day will come when you will also have to choose."

"Choose what?"

"You'll know." His body begins to fade away, warping in and out like a hologram. Then he is gone.

"Daddy . . ." I feel someone rubbing my arm.

"Hey, sleepyhead, it's time to wake up."

"Huh?" Disoriented, I try to figure out where I am.

"Elizabeth, it's me, Jackson. You're at the Hotel de Florentino on Madison, and it's four thirty on Tuesday afternoon. Time to wake up."

"Oh man, what a bizarre dream." I rub my eyes. "Yeah, hang on a sec, I need to get my head on." It all comes back.

"You okay?"

"I just had the scariest, weirdest dream of my life. At the end I was talking to my dad." *Dang. I miss him so much.* "Sit here and hold me for a minute."

Jackson sits down on the bed and holds me, his strong arms providing great comfort. "Can you remember it?"

"Definitely. It's not something I'll ever forget."

"Was Joseph in it?"

"Yeah, but he was killed. I think he was showing me the end."

"Oh, babe, I'm so sorry." After holding me for a few minutes, he says, "Listen, not to rush you, but I let you sleep as long as possible, and dinner's on the way up."

"Dinner? Wow. Okay, I'll jump in the shower."

"Good. We can talk about it while we eat."

"I'm not really hungry. What'd you order?"

"Broiled halibut, asparagus, and potatoes au gratin. And a huge pot of coffee for your thermos."

"No way," I say, salivating at the delicious thought. "Well, maybe I can force myself to eat." Wrapping my arms around him, I decide I never want to let go.

After kissing me deeply, he drags me by the hands toward the bathroom. "Now get!"

Twenty minutes later, as I click off the hairdryer, I hear a rap at the door and spy the arrival of the dining service cart. The aroma of deep, dark coffee and delicious food wafts its way toward the bathroom. I slip my scrub top over my head, set my brush on the marble vanity, and smile at my reflection in the mirror. *How did I ever live without this man?*

"Knock, knock," Jackson says, tapping lightly on the door. "Dinner is served, m'lady."

The service cart is opened to an intimate round dining table, and the steward has set everything up for us, including a vase of fresh flowers in the center. Jackson pulls out my chair, and we sit to a heavenly light meal.

Resting on the coffee table is a small brown bag.

"What's in the bag?"

"A midnight snack for the hardest-working nurse I know."

"How thoughtful." I grin and savor a bite of the delicate fish. "Were you here all day?"

"No, I flew to Port Angeles and worked until three, then flew back here to have dinner with you."

"How was work?"

"Okay. Budgeting stuff and a board meeting. Not my favorite parts, but it all has to be done."

"Sounds heavy. So are you flying back tonight?"

"No. Tomorrow evening. I've got a full day of research tomorrow at the university library, and my parents arrive about seven. I'll hang out and fly them to Port Angeles."

"So, will I see you in the morning?"

"Darlin', wild horses couldn't keep me away. I'll pick you up at six thirty, take you to breakfast, and drop you back here into bed. While you get your beauty rest, I'll do my research."

"Sounds great." I fold my hands in my lap and shrug my shoulders. "Can I please tell you about my creepy dream?"

"Start talking. I'm all ears."

For the next fifteen minutes, I describe the vivid images from my bizarre dream while he listens and tries to interpret the overall gist.

"So what do you think it all means?" he asks.

"I think I was watching the possible demise of our country."

"The symbolism does seem significant. I agree with you."

"Too many coincidences to ignore. Fifty sally ports—fifty states. Nine ballet dancers—nine Supreme Court justices. Not to mention all the rest." I sit back in my chair and hold my head in my hands. "Oh Jackson, that would mean our government is doomed."

"Possibly, or maybe it was a glimpse of what might be. You know as well as I do that dreams are subjective. So there's no way to be positive." He looks at his watch. "I hate to interrupt, darling, but I need to get you to work. We can talk more about this later. Maybe by tomorrow you'll have it all analyzed." He smiles while he moves my chair back for me.

Since the late afternoon is clear, we choose to walk the few short blocks to the hospital hand in hand. Strolling contentedly beside him, the very last thing I want to do is go to work.

Tuesday night's shift passes in a blur of unremarkable patients who ebb in and out of the department. As promised, at 6:30 a.m. Jackson meets me at the desk and escorts me to the hotel for breakfast.

"So exactly how do you get past security in the ED?" I ask as I sip my tea.

"Well, it's simple, really. My mom was in a minor car accident on I-5 about fifteen years ago and was taken to Bayside for treatment. She was okay, but needed a CT scan. Except the only CT machine was in Radiology, and it was on the fritz, so she had to wait several hours while they repaired it. She was talking with the doctor when he casually mentioned how badly the ED needed their own machine and what a huge difference it would make in diagnosing patients. A couple weeks later, Mom and Dad donated the money to have one installed. The hospital muckity-mucks will never forget my parents." He winks at me. "There are a few advantages to having the family name."

"Wow, that's really generous!"

"Yeah, that's their legacy. They give continuously to all kinds of charities, whether they're asked to or not."

"I'm looking forward to meeting them. So, what do I call them?"

"I think Rebecca and Jackson will do just fine. They're not big on formalities."

I yawn and stretch my arms. "I'm pretty beat. Do you mind if I go up to the room and get some sleep?"

"Perfect timing. Once you're tucked in, I'll head for the university and be back by four to wake you up."

"What are you doing at the library?"

"Researching paranormal activities and spooky stuff. Maybe someone else has encountered Joseph."

"So you're still taking it seriously?"

"Abbaasolutedly."

We both laugh.

He escorts me upstairs and departs. I'm asleep before the door clicks shut.

29

"Hey, Tom, where do you want me tonight?"

"I hate to ask, but do you mind taking Zone Three?"

"Nah, I've had two good days in Trauma. One day in the drunk tank won't kill me. Who's on with me?"

"Patrick. He's a newer nurse, just got off orientation. Keep an eye on him, and if you think he's sinking, let me know. I can always float someone to help."

"No problem." I turn toward the zone. "Any students tonight?" I ask back over my shoulder.

"No. By the way, congrats on your engagement! Doc just mentioned it. I'm really happy for you."

"Oh, thanks! I figured everyone knew by now."

"Mrs. Morgan. Not bad!"

I stop dead in my tracks as I think about the name again. Am I the only one not connecting the dots? I run to the locker room, drop my stuff, and run back down three hallways to the CT room. Fortunately, it's empty. I enter without notice and search the walls, but don't see anything. *Come on, where is it?*

I look all over the room until I find a small, obscure plaque attached to the back side of the giant, doughnut-shaped machine. In small gold letters it reads:

THIS EQUIPMENT AND INSTALLATION MADE POSSIBLE
BY A GENEROUS DONATION
FROM THE MORGAN FAMILY TRUST

"Well, I'll be danged." I've seen this plaque dozens of times and never paid an iota of attention, just as I pay no attention to the myriad of redundant plaques throughout the hospital. The generosity of these kind acts astounds me. Without such support, the outcomes of countless patients might have been vastly different.

Walking back toward Zone Three, I contemplate the proud heritage I'm becoming part of—people who see a need and act upon it. I can't wait to meet them.

Just one shift to go. One more shift. I enter the locker room.

"Hey, you must be Elizabeth. I'm Patrick."

"Hi, nice to meet you." I offer a hearty handshake and stuff my bag into my locker.

"I've heard a lot about you."

"Oh, that's probably not good. Such as?"

"That you're rock solid and can help me if I get stuck."

Don't brownnose me. I hate that. "We all need help at one time or another, and I got your back. Tell me what you've been doing so I have a clue."

After graduating from a private university's nursing program, the tall, lean twenty-three-year- old worked in a nursing home for two years. Lucky to land an ED job in Trauma, he's just finished a four-week orientation and is about to launch his first solo shift. A scary proposition for any nurse, especially near the beginning of his career.

"Not to worry," I assure him with a smile. "We'll survive the next twelve hours. Let's get report."

As usual, the entire department is full, although we have a few empty hallway gurneys. The first six hours fly by, Patrick manages to hold his own, and the clinic docs work rapidly through the patients, keeping the pace up.

"Zone Three, Triage," my shoulder mic squawks.

"I got it," I holler to Patrick as I turn toward Triage.

As I walk up behind the nurse at the desk, I see a stocky man of medium height standing on the other side, talking to her. He has a strained look on his face and an odd dribble of dark red blood oozing from the right side of his neck, which he's gently dabbing with a small towel.

"What's up?"

Turning, the nurse answers, "This fellow's name is Daniel, and he works construction. Thinks he got hit with something earlier today, and the bleeding won't stop." Raising one eyebrow, she adds, "Says he feels 'funny.'"

"Hi, sir." I give him a once-over. His wide eyes search the scene around him, but he doesn't turn his neck to follow his line of sight. "How's the rest?" I ask the nurse.

"Vitals are okay, except his pulse is elevated and he's got a slight temp." She stands up to face me and whispers, "I bumped him ahead of everyone else 'cause I got a weird feeling. I don't have a trauma bed open, but I think he's got a problem."

"Me, too, just looking at him." I turn back to the patient and say, "Try not to talk much, but are you having any pain?"

"No, not really. My neck just feels stiff, and I'm afraid to lay down."

Yeah, I bet you are. "Okay. I need you to stand right there, sir, and don't move. I'll be right back." As I speed into double time, I yell back over my shoulder, "And whatever you do, don't sit or turn your head."

I run back to Zone Three, grabbing a few nursing assistants

on the way, and explain what I believe is wrong with Daniel. "Move this woman out of that room and put her in the hall," I say, pointing to a door, "then clean the room stat." I turn to the remaining assistant. "Grab the narrowest, softest C-collar you can find while I get the vertical gurney. Let's go, folks. Time's essential."

While pushing the unique gurney toward Triage, I spot Dr. Bennett in the far hallway. "Hey, Doc, I think I may need you right now."

He accompanies me the remaining few steps to reception. Thank goodness Daniel has obeyed my orders and is still standing in exactly the same spot I left him. Unlocking the latches underneath the gurney, I stand it vertically. At the foot is a small metal platform which serves as a stepping area for patients getting on board. Opening the half door next to the desk, I push the gurney through and stand it beside Daniel. He starts to move, but I stop him.

"No, wait. Let me do this first." I carefully apply the soft C-collar around his neck, delicately propping his chin up and over the padded front. The nursing assistant holds a rigid slider board against the vertical mattress while I take hold of Daniel's hand. "Okay, now keep your eyes focused forward, and let me guide you sideways." Dr. Bennett, already positioned on Daniel's far side, helps guide him slowly onto the gurney's little step. Once on board, we tightly buckle the knee, waist, and shoulder straps, and I tape his forehead to the slider board to prevent his head from turning.

Dr. Bennett counts, "One, two, three," and in a coordinated effort, we slowly lower the gurney's bed into a horizontal position and push it into the inner sanctum. "X-ray first."

I have no doubt he's reached the same conclusion I have; this patient is sitting precariously on a cusp between normalcy and paralysis.

"So what's going on with me, Doc?" Daniel asks, staring

at the passing ceiling panels as we whisk him through the halls toward Radiology.

"I'm going to ask you not to speak until we get some X-rays of your neck," Dr. Bennett says. "Then I'll have a better idea, and we can talk." Patting Daniel's hand, he adds, "I'll hang out with you while we get the films."

Dr. Bennett patiently waits while the technician finishes up with a set of abdominal films, then wastes no time bumping us ahead of everyone else. Together we maneuver the hard film cases behind Daniel's head and upper back and retreat behind the lead shield when the machine fires up. Once the series is taken, the technician makes a move to clear the X-ray room for the next patient, but Doc stops him.

"We'll just wait right here while you develop those. Where's your IV stuff?"

Shrugging his shoulders, the technician points to a nearby toolbox.

"I got it," I say. By the time the films are developed, I have an eighteen gauge in Daniel's right forearm and a liter of normal saline hanging.

"Uh, Doc, you aren't gonna believe this," the tech says as he returns from the darkroom.

Dr. Bennett grabs the films and shoves them up under the clips on the light board. The back lights come on, illuminating the pictures of Daniel's neck. Sitting right between two cervical discs is a huge, sixteen-penny framing nail. Buried within the soft tissues of his neck, it has so far missed everything vital, but it's less than a micro-dot from the spinal cord. Any sharp turns or sudden movements would be disastrous for this young man.

I notice Daniel straining to look from the corners of his eyes, so I yank the most impressive film off the lighted board and hold it flat above his head. No one needs any medical training to discern the large metal nail stuck in the middle of his neck.

"Holy shit!" he exclaims.

"Exactly."

"I never even felt it go in!"

"Now, I really need you to be as still and quiet as possible," I say. "We'll be asking you questions, but you need to keep your answers brief and succinct. And whatever you do, don't turn your head."

"Okay." A single tear escapes from his eye and drips down his sweaty temple. I can see the stark terror creeping in, undoubtedly filling his mind with images of what might have been or could yet be.

"You're gonna be okay, but you need emergency surgery." Holding his hand, I use the most soothing voice I can muster. "Dr. Bennett will explain everything to you. Just listen and try to take it all in. With any luck, you'll be out of here tomorrow. Do you have any family with you?"

"Yeah, my wife."

"Good, I'll go get her."

As I wheel Daniel to surgical prep, I think about his mortally close call.

For the first time ever, I look up and give heartfelt thanks to the One who matters. "I don't know if You can hear me, God, but thank You for saving this man. Thanks for intervening."

30

"Ya doin' okay, Patrick?"

"Yeah, just thinking about the guy with the nail in his neck."

"What about him?"

"That if I'd been the one to go out to Triage instead of you, he'd be dead—or worse." He averts his pale green eyes to the floor.

"Look, Patrick. Look at me." He lifts his head up and returns my gaze. *I get it. You want to save the world. And you're afraid.* His short blond hair and cherubic face suddenly remind me of Joseph. *He's not Joseph.* "Look, there are probably half a dozen nurses here who would've missed the clues. But that's why Triage is so critical. If they think something's wrong and can't get proper attention, they'll go straight to the charge."

"Yeah, but I'd have missed it. Wouldn't have even guessed the problem." He shrugs his shoulders. "Maybe I'm in the wrong field."

Okay, I get your concerns, but no way will I let you play the victim. "Maybe you are. Or maybe you just need to be honest about your limitations and lack of experience. You've been at this for what, fifteen shifts? Hardly enough to hang your hat on."

"So how do I not kill anybody while I'm learning?"

Good question. "By sticking to the clinic side. Get used to all the normal crap coming down the pike, and ask for help when you aren't sure. With a little grace and good fortune, no one'll die, and someday you'll be saying this to another neophyte."

"Triage, Zone Three," my mic squawks.

"I got it." Happy to walk away, I end the conversation and make my way to Triage. General patient traffic has cleared out a bit, most of the hallway gurneys are temporarily stowed, and I have two rooms open, which is a miracle, given the norm. My watch shows 3:30 a.m., and I swear it's been stuck there for at least two hours.

Joseph, if this is some kind of sick trick to keep me here, I promise I will find you.

"What's up?" Repetitive though it is, I am unable to think of a more concise way to query the Triage nurse.

"Teenager," she says, pointing to a wispy shadow of a girl in the farthest corner of the waiting room. "Technically not next in line, but I bumped her ahead."

With her knees clutched to her chest, the girl rocks catatonically back and forth in her chair. Her long brown hair is pulled around to one side and loosely banded in a ponytail, although it looks mussed and needs to be redone. Even from this distance I can see her high cheekbones, pointed chin, and pale complexion. *Pretty kid.* I get the distinct impression she is trying to appear as small as possible, maybe even trying to disappear.

"See the rocking?"

"Yup."

"Been doing it the whole time."

"What's her complaint?"

"Well, first she reported spilling hot coffee on herself in the drive-through at some twenty-four-hour place."

"At three in the morning? What the heck's a young girl doing out on a weeknight at this hour?"

"Right, good question. Anyway, I couldn't see any redness on her arm. Then she hedged around, all embarrassed like and started to leave, but I talked her into letting us 'get a good look' at her arm." She lowers her voice and adds, "I'm thinking she's been raped—for real. I can't be sure, but just watching her for the past ten minutes makes me suspicious. Vital signs are mostly normal except for an elevated pulse and a temp of 99.8, but nothing else popped out."

"Shouldn't she go to Children's?"

"According to her driver's license, she's sixteen."

"Still, if she's been violated, wouldn't they be better able to handle the aftermath?"

"I get the feeling that coming in here took everything she had, and if we spook her, she'll bolt. Might not get another chance."

"Okay, I got it." I look at the transfixed young girl. "Call her up." *Not personal enough.* "No, wait, give me her chart."

I check the name and walk through the locked barrier. Some lame cover of an old Beatles tune drones from overhead speakers, and TVs at opposite ends of the room blare meaningless drivel from different stations. At least thirty people are waiting to be seen or get word of a loved one. Some have puke buckets, others hold towels over their eyes, and still others sport homemade bandages. A few are simply snoring, not yet ejected by security.

As I sit down next to the girl, I notice her petite, turned-up nose and clear complexion. I also notice there isn't much color in her cheeks. "Hey, are you Princess?"

"I hate that name," she whispers. "When I'm eighteen, I'm changing it." Rocking back and forth, she makes no eye contact.

"So what would you like to be called?"

"Sam. Short for Samantha." She rocks on. "I'm changing to Samantha."

Marking out *Princess* on the top of her chart, I replace it with *Sam*, making sure she notices.

"Agree, much better. So, Sam, I'm Elizabeth." I hold out my hand sideways to see if she'll allow body contact.

Without releasing the stranglehold on her knees, she raises two fingers to indicate a greeting. "Hey."

"I'm a nurse, and I'd like to get you out of this creepy place. I've got a private room where you can show me your coffee burn."

"Yeah, it's bad."

"Sounds like it. You want to follow me?"

"Not really." She makes no move to unfold her human pretzel.

"Well, can you show me your burn out here?"

"Not really."

My nursing brain clicks. *Something's really wrong.*

"So, what are our choices, Sam?"

"I guess I gotta come with you."

"Whenever you're ready." I stand up, holding her chart against my chest. *Come on, girl, you've made it this far. You can do it.* I wait.

She lets go of her knees and stiffly unfolds her gaunt young body, gripping the sides of the chair as she moves. I catch just the slightest wince of pain as her legs stretch out.

Interesting. And she's wearing baggy old sweats, unlike the molded jeans most teenage girls pour themselves into.

Never making eye contact, she stiffly follows me through the maze of chairs, past the Triage desk, and into the back labyrinth. Navigating around the main desk, I watch as she vigilantly eyes the new environment. At one point she freezes like a deer in headlights.

Panic? Nightmares? I wait.

Resuming her slow pace, she follows me the rest of the way to the room. I close the door and pull the drape for extra privacy.

"Have a seat on the gurney, and let me get a look at your burn."

Standing, she pulls up her baggy sweatshirt sleeve, revealing her thin forearm.

"Huh. It doesn't look too bad to me." *Like, not burned at all.* "When did this happen?"

"Earlier tonight."

"Ever happened before?"

"Not like this."

I get the feeling we're not talking about her arm anymore. "What was different?"

She sits on the edge of the mattress and puts her head down. Her voice is barely audible as she whispers, "He was mad."

"Mad about what?"

"I told him about my date for the prom."

Oh, crap. "And he thinks you're his?"

"I guess." She starts to sob quietly.

Who's the perp? "So what about your mom?"

Sam shrugs her shoulders. "She ignores me."

"Does she know?"

"Oh, yeah. All of it."

I search for the right words. "Sam, you don't know me and have no reason to trust me, but I need you to."

She stares at me, unsure. Finally, she nods.

"I think you know we need to do an exam and see what really happened, to be sure you're safe and okay."

"Yeah, I figured."

"Here's the thing about me, Sam. I'm a tough son-of-a-gun, and I'll do everything I can to protect you. But this exam could be hard for you."

"I can't take it anymore. I just wanna get the bastard."

"Now you're talking." I click my mic. "Tom, I need Dr. Bennett to room twenty-two."

"Who's that?"

"One of the nicest guys you'll ever meet." I smile. "Think you could change into this designer gown for me? It has a robe to match."

"Designer?"

"Yup! Picked it out myself at the mall."

"You're funny." She takes a deep breath, hesitating. "Yeah, I'll change."

"Okay, I'll wait right outside the door."

"No! No, please don't leave."

"Okay, I'll be right here behind the curtain."

I wait while she changes, listening for the crunch of the mattress when she climbs aboard. A quiet knock comes at the door.

"Hang on." I try to cover Sam with a warm blanket, but she pushes it away.

"Can I have just a sheet?"

"Sure." I cover her with a lightweight sheet and toss the warm blanket aside.

"Okay. Enter."

Dr. Bennett enters and barely pulls the curtain aside to peek in respectfully.

"Hey, Doc, come on in." I wait until the door is closed before I continue. "Sam, this is Dr. Bennett. Dr. Bennett, this is Sam, short for Samantha. She has a little burn on her forearm here." I barely lift the sheet to show him her arm. "And maybe another problem somewhere else."

Dr. Bennett pulls a chair up alongside the gurney and sits down, purposely positioning himself lower than Sam to allow her a perceived psychological advantage.

"Hi, Sam, I'm Dr. Bennett. What can I do for you?"

Leaning against the far wall, I watch him work his magic.

Thank goodness he's on duty tonight!

Sam immediately draws her legs up under the sheet, clutches her knees tightly, and resumes her rocking. A tear trickles down the side of her face. Her dam is about to break.

"I hate myself," she whispers. A few more tears burst forth.

"Yeah?"

"I wanna die."

"Why?" he asks softly. "What'd you do that's so bad?"

"I was born," she whispers.

"Oh." Dr. Bennett folds his hands in his lap. "Is it that you hate yourself, or maybe you hate someone else?"

"I hate . . . him."

"So how long have you hated 'him'?"

"Since I was six."

"Is that when it started?"

"Yeah."

"Why six?"

"He said he needed ten years to get me ready for my sweet sixteenth. And then I'd be free to fly away. That's what he always promised."

I think I'm gonna throw up.

"That's a long time," Dr. Bennett says.

"Yeah."

"So what happened tonight?"

"I got asked to the prom." She smiles so imperceptibly, I almost miss the sign. "First date ever."

"And he got mad?"

"Really mad." She speaks a little louder. "He tied me to the bed, like he does sometimes, to teach me things."

My stomach does a back flip. *I really am gonna puke.*

"Then he left me alone and came back with a kettle. He did this." She abruptly removes the sheet to expose her legs, revealing a horrifying sight.

"Oh, God!" I reflexively exclaim, covering my mouth.

Damn it! She's got to be in excruciating pain. Where's the bastard? I'll kill him myself!

Scalded from her knees to her groin, the fresh young skin on her inner thighs is a shriveled mass of burned and blistered flesh. Much of her pale pubic hair has been scorched away. Around the periphery of the destruction is black, charred skin, already sloughing off. Those tissues are dead, unsalvageable.

How the hell is she even coherent?

Not missing a beat, Dr. Bennett says, "Sam, if you don't mind, I'd like to make you a little more comfortable. That's gotta hurt pretty badly, and we can help the pain go away a little. What do you say?"

"Yeah, it hurts a lot."

"After you're more comfortable, we can check your legs and see how bad the damage is. Would that be okay?"

"Yeah." She grabs his wrist as he starts to stand. "Please don't tell him I'm here. He'll kill me. For real."

"What about your mom?"

"She's part of the problem."

He looks at her chart and sees the image of her driver's license. "Well, you're sixteen, and by law, that makes you an adult for medical privacy issues. So we won't say a word." He draws his fingers across his lips in a zipping movement, eliciting another slight smile from Sam.

"Thanks." She returns to the balled-up position and puts her head down between her knees. "He really will kill me if he finds me."

"I'm wondering," Dr. Bennett says as he stands, "how'd you get here tonight?"

"I drove his car."

Crap. He's probably already got a "stolen vehicle" report out. It's only a matter of time before he gets here.

"Do you have a cell phone?" I ask.

"Yeah, it's in my bag. He's been trying to call. Like the jerk thinks I'm gonna answer."

"I need you to turn it off right now," I say, "and take the smart chip out."

"Why?"

"You can be tracked with it. We need to keep you hidden as long as possible."

"Oh, I'm so stupid."

"No, Sam," Dr. Bennett says, "you're the bravest, smartest young lady I've met in a long time."

The tiny smile returns.

Dr. Bennett moves toward the door. "I need to take care of a few things, and then I'll be back. While I'm gone, I want Elizabeth to put a little IV in your arm and give you some medicine. Are you allergic to anything?"

"I don't think so." She looks up at me. "IVs don't scare me. I had one for my exam."

Exam? Why does anyone need an IV for an exam?

"Oh, really?" I ask. "When was that?"

"When I was thirteen. He took me to a clinic. Something wasn't right with my cycle."

Oh, good Lord. I'm guessing he got her pregnant and she didn't even know it.

Exchanging glances, Doc and I both know what has to be done: exams, sealed specimens, police questions, legal counsel, social workers, and uncertain foster care. All that Hell will be followed by open testimony in court, with a chance that a sympathetic judge might let the depraved bastard off—society's further humiliation of this otherwise perfectly innocent young girl, a child whose only crime was being born.

"One final question," says Dr. Bennett. "Who is 'he'?"

Her answer is barely more than a whisper: "My dad."

He nods. "Okay, Sam, I'll see you in about fifteen minutes." He hands me a sheet of orders and leaves the room quietly. It's almost 4:00 a.m.

"Tom, I need Irene," I say into my shoulder mic. "Is she still on?"

Click. "Yup, I'll send her back." *Click.* "Doc's here, we're taking precautions, changing everything." *Click.*

"Who's Irene?" Sam asks.

"She's a really cool friend of mine, actually my best friend. You'll love her. She's like a pit bull, a guard dog. I'll have her stay with you when I need to leave the room."

There's a knock at the door.

"Knock, knock. It's me," says a voice as the door pushes open a little.

"Come on in." I wait until the door is closed. "Irene, meet Sam, short for Samantha. Sam, meet Irene."

Sam takes in the obvious. At five feet two and weighing no more than one hundred pounds, Irene looks harmless enough. Her long blond hair and pretty California beach look disguise the fact that she's really an off-duty Seattle police officer pulling special security detail at Bayside. Her compact body is pure muscle, she doesn't take crap off of anybody, and she's a better shot than me, which is saying a lot. "Hey, Irene."

"Hey back, Sam." Irene looks at me. "I'll hang out here if you need to get stuff."

"Thanks. Okay, Sam, you're in good hands. I'll be back in five minutes with everything I'm gonna need for you. You'll be okay with Irene."

"What if my dad finds me?"

"Well, we already changed your name on the registration form and took you out of the computer system, so we're hoping that even if he finds the car here, we can hide you for a while."

"Wow, you can do stuff like that?"

"Yeah, they can," Irene says. "and I'll stay with you to make sure you're extra safe."

"Humph! He's huge. You wouldn't stand a chance."

"Maybe not, maybe not. But just the same, I'll stay."

Sam can't see the Glock 9 millimeter stuffed inside the rear of Irene's belt, concealed under her vest. And there's no need for her to know. Confident she'll be safe with my friend and shooting partner, I leave the room and speed to the front desk. "Tom, you'll need to get someone to cover Zone Three for a while. I'm gonna be busy with Jane Doe."

"Already did. What do you need from me?"

"Extra security. I've got a bad feeling about this. It could get ugly. Gotta go." Turning to fetch supplies, I hear a loud commotion in the reception area.

"I know she's back there!" yells a gruff male voice. "Get outta my way!"

"Sir, you can't come in!" responds the Triage nurse. "No one's here by that name."

"Look, you don't understand, she's a fuckin' problem. Always makin' up lies. I've tried to teach her, but she just doesn't learn."

Standing at the inner desk, I peer out past Triage to the ruckus. On the far side is a huge man at least six feet four and pushing 250 pounds. *Sam's right, he's a big mother.* His shoulder-length, greasy brown hair hangs over part of his prematurely aging face. Jagged lines and old acne scars decorate his forehead and high cheekbones, hiding the fact that he was probably a good-looking kid once upon a time. *Alcohol? Drugs? Rage?* All of the above.

"Look, sir, I don't even know who you're talking about. According to the computer, we don't have anyone here by that name."

"You're a damn liar!" He slams his fist down hard on the Triage desk.

No wonder she's afraid.

"I found my car in the parking lot, so I know the little bitch is here!"

"Sir, you need to lower your voice and calm down," a uniformed Seattle police officer says. He places his hand on the man's shoulder and adds, "There are sick people here."

"Don't you fuckin' touch me." The man shoves the officer's hand away, thrusting him back a step. "I know my rights. She's my daughter. She's my property, and you're hiding her."

A second uniformed officer approaches. Linking his thumbs into his massive holster belt, he says, "Look, sir, let's take this outside. If the nurse says your daughter isn't here, maybe she isn't."

"Yeah, and maybe you can eat my shit."

"Okay now, no need to get nasty. Let's keep this civil."

The giant man glances in my direction. I avert my eyes, but I know he's caught sight of me watching him. *Too late. Damn!*

He points a huge finger at me and yells through the two rooms, "I bet you're the bitch hiding her. I'll find you."

Tom wheels around to block the man's view. "Get the hell out of the front," he orders me, "and don't let him see you again."

As I turn to bolt, I have a momentary lapse of reality. For a brief moment, I see myself splattered on the asphalt next to my truck—dead. *Joseph, is that you? This is not the time!*

Tom holds my arm. "You all right?"

"Uh, yeah." My head clears a little. "Just a weird feeling. Like déjà vu or something." I see the impossible image again.

Tom continues to support my arm, jarring me out of my thoughts. "Well, go take care of the patient—the one who's not really here."

"Yeah, sure."

Ninety minutes later, after tolerating X-rays, ultrasound, and a CT scan, Samantha is sleeping peacefully with the help of a little Versed and morphine. The Burn Unit doctor evaluates her scalded tissues, diagnoses them as second degree, and orders the wound care coordinator to administer the first round of treatments. While she is asleep, I draw labs and do a quick "fem cath" to collect sterile urine, and Dr. Bennett does a pelvic exam, using the opportunity to gather the multitude of swabs and tissue samples required by law to prosecute the offender.

Bottom line is this young girl has spent sixteen horrific years being tortured by a monster—"Dad." Considering the cigarette burn scars on her back and thighs, five previously broken bones, repeated vaginal and anal tears, at least one abortion, and the scalding water poured on her legs tonight, she is lucky to be alive.

Who could survive such indescribable horror? This isn't a movie or TV show, this is real life.

Irene stays with Sam the entire time and is great consolation. Being a cop, she has a different perspective and makes certain we don't miss any critical evidence. As a bonus, she's already called her lieutenant, asking for a priority "Chain of Evidence" pickup. Then she pages the district attorney.

"You're paging him at five in the morning?" I ask.

"Yup, I want this bastard put away. Actually, I'd like him strung up by his balls on a flagpole, but in our sympathetic justice system, 'put away' will be as good as it gets."

"Truly."

"Besides, with any luck at all, he won't survive prison. There's a warrant out for him right now."

"Nice work." We high-five it.

"How long will she sleep?" Irene nods to a snoring Samantha.

"As long as I want her to." Thinking of her given name, I add, "Too bad it can't be for a hundred years like the real princess in the fairy tale."

"She's such a pretty kid, too. What a drag to have to repair all this damage."

"Yeah, it'd be nice just to wipe the mind clean like a floppy disk. You know, out with the old, in with the new?"

Knock! Knock!

I stand up to get the door, but the security guard cracks it open.

"It's me, Georgia. From Social Work."

Ugh, not you. Given what a terrible job Georgia did with Sandra, my faith in the system has plummeted. I put my finger to my lips. "Shhh. Come on in," I whisper.

"I just finished reviewing her chart, and this is revolting." She lifts her reading glasses off the end of her nose and lets them dangle on the beaded chain around her neck. I see her look at Irene and then at me, but notice she never glances at Samantha.

"Yup. Revolting."

"What's the estimated time for her hospitalization?" Georgia studies the chart again.

"Burn Unit for at least a week, maybe longer. She needs IV antibiotics, fluids, complicated dressing changes, and pain meds. She's young, her body will heal. It's the 'crazy' scars that never bleed that worry me."

"Agree. Well, I've got a little time to try and find a place for her somewhere. I'll contact the county and state agencies and see what pops."

She still hasn't taken a good look at Samantha, and I wonder why. "Can't you put her into protective custody or something?" I say. "I hate to see her go to a random home where she might get traumatized all over again."

Georgia retreats to the far corner of the room and leans against the counter. She crosses her arms and holds the chart against her chest. "Well, you know the system doesn't work like that. It's no problem removing her from the home, but no way the state will pay for a hotel for two years. So her future is up for grabs." She sighs loudly. "I have a huge caseload and I'm swamped, but I'll do my best."

Oh please! Look at this girl in front of you! And you're whining?

"Can we at least get security posted at her door while she's in the hospital? I saw her dad. He's definitely a threat."

"Dr. Bennett wrote for it on the orders, and I'll request it, too. Hopefully the hospital bean counters will agree."

"Thanks."

"Too bad," she says, finally looking at Sam. "I hate stuff like this."

"Yup." Irene and I glance at each other as Georgia departs. *I don't trust her.* "Dang, Irene. She's terrible at her job. This girl will fall right through the cracks and end up dead or on drugs, or in prostitution."

"I know. I see it all the time."

"So what can we do?" I ask.

"Hope the state doesn't let her down. And I'll try to keep my eye on her."

"Thanks. By the way, what'll happen to her mommy dearest?"

"Warrant's out for her, too. Depraved indifference. Not great, but it's a start and better than nothing."

I check my watch and see it's approaching 6:00 a.m. "Hey, what time do you get off?"

"Not till seven. I'll hang out with Sam and make sure she gets to her room safely. Why?"

"Oh, I just wondered if you want to go shoot a few rounds at the range. I was gonna pretend the target was her dad. It might make me feel better."

"No can do, but next week would work. By the way, congrats on your engagement. I hear he's a real dreamer."

"Thanks. You wanna come to the wedding?"

"Oh, partner, you know I will!"

"Wanna be in it?"

"What? Like what?"

"Like in, bridesmaid or something. But you'll have to leave your gun in the car." We both laugh quietly.

"I'd love to. Really, Elizabeth, I'm honored."

"Cool. I'll email you all the details—which, come to think of it, I don't have yet."

After scribbling a note for Samantha to call me when she wakes up, Irene and I say goodbye. She is undoubtedly the closest female friend I've ever had, and unquestionably the best competition shooter I've ever been paired with.

I check on Patrick, who seems to have survived the shift in one piece, and then speak to the nurse who covered for me while I tended to Sam. All is well, most of the patients have been discharged, and the zone is virtually empty. Signing off on the stack of charts I initially started, I carry the pile out to Tom.

"Here you go. Who's replacing me today?" My mind is already shifting to Jackson, Alder, and my quiet drive to the peninsula.

Tom smiles. "Anxious to leave, are we? Is Mr. Morgan waiting?"

"Nah, he went home last evening. It's just me, my truck, and I, but you know how I like to catch the early ferry."

"Your replacements are here in the locker room. Go give report, and have a nice four days off. By the way, what'd you think of Patrick?"

"Young. Inexperienced. But willing to learn and a fairly quick study. He just needs time. If it were my call, I'd keep him out of heavy trauma for a while. Let him get his feet wet in the back zone."

"Got it. Thanks for being honest."

"Hey, it's my butt, too."

As promised, our day-shift reinforcements are in the locker room, stowing their personal stuff. I hand off my keys and radio, snatch my own stuff, and head out, feeling for my gun at the bottom of my shoulder bag. *I really should stop and shoot at the range for a while. Catching the eight twenty wouldn't slow me down that much. I'll call Jackson and tell him.*

"Bye, guys!" I call out, waving to everyone at the desk. I head out through the triple-wide glass ambulance doors to the parking lot. Sun is coming up, and although it's overcast, it isn't raining, which is a blessing. Dialing my cell phone, I walk to the car, oblivious to my surroundings.

"Hey, Jackson, did I wake you up?" I spot my truck in the next aisle. "Yeah, I'm just getting to my truck. Long shift . . . No, I thought I'd stop and shoot a couple clips at the range. I'll catch the eight twenty and be home by ten." Searching the depths of my bag for my keys, I locate them and aim the key at the truck door lock. "Okay, babe—"

Whack!

Something hard hits the back of my head.

"Shit," is all I can muster. Soaring pain engulfs me. A monstrously strong hand grabs my shoulder, ripping my bag off as it spins me around. I'm unable to control my fingers, so my keys go flying into thin air and my phone flips from my other hand, bouncing on the ground.

Stand up! I tell myself as my knees buckle. The sky overhead swirls like cake batter in a mixing bowl. I'm succumbing to the desire to collapse, and it takes everything I have to hold on. *Fight back!*

"You fuckin' bitch. I'll fix you. You'll never hide my Princess again."

Forcing myself back from the swirling mixing bowl, I reach up and make one sweeping attempt to scratch at his eyes, unsure if I even connect. I must have hit something, because he releases one handhold and shoves me down hard on the dewy pavement with the other. I hit my head solidly on the concrete.

"You're gonna have to pay extra for that."

Turning on the ground as best I can, I grope for my bag, feeling its outer side pocket. Fingers on my Walther, I pull it out and aim as straight as I can. Considering there are at least three separate images of him swaying back and forth in front of me, I figure it'll be simpler to hit all three. Muscle memory kicks in.

Bang! Bang! Bang!

The lights go out.

31

"Listen, Jackson," a woman says, "you can't take matters into your own hands."

"I know, Mom. It just makes me so angry."

I remember that voice. Why is he angry? Who is he?

Blackness.

"I don't care what it costs! This is my future daughter-in-law. I want ICU-qualified, private-duty nursing round the clock. That means someone here every minute."

Who is that man?

"Dad, it's okay."

I recognize that voice.

"No, son, it's not 'okay.'"

Noises.

"Now, young lady, you listen to me. If one nurse needs a break, another one takes over. I don't want Elizabeth left alone for a single minute. Am I making myself clear?"

"Yes, sir."

"Dad."

Yes, I know that voice.

"Really, Dad. It's okay."

Darkness.

"Elizabeth. Elizabeth."

Oh, glory be! I'm back at the beautiful alpine mountain lake. I love it here! Wow, what a view. Look at that clear blue sky!

"Elizabeth."

"Yes?" I turn to look. *Where are you? I can't see you.*

"I tried to warn you."

"About what?"

"Danger. I showed you images of your future, but you blocked them from your mind."

"The visions were terrible, and I didn't understand. I didn't want to know."

"You are not supposed to be here."

"I know. You told me that the last time."

"No, that was Father. I am Joseph. Remember?"

"Oh, yeah. Sure I dooo. You're the one from the water. Ohhh, I feel sooo relaxed."

"Elizabeth! Pay attention!"

"What?"

"You cannot be here. It is time to stop dreaming and wake up!"

"Why? I love it here." *I feel like I'm floating on air.*

"Because I need your help, and you do not belong."

"Oh." *Makes sense.* "Where do I belong?"

"With Jackson."

"Ohhhh. Ja . . . ck . . . son. I remember him."

"Good. Now close your eyes and find his voice. He is waiting for you."

Grayness.

"Elizabeth. Hey, babe, can you hear me?"

"Yeah." *Whoa, my throat!* It's unbelievably sore and dry. "Water." *Oh, that tastes good.*

More grayness.

"And I thought maybe you should go to Europe for your honeymoon," a woman is saying, "like on one of those marvelous river cruises down the Danube, or . . ."

The sound of a chair moving wakes me.

"Jackson, she's awake again."

"Hey, babe. It's me, Jackson. Want some more water?"

"Yeah." My throat's not so dry now. "Where am I?"

"In the Neuro Unit at Bayside."

"What?" I croak.

"The Neuro Unit at Bayside. You've been here for three days. Ever since you were attacked."

A jumbled mess of memories comes flooding back all at once. "Did I shoot someone?"

"That's my girl!"

"I don't remember exactly."

"The doc said it might take awhile for everything to make sense. You were hit pretty hard, twice." Holding my hand, Jackson sits right next to the bed and strokes my forearm.

I try to raise my left arm to touch my forehead, but pain shoots through my shoulder. "Ouch! Dang!" I relax my arm. "What's wrong with me?"

"Here's the straight skinny, babe. You were hit on the back of the head with a small board. You fought back and got a piece of his face, although no one's quite sure how you managed it. Then the guy threw you to the ground so hard it broke your left hip and tore your shoulder socket."

"I guess that's why I sort of hurt. My throat's killing me. Was I tubed?"

"Yeah, sweetie. So sorry. You had to be on a ventilator because of the swelling in your brain. But it came down pretty fast, and they extubated you this morning." Tears run down his face. "I don't know what I'd do if I lost you. I love you so much."

"I'll be okay." I try to assemble my thoughts into some kind of logical order, but I still have a few big blanks. "Who attacked me?"

"A real son-of-a-bitch. Sorry, Lord, I shouldn't swear."

"Why?"

"Remember Samantha, the sixteen-year-old girl you took care of? The one with the scald burns?"

"Samantha? Oh, Sam!" *Oh, thank the Lord, I remember!* "Yeah, I do now."

"It seems her dad got it into his head that you were hiding her and decided to teach you a lesson."

"He's a big guy. Huge, I think."

"Yeah, he is." Jackson holds my hand and kisses my fingers. "But you, darling, are even bigger." He smiles broadly.

"Why, what happened?"

"First, you got a piece of him under your fingernails. And second, you shot him."

"Oh, crap. Did I kill him?" *I don't want to go to jail. I want to get married. I can't go to jail!*

"No, but two shots hit his groin and belly. He'll never pee the same again."

A voice comes from the doorway. "Knock, knock. It's me, Irene."

I'm already smiling from the news about my attacker. "Hey, Irene."

"I love that raspy voice." Bending down, she kisses my forehead, then looks around the room. "Dang, girl! Look at all these flowers and gifts! You got enough inventory in here to start your own floral shop."

"Oh, wow, there are a lot," I say, scanning the room. "I didn't even notice. I think I just woke up." I look at Jackson for guidance. "Did I just wake up?"

"Yup, about ten minutes ago."

"Any idea how Sam's doing?"

"Great," Irene answers. "Especially after she heard what happened. She never has to be afraid of her boogieman dad again. You shot off his wanger, so to speak."

I manage a little laugh at her bare-bones humor.

"But you can ask her yourself when she comes to visit. She's been checking on you every hour, every day. I think you have a new best friend, especially since you guys have something in common."

"So where's her dad now? And mom?"

"Dad's shackled and under heavy guard in a different hospital. Mom's in jail and has a few scars of her own, but she'll do at least seven or eight." She pauses and looks at me. "Thanks to you, we nailed this bastard for at least twenty rapes in the last ten years."

"What? No way!"

"Yes, way. Most of his victims were young women, college students, waitresses. And one of them, a"—she checks her notes—"Sandra, was your patient here—twice."

"Ohhhh. I remember her. We had coffee a few times. Multiple stab wounds. Really sad case."

"Yup. So girl, you truly got the bad guy, for real."

A nurse I don't recognize appears at my bedside. "Okay, folks, now that Elizabeth's awake, I need to do a few things." She shoos everyone toward the door. "Please take a little walk."

"I'll be right outside the door, babe," Jackson says, "and my parents are outside, too, waiting to meet you, whenever you feel strong enough."

"Okay."

Kissing me gently, he whispers, "Thank you, dear Lord, for bringing my beloved back to me."

The two orthopedic surgeries I underwent to repair my hip and shoulder were successful, but the docs tell me I'll be in the hospital at least another week because of all the physical therapy. The hairline fracture in my skull is healing, and fortunately the swelling in my brain never recurred.

Jackson Sr. is definitely Jackson's father, as they are almost identical in features, size, and demeanor. Aside from a twenty-five-year separation, the biggest difference I can tell is that Jackson Sr. speaks with a Texas twang. Jackson's mom, Rebecca, reminds me of Katherine Hepburn with her tall, statuesque shape, beautiful auburn hair, and overall classic style. Her hazel eyes continuously sparkle and seem to change color slightly, depending on what she's wearing. Her compassion and kindness shine brightly through her peaceful features, putting everyone she meets instantly at ease.

Jackson's dad arranges for me to be moved to the top-floor VIP suite, which I didn't even know existed. Consisting of a bedroom, kitchenette, and a sizable sitting room with a fold-out sofa, it affords plenty of room for the constant stream of visitors and well-wishers. Large picture windows offer breathtaking views of West Seattle, the harbor, and the Olympics in the distance, definitely a bonus during my recuperation.

Using the full extent of his clout, he also manages to get Samantha moved to the large room next door and hires a top plastic surgeon to treat her burns. Hopefully, with a few revisions, the long-term scarring will be minimal and she'll have a chance at some semblance of normalcy. Dr. Bennett and my boss, Angela, visit every day, double-checking all the orders for Sam and me, ensuring nothing is missed. All in all, the outpouring of love and support from everyone is pleasantly overwhelming.

Jackson rarely leaves my side. Even when obligations of his church call him, he isn't very far. Considering my injuries, we decide to push our wedding date back to the end of May, mostly because I want to be able to enjoy our honeymoon. His delightful mom and dad, as well as Mike, Sally, Roger, Nan, and Irene, keep Samantha and me occupied with cribbage, Monopoly, and crosswords, although I usually last only a few hours between naps, so it's doubtful I'm much company.

Rebecca loves diversions and schemes up several events to keep Sam and me entertained. Since neither one of us can leave the confines of the hospital, Rebecca arranges for a personal shopper to come to our world one afternoon with samples of clothes, shoes, and accessories for both of us. After all the pain and procedures, we're like little kids in a candy store, playing dress-up with beautiful items. It does my heart good to see Samantha laughing and enjoying herself a little.

During the miniature shopping spree, Sam finds several things she likes and sets them off to one side, but then sheepishly hands them all back to the lady. "I don't have any money. You probably know my dad's in jail."

The woman doesn't miss a beat. "Oh, darling, I thought you knew. These are all part of a donation from the Seattle community. Sort of a congratulations to Elizabeth and you for your bravery in fighting crime." She smiles and nods in Rebecca's direction.

"Oh, I didn't know." Sam puts her head down and sniffs back tears. "I'm so sorry he hurt so many innocent people. I never knew about the others."

This girl is gonna blame herself for everything if someone doesn't help her. "Sam, I think we hit the jackpot!" I exclaim. "I love these!" I hold up a summer dress and shorts. "Which ones are you choosing?" *Come on, come back to life.*

She looks up at me, swiping her long eyelashes with the back of her hand. "Well, I do kinda like these shirts." She points to a few spring outfits.

"Good," Rebecca says. "Done! We'll take all of this stuff, and please tell the mayor we appreciate his city's generosity." She escorts the lady out.

I'm not fooled for a minute, but I'm absolutely in love with how respectful Rebecca is of this young girl's pride. I can learn a lot from Jackson's mom.

No time like the present. "Sam? I know we haven't known each other very long, but seeing as how we're kind of connected, I have something to ask you. Would you mind being in my wedding?"

"Me?" Her beautiful dark eyes widen to the size of walnuts. "You want me to be in your wedding?"

"Yup, you and Irene. I need two bridesmaids, and you're the ones I want." *Please say yes.*

"Wow. Ah, yeah, sure. What do I do?"

"Almost nothing, dear," interjects Rebecca as she gracefully reenters. "Your job is to stand next to Irene in a beautiful dress and look gorgeous, which will be easy for you."

"Gorgeous? Gorgeous." She says it so softly it's barely audible. "I'd . . . I'd really like that. Thanks for asking."

I hug her as best I can manage with my shoulder still wrapped up.

Taking charge of the wedding plans, Rebecca forges ahead, meticulously organizing everything Jackson and I ask for. But I still lack a wedding dress.

On the afternoon of the day before our discharge, three men and a French lady arrive with numerous garment racks full of wedding gowns and bridesmaid dresses. It is a sight to behold. Samantha, Irene, and Sally are kind enough to add their opinions, and soon I've selected the gown of my dreams.

"I love this one. It's so beautiful!" Discreetly searching for the price tag, I notice there isn't a tag anywhere on any of them. "I hate to admit this, but I'm on a budget. How much is it?"

"*Deux,*" the lady responds.

"Two hundred? Really? I can afford that."

"*Bon.*" The woman exchanges glances with Rebecca, and both smile.

"I'm so glad you love this," Rebecca says. "It's just perfect!"

I get a funny feeling the "two" isn't what I initially

thought. *Oh well. At this point, I don't care.*

After Irene and Sam choose their dresses, the lady takes all the necessary measurements. "I will zend zee bill," she says, giving me a peck of a kiss on one cheek. Snapping her fingers, she flits off with the three men caravanning behind her, pushing the racks of dresses.

"That was so darn fun, Rebecca. Thank you for arranging all of this. It's the sweetest thing anyone's ever done for me."

"It was just as fun for me. I've been waiting a long time for my son to get married, so trust me, I'm in heaven, too."

"Knock, knock. It's me, Georgia from Social Work."

"Come on in."

"Hi. I'm looking for—" She glances around the room. "Hey, Sam, I was looking for you. Wow, look at all these flowers! My goodness!" One eyebrow rises as she scans the cards and three-dozen bouquets placed on tables, counters, and air vents. "Aren't you the popular one."

"Hey, Georgia." I get a nasty, dry taste in my mouth. "What's up?" *Don't you dare spoil our fun.*

She removes her glasses again and puts one earpiece in her mouth like she's deliberating. *She thinks she's important.* "I just came by to talk to Sam about where she's going tomorrow. I've got a family that thinks they can take her."

That's it? That's the best you can do? I can feel the hair standing up on the back of my neck. "What kind of family?"

"Oh, ah, it's really not your concern, Elizabeth. This is between me and Sam."

Watching Sam, I can see her heart disconnect and plummet to the basement. The tiny spark of happiness she's experienced this week is about to be extinguished, and she knows it. I know it, too. I also know she doesn't have the confidence or skills to stand up for herself—not yet. "Sam, do you mind if I ask Georgia questions about where you're going?"

She shrinks into the chair. "No."

I turn back to Georgia. "So whaddaya got for her?"

"Well, if you must know." She crosses her arms. "It's a home in Puyallup. Married couple, one biological teenage son and three foster kids. She'll have to share a bedroom with another girl, but it should be comfortable enough."

Easy for you to say. I hate this woman. "Sam, what do you think?"

Sam shrugs her shoulders.

"I'll tell you what," Irene says. She stands up and walks toward Georgia. "Don't give an answer yet, Sam. I'll drive down there right now and check it out. Be back in two hours."

"You don't need to check it out." Georgia postures, hands on her hips. "I already did. It's sufficient, and she'll be safe."

"I'm sure you did, Georgia, but you know the old saying, 'Two heads are better than one.' I wanna see for myself." Irene snatches the paperwork from Georgia's fingers, and she's gone before Georgia can grab for it.

"This is entirely unacceptable," Georgia huffs. "She took my paperwork. I can get her fired for this."

Oooh, aren't you the haughty one? "Fired? From the Seattle Police Department? I don't think so. She's one of the most decorated cops they have."

Rebecca stands and elegantly says, "My dear Georgia, I believe you have outstayed your welcome."

"This is ridiculous!" She points a finger at me and then at Sam. "If you have nowhere to go tomorrow, don't blame me. I tried."

"Ta-ta, dear," Rebecca says.

Samantha's big brown eyes fill with a vacant, empty look. *Don't go away. Please don't hide. The world's not that bad.*

"I say we go for a little walk and get our afternoon therapy out of the way while we wait to hear from Irene," I offer. "I'll race you to the end of the hall and back."

"Nah, I think I'll take a nap." Sam rises and walks to the

door. "Thanks for standing up for me. Nobody's ever done that before."

"We'll figure this out, sweetie. I promise."

It's Rebecca's turn to speak. "Each of you take a nap. You need one. I'm going for a walk, and when Irene returns, we will discuss this further. Come on, Sam, I'll walk you next door. Now rest, Elizabeth."

I hate to admit it, but I'm definitely tired, and a nap will be a welcome respite. I've been off all narcotic painkillers for two days and am sleeping better with fewer nightmares. I swallow two Tylenol and doze off.

When I open my eyes, I'm standing in an oversized cathedral prayer room at the edge of a capacious pool of serenely undulating water. Resting my elbows on the waist-high side of the marble pool, I lean over, curious. Having neither a fixed shape nor a defined bottom, the pool's dimensions fluctuate rhythmically. I somehow understand the size is limitless. Within the rocking water are millions of small ovoid objects, each one gently illuminated from within.

Through the warm, dim light, I hear faint music, like a monks' choir chanting from a distant hillside chapel.

"Ooomaaaaa . . . ingaaahhh . . . doughmoh," the deep, harmonizing voices sing.

Beautiful. I wonder what it means?

My surroundings seem vaguely familiar, yet unrecognizable. A relaxing peace fills me, a peace I don't understand. As I lean over the edge of the pool, I begin to rise ever so slowly.

I'm not afraid.

Floating in the air, I see my full-length white robe billowing around my legs. I stretch out my arms and allow myself to be carried out of the room and down a long marble hallway, drifting past countless archways. When I reach the last archway, I am settled gently to the ground.

"Elizabeth. You came."

I turn. "Joseph." I put my hand to his cheek. "I don't know how I got here." *What a beautiful young man.*

"You are dreaming."

"Yes, I must be."

"I have brought you here to warn you. Now your linear timing becomes essential. The Tenth has been started. With it, the darkness begins."

"What is it?"

"I only know it as the Tenth. And I know its presence in our world is unthinkable."

"What will it do?"

"Signify the beginning of humanity's destruction, the destruction you already witnessed."

"Can it be stopped?"

"It must be. It has no passage. It cannot be allowed to try."

"How do I stop it?"

"You will know."

"How? When?"

"When it is time to choose."

"Choose? Joseph, what will I be choosing?"

"You will know."

Joseph and the dream-like surroundings vanish as I'm jarred awake by a ringing noise. I sit up in bed as the ringing continues.

Dang cell phone!

I fumble for the phone and answer.

"Hello."

"Sorry. Sounds like I woke you up."

"No, that's okay, Irene." I try to collect my thoughts. "What'd you find out?"

"It's a dump, a real dump. A rundown doublewide trailer in the back of a depressing trailer park. I caught sight of the couple, and this would be bad for Sam. Dad hasn't shaved in a week, has a huge beer gut on him, and mom's a chain-smoker. Kids were doing homework on the porch . . . in the rain. I took a bunch of pictures."

"Damn that Georgia anyway." *I hate the frigging welfare system!* "Thanks for checking. Are you coming back?"

"Yeah. Rebecca invited me for dinner. What are you gonna do about Sam?"

"I don't know." The old anger begins to rear its ugly head, and I can feel my blood pressure rise. "See you when you get back."

"Hey, darling, are you awake?" Jackson pushes the door open to my bedroom. "I heard your phone ring."

"Yeah, I'm awake, and I'm peeved. That was Irene." I tell him what she found out.

"Well then, there's only one solution."

"What?"

"We take her to Port Angeles with us."

I stare at him. "Are you kidding?"

"Not at all."

"Jackson, she needs a family. A mom and a dad. She needs advocacy, dependability, and no more abuse. She needs love, nurturing, and care. And she'll need years of counseling."

"Exactly. She needs us."

"You're serious about this, aren't you?"

"Look, Elizabeth, this is what I do for a living. I counsel people, help bring them back from the depths of Hell, and show them another way. She can finish out the school year via distance learning and start again as a junior in the fall. No one ever needs to know her past."

"So you've worked it all out, have you?"

"No, not at all. But I'd rather offer her us than have her go live with a loser family and end up dead, or worse."

"It's a lot to think about. A huge responsibility."

"Yeah, but think of the reward. The opportunity to save a life. The opportunity to choose."

Choose. Joseph keeps saying that I'll have to choose. Is this what he meant? Is she the Tenth? No, she can't be. That wouldn't make any sense.

"What if she doesn't want to come with us?" I ask.

"Why don't we just ask her? If she's unsure, we can make it for a finite period, like a week or a month or until the end of the school year. If nothing else, we can buy her a little time until the system can find her a good home."

"We . . . could do that."

"We'll know soon enough if it's gonna work or not."

"I just don't know much about parenting. I mean, I didn't have a mom for very long, and I suck at personal stuff."

"That's precisely why you two hit it off so well. There are a lot of similarities."

"I was never abused," I say, defending my parents.

"Of course you weren't! But you suffered a bunch of losses and were isolated, alone with your sadness and anger. That's the similarity."

I nod. "Yeah, I get it." *Why not?* "Okay. I'm willing to try it."

"Good! Now, can I please kiss you?"

"I'll be mad if you don't."

We hold each other in an awkward embrace, since I'm still unable to raise my left arm all the way or stand comfortably with my head back. Nevertheless, it's marvelous to hold him against my body and feel his warm strength flowing through me.

Six weeks until our wedding—I'm sure glad it's not any longer. I can't wait to make love to this man.

There's a tap at the door.

"Hey, kids," Jackson Sr. says. "Sorry to interrupt, but your mom and I want to talk with you both."

"No problem, Dad. I'm just helping Elizabeth remember why she's marrying me. What's up?"

"It's about Samantha."

"Oh no, what's happened now?" I ask.

"Nothing—don't worry." He lowers his voice. "But I decided to have an investigator do some checking."

"Oh, Dad, you shouldn't have done that. She has a right to privacy."

"Yeah, I know. But I wanted to be sure."

"Sure about what?" I ask.

"Her. Turns out, she's a pretty bright, straight-A student, which probably was no easy task, given what she's gone through. Also, she never exhibited any rebellious behavior toward anyone. Everyone interviewed thought she was a smart introvert who simply couldn't relate to other kids. Her teachers either missed the clues or didn't care. A little sickening, but that's another story.

"Anyway, your mom and I decided to do something for this young lady to help protect her. She needs a strong advocate, so I retained legal counsel who will guide her through the depositions and trials. He'll take care of whatever she needs. And, uh, we set up a small trust fund for her, should she decide to go to college. It's not huge, but it should be enough to take her anywhere."

"Wow, Dad. That's amazing."

I'm stunned. Once again, this family's kindness and generosity blow me away. "That's so kind. I know she'll appreciate it." I look at Jackson. "Babe, why don't you tell them what we're planning?"

After Jackson explains what we've discussed, his parents help us figure out a few extra details. "Since she's already sixteen, temporary custody shouldn't be an issue," his dad says. "I'll take care of the legal side."

He's already dialing Sam's newly retained attorney.

32

Having accomplished our afternoon routine of exhausting physical therapy and painful dressing changes, Sam and I ready ourselves for the big farewell dinner party Rebecca has planned. She's invited a swarm of people, and even Jackson's sister is flying in. I have no idea what is ordered for the meal, but figure it will be fabulous.

Just before the dinner is set to begin, Angela, my boss, peeks her head around my door. "I want to speak with you for a few minutes. Do you feel up to it?"

"Yeah, sure. If this is about my sick leave or something, I can work it out with personnel."

She laughs and shakes her curly head of blond hair. "No, it's not about sick leave. I'm here to offer you a different job."

Oh, dang. I'm being fired 'cause I shot the guy. "Really? Like what?"

"I know you're never around during day shift, but you must be aware that my assistant, Becket, recently left to manage the ED at Pacific General in Tacoma. I've been advertising to fill his position for three weeks. So far, I haven't found anyone I like or want."

"I read the bulletin."

"It requires a master's degree, plus at least three years in Trauma. That really narrows the field, and your name keeps popping up as a serious contender. It's all management-related, so you'd be off the floor. The job is primarily planning, budgeting, reports, staff meetings, negotiating with unions, and boring stuff like that."

I can see myself doing that. "I wouldn't mind getting away from the grind, but it's five days a week, eight hours a day, isn't it?"

"It is. But if you're interested, I'd say the schedule's negotiable."

"I doubt if it's negotiable enough. You know I live on the peninsula, and it's a three-hour commute each way with the drive and ferry ride. There's no way I can do that every day, and no way I can stay over here for a week at a time, especially since I'm getting married."

"What if it's four ten-hour shifts?"

"That'd still be tough."

"What if you could do part of it at home from your computer?"

"Okay, I'm listening."

As Angela spells out what she has in mind, I have to admit, it's tempting, especially given how exhausted I am from the injuries. The thought of running all over the Trauma Ward is not appealing, and her offer is like a chocolate carrot dangling in front of my face.

"The salary and benefits package are substantial," she explains. "Of course, you'd no longer be union."

Now I'm hooked. "Dang, I'd really miss that." I hate the union. It's a drain on my income and never fights for what's important, anyway. "What's the salary?"

"About forty percent more than you make hourly, plus four weeks a year off."

"Can I have a few days to mull it over and talk to Jackson?"

"Of course. If you tell me you're interested, I'll hold it for you."

"I'm interested."

"Good." Reaching for the door, she adds, "I'm really sorry about what that creep did to you, Elizabeth, but I'm really proud of how you handled yourself. Every woman should know how to defend herself like that. My hat's off to you."

"Thanks," I answer with a self-conscious grin. "It was all muscle memory and reflex."

"Well, you're alive because of those reflexes. Anyway, a job's waiting for you when you're well enough to return, whatever you decide."

"Thanks for the generous offer. I'll be in touch."

As she departs, Jackson sticks his head around the corner.

"Did you hear all that?" I ask him.

"I wasn't trying to, but yeah, I caught most of it. Nice offer."

"I always figured management was coming. That's why I went to grad school. Maybe the timing is right, considering everything. What do you think?"

"I think it's a nice offer, and you need a few days at home to mull it over. You'll reach the right decision."

"Well, taking it might be easier on Sam. Especially the day-shift schedule."

"Speaking of Sam, do you feel rested enough to ask her?"

"Sure, before I chicken out." A nervous fear of rejection is looming.

"Good. Be right back."

A few minutes later, he returns with Samantha and explains what we have in mind while I sit quietly, observing her reactions. He doesn't gloss over anything, but thoroughly describes our housing, work schedules, school, expectations, goals, and possible snags in forming a new family unit. Jackson never mentions what Irene discovered in Puyallup, nor is there a need. Sam listens until he's finished. The only reaction I can discern is that perhaps her big brown eyes grow in size, if that's possible.

"So, what do you think?" I ask. "You'd be mostly staying with me at my cabin until Jackson and I are married next month. But after that, we can all be together and work things out as a family."

She doesn't speak.

"Listen," I say, "if it doesn't work or you don't like it, we can figure out something else. You're sixteen years old. It probably seems foreign, but you can pretty much make your own decisions at this point."

Silence.

Come on girl, say yes. "Isn't it worth a try?"

She responds with an almost imperceptible nod.

I'm not missing that opening. "Good, then it's settled. We leave this 'hotel' in the morning and head home. Wait until you meet my dog!"

"Great! Fabulous!" Jackson exclaims, clapping his hands together. "We have a lot to celebrate and be thankful for, so let's get the evening started. Also, heads up, I think my mom went a little overboard on the party plans."

Jackson leaves the room, and Sam and I are alone for a moment. I limp toward her, take her hands in mine, and put my forehead to hers, whispering, "We're not perfect, but we'll do everything we can to make this work, and you'll be safe."

"I know," she whispers.

True to form, Rebecca has left nothing to chance for our farewell celebration. Arriving ahead of the other guests, Jackson's sister, Jillian, and I have a brief opportunity to get acquainted. She looks just like Rebecca and is as kind and solid as Jackson. I like her immediately.

Every morsel of delicious food, catered from one of Seattle's finest restaurants, is served buffet-style on elegant china, with white linens and polished silver. After ten days of hospital food and plastic trays, Sam and I thoroughly enjoy the spoils and splendor. The extensive guest list includes family, friends, staff members, and even the hospital CEO and his wife. Entertaining though it is, I'm relieved when folks begin to leave. Apparently sensing I'm about to poop out, Rebecca waves her magic wand and whisks away the caterers, bartender, and all evidence of the party. The only item left is a large remnant of the double chocolate layer cake, which I assume will also vanish soon enough.

Once again, Jackson sleeps on the fold-out couch in the sitting room, while the out-of-town guests lodge at the family's favorite place, the Hotel de Florentino. The next morning, Mike and Roger load up my truck with flowers, gifts, and personal belongings and head out to the peninsula to get things ready for our return. Since I can't climb into the airplane or sit comfortably upright for any length of time, Jackson's parents have hired a stretch limo to get Sam and me home. Royalty never had it so good!

The next few weeks are a whirlwind of settling into a routine with Samantha, getting her acclimated to life on the peninsula, and helping her finish her academics for the school year. Taking life one step at a time, she and I learn to trust each other more, bonding as a tiny family unit. All I want is for her to feel safe and secure in me, Jackson, and our home.

Through Jackson's mentoring, Samantha attends church and joins the youth group, which is full of great kids who accept her without any questions. As intelligent as Sam is, she easily finishes her academics from home and will be ready for the start of her junior year at Port Angeles High School in the fall.

In addition to attending Bible study classes, my days are filled with relentless physical therapy. As physical activities become easier, I can soon maneuver in most situations, including stairs, trucks, and floatplanes. Tackling the steep steps into *Ladybug* means we can introduce Sam to our Canadian home, the biggest surprise of all.

Everyone decides Sam's middle name should be Stoic, because through her endlessly uncomfortable burn treatments, she never issues a single complaint.

"Doesn't that hurt, sweetie?" I ask one day while I watch the nurse change her dressings.

"Yeah, but I try to ignore it." She shrugs her shoulders a little. "I'd rather think about my life right now, you know, with you guys. Like the old stuff's a nightmare I woke up from." Looking at the ceiling, she whispers, "I'm the lucky one who got to wake up."

Astounded by the healing power of her young spirit, I marvel at her conscious decision to elect positive thinking over the depressing alternative. Sam's resiliency is far more than mere survival. She is vibrantly alive!

Although Joseph hasn't surfaced since my last dream in the hospital, Jackson and I decide it's prudent to alert Samantha to the remote possibility that my mountainside home might be subject to weird power outages and isolated thunderstorms. We gloss over the details and chalk it up to the possibility that my cabin might be haunted, which Sam seems to think is quite cool.

Two weeks after discharge, I accept the position as assistant director of the Emergency Department at Bayside. Angela agrees to having me in the office 7:00 a.m. to 5:00 p.m., Monday, Tuesday, and Thursday. I'll work at home an additional ten hours each week and on occasion be required to attend random meetings. Aside from all the other positive benefits, the deciding factor was being able to continue a normal family schedule, especially with Sam in our lives.

Rebecca manages every detail of the wedding, reception, and honeymoon planning, allowing Sam and me to focus on healing. She books Jackson and me passage on a European river cruise, starting from Amsterdam and traveling on the Rhine and Danube all the way to Budapest. Initially I am concerned about sitting upright in a cramped cabin seat for the ten-hour overseas flight, until I learn we'll be in first class with foldout beds. *I can handle this!*

The wedding and reception are fabulous, but I'm glad we have two photographers, because afterward I don't remember much—it all happens so fast. On the other hand, our honeymoon is a different story. It feels incredible to have Jackson all to myself for two full weeks, and every detail of our time together is embedded in my mind. Granted, we miss a few cruise events, like dinners with the captain and bus tours to cathedrals, but making love to my husband always takes precedence. I just can't get enough of that delicious man.

We're contentedly happy when we return to Port Angeles, and I'm not a bit surprised to discover I have a bun in the oven. Based upon my calculations, we must have conceived on our first night together.

Our pregnancy thrills Jackson, making him all the more protective of our family nuclei. When the time comes for me to return to work, he insists on flying me to and from Seattle for my shifts. Since the turnaround is limited on Monday evening, we agree that I'll spend one night a week at the Hotel de Florentino. My reservations there are already scheduled through the end of the year.

July and August are warm and spectacular, and filled with long walks and picnics on the beach at our home in Canada. During one such outing, Sam seems deep in thought.

"What's up, Sam?" I ask.

"Oh, nothing." Samantha takes a deep breath and looks up at the sky. "It just seems too good to be true. I feel so safe here."

"Well, that's good," Jackson says. "That's the idea of having a home. A safe haven."

"Yeah, I guess. But it's not just about the house . . . it's you guys. I trust you."

I reach out and grab Jackson's hand. *We made the right decision.*

"Plus, I never want to see my creepy parents again, and I don't think they can find me here."

I reach out my other hand and take hold of hers. "I'm pretty sure they'll never find you."

In midsummer, Samantha and I start meeting once a week with Madeline, a crisis counselor. Sam refuses to go to the meetings alone, and it's an arduous process, but worth every moment. Even though my interaction with Sam's dad was substantially less than hers, I find it's helpful for me as well.

By early September, Samantha is involved in junior-year classes and is making new friends easily. Our glorious summer sunshine has come and gone too quickly, all too typical of the Pacific Northwest.

In mid-September, Sam's mom is prosecuted for aiding and abetting a criminal, as well as depraved indifference and child abuse. To our relief, she pleads down to seven years, saving Samantha the exhausting, emotional ordeal of appearing in court. Sam's dad is still awaiting his trial, but word is, he now pees through a tube in his side and will never walk correctly again. Can't say that he gets one iota of sympathy from any of us.

One day after our counseling session, I ask Sam to hang out in the waiting room for me while I meet with Madeline alone.

"I think there's someone else I'd like to bring into this equation," I explain to Madeline. "It might help Sam."

"Okay, I'm open." She leans her slim hips back against the edge of her desk and puts her hands in the pockets of her tweed wool slacks. "Who is it?" With her doctorate in psychology, Madeline's been practicing for over twenty-five years, which puts her age at the top end of mid-fifty, but it doesn't show. Her flawless complexion and tight skin is that of a young woman. The only giveaway to her years is the wisdom she uses in skillfully managing clients. I chose her because she knows how to get right to the heart of an issue without making the situation worse. And because both Sam and I trust her.

"A young lady named Sandra. She was a trauma patient I had at the hospital."

"And?"

"She was brutally stabbed and raped by Sam's dad."

"Oh no."

"But that's not the worst of it. It's unusual for me to get involved with my patients after they leave the ED, but for some reason I felt a connection to her and kept checking up on her. We had coffee a few times until she was discharged. Then we lost track of each other. I think she kinda closed up."

"I get the feeling there's more."

"Yes, but it's confidential."

"I'm a professional, Elizabeth. Anything you tell me is in strict confidence."

"Okay." I take a deep breath. "When he attacked her, he did a great deal of damage to her abdominal cavity and all the organs. She spent hours in surgery and barely survived. But he also impregnated her."

"How sad."

"Yeah, and to her credit, she couldn't bring herself to take the morning-after pill. So the pregnancy continued."

"And then?"

"By her sixth month, her mom and friends had sort of deserted her. Apparently she fell into a deep depression and decided to have an abortion. The saddest part is that she had my number, but never called me. If I'd had any clue, I would have reached out to her."

"You can't blame yourself. That was her decision. You know as well as I do how damaging depression can be."

"I know. And I also know this isn't about me." I take a deep breath. "Anyway, she went to a crummy clinic where they didn't do much of a history or physical exam. Without thoroughly understanding her background, an untrained technician administered a drug to expel the contents of her uterus. But it's known to have terrible side effects, not the least of which is massive internal bleeding. Long story short, her uterus ruptured, and she went into cardiac arrest."

Madeline rubs her hand over her face and shakes her head. "Oh, Lord. When will we ever learn?"

"I don't know. That's a question I ask myself every day." I lower my head and say a silent prayer for her unborn child. "Anyway, the outcome was that in order to save her life, the surgeons had to do a hysterectomy and remove part of her intestines. So she can never have another child—and the baby died."

Madeline takes a deep breath. "So what's your plan?"

"Well, I'm pretty sure our attorney can find Sandra. If she'll agree, I'd like her to meet with us, especially Sam. I think the two of them have a lot in common, and it might help them each to understand what happened to them. I doubt Sandra knows that Sam's dad attacked me, which might help her as well."

"At a minimum, it might be cathartic for you all to talk about the monster and how his savagery changed your lives."

"Right, I agree. I'll get on it and set it up."

Although reluctant at first, Sandra does agree to come to the meeting. Ten days later, we're back in Madeline's office. Sandra's hair is still dyed blond, although it's longer now and looks recently styled. Her pretty hazel eyes are covered in heavy eyeliner and purple shadow, and they repeatedly dart about, as though on a vigilant watch. *She's still afraid.*

Through Madeline's skillful guidance, Samantha and Sandra find out about each other and how powerless they were during their terrifying ordeals. Similar horrors connect us all in a strange sort of sisterhood, giving a modicum of relief that we are definitely not alone in our recovery.

A few weeks later, Sandra arrives at our meeting with

brown hair. Granted, it's died over the blond, but it's almost back to the original color. Aside from a smidge of mascara and blush, she isn't wearing makeup. For the first time, her eyes seem to have a bit more life in them. She looks better. "I like your hair, Sandra, and your makeup. It all looks more natural."

"Oh, I'm glad you noticed." She takes a deep breath. "It took some courage, but I think I'm done hiding." After our session, she pulls me aside. "Elizabeth, I owe you some thanks."

"No, you don't."

"Yeah, I do. So let me get this out. You're the closest thing I have to a real friend, and I'm grateful for everything you did, all the way back to the coffee you brought me in the hospital. When your attorney called me two months ago, I absolutely didn't want to come. But I'm so glad I did." She takes a deep breath. "I can finally close my eyes again and get some real sleep."

"I'm glad to hear that."

"You know, I used to blame myself for what he did to me. Like I should've been able to stop him or prevent the attack." She shakes her head.

I hug her tightly. "Nothing could be further from the truth."

"Yeah, I think I finally get that."

"Sandra, the monster was twice your size and whacked you from behind, just like he did to me."

"Trust me, I know that now."

"The important thing is to learn from it all and never be a victim again. I'm glad you're taking self-defense classes and learning to protect yourself."

"I have you to thank for that, too, Elizabeth. You gave me the courage."

We hug again. "See you next week, Sandra. Drive safely."

During my early November OB/GYN appointment, an ultrasound discloses that Jackson and I are having a baby boy. Even at five months gestation, he is adorable. My due date is reconfirmed for the end of February, and everything is on track. Jackson's parents come up for Thanksgiving, and Rebecca helps me decorate the empty front bedroom for the baby, which is exactly what Jackson designed it for in the first place.

Although my boss, Angela, isn't thrilled about me being on maternity leave for four months, she agrees to it, especially when I offer to work from home during my time off. I redouble my efforts to get as much work done in advance as I can to avoid leaving her hanging on my projects.

By mid-December, my belly is pretty huge and I don't feel much like long-haul flying, so we opt to stay put for the Christmas holidays, mostly at our home in Canada. Jackson's parents are in Asia finalizing some major deal, and his sister is holding down the business in Texas. Aside from traveling back and forth to Port Angeles for Jackson's church services and perishable groceries, the three of us enjoy a quiet holiday season.

Jackson and Sam manage to find the perfect tree in the nearby woods and set it up in the living room bay window. After stringing it with lights, Sam and I decorate it with homemade ornaments.

"I'm thinking these looked a lot better in the magazine," Sam says.

"Yeah, but still, they are pretty unique." I hand her a purple Styrofoam egg to hang. "Maybe it's just a matter of practice."

"Maybe, but I don't think I'll show my art teacher." We both laugh.

"I think they're all magnificent!" Jackson says. "The best ornaments I've ever seen."

On Christmas Eve, following the afternoon service and an early dinner at Café Garden, Jackson flies me, Sam, Mike, and Sally back to our coastal home so we can all be together on Christmas morning. The lightly falling snow and a few remaining rays of daylight complete the enchanting scene, reminiscent of a Currier and Ives painting. Alder runs through the snow, tossing it up with his paws, biting at the falling flakes, and rolling on his back in the thicker patches. As I lean against a front porch post and absorb the quiet beauty of the evening, I am filled with awe and the deepest gratitude.

Thank you, God, for allowing this to happen. Thank you for saving me. Thank you most of all for this beautiful life inside me. I rub my hands over my engorged belly, trying to feel all of my baby's wonderful features.

"Elizabeth, it's time!" Samantha calls out from the open front door. "You said I could, as soon as we got back. Can I, please? Pleeeease?"

Turning, I answer, "Oh, okay. I did promise." *She's so excited!* "But just one. And wait till I get there. I want to take pictures."

"Okay, but hurry up!" She waves her hand, signaling me to come inside. "Come on! Jackson's making hot chocolate."

Sam has conned us into allowing her to open one gift tonight, as a prequel to the rip-and-tear of tomorrow morning. Sitting around the fragrant fir tree, we all watch while she selects one present out of the many waiting for her eager hands.

"This is the one. I just know it!" She picks up a medium-sized box and looks at me. Not wanting to give her a clue, I give her as blank a stare as I can muster. Since Jackson doesn't know what is in most of the boxes, he's of no help. "It's got to be them."

"Only one way to find out," Mike says.

"Yeah, I guess." Sam shakes the box again.

"Wait," Sally says, "what about this one?"

"No, I feel it!" Undaunted, Sam hugs the box to her chest. "This is the one."

Sam seems to savor every moment, carefully undoing the wrapping paper one corner at a time, as though this is her very first Christmas. Despite the suspense, she doesn't hurry. *Maybe it is her first Christmas.* With the paper all but off, she takes a deep breath and tightly squeezes her eyes closed, as if she's plunging into icy water.

"Yippee! I knew it!" Her face lights up like a diamond in the sky. "Boots! My cool boots!" she exclaims as she removes the fur-lined black suede boots from their box and holds them up for everyone to see.

For two months I've watched her admire them longingly in the local shoe store window and knew she wanted them about as badly as I wanted my baby to arrive safely. *What a sight! She's gonna love the rest of her gifts tomorrow morning.* I can hardly wait.

"I know it's only Christmas Eve," Jackson says, "but I have to say that this is about the best Christmas I could imagine."

"Hear, hear!" Mike says.

Sam crosses the room to Jackson and puts her lithe arms around his neck. "Thank you, Jax. I love you guys so much."

This is the first time she's ever hugged him or said those words to either of us. Crossing to me next, she repeats herself. By the time she's done, not a dry eye remains.

After hot chocolate, Christmas carols, and a few hands of Uno, it's time for bed. I'm tired and know Samantha will undoubtedly be up early. When I tuck her in, I find she's wearing her new boots in bed. "You sure you want to sleep in those?"

"I'm never taking them off," she answers with a wide grin.

"Works for me." I kiss her forehead. "Sweet dreams."

A few minutes later, as I lay in bed next to Jackson, I say, "We still don't have a name for our baby."

"I know."

"So you haven't decided?"

"Not yet. I'm still considering," he responds.

"Well, I've given you my opinion, and need you to make up your mind."

"I just think another Jackson is too much. I'm hoping it will come to me."

"Okay. Maybe you'll have a revelation or something."

He rolls over and kisses me. "Good night, my darling. I love you."

"Night. Love you, too."

I stand alone on a single stone suspended thousands of feet in midair, exactly in the middle of an enormous crevasse. Miles from either side, I sense an urgency to step in one direction or the other, but am unsure which way to proceed. I wait. A breeze swirls gently around me. Although feeling peaceful, I'm deeply confused.

"Elizabeth."

"Joseph, is that you?"

"Yes."

"What am I doing here?"

"This is the point to which everyone involved must eventually arrive."

"Everyone involved?"

"Yes."

"Am I involved?"

"Only indirectly. But it is important that you understand."

"Understand what?"

"How death is dealt with."

"Is this where I will come when I die?"

"No."

"Then why do I need to see?"

"Because you facilitated the deaths of others."

"What? When?" I ask.

"Many times. And you need to understand what awaits them."

"I don't remember."

"Because each one seemed insignificant."

"No! It can't be true."

"Yes, it is."

"I don't understand, Joseph. You're confusing me."

"Follow me."

Without pausing to consider, I move one foot and find myself back in the warm air of the cathedral prayer room, overlooking the deep, dark, pliant pool of undulating water. Once again I see the countless millions of small ovoids lit faintly from within. "I've been here before."

"Yes."

"What is this place?"

"Look deeply into your soul, and you will find the answer."

I can't perceive what he expects me to comprehend. "I . . . don't know."

"Feel the life within you."

I look at my swollen abdomen and instinctively put my hand underneath it. I can see the light from within my belly and know that the light is my baby's soul. Looking into the pool, I see the millions of floating lights, now glowing brighter in response to my own baby's life. "Are they all souls?"

"Yes."

"Waiting to be born?"

"No."

"Then who are they?"

"Souls without sin. Souls denied the natural cycle of life."

"The unborn."

"Yes, Elizabeth. The truly Pure. All of them."

"Is this their Heaven?"

"No, this is their Holding, where they wait."

"For what?"

"To be claimed."

"Claimed?"

"Claimed by their parents."

"I don't understand."

"Some parents desperately want to claim. Some parents remorsefully claim. And some simply do not."

"But who wouldn't, if these are their children?"

"Those who elect not to."

"Elect not to?"

"Yes, those from your earth-realm who disregard life."

Oh my God! I feel a dark terror.

"And those who have lost count."

"Lost count?"

"Yes. Millions of souls are created for nothing. Without thought."

The dark terror grows, threatening to suffocate me. I hear myself screaming. "Joseph, please let me go! I don't want to know. I don't want to be here anymore."

"Not until you understand."

"Understand what?"

"The Tenth is almost upon you. You will have to choose. If the Tenth breaks through, all will be lost."

"Please let me go. I beg you!"

A wave of energy moves through the room, bringing me a welcome respite from the terror.

"*JOSEPH, LET HER GO.*"

"Father!"

"*RELEASE HER.*"

"But she must choose," Joseph says defiantly.

"YOU DO NOT UNDERSTAND, MY SON. YOU HAVE NEVER UNDERSTOOD. SHE ALREADY HAS CHOSEN."

———————

Feeling nauseated, I roll over on my side. "Jackson, I'm sick." I sit up on the edge of the bed, panting. "I'm gonna throw up. Hand me something!"

Rolling toward me, Jackson realizes I really am ill and quickly puts the wastebasket in my hands. I rapidly upchuck dinner and the hot chocolate. *Nothing ever tastes good coming up.* "Ugh, dang. I hate to throw up."

"Babe, you're covered in sweat. Your nightgown is drenched! You think it's indigestion? Or the baby?"

"Maybe a little of both. But I had a terrible dream with Joseph. Could be that."

Jackson hands me a wet washcloth and helps me to the bathroom. I clean up and rinse my mouth out. "Vomiting has to be one of the worst things in the world," I complain.

"You want some tea?" he asks.

"Yeah, maybe. Let's go downstairs for a few minutes."

Jackson makes a pot of mint tea and puts a dollop of honey in the bottom of the cup for me. I sit on a stool at the granite island and look around at the familiar surroundings of our beautiful kitchen. *This is real,* I tell myself. *Not that place with Joseph. You don't need to be afraid.* I want to stop shaking and get my stomach right side up.

"Maybe this will help your tummy to calm down," Jackson says, handing me the hot concoction.

"Maybe." I try to pull myself out of Joseph's realm. "But I need to tell you about my dream before any of it fades."

"Okay. I'm all ears." He sits down on a stool next to me so that our knees touch.

"I think I understand a few things about Joseph, maybe even what his purpose is."

"Wow. It'd be nice to have some real answers."

"Maybe, possibly." I think for a moment, then square my shoulders. "What Joseph showed me scared the crap out of me tonight. Really scared me. I felt a terror I've never felt before. I think that's why I got so sick."

"Oh, babe. I'm so sorry." He rubs my forearm. "I wish I could make it all stop."

"Me, too." I take a deep breath. "Jackson, at the end, when I was really frightened, another voice spoke. This time, I'm absolutely certain it was God. Our God. And He's angry."

"At you? Why would God be mad at you?"

"No, not at me. His voice filled me with peace." *Thank goodness.* "It was like God was counteracting Joseph."

Jackson nods thoughtfully. "I always wondered if Joseph was a good boy." He looks up at the ceiling. "Hmm. That's interesting."

"He commanded Joseph to . . ." I try hard to remember all the words. "To release me. Definitely commanded. He was God."

"So, that would mean Joseph does have a will. A will of his own."

"Yeah, and he's using his will to control me and my dreams—he's causing them. I think that's why God's mad. I'm certain now that Joseph's broken the rules, and we aren't supposed to know about their dimension."

"We've got to get him out of your head."

"Yeah, we do." I try to remember the dream. "But Jackson, after tonight, I believe there really is something I'm supposed to do. I just don't know what it is yet."

"Well, I'd like him out of our lives. Think about the power he has, what he's able to do. I mean, the storm, the earthquake, the downed tree. Then there's the bending time thing."

As I think back over the list of events, I also remember another side. "On the other hand, he did bring us together, and he did try to warn me about the assault, so maybe he's not a bad guy."

"Maybe not. But I'd sure like him to leave us alone now, at least until the baby comes."

"Yeah, me too, I guess."

"Okay. Whenever you're ready, tell me about your dream. Start from the beginning, and try not to leave anything out. Even the smallest detail could be important."

As bizarre as the dream sequence sounds, I try to carefully describe all that I saw and felt. Jackson patiently listens to my ramblings. At the end I say, "I can give you my interpretation on a few things, but it may not be accurate."

"Try me."

"I think Joseph is some kind of tool or guide for souls. Souls of unborn babies."

He considers this. After a moment, he says, "One of my foundational beliefs is that all innocent souls go to Heaven to be with God. Period, no questions asked. It would be hard for me to accept that God would punish them for something totally beyond their control."

"I don't think they're being punished. I'm not sure the souls even know they're in that place. Joseph keeps calling it a 'Holding.' So what if it is?" I shake my head. "I'm just thinking out loud."

"Okay, let's say that's true. What's the point of keeping them in pods in a pool?"

"No clue. Except water is essential for life, and the womb is filled with amniotic fluid, a type of water. Maybe the pool is God's womb." *Oh, I wish I hadn't said that.* "Probably a stupid idea, because honestly, I don't know."

"No, wait, I think you're on to something. Just think of our rite of baptism, a symbol of our rebirth with Christ."

"Yeah, and what if these souls aren't there for themselves?" My thoughts are speeding up. "I mean, what if they're in Joseph's world waiting for their parents, the ones who conceived them?"

"For a reunion? Like they have to wait for their parents to catch up to them?"

A light goes on in my head. "Exactly. A reunion."

"Well, that's cool. So they'd all enter Heaven together."

"Or not." A feeling of anxiety creeps into the back of my mind. "What if it's a test for the parents?"

"What kind of test?"

"To see if they're worthy." I stare at a blank spot on the wall. "A test of their worthiness in accepting Grace."

"Dear God, Elizabeth!" Jackson exclaims in a whisper.

"Dear God is right." Another wave of nausea sweeps over me. "Dang, Jackson. Think about how casually people have sex. How casually a soul is conceived . . ." My stomach turns over. "Crap, I'm gonna be sick again." I run to the sink and retch up my tea.

Jackson stands with me, rubbing my back. "Babe, what can I do for you?"

Tears stream down my face as I brace myself against the counter and retch again into the sink. Through a mouthful of spittle, I whisper, "Think of all the abortions—the millions, if not billions, of abortions."

Handing me a wet towel, he says in a low voice, "I have. I do. I pray about it every single day."

I look at him sideways from the depths of the sink. "Where does it start?"

"Where does what start?"

"The soul."

"I don't know. No one except God knows the answer to that. But you know I've always believed it starts at the beginning."

"So, with conception?"

"At least."

I cringe. "Think of what that could mean." I stand and sob into his shoulder. "What if the other dimension I saw is real?"

"Then you got a glimpse of the road to Heaven." He holds me tightly until I calm down and the nausea subsides.

"I need to sit down."

He guides me to a nearby chair, where I collapse. "Jackson. Think for a minute. What if all those parents—mothers *and* fathers—are required to come together at some point and acknowledge the souls they've created, but don't recognize? What if those parents have no clue?"

"Even worse, what if they don't care?"

"Exactly. And what if the chasm is their final opportunity to decide? A kind of test. And if they fail . . ."

"Then Hell must be a really big place," he says sadly.

We sit in silence for what seems like an eternity. Gradually my stomach settles down, and my head begins to clear.

Quietly, I speak. "I still don't understand what 'the Tenth' is. But it keeps coming up, and it scares me. Joseph said again that I'd have to choose. But the other voice said that I already had. Help me, Lord! What did I choose?"

"I don't know." He lowers his head.

As if in answer, my baby kicks my ribs violently. Thoughts fly in crazy circles. *Please help me, God! What if this is like* Rosemary's Baby *and I'm carrying the devil? Stupid thought. Sorry, baby.*

Wait! I grab Jackson's arm. "What if our son is 'the Tenth,' like the anti-Christ or something?"

He laughs a little. "Not possible."

"Why?"

"Because he was conceived out of pure love by two people who desire to love another."

"Oh." *He's right. He's got to be right.* "Yes, of course. Of course."

"Whatever 'the Tenth' is, I think you'll know it when you see it."

"That's scary."

"Well, if it was in fact God you heard in your dream, that should give you great peace."

"Why?"

"Because you've already chosen, and your destiny is sealed. God already knows your answer."

What a thought. "I hope I made the right choice."

"Have faith, Elizabeth. God is on our side, and He's protecting you. Don't worry, eventually it'll all be clear."

The clock strikes 3:00 a.m., and I need more sleep.

"Merry Christmas," I say. I snuggle next to his warm body and drift off.

35

Christmas morning comes so early that the sun isn't even breaking through the towering fir boughs in the east. Unable to wait, Samantha runs through the house in her new suede boots, waking everyone with the "news" that the big day has arrived. Jackson and I hug each other in bed and decide that Samantha's honest joy is the best Christmas gift anyone could possibly hope for. We don robes and slippers and make our way down to the living room.

"Sam, time to test out those new boots! Take Alder out for a long morning run while I build a fire."

"No problem. Come on Alder, let's go!" Ankle deep in snow, she runs through the backyard while I pop a large, candy-cane-shaped pastry in the oven and make coffee.

"How's your tummy?" Jackson asks as he kisses my neck.

"Better, thank goodness. I'd hate to ruin the day for Sam."

When Sam and Alder return, they are covered in freshly fallen snow. "These boots are awesome. Look, my feet aren't even cold!" She points to her toes.

"Isn't that a bonus?" Jackson teases.

"Ha, ha."

"Actually, they're quite nice," I say. "I may have to get a pair myself."

"Cool. Then we could be twins."

While we politely wait for Mike and Sally to join us, Sam strategically positions herself on the rug in front of the Christmas tree, guarding and rechecking all the gifts. Picking through the massive pile, she casually blurts out, "Oh yeah, by the way . . . I know what you should name your son."

"Oh, really?" I ask.

"Yup. It's perfect."

"Well, don't keep us in suspense. What's the perfect name?"

"King Arthur." She looks up at us in total sincerity, her long brown hair pulled around to one side, as usual. "Well, without the 'King' part."

"Hmm, Arthur. Arthur Howard Morgan, the first." I look at Jackson. "Not bad."

"See, you guys are like the king and queen of the magical kingdom, and your son will be the prince. You know, like Prince Arthur who pulled the magic sword out of the stone and changed the world?"

Jackson and I exchange glances.

"Because he will, you know. He's coming to help you choose."

Her words hit me smack dab in the heart and, judging from Jackson's reaction, have the same effect on him. Someone is sending us a direct message. *Okay, what is it we're supposed to do, God? I'm listening. We're listening.*

"I think that was the epiphany I was waiting for," Jackson says, nodding to me.

"Seriously? You like it?" Sam asks. "Cool."

"Yeah, I do."

Already redirecting her focus, Sam is organizing the piles of wrapped packages and seems to have momentarily forgotten our discussion.

Jackson raises an eyebrow at me as he casually stokes the fire. "So, Sam, when did you happen to think of the name?"

"Oh, I dunno." She picks a present out and shakes it. "I think it came to me in a dream last night. A boy told me." She looks up from her position on the floor. "He said it was important."

"Have you ever dreamed about him before?" I sip my coffee nonchalantly.

"Maybe. He seemed sorta familiar." She examines another package. "Hey, Sally! Merry Christmas!"

"Merry Christmas to you, too."

"Coffee's in the kitchen," I say. "Help yourselves."

Soon we're all gathered around the tree. Jackson gives Samantha the task of handing out gifts to everyone as equally as possible. Considering that most of them are for her, things are a bit lopsided. It's sheer pleasure watching her act like the innocent little kid she's never had the opportunity to be before. And she scores big time, too: a laptop and printer from Jackson's parents, some beautifully bound books from Roger and Nan, a leather jacket from Mike and Sally, and a few things from us as well.

"That's it," she announces when the space under the tree is empty. "All done. No more presents!"

"I'm not too sure about that, Sam," says Jackson. "What about that tiny one hanging from the back branch?" He points to a little blue package with a velvet bow.

"Ooh, what's this?"

"No clue. Who's it for?"

"Me," she answers.

"Well, you should probably open it, then."

Carefully, she undoes the bow and wrapper and

withdraws a small velvet jewelry box. As she opens the lid, she lets out a huge gasp. "Oh my gosh, it's beautiful!" Seemingly shocked, she sits back down on the floor and starts to cry. "It's so beautiful," she whispers.

"So are you, sweetie," I say. "It's from both of us."

"Let's see what it is," Mike says.

Sam holds up the delicate gold chain. Dangling from it is a simple gold cross with a sparkling diamond set in the middle. "Will you put it on me, please?" She scoots over to the front of my rocking chair.

"I'd be honored."

After I attach the clasp, she walks to the mirror in the hall. I watch her as she studies her reflection, rubbing the cross between her fingers. Speaking mostly to herself, she says, "I love it. It's the best present of all."

"All right, everyone," Jackson says, "Time for breakfast!"

We finish a late breakfast and go for a trek around the property in the snow, which is now at least eight inches deep and falling hard. Under thick, low clouds, it's a lovely sight watching the snowflakes hit the calm water in the bay. Taking a shortcut through the woods, Sally and I reach the house ahead of the pack.

"Sally, I think Joseph's been in contact with Sam."

"Oh, no." She shoots me an intense look. "What happened?"

I repeat the conversation we had about the baby's name and the suggestion Sam made. "She seemed really casual about the whole thing, like she was just relaying an innocent message."

"Well, that's good. At least he didn't freak her out."

"I guess not. But I had a terrible dream early this morning. It was so bad, I vomited when I woke up."

"Oh, bless your heart, are you okay?"

"Yeah, but it was awful. I think I know what Joseph does."

When I finish telling Sally about my dream and what I figured out, she just stares at me.

Finally she speaks. "I'm pretty reserved about my opinions, but I don't mind telling you, I'm very opposed to abortion. For forty plus years, abortion rights advocates have crammed lies down our throats that life in the womb isn't significant, that it's only tissues."

"Sally, I was one of their believers. I mean, I knew late-term abortions were wrong, but didn't care one way or the other about the early-term ones. Honestly, until I had the epiphany in the ED, I never gave the subject much thought. But when I saw that baby girl in the towel, everything changed. I knew it had a soul."

"The thing that bothers me the most," Sally says, "is watching our country move away from morality and into the horrors of Hitler's Nazi Germany or Stalin's Russia. It starts with early abortions, then late-term, then getting rid of a newborn with defects, then older kids, then elderly adults. Anyone who's a drain on society."

"What a horrible thought."

"There've been lots of dark times in our humanity, but those were some of the worst. So many were murdered, eventually the population became numb and life meant nothing. Our country's moving in the same direction."

"Yeah, I agree. We're adrift." Since I started paying attention, even I can see our disinterested attitudes snowballing.

"America used to be different." She shakes her head. "We used to believe in God. Our laws used to count every life as precious, including life in the womb. But in one single generation we allowed immoral leaders to erode our society. In doing so, we threw away the value of life, and with it, God."

"Not everyone did," I say softly. *I just found Him.*

"No, but since the vocal minority is the underbelly of the engine that gets the grease, we're a lot more likely to save a newt than a baby's life." She lets out a sigh. "It makes me sick."

"Yeah." I rub my hands over my belly. *Don't worry, Arthur. You'll be loved.* "Me, too."

Sally sits back and puts her hands up over her head. "I can take a little comfort in your dreams. It's good to know the millions of violent murders aren't forgotten, and the guilty are tried. Ha! Just imagine their surprise when they reach the chasm and come face-to-face with their crimes. I just pray the prisoner list includes everyone who facilitates the murders as well."

"That list would include me." I look down at my hands. I can't see the bloodstains, but I know they're there.

"Why?"

"Because I've handed out hundreds of 'morning-after' pills. That means I've helped abort hundreds of innocent lives." I feel sick again. "It's mind-boggling."

Sally lowers her arms and crosses them. "Yes, it is. But the important thing is that now you know. For some reason, you've been given a glimpse of another dimension most of us don't even know exists. You got to experience the truth. I have faith that God will base His verdict about you on what you do from this point forward. You can choose to either continue to be a part of the problem, or you can choose not to."

Choose. That word comes up over and over. "Considering the life inside me, that decision's a no-brainer." *Please forgive my arrogance, God. I didn't understand.*

"So, Elizabeth, what do you think 'the Tenth' is?"

"That's still a mystery. I have no idea."

The back door opens, and Alder comes charging in, followed by the rest of the gang, all covered in snow. "It's great out there!" Sam exclaims. "We made snow angels and a big snowman. I need a carrot for his nose." She opens the vegetable bin in the fridge.

"Help yourself. I'll get the camera," I say as she runs back outside.

"We can talk about this some more later," Sally says. "I'll fill Mike in. By the way, I kind of like the name Arthur. It has a nice ring to it."

"I do, too," Jackson says as he puts the standing rib roast in the oven. He checks his watch. "Christmas dinner will be ready at three o'clock."

As hours drift by and the roast slowly bakes, the delicious aroma fills the house. By late afternoon, the snow is falling much harder, and it's decided that Mike and Sally will indeed be spending one more night with us. No sense risking an evening flight across the pond in bad weather.

"Yay! I'm so happy you're snowbound with us," Sam says. "Now we can play a ferocious game of Monopoly."

"I'm for that," Mike says, "but I get to be the car."

"Deal. I'll go set it all up."

The game does indeed keep us occupied well into the night. When I tuck Sam in at eleven, she puts her hand on my belly, feeling the baby move. "I've always wanted a little brother. Hang on, Arthur, you're almost here."

"Ha, ha! Don't rush it, Sam. Arthur still has two months, and we both need it. Especially me. I have a lot of shopping to do."

———※·※———

Someone pushes against my shoulder. I'm so sleepy, I don't want to wake up yet.

I feel another nudge. "Elizabeth. Elizabeth."

Opening my eyes through the fog of sleep, I realize Samantha is standing next to me at the edge of the bed, her long pink nightgown silhouetted against the darkness. She's shivering badly.

I reach for Jackson, rousing him.

"Hey, Sam, aren't you cold?" I ask, sitting up. Meanwhile, Jackson gets up and puts my robe around her shoulders.

Sam doesn't seem to notice. "Prepare and make ready!

Arthur is about to arrive. Prepare and make ready!" She raises one arm and points to my belly. "He comes early to save the Tenth."

"She's asleep," Jackson whispers. "Sleepwalking and talking." He waves his hand in front of her eyes, but she doesn't blink or flinch. "Like she's in a trance."

"Look at her feet," I whisper, pointing to her reddish toes. "They're wet and bright red, like she's been standing outside in the snow or something."

"Joseph understands now," Samantha says. "He knows Arthur is coming to help slay the dragon."

Arthur slay the dragon? "What dragon?" *What the heck is she talking about? Joseph, what have you done to her?*

"Prepare and make ready. Arthur comes early, to save . . . aaahhh . . ." With that final word, Sam faints, collapsing on the floor.

"Dang, girl!" I say, grabbing for her.

Kneeling by her side, Jackson lifts her petite body and carries her back to her bedroom.

"She's freezing," he says. "Ice cold."

Together we tuck her back under the warm covers and put her favorite stuffed animal under her arm. I fetch more blankets and pile them on top. She stirs a little and rubs one eye. "Hey, guys, what's going on?"

"Nothing, dear. You were talking in your sleep and cried out. We're just checking on you."

In a suspicious reflex, she grabs the covers and pulls them up tightly around her neck. "What happened?"

"She's frightened, Jackson. We should just tell her the truth."

Sam relaxes her grip on the sheets a little. "The truth about what?"

I sit on the edge of the queen-size bed while Jackson pulls a chair up and sits on the other side.

"It sounded like you were having a nightmare," he says. "Can you remember anything about it?"

She takes a deep breath and closes her eyes. "Not really. Except, I'm really cold." Her teeth start chattering uncontrollably.

"Yeah, you're shivering," I say. "Actually, you were sleep-walking. Have you ever done that before?"

"I was?" She looks up at the ceiling. "No, I don't think so. Where did I go?"

"You walked to our room and woke me up."

"Oh, sorry. I didn't mean to bother you."

I lay a hand on her arm. "We're not mad at you, darling. Just trying to figure out what you were dreaming about. I think it's important."

"Why?"

"Because I keep dreaming about a young man in a faraway land who tells me stories about babies, and other things." I pause, waiting for her reaction. "I think maybe it's the same one who told you about the name Arthur."

"Yeah, now that you mention it, I do remember a boy. He's about fifteen or sixteen, with blond hair . . . and he wears a kind of long robe or something."

"It might help us to understand Elizabeth's dreams, if you can remember any of yours," Jackson says.

"It's kind of hazy. But I remember it was really cold. And from somewhere I could hear the sound of water."

"I always hear water, too, like a waterfall."

"Maybe." She shrugs her shoulders under the covers, and her chattering teeth calm down a little. "The boy seems nice, but kinda sad, I think. Like he's got a big problem. I'm not too sure."

"Did he take you anywhere in your dream? Like down a long hallway or outside into a green meadow?"

"I only remember one place. It was winter, icy cold. I was standing on a narrow stone path that had come to a Y, and I had to choose which way to go. To the left it went down into a creepy, dark forest filled with fog. It looked even colder down there. Ugh!" She shudders. "The other path, going to the right, went up toward a low hill. I could see the sun rising, and it seemed warmer."

"What did you do?" I ask.

"Honestly, I just wanted to leave. You know, run away. I didn't want to choose. I felt alone and afraid."

"It's okay, sweetie. It was just a dream," I say, holding her hand.

"Do you remember what happened?" Jackson asks.

"Yeah." Sam looks down at the covers and swallows hard. "I saw my dad's face in the foggy darkness and started running as hard as I could in the opposite direction."

"Oh, Sam, that's so scary," I say.

"Yeah. I never want to see my dad again. But that's when I saw the boy. He stopped me on the path and said that I needed to warn you."

"Warn me? About what?"

"That your baby's coming soon. He said it has to." She looks at the ceiling again. "He said, 'Tell Elizabeth to prepare and be ready.'"

"Arthur still has two months. Did the boy say what I'm supposed to be ready for?"

"I don't know. I woke up here, and you guys were looking at me."

"Well, everything's okay now. You're safe and back in bed." I pat her hand again and pull the comforter up around her shoulders. "By the way, where are your new boots?" I ask, joking.

"Huh, I don't know." She sits up and feels her feet. "I had them on when I went to bed."

"Don't worry, they're probably downstairs in the living room."

"No, I remember. I wiped them off and everything just before I got in bed."

"I'll find them for you," Jackson says.

"Thanks." She smiles but seems uneasy. "Leave the hall light on, will you please?"

"Sure." I leave the door ajar, and Jackson goes downstairs to look for the missing boots.

I guess I'll make a cup of boring tea. I waddle down to the kitchen, and as I'm putting the kettle on, I notice the back door ajar. "Jackson? Jackson?" I whisper loudly out the back.

"Yeah, I'm out here." His response comes from clear across the yard. He's near the edge of the forest, and I can see the flashlight strobe moving back and forth, searching the ground.

I step out onto the back stoop so he can hear me better. "What are you doing out there? There's no way her boots would be out there."

He continues to move his light back and forth on the ground as he returns to the house, holding Samantha's black boots up with his hand. "I found one pair of footprints matching these boots leading over there, toward the woods." He points with his light. "And where she stopped, I found two more sets of prints within a small area. One set was medium-sized, and the other was huge, probably a man's, with Vibram soles."

"You mean someone's here? On our property?"

"I'm not sure. Where all the footprints converge, there seems to be confusion, like they were moving around each other or something. And I found her boots in the middle of the mess. But here's the weird thing. Aside from her boot prints leading from the house to the forest, I couldn't find another single print leading up to the converging spot, and none leading away. It's like the two others just dropped in from the sky. And there are no footprints from Samantha walking back to the house. Even if she was barefoot, there'd be clear prints. But there's nothing. Nada."

Now I'm freaking out. "Can we call someone to make sure her dad is still locked up?"

"My thoughts as well. Let's go back inside. I'll turn on the security system."

Turning off the teakettle, I find my Walther in its fanny pack and buckle the pack around my shoulder. No way it will fit around my bulging waist at this point. *If he's escaped, I'm killing the bastard this time. No ifs, ands, or buts.*

I have a sudden thought. "Jackson, you don't suppose this is another one of Joseph's attempts to isolate us and communicate, do you?"

"I considered that, except that he's already communicated. Seems like he's been communicating without any problem." He dials the phone. "Yeah, hi. Sorry to call so late, but I need some information about a prisoner . . . Sure. This is Pastor Jackson Morgan . . . No problem, I'll wait."

We wait while they validate the information Jackson gives them. Apparently murderers and rapists are entitled to "privacy." *What a crock! I like early America better, when criminals were locked in stockades in full public view.*

"No problem. Oh, I see. When? . . . It's confirmed then? . . . If you don't mind my asking, what happened? . . . Really? How's that possible? . . . You're right, it is weird. Well, thanks so much," Jackson says. "Oh, one more thing. What kind of shoes did he wear? . . . Yeah, you're right, stupid question, but I need to know . . . No kidding. Okay, I appreciate your help." He clicks the phone off and sets it down.

"He's dead. About an hour ago."

"Huh?" I suck in a breath that feels like icy fingers going into my lungs. "What happened?"

"Severe hypothermia. He froze to death."

"What? How the heck did he freeze to death in prison?"

"They have no idea. He was found in his bed frozen solid. And he had traces of sap and fir trees in his hair."

"What about his shoes?" I'm afraid to hear the answer.

"Supposed to be sneakers, except that tonight the guards found boots—with Vibram soles. And they were wet."

I sit down hard on the chair. "You think Joseph caused this?"

"Oh babe, I'm just a pastor. This is way above my pay grade."

"This gets more bizarre by the minute." *To heck with tea, I want a drink so badly I can taste it.* "I want some brandy."

"No can do, darling. Little Arthur wouldn't like it." He puts his arms around me. "We'll figure this out. I promise."

The day after Christmas is clear and bright. Before breakfast, Jackson takes Samantha for a walk and explains what happened to her dad as delicately as possible.

"It's okay, Jackson. I already know. The boy in my dreams came back again last night and told me I didn't have to be afraid anymore."

"What are you talking about?"

"Joseph. The boy I've been dreaming about. He killed him."

"Samantha! You don't mean that."

"Yes, I do. He did it. Right over there." She points to the area near the forest where Jackson found the footprints and located her black boots. "He made him freeze to death."

"Sam, your dad was in jail. There's no way he could get here and then freeze."

"But he did freeze to death, right?"

"Yeah, he did," Jackson admits.

"And you found footprints right over there, right?"

"Yeah."

"Trust me, Joseph brought him here and made the cold wind freeze him."

"Honey, this is crazy."

"No, it's not crazy. It's Joseph. And he's gonna make the other one fry."

"Your mom?"

"No, my mom's bad, but not like the other one. The other one's really bad, pure evil. Joseph's gonna make the lightning strike her. She'll catch fire and burn from the inside."

"Who are you talking about?"

Samantha shrugs her shoulders. "What? Uh, I dunno. Just a thought that popped into my head." She shakes her head and seems confused. "At least I don't have to worry about testifying in court."

While they're out walking, I take the opportunity to bring Mike and Sally up to speed on the events of the night, including the discovery of Sam's boots at the edge of the forest. Like us, they have no explanation for the footprints or how they might connect to the freezing death of Sam's dad, other than the likely involvement of Joseph. The only thing we can all concur on is that it's a blessing her dad is most definitely dead.

"Wait till I tell you about my conversation with Sam," Jackson whispers in my ear. "I think Joseph is taking matters into his own hands."

36

"Ready to go, Elizabeth?"

I hear the floatplane's engine running. "Yeah, I'm just calling Dr. Hudson's office to see if they can work me in." I hold up one finger. "That's great. Thanks so much. See you at two." Turning to Jackson, I ask, "Can we make it to Dr. Hudson's office by two?"

"Sure, if we drop Mike and Sally off and continue straight on to Seattle."

True to form, Jackson lands at Boeing and gets us to the appointment with fifteen minutes to spare.

"So, what brings you in here ahead of schedule?" Dr. Hudson asks. "I just saw you last week."

"Doc, I've been sick, vomiting. Not sleeping well, either. Just wanna be safe, rather than sorry."

"No problem. I'm happy to check things again." Dr. Hudson looks at my chart. "You lost two pounds since last week. Are you dieting?"

"Yeah, right." *Oh wait, he's serious.* "No, no way."

"Put your feet up here, and let me see."

Even with thick wool socks on, I can feel the cold steel stirrups as my heels settle in. *There is no dignity in childbirth.*

He feels my lower abdomen with one hand while he pushes ever so gently with two fingers of his other hand. "You've dropped a bit. Rather, the baby's dropped, head's down. Do you feel any different when you're walking?"

"Like I've got a football stuck between my thighs and I'm trying to hold it up."

"Good analogy." He smiles. "I want to run some labs and have the tech do an ultrasound. Stay put, and I'll be back in a few minutes." He opens the door and lets Jackson and Samantha back in. "She's fine, baby's fine. But I want to check a couple things before you leave."

"Thanks, Doc," Jackson says.

After the lab tech draws several vials of blood, the ultrasound tech comes in and dims the lights for the scan. Once my belly is slathered with slippery gel, she has no difficulty locating the baby's strong, steady heartbeat. We can see little Arthur upside down in my womb, moving his arms around and kicking his feet.

"He's so cool!" Sam says. "I love him already."

"Ooh, I felt that one, Arthur." I laugh as he nails a rib.

As the tech is finishing the scan, I feel a dribble of water oozing from between my thighs, like I just unexpectedly urinated.

"Dang, I think I just peed on the bed. Sorry."

She lifts the paper sheet and looks down. "No, that's not urine. I'll be right back."

She and the doc return a moment later, and he takes another look. "Young lady, your water just broke."

What did he say? That can't be right. "Why? Why'd my water just break?"

"I guess because this little guy is ready."

"But he needs more time!" I feel tears welling up as emotions flood my system. Mostly, I'm fearful of losing my precious cargo. "Please don't let him die."

"Hey. Hey, Elizabeth," he says, patting my arm. "Calm down. He'll be just fine. But I want to get you to the hospital."

Although Dr. Hudson's office is less than two blocks from Bayside, an ambulance is summoned to transport me directly to the OB Ward. Before the medics arrive, Dr. Hudson's nurse inserts an IV in my arm and starts running a small bag of fluids. Since I'm not having any cramps or contractions, no one is sure how fast the baby is coming or how long I have. Nevertheless, Jackson takes a few moments to alert his family and update all the usual suspects, promising to call back when we have more information.

Meanwhile, I'm lost in thought about Joseph's recent warnings: *Prepare and make ready. Arthur comes early.* And his words from months before: *Now your timing becomes essential.* What possible reason could there be for my baby to leave the safe haven of my womb to make an early entrance into this scary world?

Jackson, Samantha, and I pray together, asking God to allow for Arthur's safe passage. *Please God, it has to be all right!*

At 6:00 p.m., Dr. Hudson arrives at the hospital and writes a few more orders for my care. Soon after that, things happen fairly quickly. By 8:00 p.m. my cervix is dilated to six centimeters with a few contractions. By nine it's expanded to eight centimeters, and contractions are progressing to unbearable. By ten thirty I'm in full-blown labor.

At 11:00 p.m. sharp, Arthur enters the world, and somehow I manage to hang on through it all. While Dr. Hudson is suturing my episiotomy, a nurse lets me hold Arthur for just a moment.

"Hi, Arthur," I cry. Inspecting him more carefully, I notice he looks dusky. "He's a little blue, isn't he?"

"Yup, and we gotta go," a male voice says from behind a face mask.

"Wait, what's wrong with him?"

"I think he has a pneumothorax."

"What's that?" Jackson asks.

"A hole in his lung," the masked man says. "Probably sucked in a little amniotic fluid in the birth canal. He may also have premature lung disease. I'll know more in a few minutes. But right now, we need to hurry." Then he dashes out of the room with my newborn son in his arms and Jackson on his heels.

"Arthur's in good hands," Dr. Hudson says from his seated position down between my knees. "That's Dr. Daylen, the head neonatologist." I can feel him tugging at my numb groin with a suture line. "We knew he'd be a preemie and a small fry, but five pounds isn't bad. Problem is, he didn't cry real loud, and he didn't pink up. Initial APGAR score was five out of ten, but then dropped down to a three. We prefer the score to go the other direction."

"What happened?"

"Not sure. But if I had to speculate at this point, I'd say maybe you developed a late case of gestational diabetes or something. I had 'em draw some more labs right before you delivered, so we might learn something from that."

"I did everything you told me. I didn't cut any corners."

After clipping the last thread from the sutures, he stands up and looks at me in a fatherly way. "Look, Elizabeth. You know as well as anyone that these things just happen. The important thing is that he's going to be fine." He rips his gloves off as he walks around to my side of the bed. "Have a little faith in God and in the guys working on your son."

"Okay." Sobs come over me again. "It's just not what I expected."

"No, I'm sure it's not. But in a few weeks, it won't matter. Really." He pats my hand and clicks a buzzer, summoning a nurse. "Mrs. Morgan can have whatever she wants, and I think there's a sweet young lady in the waiting room who might want to come in for a visit."

Samantha keeps me company while Jackson runs back and forth between my room and the Neonatal Intensive Care Unit, or NICU, relaying information and updates. When Dr. Hudson returns to check on me at around 1:00 a.m., I'm borderline hysterical.

"Give her five of Valium," he orders the nurse.

I don't really want it, but I take it anyway. Two more agonizing hours pass while we await confirmation on Arthur's diagnosis and prognosis. At 3:00 a.m., Dr. Daylen and a woman in a white lab coat return to speak with us. He sits on a stool next to my bed.

"This is Dr. Thompson, our pediatric pulmonologist," Dr. Daylen says. "She and I have been working on your little guy. He's a real fighter."

"Oh, God," I cry. "Please tell me he's gonna survive."

"Absolutely. He'll be okay, but he's pretty sick. He has a pneumothorax, so we put two tiny chest tubes in his side to help keep the right lung inflated so it can heal. And he does have premature lung disease, so I intubated him to keep positive pressure up. At first we thought maybe we could manage his oxygen with a hood, but that didn't work. He's in an incubator and has a lot of lines in him, but he should be out of here in two or three weeks."

"Oh my God, I feel so bad." I start sobbing again.

"Listen, you two," Dr. Daylen says, "you didn't cause this. And one thing I've learned over the years is that parents need to maintain a positive attitude. I know it's tough, but he needs you to keep hope alive. These little ones can tell if parents are pulling for them."

"Okay." I squeeze Jackson's strong hand. "What about nursing him?"

"You'll be able to once he's ready. But right now we're feeding him through a tube so he can rest and gain a little strength. Have faith, though. It won't be long before he's in your arms, sucking away."

"Can I see him?"

"My dear, he's your son," Dr. Daylen says. "You can see him right now, if you feel up to it."

Someone brings me a wheelchair, and once I'm seated in it, Jackson pushes me down the hall toward the nursery. Passing the regular unit, I see all the precious babies bundled up in pink or blue swaddling cloths with their little knitted caps on and wonder why my Arthur has to be different. I feel helplessly devastated that my baby isn't in one of those open bins.

When we round the corner to the NICU, my heart sinks even deeper. Through the large glass viewing windows, I see about fifteen fully enclosed incubators, each one the temporary home for a miniature human being fighting for its life. In exchange for the dark, warm, protected environment of their mother's wombs, these tiny humans have been catapulted into a sterile, Plexiglas barrier under bright lights. Objectively, I know the purpose for every piece of equipment and understand the necessity of methodically buying precious time for each baby. Subjectively, it's breaking my heart.

All he needs is a little time. A few days, and he'll be out of the woods. Please God, watch over him! A younger woman in a robe walks up to the window and puts her hand on the glass. "That one is mine," she says softly, pointing to a baby a few feet away. "She had a bad infection when she was born, but she's okay now. The doctors here saved her life. They're amazing! Which one is yours?"

"I can't tell from here." I look at Jackson. "Which one is Arthur?"

Jackson clicks the intercom and asks for our son. Dr. Daylen and Dr. Thompson are huddling around his incubator, but respectfully back away long enough to allow the nurse to wheel it over to the window so we can all see. *He's perfect! Oh, thank you, God! He's perfect!* I start crying again.

Jackson kneels down next to the wheelchair and puts his arm around me. "Hey, he's going to be okay. This isn't your fault. God will see us through this."

Samantha joins us at the window. "Aw, he's about the cutest little thing I ever saw!" She kisses the top of my head. "Way to go, 'Mom'! You did perfect!"

"He is pretty amazing, isn't he?"

"Look at that turned-up nose and all that black hair," she says. "Well, maybe he doesn't have that much hair yet, but it sure is black."

Although her enthusiasm lightens my heart a little, an unquenchable thirst is growing from the depths of my belly and heart. I want to reunite with the baby who has lived within me for seven months, yet my arms sit idle, denied what they yearn for. I long to caress him and hold his warm little body to my bosom, but it is not to be. As though caught in some type of cruel torture wrenching our bodies apart, I feel the desperation of our separation.

Making the physical division even harder, I can feel the precursor to my breast milk beginning to flow toward my nipples. My body is ready to receive Arthur, to feed, nourish, and adore him. He just isn't ready for me.

I want him back! screams my soul. *He left before he was ready. Before I was ready.* Tears stream down my face as I cry openly.

Without warning, a vision appears next to Arthur's incubator. Joseph. All aglow, his serene face is smiling at me. *"Elizabeth, I was right,"* his voice says in my head. *"Arthur is the one. He arrived at the perfect moment."*

The one? The perfect moment? "Joseph, what are you talking about?"

Joseph looks down at my son in the incubator. *"Yes, Arthur is the one. He will fulfill his destiny."*

"Hey, kids," a cheerful voice greets us from behind. "They told me I'd find you here."

Pulled from my exchange with Joseph, I look around and see Dr. Bennett approaching. I look back toward Arthur, but the image of Joseph is gone.

"Hi, Dr. Bennett!" Sam says, throwing her arms around his neck and giving him a big hug. "Look at Arthur! Isn't he amazing?"

"Yes, he certainly is. And I understand he's got a lot of fight in him."

Jackson vigorously shakes Doc's hand. "Thanks for stopping by. We really appreciate it." He puts his other hand on my shoulder. "This is hard for us, you know."

"Well, don't tell anyone," he says as he winks at me, "but I've been checking on you guys since I came on last night at six. Been up here about every hour to make sure things are moving in the right direction. Daylen's a pretty sharp guy, doesn't miss much."

From the wheelchair, I look up at him through flooded eyes. "Thanks for being here. It means a lot." I bury my head in my hands. "I just don't want him to die."

Dr. Bennett squats down on his haunches next to my chair and holds my hands. "I have to believe God's plan was for Arthur to be born at precisely eleven p.m. on December twenty-sixth, and not a moment later. But not so he would die, so that he would live."

Eleven. The perfect time. The eleventh hour? What am I missing?

Dr. Bennett continues, "Why he needed to arrive early, I haven't a clue. But I'm absolutely certain there's a reason. And eventually, maybe God will make it known."

"You're right," I say. "I know. It just hurts." *Hurts to see him suffer, hurts not to hold him, hurts to watch them poke and prod him. God, take me in his place! I scream to myself. I can take the pain. Please don't put my child through all this.*

"Listen, Elizabeth. You're one of the toughest fighters I've ever known. You've survived some of life's most wrenching heartbreaks and a bad physical assault. And you came through stronger for it. According to what I've seen, your little guy in there"—he points through the glass to Arthur—"is cut from the same fabric, and he isn't about to give up. Seems like he's just like you."

"Hey, Doc," Jackson says as Dr. Daylen comes through the double doors of the outer NICU area.

Dr. Daylen pulls his mask down to give us a welcome update. "I just finished a couple other tests, and aside from his lungs, all his systems and organs seem to be functioning perfectly. I'm pretty pleased about his progress, and you should be, too."

"Thanks, Doc." I can see tears on the side of Jackson's face as he shakes Dr. Daylen's hand. *Oh, Jackson, you're just as worried as I am.*

"Now, I have some orders," Dr. Daylen says. "Everyone needs to get a few hours of sleep, including Arthur, and especially Elizabeth. I want all of you rested and ready to go by noon. That's when you'll learn how to scrub, gown, glove, and mask so you can enter the NICU and help take care of your baby. So scoot."

As hard as it is to turn away from my son, I know the advice is solid. As he escorts us back to my birthing room, Dr. Bennett says, "You might not see me much, but I'll be around."

"I really like him," Samantha says after he leaves. "Probably the coolest doctor I've ever met."

"Yeah, he is," I concur as I stiffly get into bed. Letting

myself relax a bit, I'm aware of how tired and sore my lower back and pelvis are. The local anesthesia Dr. Hudson injected before he repaired the episiotomy is wearing off, and my groin is starting to sting a little. "Jackson, could you please ask the nurse for a pain pill? I think I could use one."

With the extra blankets and pillows the staff provides, Samantha gets comfortable on a foldout chair, and Jackson curls up on the love seat. Thirty seconds after swallowing a single Percocet, I'm sound asleep. It's a difficult end to a very long day.

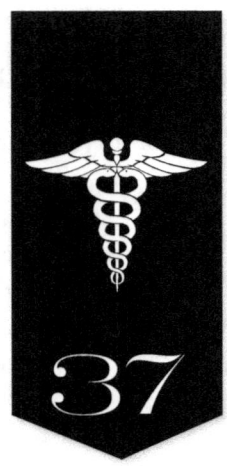

37

The next fourteen days are fraught with periods of anxiety, stress, and desperation, interspersed with prayer vigils, hope, and fleeting moments of confident peace that our son will survive unscathed. For every high, there is an equal low, the gamut circling in a never-ending pattern, always bringing us back to an unsure footing.

Jackson's parents cut their Asia trip short and fly back to Seattle to lend much-needed support, for which I am deeply grateful. Not wanting to leave the hospital's proximity, we all camp out at the Hotel de Florentino, although I rarely leave the NICU. When I do, it's to migrate catatonically to my office and make a weak effort to focus on a few projects. However ineffective I am, work is at least a diversion whenever worry overcomes me. Truth be told, I have a nagging feeling I will never want to return to my job after I get Arthur home.

Talented teams of nurses and doctors meticulously care for Arthur and the other neonates in the NICU, most of whom are premature. Fighting against overwhelming odds, these tiny people battle to overcome rare medical problems and life-threatening hurdles. For some, each successive heartbeat is a gift, every breath a defiance of death. As these miracles of life not only survive, but thrive, I begin to comprehend the relentless power of the human spirit, even in someone weighing only two pounds. These little ones desperately want life. All they need is a chance.

For Jackson and me, it is wondrous to watch Arthur gain half an ounce here, a quarter of an ounce there. Watching him kick his little legs and stretch his arms, I get the feeling he is letting the world know he will soon be a force in the universe. Gradually the tubes and lines are removed, first one chest tube, then the other. At last he is extubated, allowing his lungs the opportunity to breathe on their own.

Once it is determined that he can support his own respirations, the next step is to introduce him to fluids. Jackson and I watch spellbound as his tiny mouth surrounds the miniature rubber nipple and he drinks his first drops of warm, sterile water. Although his suckling reflex is present, he still isn't quite strong enough to latch on, so the feeding tube stays in for a few more days.

"Are you ready for this?" Dr. Daylen asks as he finally disconnects Arthur from the feeding tube. "I have to leave this one tiny IV line in his scalp, but otherwise, he's on his own. Here you go, Mom." He gently places Arthur in my arms.

"Oh, Jackson, he's so perfect!" The reunion is pure heaven for us as we cry, laugh, admire, snuggle, and love this little boy God has blessed us with. After pumping my breasts for three weeks, it is total ecstasy to feel him suckle and nurse from me. I can immediately feel my uterus responding in reflexive acknowledgment of the real thing. The miracle of life, my son at my breast.

By the twenty-third day, Arthur weighs almost six full

pounds, and we anticipate taking him home the next morning. But alas, a routine lab test reveals a moderate case of jaundice requiring treatment, so Dr. Daylen decides Arthur needs to sleep under fluorescent lights in the neonatal step-down unit for at least another forty-eight hours. I'm bummed, but know it's important to resolve all of his medical issues before we take him home.

At five thirty on the afternoon before Arthur's planned discharge, I'm in my office trying unsuccessfully to concentrate on a department budget report when I hear a knock at my door. "Come in," I holler.

"Hey, Elizabeth. How's it going?"

"Hey, Tom. Are you charge tonight?"

"Yeah."

"You're here kinda early." I look at my watch. "Aren't you?"

"Yeah, but I need to ask you a favor."

"Okay."

"I know you don't work the floor anymore, but I need to get out of here by about five thirty in the morning. My son's having his tonsils removed at Children's, and we need to be there by six thirty at the latest. That means I need to leave here about an hour early."

"Okay. Who's on day shift? Maybe they can come in a little early."

"I've called everyone. I've begged, pleaded, and offered to trade extra shifts. But it's last minute, and I can't find anyone. The day-shift charge has a three-year-old and can't drop her off at daycare any earlier than normal."

"Okay, so what do you want from me?"

"Can the department live without a charge nurse for an hour?"

"No. You know that's not possible."

"What about Angela? I've been trying to call her."

"She's in Chicago at a meeting." *Here it comes.*

"Any possibility you could come in at five thirty for an hour? I mean, you're here all the time anyway with your baby upstairs."

Ooh, that hurt. "I'm technically on maternity leave," I reply dully.

"Oh yeah, I guess you are." He leans against the door. "Look, my back's up against the wall. I don't want to call in sick, but if I can't leave early tomorrow, then my only other option is to get violently ill, right now. My son is just as important to me as anyone else's."

That hits home. *What the heck?* "Okay, I'll cover for you. Call the day-shift charge and tell her I need her to be here promptly to relieve me. I'm still only three and a half weeks postpartum, and I'm taking my son home tomorrow."

"Thanks. Will do."

Jackson is upstairs in the nursery. Riding the elevator to find him, I wonder how I've gotten myself sucked into tomorrow morning's early duty, brief though it might be. Working the floor is absolutely the last thing I want to do before I take my son home.

I find my husband sitting in a rocker, holding Arthur to his chest and singing to him softly. *What a picture of love!* I stand quietly at the door, just taking it all in. *Thank you, God, for saving our little family.* I have so much to be grateful for.

He looks up when he hears me. Sensing something is not quite right, he says, "You look worried. What's happened?"

Bless his heart, he thinks it's Arthur. "Oh, babe, it's nothing. Just that Tom asked me to come in early for him in the morning to cover his shift." I explain the situation.

"Hey, it's only an hour. We'd be here by six thirty anyway, so no problem. Tom's got a lot on his plate, too," he says cheerfully. "I'll get up and tag along, 'cause according to Dr. Daylen, Arthur's supposed to be released by eight or nine. You'll be done by seven at the latest, so we can hightail it out of here as soon as we get the green light."

"Thanks for cheering me up. For some reason, I just don't like the thought of being coerced into covering his final hour."

"You'll survive." He hands me our little bundle of joy. "I think he needs you, Mommy."

Putting Arthur to my breast, I revel once again at the satisfying sensation of nursing the tiny human Jackson and I have been blessed with. *God and His divine creation of life! What a marvel.*

While I nurse, Jackson gets out his notepad to go through our predeparture checklist for tomorrow morning. "Mom and Dad are already back in Port Angeles. The cleaning crew finished up in Canada and cleaned your cabin this afternoon. Mom and Nan went grocery shopping and also got everything on the list for Arthur."

"That's so sweet. I'm sorry we had to impose."

"Nonsense. They were happy to do it. Besides, you know how my mom loves to shop." We both chuckle. "And *Ladybug* is back at Boeing Field, fueled and ready for our departure—hopefully tomorrow morning."

"Yeah, I'm ready to leave, too. Much as I've grown to love these folks up here in the NICU, I'd like to put this behind us."

"By the way, I bought a few extra items."

"Yeah? Like what?" I ask.

"Call me crazy, but I bought three extra car seats, one for the plane, one for your truck, and one for each of my vehicles, totaling four in all. I also bought a crib, bassinet, and playpen for your cabin, as well as similar items for the rectory."

"Oh, Jackson, isn't that a little overkill?"

"Well, I didn't figure I wanted to pack up all the stuff every time we switched direction, so I just got extra. Besides, for some reason, I think we'll need it all."

"It's fine. Actually, it makes a lot of sense."

An hour later, with Arthur soundly sleeping in his hospital

bassinet, Jackson and I head back to the hotel. "I think our last meal should be in their restaurant, at our favorite table. What do you think?"

"Sounds perfect, but I need to run upstairs for a minute. Can you get the table?"

"Sure." Taking a detour, I stop at the front desk.

"Excuse me, sir."

"Yes, Mrs. Morgan? What can I do for you?"

"I was just wondering if I could see the bill for our room, please."

"The bill?"

"Yes."

"I'm sorry, Mrs. Morgan. I don't understand."

"The bill. You know, we've been staying here for over three weeks, and I just want to see the bill."

"But, madam, there is . . . no bill."

I frown. "Don't be ridiculous. Of course there is. And I'm rather certain it's quite a bit, not that I care, but I just want to see it. Come to think of it, I don't even know how much a room costs here."

"Mrs. Morgan, I apologize. Perhaps there is some confusion."

Now we're getting somewhere. "Good. I'd just like to see it, even if it's not totaled."

"Mrs. Morgan. Ahem." He puts his hand to his mouth and clears his throat. "There is no bill. There never is."

What? Oh yeah, like we're just so nice they don't charge us for staying here? Wait . . . "Why? Why isn't there ever a bill?"

"Ah. Here comes Mr. Morgan. Perhaps he might be able to assist you."

"Assist you how?" Jackson asks from behind me.

I turn to face him. "I was just asking if I could see the bill for our room charges, because I'm sure it's quite a bit. But he said there isn't one."

"Thank you, sir," Jackson says. "I'll take it from here." He offers me his elbow and escorts me to the dining room. "How about a glass of Chardonnay?"

"Jackson!" I yank my hand out of his arm. "You know I can't drink! Now what is going on?"

"Nothing."

"Bull!" I whisper. "Tell me."

"My parents like staying here."

"Yeah, I got that."

"So they invested in the hotel about twenty years ago."

"You mean . . . like, they own it?"

"Not entirely. Let's just say, partially. Enough so that they can walk in whenever they want and have a say in how things are run." He winks at me. "It's better than owning a condo."

"Not funny! Why didn't you tell me? Why the big secret?"

"Honestly, it never came up. I never think about it." He takes hold of my shoulders and turns to face me squarely. "Look, my parents' holdings and investments are vast—so vast that I can't keep track, nor do I want to. I don't take things in life for granted, but sometimes—sometimes I forget about the things they have that I'm familiar with. Partly because my folks never flaunt their wealth or advertise what they have, even to family members."

He's right. "No, they don't."

"Still love me?"

"Yes, of course I do. But do me a favor. If you think of anything else you 'forgot about,' would you please fill me in?"

"Agreed. Dinner?"

"Yeah, I'm starving."

38

Our 4:30 a.m. wake-up call comes with the aroma of freshly pressed French roast coffee, delivered with warm croissants and the morning newspaper. I've only slept about five hours because I keep imagining myself taking Arthur home and being his mother for the next fifty years. A nightcap probably would have helped to quiet my mind, but since I'm nursing, such indulgences are out of the question.

After parking the car, Jackson escorts me through the Emergency Department entrance and then heads upstairs to feed Arthur. We still have a few bottles of expressed breast milk, so Jackson can fill in for me once in a while.

Tom, who looks noticeably relieved to see me walk through the triple-wide doors, immediately gives me report. As usual, it's been a crazy night full of overdoses, gunshots, stabbings, heart attacks, car accidents, drunks, addicts, suicide attempts, and a few other interesting cases thrown into the mix. At this point, things are down to a low roar, and many of the beds are idle, thank goodness.

"Who's in Trauma?" I ask.

"Linda's in T-1 and doing fine, but still swamped. And some agency nurse I couldn't put anywhere else is in T-2. And she sucks."

"Why?"

"Bad attitude, incredibly lazy. Won't get off her butt to do anything. Lots of near misses, and I've been covering for her all night. Really ticks me off."

"Okay, I'll watch her. Anything else?"

"Nope, that's it. Thanks for covering for me. My son appreciates it, too."

"No problem. Good luck!"

I check the stack of charts which Tom has already organized. He's good at his job, and for that I'm grateful.

"Please tell me you're not coming back to work on the floor already," Dr. Bennett says as he rounds the corner of the desk.

"Nah, I'm just covering an hour for Tom so he can take his son to Children's for a tonsillectomy."

"An hour? Not a bad shift."

"That's all the time I've got to spare. By seven a.m. sharp, I need to be upstairs with Jackson, getting discharge instructions on Arthur. He goes home today!"

He gives me a wide smile. "Fantastic."

"Yeah, it is. I never knew I could love something as much as I love that little guy. It's the most amazing feeling."

"Indeed. I love being a father."

"I mean, think about it. They are so perfect. So ready. All they need is a little nurturing and care, and they'll blossom into a wonderful life. Any of them could literally change the world."

"Yup. Just think what a few key players have done throughout history. Maybe you have a little Socrates or Galileo upstairs. You never know."

Ring! Ring!

A red light starts flashing at the same time we hear the call.

"Hold that thought." Dr. Bennett picks up the receiver to the medic radio. "Bayside here. Go."

"Medic unit nine. Inbound with thirty-one-year-old pregnant female, multiple stab wounds . . ."

My mind flashes to Sandra's vicious attack and Samantha's dad. *Surely it's not related. Pay attention!*

"Found at home in her bathroom . . . in left AC, normal saline open, vital signs . . ."

How far along is the baby? Focus!

Can't find the baby's heartbeat. ETA three minutes."

Oh God, the baby! I feel something warm oozing from my nipples. I glance down and see that my scrub top is wet. I'm lactating. *Pay attention! It's not Arthur!*

We can already hear the sirens on approach. I click my shoulder mic. "Trauma Two, medics on approach. Get ready!"

I don't see any sign of response from the nurse in Trauma 2, so I speed back to ensure she's heard my squawk. "Did you catch that?" I ask as I burst through the doors.

"Yeah, yeah, I got it," says an enormous woman sitting on a stool, wearing scrubs at least three sizes too small. She makes no movement to prepare for the incoming patient or meet the medics.

"You only have one patient in here. Don't you need to be doing something?" *Like, get off your rear and move toward the ambulance doors?*

"Nah, they'll bring it to me."

"Patient is pregnant. It's possible we might need an incubator. Did anyone show you where those are kept?"

Continuing to obliquely sit on the stool, she seems nonplussed by my urgings. Her only movement is to reach into a small bag on the desk and withdraw a candy bar. "Yeah, I know where they are. I'll get one if I need it."

"I don't think we've been introduced. I'm Elizabeth, the assistant manager of this department."

"Hey, how ya doing? I'm Bunny," she says through a thick bite of caramel chew.

"I'm not impressed. Now get up and go get the incubator, before I fire you!"

Taken aback, she stands up, throws the remnants of the candy bar back into the bag, wipes her hands on her scrub pants, and swaggers out the door. Through chocolate-covered front teeth she spits, "You can't fire me, you know. I work for the agency."

No, but I can sure cancel the agency. "Go get the equipment!" I can hear the medics rounding the bend in the hall and Dr. Bennett barking orders to me from their side.

Pay attention! I tell myself. *You're charge nurse. You have to take his orders.* "Right. OB, ultrasound, anesthesia. I missed some of that, Doc. Can you repeat it?"

He repeats his instructions.

Instinctively I grab the head of the gurney to move it alongside the trauma bed and feel an electric current zap me from the metal side rail. As the painful shock runs through my body, I withdraw my hand instantly. "What's wrong with your gurney? I just got shocked!"

"I know. And I don't know," the medic says. "It's been happening since we loaded her up. Some kind of weird static."

"Well, let's get her transferred as fast as possible. I can't take much more of that." *Ouch!* I get shocked again.

Realizing there is no other nurse to cover the Trauma room, I pick up the phone hanging on the wall and dial the house supervisor. "Hey, it's me, Elizabeth. I'm charge right now, but there's a worthless agency idiot pretending to be a nurse in T-2. She's dangerous."

"Yeah, Tom complained about her, too."

"Medics just brought in a pregnant stabbing victim. I can

manage the patient, but I need you—or someone—to cover the department as charge."

"I'm right down the hall. I'll take over. You deal with the patient."

We hoist the patient to the trauma bed, and RT assumes control of the patient's airway, augmenting her breathing with a large, rubbery face mask. Her long, unevenly layered brown hair is greasy and matted with tangles. *Shampoo and a brush would do her a world of good.* As I clip the oxygen saturation monitor to her index finger, I notice her jaggedly uneven fingernails. Old red polish has grown out or chipped off, and grimy dirt is smashed underneath the nail ends. I glance at her bare feet and see that her toenails are overgrown by at least half an inch. Shaking off my repulsion, I refocus and strip away her bloody clothes.

"Where did you say you picked her up from?" I ask the medic.

"Her home. It's a walk-up apartment in the projects. Why?"

"She looks dirty, like an indigent. Clothes are dirty, too."

"Yeah. I hate to say it, but the apartment was a pigsty."

"I wonder if she bathes."

"No clue."

I look again and realize it's more than that. *She's really scummy looking.* I put new leads on her chest and hook her up to the monitor. *Creepy looking. Not drugs . . . not alcohol . . . from the clubbing of her fingers, she's a heavy smoker for sure.* But something about her makes me pause.

From the corner of my eye I see Bunny return from Supply, casually pushing the incubator through the doors to the back corner of the room. She passes the organized chaos surrounding the patient and plops herself down on a stool, making no effort to assist in the lifesaving efforts.

She's completely worthless! Maybe it's better if she stays out of the fray. I turn back to the patient. *Focus!*

Based upon the size of the patient's belly, she has to be full-term. I count at least three one-inch knife wounds just above her pubic area, and multiple smaller puncture wounds higher up in her abdomen. Given how compressed the bladder becomes with pregnancy, it's likely the bladder has been hit. Wasting no time, the Trauma team puts in another IV line, draws labs, starts fluids, and inserts a urinary catheter, which immediately fills with blood-tainted urine, confirming my suspicions.

Glancing up at Bunny again, I stop dead. In place of her 300-pound body is a mass of red-hot coals. Watching the heat rise, I remember what Joseph said about evil in its purest form. The mass suddenly morphs from coals into the image of the small dark man in the theater. *Maestro!* The sound of cruel, screeching laughter hits my ears, assaulting my senses. I instinctively put my gloved hands to my ears and cry out.

"Elizabeth?" Dr. Bennett says. "You okay?"

His question startles me out of the vision. "Yeah, sorry." I shake it off. *Not now, Joseph!*

The senior OB resident arrives and positions herself between the patient's legs at the end of the breakaway gurney. Meanwhile, her OB nurse attaches the fetal heart monitor and uses the portable ultrasound to check the baby's status. Miracle of miracles, the baby still has a strong heartbeat. *Thank you, God!*

"I don't think the baby was hit in the attack," the OB doc says. "But I see a small knife wound around the vaginal opening. The thrust must have caused her water to break— hours ago." The doc looks up. "She's not dilated at all. She needs to deliver immediately. It'll have to be C-section."

"Agree. No doubt she's got some internal injuries." Dr. Bennett examines the rest of the patient in his normal, methodical manner. "Everything else seems okay, except for the glaring stab wounds. If we open her up for the C-section, we can repair whatever got hit in abdominal cavity at the same time."

The unit secretary speaks from behind the curtain. "Her

name is Evita, but she goes by Eva. Here's the labels," she says without looking. She hands them to a medic, who hands them to me. "And I've got paperwork ready whenever you need it."

Partly speaking to himself, Dr. Bennett says, "Look at the angle of these wounds." He puts a finger into one of the shallow wounds.

I lean over to look.

"See how these two here are only about half an inch deep? And see how this other one angles up? Almost like her attacker was upside down, stabbing upward. Hmm. Or maybe she was lying down and he was at her head, stabbing and pulling toward her midline?" He mimics the possible attack position.

"That's weird."

"And see how they're mostly superficial, like the perp hesitated?"

"Yeah, same with the vaginal wound," the OB doc says.

Dr. Bennett picks up the woman's hands, examining her arms. "Hands are grimy and she's a smoker, but nothing else. No defensive signs on her hands or forearms."

"You mean she didn't even try to defend herself?" Having been attacked recently, I can safely attest that my natural instincts were all about defense. "Maybe she was passed out. A junkie?"

He takes another look. "No track marks." Lifting the oxygen mask, he sniffs. "No alcohol on her breath."

The OB stands up from her seated position between Evita's legs and rips off her soiled gloves. "Not to interrupt, folks, but I'd like anesthesia to get the spinal started. The baby doesn't have much time, and it's possible the umbilical cord got hit. Is the OR open across the hall?"

"Yeah, it's open."

"Good. We can do it in there, save a little time."

Dr. Bennett stands up straight and looks at me. "I think maybe she did this to herself."

"You mean, like suicide? Suicides usually don't stab themselves. Why would she use a knife?"

"No, not suicide." He leans toward me and says quietly, "I think she was trying to kill the baby."

"Anesthesia's here. What do you need?" a man says as he enters the room.

"What?" I sputter. "Why would she do that?"

"No general," the OB doc says. "She needs a spinal, as fast as you can."

"Sure, no problem." The anesthesiologist turns and heads for the OR. "I'm ready. Let's roll!"

Almost in a whisper, the OB doc leans over toward Dr. Bennett and me. "I agree. She was trying to kill it."

"Ugh, what's the big deal?" Bunny mutters.

Having momentarily forgotten about her, I see now that she has moved closer and is hovering beside me. The little devil has been eavesdropping.

"What did you say?" Dr. Bennett asks, looking up at Bunny.

"Nuttin', just 'ugh.'"

Doc looks down at the wounds again, shaking his head. "Yeah, I can't explain it, but I think she did this to herself."

"So?" Bunny says. "Maybe she didn't want it. Her right, ya know."

You witch. Firing's not enough. Now I really want to hurt you! I turn to face Bunny squarely. "In case you haven't noticed, this baby's full-term and very viable." *After everything I've been through in the last three and a half weeks with my own son, don't push my buttons.*

"Don't matter how 'full-term' the tissues are," she spits through another mouthful of chocolate, "it's not a real baby till it's born."

"Tissues?" Dr. Bennett and I say simultaneously.

Again, the Maestro! "What kind of heartless monster are you?" I add.

"Ha! It's the truth! I work full-time at Planned Prevention, and according to our mandate, a fetus is only tissues unless it can walk home." She laughs again.

Before I have time to smack her, the patient begins to rouse. "Stop! Help me, please."

"We're here," I say. "You're in the hospital." I stroke her grimy, pocked forehead as we begin wheeling her out of Trauma. Her acne-filled face is a maze of deep, bulging blackheads. "We're taking you to the operating room. You'll be okay. And we can save the baby."

"No!" She grabs my arm, then pulls the oxygen mask aside. "I don't want the damn thing!" This is my first glimpse of her nose, and from its odd angle and uneven thickening, it's obviously been broken—more than once. *Childhood accidents? Spousal abuse?*

I look at Dr. Bennett, who is pushing alongside the gurney, and shake my head. "She's hysterical. Can I give her something?"

"Not till I get the baby out," the OB doc says from the scrub sinks, "and I've cut the cord."

"I don't want the fuckin' baby!" the woman screams. "Kill the shit!"

Following behind the gurney, Bunny says, "Hey, you gotta do what she says, ya know. Law says her body, her rights. Her choice."

Choice? "Get out of this ED!" I scream at her as I grab a mask at the OR door.

"No!" Barging her way alongside, she starts to enter the OR. "I'm gonna make sure you do what she asks. It's the law."

"Yeah, my body!" Evita says from under the mask. "I can do what I want. I have rights." She laughs a cruel, terrible laugh that sends shivers down my spine.

"I'll help you kill it, lady," Bunny says. "Don't worry."

"You're relieved! Now!" I yell. "Get out of here!"

Joining the ruckus, the house supervisor grabs Bunny by the arm and pushes her massive body out the OR doors. "Leave now! I'm reporting you to the state."

"For what?" She stands firm, fists on her hips. "More like, I'll report you guys for ignoring a patient's rights. Wait till the newspaper hears about this one! Ha!"

As the OR doors swing shut behind me, I click my shoulder mic. "Security! OR, stat. Security!

"All right, folks, let's roll her to her side," says the anesthesiologist. "I need to get the spinal in."

"No, I don't want this fuckin' baby!"

Through the glass windows, I watch security officers arrive at the OR doors and grab Bunny. Then I hear the supervisor order, "Call the police. I want her arrested."

I bump open the OR door with my hip and add from under my mask, "We might want the police for the patient as well. Attempted suicide—attempted murder."

I hear the docs arguing with Evita and turn my attention back to the critical situation.

"You're tryin' to trick me. I don't need your damn numbing stuff! I want the little shit to suffer. Just get the thing out and kill it! One way or another, it's gonna die today!"

"Look, this isn't about your baby," the OB doc says, leaning over the patient's head. "Your uterus and bladder are badly damaged. You're bleeding internally. I can't fix it from your vagina. I need to open you up. You wanna feel the incision, or be numb? Or you can just bleed to death. Your call." She and Dr. Bennett leave the room to go scrub.

"Bastards. You're all bastards!"

Yeah, yeah, we're all bastards, trying to save your pathetic life.

"Look, lady, I'm just a nurse," I say, "and I don't know all of what's going on with you, but this isn't just about your baby. You might die if the doctor doesn't repair the damage from the stab wounds. You're losing a lot of blood." As my hand rests on the metal edge of the OR bed, I feel another sharp shock zap through me, traveling all the way from my fingertips to my toes. "Ouch!" I reflexively pull back. *Dang! What is causing this?*

Apparently something starts to sink into her sick brain, because she lets us roll her to her side. Avoiding the side rails, I grab her dirty, bloody knees and pull them up as close to her chin as possible to flex her back into a convex shape. The anesthesiologist has the spinal inserted and taped down within two minutes, and we roll her back into a prone position.

"Don't forget, I'm awake, and I'll remember! You kill that thing before you cut the umbilical cord. I'll sue the crap out of you if you don't."

"Yeah, yeah . . ." *What's wrong with this woman? What's wrong with Bunny?* Thoughts flood my brain. *How depraved can people be? They're nothing more than cold-blooded killers.* Tears fill my eyes, tears for all of humankind. I push them back. "Yeah, yeah. I hear you." *I'm not even supposed to be working here today. Oh God, please take me out of this insanity!*

Both surgeons enter the OR at the same time, masks on, hands in the air, awaiting sterile towels, gowns, and gloves. I'm certain they've both overheard the latest verbal exchanges with the patient. I search Dr. Bennett's eyes for help. *We can't kill an innocent baby, can we?* Backing away from the gurney, I watch while the circulator washes the woman's belly and the scrub nurse creates a sterile field around the patient.

Quietly I exit the OR and run back to the Trauma room. Grabbing the incubator, I roll it down the hall, making sure it has all the necessary resuscitation equipment within easy reach. When I near the scrub sinks, I push it to the side, wash my hands, and don a clean mask, booties, and gloves. Reentering the OR, I see the two surgeons prepping the woman's belly for the incision. It will take a few more minutes for the spinal to take full effect. Racking my brain, I weigh possible options.

Dr. Bennett looks up at me through his magnifying glasses

and barely shakes his head. He is definitely signaling me. *What? What am I supposed to do?*

Then, as casually as if he's ordering a cup of coffee, he asks Evita, "How do you want it killed?"

"Huh?" I almost fall over. *Surely he won't kill the baby! Oh please God, he's a doctor! He's a Christian!*

"Stick some scissors into its neck, or crush the skull or something. That's what he did the last time."

Oh Lord, she's done this before. What kind of devil monster are you? I flip the intercom record button to the *On* position.

"Really? Last time?" he casually says. "How many have there been?"

"This makes ten. Ten little bastards!" she cackles.

Dr. Bennett's face turns pale, then his eyebrows narrow above his magnifying glasses. "Always wait until they're just ready to be born?"

A peal of laughter pours out of her. "That's the fun of it. Watch them squirm and burn!"

"But I'll bet you never did this by yourself before, did you?"

"No. My baby left me. They took him away. The winter snow angels took him away." She pulls the mask away from her face and speaks in the creepiest voice I've ever heard. "But he'll be back."

She's bonkers. She needs to be locked up and never released!

"Oh, that's interesting. By the way, after it's dead, do you want the remains?"

A sterile curtain has been put up, separating the woman's head and neck from the rest of her body. She is unable to see that Dr. Bennett holds a scalpel and is looking at me. The OB doc has her back to me, but I can tell she's started cutting and cauterizing the woman's skin and tissues.

"Are you crazy?" Evita says. "I just want to see the shit kick and squirm. Then kill it. Cut it up into little pieces and flush it down the toilet or throw it in the trash with the rest of the garbage."

I'm starting to feel lightheaded. *I've got to get out of here.* I push against the OR door.

"Elizabeth, wait!" Dr. Bennett says.

I pause at the door, dazed.

"Okay, Evita, whatever you want." He looks up at me and almost indiscernibly makes a tiny sign of the cross on his chest with his empty hand. If I hadn't seen him do it before, I'd have missed the action entirely. "Elizabeth!" Dr. Bennett repeats, yanking me from my stupor.

"Yeah, I'm right here." I look down, fighting back tears.

"You know how to dispose of the remains, right?"

What? I'm not gonna be complicit in this murder . . .

"Right?" he repeats.

The light bulb in my brain goes on. I slap the intercom record button to the *Off* position. Fumbling for convincing words, I respond, "Oh, yeah. 'Course I do."

"Okay, good. Why don't you go get what you'll need. The bag, you know, your bag and stuff for the transport. And call the morgue . . . 'Morgan' . . . upstairs, and tell him you'll be coming with a dead baby in five minutes."

The OB doc still has her back to me, but looks up and nods to Dr. Bennett in some type of agreement.

"Got it. Be right back." A tornado starts in my brain, quickly processing every possible scenario I might encounter. Moving as fast as possible, I speed to my office and grab my belongings. It's 5:55 a.m., and thank goodness the day-shift charge nurse has already arrived. "I'm in the middle of a huge emergency and don't have time to talk," I say, "so no report today. Tom left a pile of charts there. Throw them into my office when you get time. Gotta go!" I toss the keys and radio as I run by the desk.

"I'll take care of the report," the house supervisor says

from the hallway. "And I'll make sure that Bunny—whatever she is—never works again, anywhere."

Running back down the corridor, I drop my bag and jacket at the OR door next to the incubator. Blessedly, no one is in the area. I search through the incubator cart, snatch any items I might need, and shove them into a white plastic "patient belongings" bag. After grabbing two warm blankets from the wall warmer, I take a deep breath. I'm as ready as I'll ever be.

Through the glass window in the OR door, I see Dr. Bennett lifting the slime-covered baby out of the woman's womb. It is 6:00 a.m. on the nose. "Oh, God bless!" I murmur to myself. "It's a girl. A sweet little girl."

Poised next to Dr. Bennett is a translucent image of Joseph. His voice comes from inside my head, and his words are crystal clear: *"The Tenth has arrived. It cannot pass. Arthur will need her. You . . . must . . . choose."* The image fades, and the voice is gone.

Joseph, what have you done? I don another mask and gloves and push back through the OR door. "I'm back."

"Good," Dr. Bennett says. To the anesthesiologist he orders, "As soon as I cut the umbilical cord, give her ten of Versed."

"Right."

Clever. Since Versed causes temporary amnesia, the patient won't remember anything from the time she's given the drug until it wears off.

The OB resident says, "She's past her due date. This baby's starting to decline. Must be in her tenth month."

Tenth month? This is her tenth child. Tenth month, tenth child. The words swirl around in my brain, as if echoing through the deepest canyons. The Tenth! Oh my God! Joseph's words. All his cryptic messages and confusing words now make sense. Joseph's a Sixth. The Sixth of Nine. Nine! One of them for every month of human gestation. They are the guides and caretakers of the souls of the unborn. Their realm takes care of them until they would have died naturally if they'd

been given life. And their parents must come to the chasm to acknowl-
edge them. That's why he's sad. There are millions more of them now
than there used to be. And Joseph's warning is that there is no guide
or caretaker in the Realm of Holding for the fetus beyond nine months.
Like a womb, the divine system of protection wasn't designed that way.
Holy God! I get it, Joseph!

"Let me see the little shit's dead body!" Evita garbles
through the oxygen mask.

Slowly, deliberately, the anesthesiologist pushes down on
the curtain across the woman's chest so she can catch a glimpse.
Keeping the mask on her face, he increases the oxygen flow
briefly to hyper-oxygenate all of her tissues, including the baby.

"Everyone out of here!" Dr. Bennett barks to all the extra
staff, "including you." He indicates the surgical nurses and
the OB resident. "Give us thirty seconds." Everyone complies,
departing to the sterilization room.

Dr. Bennett holds the baby low above Evita's belly, closer
to her groin, making it difficult for her to get a clear look at
the umbilical cord. Clamps are placed on the umbilical cord in
multiple locations, but I doubt she can see the two closest to
the baby. She also can't see that Dr. Bennett has just cut the cord
near the baby. He signals the anesthesiologist to give the Versed
as he cuts the now insignificant cord nearer to the placenta.

Without warning, there is an electricity surge and power
spike. Lights flicker off and on. Then some type of static charge
shoots from the ceiling in the center of the room and hits the
woman's belly. Dr. Bennett hunches his shoulders down and
lurches to the side, ducking the bolt and protecting the baby. The
charge seems to flash up, causing a burst, then dies back down,
disappearing into thin air.

"What the hell was that?" the doctors ask in unison.

"Joseph!" I whisper loudly. "Joseph, if that's you, stop this
instant!"

"Knock her out!" Dr. Bennett yells to the anesthesiologist.

"Knock her out. Intubate her!"

"What's wrong?" I ask from the door.

"Her belly's on fire. The uterus is burning up!" He does a quick suction on the baby's mouth and nostrils, then bundles her up in a sterile towel. Zooming around the end of the bed, he hands her to me. "You know what to do, Elizabeth. I got your back."

"Me, too," the anesthesiologist says.

We're the only three people in the room besides an unconscious Evita and the baby.

He puts a few small tubes into my pocket. "Here's amniotic fluid and umbilical cord blood. Test these for everything—including DNA." He stops and adds quietly, "Get Irene to run it."

39

I check my watch. 6:02 a.m.

"Jackson, it's me. Listen, I'm in the car, driving back to
the hotel." *Try not to sound hysterical.* Balancing the phone on
my shoulder, I suction the baby's nostrils and mouth out again
with a bulb syringe. *Come on . . . cry!* I wipe her eyes and face off.
Come on, girl, give me a good cry. "Oh, thank God!" Tapping her
back, I make her cough a little more. "No, nothing's wrong with
me. Listen, meet me there. . . . No, I can't wait. Meet me there as
fast as you can."

I throw the phone into my pocket and pull into the circular
drive of the hotel. Holding the baby tightly, I slam the car into
park, jump out, and grab my coat and bag.

"Welcome back, Mrs. Morgan," the doorman says.

"Thanks." I bolt past, hurrying to the front desk. The clerk
is assisting another guest, but I interrupt, half screaming, "I
know we checked out, but I need the key to my room! Now!"

"Excuse me, sir," he says politely to the guest. "Yes,

ma'am. Do you need bags brought up?"

Ignoring his question, I snatch the key and run to the elevator, punching the button multiple times. *Come on . . . hurry! I check my watch. Six minutes! Hurry!*

When I reach the room, I rush in and kick the door shut. Dropping everything on the floor, I rush to the bathtub and turn the faucet on, filling the tub with warm water. I lay the bundle on the soft bath mat and carefully unwrap the sterile cloth. Taking an infant-size ambu bag, I give the baby a few tiny puffs of air to inflate her lungs a little more. Then I carefully lift her into the warm water atop a large bath towel lying in the tub. Sponging her carefully, I clean all of the placenta slime from her body.

Her cries are music to my ears. She lets out a louder cry and pinks up nicely. Glory be!

Five minutes later, Jackson walks into the room to find me in the bathtub, sobbing gently, a newborn baby resting against my chest. "What in Heaven's name is going on?"

"Oh, Jackson, I don't even know where to begin."

He kneels down beside me and rubs the tiny girl's wrinkled skin. "Who is she?"

"Ours. She's ours." I start at the beginning and tell him every detail. As I chronicle the saga, I put the infant to my breast, and she begins to suckle. "Let's hope she likes my breast milk."

"So," Jackson says slowly, "we need to get her out of here and back to Canada. And we need to contact Irene. Maybe she can meet us at Boeing Field."

"What about a birth certificate? What about the people who know I only had a boy?"

"My dad's attorneys can take care of the legal stuff. We'll figure the rest of it out as we go. Right now, I want to get you and her as far away from this place as possible."

"Agreed."

"You think she can make it?"

"Yeah."

While I nurse, Jackson packs up every possible shred of evidence that anything unusual occurred in the hotel room and puts it all in plastic bags. Then I bundle the baby up, and we walk as casually as possible through the lobby.

"Oh, Mrs. Morgan! Is that your new baby? How adorable!"

I stop cold. *Of course. It's natural. Everyone will assume this is my baby.* "Yes, thank you. We finally get to take him home! I'm so relieved."

"I didn't know you had the baby with you earlier. I'd have had the bellman assist you."

"Oh, no problem. Sorry I was in such a rush," I fumble. "I didn't mean to be rude. New mother jitters."

"Not at all, madam. You have a wonderful day, and enjoy that young lad."

Once in the car, we have to figure out how we will manage Arthur's discharge while still caring for the new baby, who's wide awake and looking at everything.

"I think it's better for me to go up, Jackson. I can hunt down supplies and pilfer everything we might need. Can you manage her while I run up?"

"Sure. If you're gonna be more than fifteen minutes, just come back and check on us." He kisses me. "Good luck."

"Okay, babe. I'll be right back." While I'm waiting in the neonatal unit, I scrounge for everything I can think of and stuff my bag full of supplies. I've never stolen anything before and hope God will forgive this one transgression. *It's not really stealing,* I reason, reaching for an oxygen saturation monitor. *I'll return everything in a few weeks, and they'll never be the wiser.*

Jackson manages to track down Irene and, bless her heart, she meets us at the Boeing hangar. As I relay a brief version of the story, I feel like a spy passing secret documents to a government agent. *What the heck has happened to my boring, mundane, isolated life?*

"What a story!" She shakes her head. "Yeah, I can get this

stuff tested. I've got some favors I can call in. Hopefully have some answers in a few days. I'll be in touch."

"Thanks, Irene. You're the best."

"I'll check on the nurse and baby's mom, too," she says. "Maybe something will pop."

An hour later, we're landing on the bay in front of our Canadian home, bringing two new babies into the house. "What do we tell your parents and Samantha?"

"The truth."

I sigh heavily. "I don't know if I'm up for this."

"I'll handle it. Let's get our kids inside."

I grab his arm. "What's her name? What shall we call her?"

"Kathleen. Named after the woman of my dreams."

My middle name.

Jackson Sr. wastes no time in having his personal attorney draft the necessary documents of birth for Kathleen, eliminating future legal hassles. Aside from bringing Mike, Sally, Roger, and Nan into our confidence, we don't say a word to anyone. Mostly we just keep to ourselves, and I stay at home in Canada while Jackson travels back and forth for work and to take Sam to school. We have to be a bit crafty with the people we know well, but it's amazing what people will believe if you tell your story correctly. Convincing our casual acquaintances that I actually had twins is quite easy, considering both babies weigh essentially the same, and have dark hair and deep brown eyes.

A week later, I get a call from Irene. "Hey, Elizabeth. How's it going?"

"Okay. A little busy with two babies, but we're managing. Did you find anything out?"

"Yeah. But I don't want to talk about it over the phone."

I can feel the hair bristling on the back of my neck. "Oh. Well, I'm not sure I want to leave home right now. Is there any way you can come out here?"

"Yup. I can be there tomorrow around noon. Would

Jackson be able to get me across the water?"

"Absolutely." Since I haven't been out of our cove since coming home from the hospital, I'm delighted at the prospect of Irene's company. "And please pack a bag so you can spend a night or two."

Waiting expectantly on the porch with the babies the next day, I watch as Jackson maneuvers the plane alongside the dock. It's a cold, gray, wintry afternoon, and icy rain is expected by nightfall. Irene sits in the nursery with me, patiently waiting to tell us what she's uncovered, while I feed both babies and tuck them in for their naps. Then we quietly exit and move downstairs to join Jackson in the kitchen.

"Listen, I couldn't bring myself to tell you this on the phone, but I got some pretty unexpected information on the biological mom and Kathleen."

"Yeah? How unexpected?"

"Very. But you both need to sit down and try to not freak out. By the way, where's Sam?"

"At a church sleepover. Why?"

"Because she doesn't need to hear this."

Irene's words cause the hair to prickle on my neck again. I watch as she withdraws a little notepad from her vest pocket. She looks at us both and takes a deep breath. "First off, the mom was linked to nine previous unsolved dead baby matters, like newborn body parts in dumpsters and newborns who were found in trash bins, having been tortured to death."

"Oh, God. I might throw up." *This is so personal.*

"Wait, hang on." She looks at Jackson, who's still standing. "Really, Jackson, you might want to sit down."

He sits.

"We always had the DNA links between the babies, but never could find the parents."

"So, I'm assuming it's Evita and now you have her, right?" he asks.

"Yeah. By the way, her uterus was completely fried by the electrical explosion. Had to remove it, as well as part of her intestines and her bladder. She'll never be the same."

Jackson and I exchange glances. We know perfectly well what caused the frying.

"Anyway, she's locked up, nuttier than a fruitcake. Hopefully she'll get the death penalty, but I'd be happy if she'd just miraculously die in prison."

"You won't get any argument out of us," I say. "Sorry, but I can't say that I feel much sympathy."

"Right, me neither." She looks at her notes. "But there's more."

"Okay. Like what?" I have a bad feeling in the pit of my stomach.

"It's the biological dad." Pausing, she looks from Jackson to me, then back to Jackson. "Same one on all the babies. And . . ." She pauses yet again. "It's the same as Samantha's."

"Oh, God!" I curl up into a ball.

"Yeah," Irene whispers. "They're half sisters."

Her words burn and sear at my heart as the room spins around me. *What kind of bizarre nightmare am I in the middle of?*

"Jackson!" Everything goes blank.

When I come to, I'm on the floor, looking up at their faces and the ceiling beyond.

"She'll be okay. She just passed out," I hear Jackson say. "Too much for her."

"Sorry, Jackson," Irene says. "I couldn't think of a delicate way to tell you, other than to just say it."

"Hey, guys." I feel a cold cloth on my forehead. "What happened?"

"You passed out, babe. Probably from the shock." He gives me a sip of sherry.

"I'm not supposed to have any alcohol," I say, wiping my lips and sitting up.

"I don't think a sip will hurt the babies, darling. And it'll do you a world of good."

"Irene, who else knows about this?" I ask.

"Not a soul. Sam's records are sealed, per her attorney and the court. And here is the only copy of the records relating to Kathleen." She hands Jackson a sealed envelope. "In all likelihood, no one will ever think of connecting the dots."

"What do we do?"

"Nothing." Jackson stands up, throwing his arms into the air. "This doesn't change anything." I've never seen him upset like this. "We continue loving Samantha, Arthur, and Kathleen, and we move on with our family and our life."

"Just like that? We never tell her? Never tell them?"

"No, we just leave it alone. There is no reason for them to find out. Not now, not ever."

It seems logical enough. Simple, in fact. Irene agrees. We seal our silence with a toast of wine and throw the glasses into the fire pit, watching the crystal flicker in the heat.

40

THIRTEEN MONTHS LATER

"Elizabeth! Elizabeth!" Samantha screams as she runs down the dock from Jackson's floatplane, waving a letter in her hand.

"Did you find out?"

"I got in! I got in! Can you believe it?" Jumping all around the beach, she shouts at the top of her lungs. "I got in! I'm going to Harvard!"

"Oh, Sam, I'm so proud of you!"

Grabbing my hands, she pulls me around, and we dance on the front porch together, hugging and kissing each other. I've never seen her so elated.

"I never had a doubt," Jackson says, kissing the babies. "You're brilliant!"

"Thanks," Sam says. "Thank you both for having confidence in me."

"Have you decided yet what you want for your graduation gift?" Jackson asks.

"Not yet, but I will." She jumps around some more. "You

know, I might need some extra clothes and stuff." I can almost see her mind switching into preparatory gear.

"I imagine you will. I needed lots of new clothes when I went off to college. Don't you worry, Rebecca and I will take you on a shopping spree before you leave."

"Cool. Wait till I tell Uncle Mike and Aunt Sally! Wait till I tell the world!" She spins around again on the porch.

Jackson opens the door for us as we walk into the house. "So, have you figured out what your major should be? What you're interested in?

"Oh, that. Yup! Biochemistry. Premed."

"Wow, that's great! Kind of heavy, though. It might be a heck of a load. You can always go into nursing, you know," I say with a wink.

"Nah. It's gotta be neurogenetics."

"Really? How'd you come up with that?"

"Joseph and I worked it out." She strolls in, absentmindedly patting Alder. "Got to be neurogenetics."

I stop dead in my tracks. "What? What did you just say?"

"In my dreams." She casually picks up an apple from the bowl in the front entry and shrugs her shoulders. "Joseph and me. We worked it out."

"Worked out what?"

"Now, Elizabeth . . ." She turns to look at me, casually pulling her beautiful, long brown hair to one side. "I know Joseph told you there's a darkness coming."

I stare at her in blank silence. *I don't want to hear this.*

"You may not want to hear it, but you need to."

"Did you just read my thoughts?"

"Yeah, I did. Joseph taught me how." She rubs the apple on her shirt. "And he can teach you, too, whenever you're ready."

Jackson looks at each of us, probably wondering why the conversation seems one-sided.

"I don't want him to teach me."

"Someday you will." Sam shrugs her shoulders. "Anyway, you must know that Kathleen isn't the only Tenth. That means the darkness is still coming, and the evil will only get stronger."

"Oh my God. You mean there's more of them?"

"Yeah, and they're being created for a reason. A very bad reason." She takes a bite of apple. "But Arthur and Kathleen are special . . . extra special. They're here to fight the darkness, and neurogenetics is the best way I can help."

———◆———

THE END

ABOUT THE AUTHOR

 **Joanne Moudy** graduated from the University of Colorado with a degree in Fine Arts. After owning a successful business she entered the military and proudly served as an officer for nine years. At the age of forty-one she returned to college to earn her degree in nursing, and specialized in emergency nursing until retirement.

Joanne has three children and four grandchildren and lives with her husband in Arizona.

Her gripping supernatural saga continues in *The Gathering*, due out summer, 2014.

Visit her Web site at www.gatedcreative.com.

HOW TO ORDER

You are invited to continue your journey with Elizabeth, Jackson, Joseph, and Samantha by visiting our Web site:

www.gatedcreative.com

Where you can:

- Communicate with the author.
- Share your thoughts on *The Tenth* and find our what other readers are saying.
- Find out about group rates for purchasing *The Tenth* for book clubs and organizations.
- Find out about inviting the author to speak to your club or organization.
- Get sneak peeks at the sequel, *The Gathering,* due out in summer, 2014.

All of this and more at:

www.gatedcreative.com

Thank you for reading *The Tenth*.